THE HERO SLAYERS FACE THEIR DEMONS

THE HERO SLAYERS FACE THEIR DEMONS

O. S. Marrow

Podium

Published in 2025 by Podium Publishing
www.podiumentertainment.com

Podium

THE HERO SLAYERS
FACE THEIR DEMONS

CHAPTER ONE

New Normals

Arzak clearly had the sense that something was horrifically, game-changingly, world-shatteringly wrong, but she also had the good sense not to pry. If she had, I wouldn't have told her, and I'd toyed with the odd lie to get her off my case— that I had a stomach bug, or some sort of disease of the groin, perhaps; anything that wouldn't invite any follow-up questions. But she didn't ask again after the first time, only keeping a close eye on me on our journey back to Lore's farm.

I still didn't know if I believed it myself. The idea that I might have the blood of Players in me—the people who I'd learned to hate with a passion, over these past few months—I couldn't quite cope with. Part of me was in denial; the other part was screaming. Silently, of course; I didn't want to give Arzak any more suspicions than she already had.

Even once we arrived back on Lore's farm, I knew I was being oddly quiet. Mostly because Val kept telling me so. Now that I was back around her, I realized I had to act more like my normal self. While Arzak had the good sense to not interrogate me on what was the matter, Val . . . Well, it wasn't often that the phrases *Val* and *good sense* were used in the same sentence without *doesn't have* in between them.

And so, I'd thrown myself into training up alongside her. When I said *training up*, I meant the *Worldbending* and *Knifework* skill trees, really—the idea that I'd tell Val about my new *Needlework* skill was about as unlikely as me telling her about my Player ancestry.

While I eked out experience in my main combat skills—even with the *Sisyphus* bonus, there was only so much experience I could get without an enemy to fight—Val worked on her *Healing*. In the past, she'd only used it to battle hangovers, but now that Tokas had betrayed us, there was a very substantial demand for a healer in the party once more.

"A broken bone?" Val suggested.

"What?" I replied, concentrating on flicking a portal between two locations as quickly as possible—something I still hadn't quite got the knack for.

"If you let me injure you, I can *heal* it," the sorcerer said. "How am I supposed to get *Healing* experience if I have nothing to bloody *heal*?"

"And your opening suggestion was that you snap one of my bones, was it?"

Val shrugged. "I thought we'd haggle."

"I'm not haggling."

"OK, what about a flesh wound? Nothing mortal, just—"

"You're not injuring me, Val," I interrupted.

The sorcerer tossed her head back, rolling her eyes. "Come on, you've got to give me *something* to *heal*."

"No."

"Anything, please. Or do you want to face the next Player alongside a healer whose ability stretches, at best, to fixing an upset tummy?"

I sighed, closing my pair of portals; this was clearly a conversation that Val wasn't giving up on anytime soon. "Why don't you injure one of Lore's sheep instead of your friend?" I suggested.

Val blinked at me. "Hurt one of *them*?" she asked, looking over at the surrounding field full of what Lore affectionately called his *babies*.

"You know, there was a time not long ago that you suggested I tried cutting a sheep in two."

"Well, that was before I got to know them, wasn't it?" The sorcerer grabbed one of the sheep as they passed by and rubbed it affectionately on the head. It didn't seem to notice. "And besides, I think Lore would kill me if I did. Or try to."

"Either way, you'd have something to *heal*," I said.

"I'm not hurting Lore's babies," Val said, metaphorically putting her foot down.

I sighed again. I'd never been one for sighing all that much, but that was before I'd met Val. "You can slap me."

"Slap you?" Val repeated. "That's it?"

"Either that or you get me drunk. Again."

"I think we've already drunk all of Lore's supplies."

I gestured a thumb toward the dirt road. "I could pop into town? Get some more?"

Val's eyes lit up. "Ooh, maybe more of that ruby ale that—" She caught herself. "No, wait, stop. I'm not fixing any more hangovers. Do you know how much experience I get for those? It's only in the double digits."

In the distance, someone shouted. My head snapped to face them, though

I noticed Val didn't have the same reaction; clearly one of us held more anxiety than the other.

Across the field, Seld—Lore's farmhand—grabbed his behind as though pained. Nearby, a sheep munched on grass almost *too* casually. "Lore!" Seld shouted. "They're doing it again! They're headbutting me!"

The owner of the farm popped his head out of the farmhouse. "Who is?"

Seld pointed at the nearby sheep. "She is."

Lore looked at the sheep, peacefully chewing grass. "Are you sure?"

"I've told you, they only do it when nobody's looking!"

I glanced to Val, who shrugged. It wasn't that neither of us believed Seld, but neither of us had actually seen it happen. In fact, nobody had; if these sheep really were bullying the farmhand, they were doing a good job of doing it subtly.

Arzak and Corminar watched from the porch of the farmhouse. From the looks on their faces, neither of them had seen the incident unfold, either, though that was likely because they were hard at work.

The orc, who had been so delighted that I'd liked her gifted purple scarf so much, was working unashamedly on her own *Needlework* to produce me a purple sweater which I didn't have the heart to tell her was a bit *too* much purple. Val didn't make anything of Arzak taking up *Needlework*, but I didn't trust the sorcerer to treat my new crafting skill the same way. She'd probably use the different specialism—sewing versus knitting—as a reason to insult me but not Arzak.

At the orc's side, Corminar sat with furrowed brow, an array of flowers, roots, and monster parts in front of him. I'd asked him a few days ago where the monster parts had come from, and he'd stopped what he was doing, looked up at me, and with a raised eyebrow had replied, "They are from monsters, Styk." I hadn't pushed the matter further.

The elf selected three particular ingredients—without access to the *Alchemy* skill tree, I had no idea how this process worked—and placed them into a small stone mortar. He picked up the pestle, and then paused, just before beginning to crush, and looked up at me. "Would it matter if your mana potions made your vision blurry?"

"I'm sorry?" I asked, confused.

"Please, don't be. I ask only because I could provide you with a potion that both increases your mana *and* your maximum mana, if only you were not too attached to your vision."

"I'd like to see, Corminar, if possible."

Val opened her mouth, and I immediately knew something annoying was about to come out of it. "You'd like to see Corminar?"

"So many would," the elf agreed, unconsciously fiddling with his long, lush hair.

"No," I replied, voice strained, "I'd like to see, Corminar. I'd like to see, *comma*, Corminar."

"I quite like seeing Corminar," Lore shouted out from somewhere inside the house, clearly having missed much of the subtext—and, indeed, *text*—of the conversation.

"Perhaps I shall create you a handful of these such potions. We shall see how much you get on with them."

"How blind are they going to make me?" I asked. "And for how long?"

"Your vision will be just a little blurry, that is all," Corminar replied.

I waited for the answer to the other question. It became soon apparent that it wasn't coming. "And for how long, Corminar?"

The ranger mumbled something I couldn't quite hear.

"What's that?"

"Five."

"Five what?" I asked. "It better not be years."

". . . Days."

I met the elf's gaze and held it.

"I shall create the normal potions, shall I?" Corminar asked, picking out one of the three ingredients from his mortar.

"Yes. Please." I turned back to Val and was surprised by a slap in the face. Staggering backward, I cradled my cheek with my hand. "And what in the hells was *that* for?"

Val furrowed her brow. "*Healing?* You said I could?"

"I thought you'd give me some warning!"

"Well, then, specify that next time," the sorcerer replied, then touched one of her soft hands to my cheek. As the warmth of her *Healing* magicks *healed* what little injury had been done to me, I looked up at Val, and she suddenly seemed unable to meet my gaze.

"And did you . . . err . . . get lots of experience from that?" I asked her.

Val whipped her hand away from my cheek with more speed than was perhaps necessary. "No."

I sighed. Again! And then pulled my dagger from my sheath. "Alright," I said, holding the blade over the back of my arm, "if you really need a flesh wound, then I guess I can give you—"

An almighty noise erupted across the farm, making me almost drop my knife in my scramble to cover my ears. Sheep scattered, running as far as the fencing would allow, while Seld did his best to avoid the charging animals.

It took me a moment to recognize the intense din that was in danger of making my ears bleed. It was the shriek of a banshee—a truly unsettling, bone-chillingly awful sound that, admittedly, I was responsible for. The latest of my *Worldbending* abilities, my *Shrill Perimeter*, was alerting us that trouble had crossed its boundary.

I'd only been able to place one of these perimeters, I'd discovered, and the radius wasn't all that great. So I'd placed it on the dirt road into Lore's farm, rather than on the neighbors' fields or at the tree line to the north, hoping that whoever brought trouble would approach us directly. It looked as though that gamble had paid off.

Danger had found us once more.

What a relief.

CHAPTER TWO

Prickly People

A group of elves, each wearing a long crimson robe and a bow over one shoulder, ambled up the road to Lore's farm. All pairs of eyes gazed upon the house, none of these visitors giving Val and me a second look. Every one of them had long hair twisted into a tight braid, as though to keep it out of the way in case of trouble. But were they seeking the trouble, or bringing it?

"We seek Corminar Cladenor," one of the elves said, gesturing for the group to halt a good twenty yards from Lore's house.

My elven friend stared back at the new face, considered the man without expression, then slowly placed his potion ingredients back down on the small wooden table in front of him. He matched the visitors' pace as he strolled down from the terrace and onto the yard.

Corminar stared the visitors down for a moment in silence, as though daring them to speak first. They didn't.

I placed a hand on the hilt of my dagger. Back over at the house, I could see Arzak doing much the same with the sword leaning against the side of her chair.

"I must admit," my elven friend finally said, "what with all that has happened of late, our deal had rather slipped my mind."

It wasn't until this moment that I realized who these visitors were. There was only one group—as far as I was aware—that Corminar had outstanding business with. And it wasn't the type of faction that you much *wanted* outstanding business with, either. The elves standing on the road to Lore's farm were, surely, members of the much-feared Red Thorn—elves that had been exiled from the Dawnwood, operating in industries best kept in the shadows.

The elf in charge, an older man with hair starting to gray took a step forward while the rest of his contingent remained behind. "How unbecoming of you," he said, meeting Corminar's stare. "And just what events might have kept you from fulfilling our bargain?"

"I do not think you would believe me if I told you."

The older elf raised an eyebrow. "No? You think I would not believe that you were busy delivering justice to a Player that had overstayed their welcome?"

Corminar's right eye twitched. This was about the only giveaway I'd noticed him having, when it came to his emotions. "You—"

"We are informed sufficiently about the world around us to understand that the general consensus concerning Players is not rooted in reality. We would be rather terrible at our jobs if this were not so."

Ugh. Why did elves all talk like this?

There was silence once more as Corminar considered these words. A sheep *baa-ed* in the distance. Lore stuck his head out of a window to see what was going on below, but snapped his mouth shut before saying anything that might have gotten Corminar in trouble.

"Elandor, I—"

The older elf held up his hand. "I am not present to listen to excuses; I am here to uphold the name of the Red Thorn. If it were known that we allowed you to escape a bargain, then our name would mean nothing. Do you not agree?"

"Perhaps we can strike a new arrangement," Corminar suggested. "One that grants me my life while demonstrating that the Red Thorn cannot be trifled with."

"If you do not have the mala with you," Elandor said, "then I believe it would be simpler to deliver our own form of justice now and be done with the—"

"Kill him?" Val shouted from the other side of the wooden fence, apparently able to keep quiet no longer. "You can kill him over my dead body."

Elandor raised an eyebrow, making no effort to hide the smile that crossed his face. "Such terms would be acceptable to us."

Corminar flung a hand out to signal Val to stay out of this, that he had it under control, but it was too late. The sorcerer was already moving.

Realizing what was about to happen, Arzak grabbed her two swords and stood, ready to defend herself. Lore's face disappeared from the window above.

"No," Corminar said. "No!"

Elandor's fellow elves, remaining strangely calm, responded in kind, and pulled their bows from their shoulders. What was it with elves and *Archery* skills? Why did they like it so much? Was it the wood involved?

"I had hoped it wouldn't come to this," Elandor said.

Corminar opened his mouth to reply, but was cut off by me opening a portal underneath him and sending him tumbling back onto the porch, where his bow was waiting. A single arrow, that would have struck him firmly in the chest, soared over his head.

Arzak stepped off the porch, parrying away the shot of another Red Thorn ranger with expert timing. "You not want this?" she said. "Then stop!"

Val stood at my side with her arms stretched out at her sides, then suddenly clapped them together. A summoned gust—though *gust* was maybe underselling the strength of this blow—billowed across the road and caught the group of elven archers, blowing two of the five from their feet.

"Val, we—" Arzak started, but was cut off when an arrow caught her in the shoulder.

Up above, Lore appeared back at the window, this time . . . leaping through it. He met the dusty ground hard, greatsword in hand, then rose to leap once more—this time at the members of the Red Thorn group who were still standing.

As Lore attacked, his sheep's heads suddenly snapped to him, their eyes wide. Most of them were fenced in, but a few—Lore's favorites—were able to wander the farm at large. It was those ones, now, who began to charge at our new enemies.

In these last few seconds, I had gestured one hand to the leader of this enemy group, opening a portal at his side and linking it to one at Arzak's side, expecting her to strike through it. But the orc didn't move, her only efforts concentrated on defending herself.

As Lore charged the enemies, so too did a pair of his sheep, from the elves' other side. He swung his sword forward at Elandor, but the older elf—a smile still on his face—simply stepped backward, out of reach. "Thorns," he said, "concentrate your fire on this man, if you will."

The three archers still standing pivoted to point their bows at Lore, and he had just enough time to blink, dumbfounded, at them before they fired.

I was quicker, though. I flicked one of my portals to the space between Lore and the agents of the Red Thorn, catching their fired arrows with it, and sending them shooting instead into empty air and the dusty ground.

The closest of the sheep reached Elandor at this point. While the older elf had expected the attacks of the Slayers, it seemed he hadn't anticipated the sheep attacking him, too. This sheep headbutted the elf at the back of his legs, sending him tumbling backward to the ground.

To Elandor's credit, he adapted the fall into a backward roll, landing on his feet once more a moment later. He had more agility than I'd expected of an elf his age. With a furrowed brow, the older elf glanced down at the sheep, then flicked his fingers.

In the blink of an eye, Elandor was standing much further down the road, out of range of the conflict. He left a purple glow where he'd been standing just for a moment—the familiar purple glow of *Worldbending* magicks.

Lore turned his attention to the five elven rangers, then he charged at them. I wasn't quick enough to block the arrows this time around, but Val was on it. The sorcerer sent another blast of air at the enemies—one with enough force to push the fired arrows off-target or to mess up the rangers' aims.

The barbarian leaped into the air, sword raised, and one of the rangers dropped their bow to the ground. In the same movement, they pulled a dagger from their waist and held it up to meet Lore.

"Lore!" I shouted, admittedly for no particular reason, before draining my mana some more to open another pair of portals. I caught Lore before he could meet the hidden blade, sending him rolling onto the ground at Arzak's feet.

The orc looked down at Lore, then up at me, and nodded.

This was a signal I knew, by now, all too well.

With another flick of my hands, I opened another pair of portals once more—one at Arzak's side, the other behind the group of enemies. She stepped through it, dropping one sword to the floor and holding the other high, then grabbed at the nearest elf. She held the sword to their neck, and then . . .

"Enough!" she roared.

The farm fell silent but for a sheep turning to charge at Elandor. With a whistle from Lore, they too came to a halt.

Arzak pulled the enemy elf away from the rest of the group, blade still held to their neck, and then turned to face down their leader. "We do this, we kill some of you. You kill some of us. Nobody win. There is better way."

Elandor considered her carefully before speaking. "Pray tell."

"We do better than mala," Arzak said. "And we do it for free."

CHAPTER THREE

Haggle with Care

"Tell me . . . *more*," Elandor said, gesturing for the elven rangers *not* currently being held at the edge of a sword to stand down. They lowered their bows at once.

"If release this one," Arzak said, nodding to the elf in her arms, "you attack again?"

"We will not," the enemy leader replied. "You have my word. And as Corminar will attest, one's word is sacred in this business."

The orc considered Elandor for a moment before releasing her captive, pushing them back toward the rest of the group.

"Please," the elf said, gesturing for Arzak to continue, "you were saying you would deliver unto us a mala, and that Corminar would be returning our up-front payment?"

"No," I blurted out. I didn't quite know where Arzak was going with this. Maybe she was lying, just trying to get us out of trouble. But there was a chance she was being honest—she wasn't one for deception, normally—and that she truly intended to free Corminar from his debt in this way. I couldn't have that. Not a mala. No life was worth a mala getting into the wrong hands, not even Corminar's.

Elandor raised an eyebrow. "So quick are you to rescind your offer. Is it your wish that we resume our skirmish?"

"Not a mala," I added. "We'll get you something else—something worth the same, or more—but we won't get you that."

"Ah, but you see, it is not the monetary value with which we are concerned. My masters in the south require the creature. They have need for it. We must retain our alliance with this confluence of power if our business is to survive." Elandor sighed. "Perhaps I speak too plainly."

"*This* is plainly?" Val retorted.

"It is in your interest to deliver the mala to us. Beyond this, I can say no more."

Arzak looked to me, as though allowing me to make the call. Perhaps she really was shedding herself of the responsibility of leadership.

"We can't."

"You cannot, or you *will* not?"

I shrugged. "The result is the same. What else can we get you? Surely there's another way we can pay off what Corminar owes?"

"Gold, maybe?" Val asked. "We could do a bank heist for you?"

Arzak, Lore, and I shot Val a perplexed expression, while Corminar seemed completely unfazed by the suggestion.

"It would need to be . . ." Elandor said, taking a good deal of time about his response. "We have gold. A more than sufficient amount, even. Riches do not interest me."

"Then what?"

"There are things in this world that have no value. That gold cannot buy. For most"—he shot Corminar a meaningful look—"a mala is one of them. But perhaps there are . . . equivalents?"

I shot Val a nervous glance; I did not want to think about what Elandor considered equivalent to a mala.

"Go on, then," Val said. "Like what?"

"I would ask you to use your imagination," the group's leader replied, "yet I expect that would only lead to a misunderstanding. Consider the—"

One of Lore's sheep headbutted him again.

Elandor scowled down at it. "If you do not restrain your beasts, then I will be forced to—"

An earsplitting whistle rang out, coming from Lore's mouth. "Oi, Daisy! Come here, girl."

The sheep baa-ed one more irritable baa at Elandor, then turned to strut toward the barbarian.

"Where was I?" the elf asked.

"You were being insulting and telling us what we could get for you," Lore answered with a helpful smile.

"Ah, yes." The old elf strolled back and forth, as though for show, his hands clasped behind his back. "Equivalent in perceived value to a mala, it must be—for the Red Thorn to retain their image. Perhaps an elderbeest, I might suggest. Or a grayback. Or, if you are feeling particularly adventurous, a bogspawn. Any of—"

"Are you sure we can't interest you in a bank heist?" Val asked, clearly eager to move away from the idea of bogspawn; after all, she'd already seen one firsthand, and she knew damn well we couldn't control or overcome one.

"I have already been far kinder to you than I might have been with any of our other contractors—you have Corminar's history to thank for that. I do, however, still have the Red Thorn's image to maintain—you must be seen to suffer for your sins. Paying off this debt . . . it will not be easy. But the alternative, I think you will find, is far worse."

"We shall get you your creature," Corminar said.

"*Which* creature?"

"Allow us to worry about that," the elven ranger said. "I assure you, you will not be disappointed."

Elandor stared Corminar down for quite a bit longer than was comfortable, as though searching his eyes for any sign of a lie. "Very well," he eventually said, "but you must understand, we cannot take you at your word. We learn from our mistakes, Cladenor."

"I assure you, I, too, learn from my mistakes. I would not cross you a second time."

"Be that as it may . . ."

Corminar pushed his hand down the top of his shirt, pulling from it a brass locket. "I still have my birth seed," he said. "If I were to give that to you, might that serve as suitable assurance that I intend to deliver?"

"And just what might any of us elves do with a birth seed?" Elandor responded. "You know as well as I that it is powerless outside of the Dawnwood. You might as well hand me a rock, for all that is worth."

Corminar said nothing, his face stoic but—unless I was imagining it—a shade paler than usual.

"No, I think I have seen for myself just what one member of your party values above all else," Elandor said.

"It is *my* debt to pay, not—"

"Did I not see your . . ." Elandor searched for a word. ". . . *friends* all hurry to your aid? Did they not all bare weapons against me? They share in this debt now."

"You will *not* take from—" Corminar started, but was cut off when Elandor thrust a hand into the air, snapping his fingers into a clenched fist. At the same moment, purple glows illuminated all around the farm. Portals.

Val glanced to me for a second, as though she thought I was responsible.

A chorus of animal squeals followed, as each and every one of Lore's sheep fell through their own portal. But where they ended up . . . I couldn't see. This Elandor was far stronger in the magicks of *Worldbending* than I was.

When I looked to Lore, I could see Arzak was already holding him back—a job easier said than done.

"Oh, do not worry yourself, human," Elandor said.

"Where are they?" Lore shouted, globules of saliva arcing from his mouth. "What have you done with them?"

"A . . . pocket space, you might call it," the older elf replied. "A place in which time passes slowly. A second in there might even be a day out here, in the real world. If you complete your quest quickly, your precious flock might not even notice that they are in there. If you complete it slowly, however . . . Well, I must inform you that they are not *alone* in there . . ."

"You . . . you . . ."

"You will have your prize," Corminar said, stepping in front of Lore before he could finish whatever insult was about to come out of his mouth. "I assure you of that."

"See that you do," Elandor replied. "For it is not only the lives of sheep that are at stake." With that, the older elf turned and gestured for the elven rangers to follow, which they did at once. They were well trained. Only once he was half-way down the road did Elandor turn. "Oh, and I assume you still know where to find me?"

Corminar nodded.

"Very good." Once more, Elandor turned and ambled away.

"So, Cor," Val said, watching the Red Thorn contingent stroll down the path and out of sight, "what's this creature you want us to go capture?"

The elven ranger kept his eyes fixed firmly on the spot where Elandor had disappeared. "I do have one lead. One that I received during my acquisition days."

"Yes . . ." Val prompted him.

"We will need to fetch an artifact first, if we are to control it."

"Cor, will you just tell us what we're gonna be doing?"

"Yes," Arzak echoed. "Tell. Now."

Corminar sighed, licking his lips as though he didn't want to speak the words. "We shall acquire a depth-raider."

"Ah." Arzak furrowed her brow.

"Yeah."

"You know," Val said, "I'd really rather we just went and robbed a bank."

CHAPTER FOUR

Golden Horizons

We left Tanar that very afternoon, wanting to be seen to make good on our verbal agreement with the Red Thorn. Corminar was convinced they'd be watching, and—based on their knowledge of the Player we'd killed—I was inclined to believe him.

Lore left Seld in charge of the farm, but the young farmhand seemed a bit clueless about what to do when . . . all the sheep were stuck in some alternative "pocket" world. He seemed almost as distressed as Lore about the "sheep-napping," as he'd called it, which made me wonder what he'd have called it if Elandor had taken baby goats instead. Finally, Lore, fighting through his own torment, calmed the farmhand by telling him he could head into town and start planting those crops they'd spoken about. Seld seemed a bit more focused after this.

The five of us left Lore's farm in the vicinity of the small town of Tanar, and headed south to the seaside town of Birrow, where we were going to board a ferry. For the first time in my life, I was going to leave the Gentle Tundras.

Corminar's lead on a depth-raider—whatever that was—had us crossing the Iron Sea, making for the midst of the Goldmarch. The Goldmarch was the Tundras' neighbor to the south, still under centralized authority, and known above all for its riches. Here, we'd track down his contact and get the latest information as to its whereabouts, but also—more importantly—a lead on the artifact that could control it.

Val, who'd been uncharacteristically quiet on our journey to the coast, seemed particularly riled up by any talk of this artifact, the name of which Corminar had, almost intentionally, avoided saying.

We reached Birrow in the midafternoon a few days later, and set our eyes on the ferry itself, a boat that was almost as large as the—admittedly quite small—buildings of this fishing town. For all that its size made it seem majestic, the array of different color wood in the hull and patchwork fabric in the sails made it . . . not so majestic. Not that it mattered; the next nearest ferry was all the way in Ironview, and we didn't want to add any more days onto this trip that were absolutely necessary, for the sake of Lore and his missing sheep.

"Big guy, ain't you?" the captain of the *Birrow–Last Soil* ferry said, her eyes glistening, mouth agape, as she stared up at the barbarian. "And handsome, too."

Corminar put a hand to his chest. "Well, I don't know about *big*, but—"

"She talk about Lore," Arzak said, and the elf suddenly hurried aboard the large wooden vessel.

"I should charge you double, big lad," the older captain said. "Big, strong lad."

Lore blushed, and he too hurried on board. As he passed the captain on the ramp to the ship, the woman moved to touch him on the rear, but a dirty look from Val made her stop midway. Instead, the captain held up her hands as though to protest her innocence, then suddenly pulled out her spyglass to take a look at *something*—in reality, nothing—she'd seen in the distance.

I was the last of our group to board the ship, and I was surprised by the sensation of the floor moving beneath me. I felt unsteady, and something about the vessel gently bobbing up and down in the water made me feel a little queasy. How did sailors cope with it?

Our group amassed toward the rear of the ship, Corminar sitting atop a barrel and pushing dried leaves into a pipe. From the looks of Lore, standing next to him with another empty pipe in his hand, he was hoping the elf would share.

"So," I ventured, gulping down the acid that was rising in my throat. "Depth-raiders. You still haven't told me what they are."

Corminar looked up at me, then caught sight of the smiling Lore standing next to him. With a sigh, he handed his bag of pipeweed over to him. "They are dangerous creatures indeed. Not mighty of frame or stature, but able to harness a power unlike anything else."

I raised an eyebrow. "And . . . should we feel comfortable handing one over to the *Thorn*? I know we said no mala, but I don't exactly wanna hand over something just as bad. You say depth-raiders are small but powerful? That sounds like the same thing."

Corminar shook his head. "It is no mala, that is for sure. From what you have told me, there is no power in this world as strong as those creatures. The depth-raider, however, might be a member of the same league. These beasts—not much larger than a mala, in fact—can sense great power, and seize it for their own. Most would find them not dangerous in the least—they've even been kept as pets—but once a man with power appears nearby . . . Let us say only that I have seen communal bathrooms less disgusting."

"OK," I said. "New question, then: if they're as dangerous as this, why did we just volunteer to go catch one? We've just escaped one life-threatening situation; do we really need to go throw ourselves into another?"

"It what we do," Arzak said. Lore nodded his agreement, his eyes on the captain who'd taken a fondness to him, who was at this moment undocking the ship.

"You forget the artifact we seek," Corminar added. At mention of this, Val turned away and ambled over to the edge of the ship, looking at the coast. "Though this creature is strong, it has a notable weakness. Its powers are rooted in magicks of nature; an artifact which nullifies these magicks can render the beast inert. Therefore, we must first find ourselves a witchfinder's clasp."

My eyes darted over to Val. "A what?"

"A witchfinder's clasp," Lore repeated, loudly and slowly.

"No, yes, I heard it. I just don't know what that is."

"It is a metal binding," Corminar explained, "reforged from a witchfinder's blade. At least, a blade that has been stained by the blood of witches. There is a power in witch blood, you see; it is not just tradition that necessitates the slaying of—"

"Corminar," Arzak said.

The ranger's eyes darted to Val as well. "Yes. Of course," he said. "The heart of the matter is this: we do not even *consider* fetching this beast until we have a witchfinder's clasp in hand. One that we have . . ." He shot a nervous glance at Arzak. ". . . tested."

While Corminar, Arzak, and Lore discussed the whereabouts of his informed contact, I slinked off to the side of the ship, and I tried my very best not to throw up.

"Did they send you to see how I was?" Val asked.

I said nothing, mostly because a fresh wave of nausea swept over me as I saw just how far away the land had become.

"Tell them I'm fine."

"I . . ." I started, then steeled myself to ask the inevitable question. "Why would they send me over for that?"

Val sighed. "I suppose it's time for . . ." She seemed to lose faith in that sentence. Meeting my gaze with an almost pained effort, she continued, "There's something you don't know about me, Styk. Something that might . . . push you away, if you were to find out."

I couldn't help but think of my own secret—that of my newly discovered ancestry. "Yeah, you and I both," I said.

Val couldn't seem to help but smirk. "That you sew?"

"Arzak told you, huh?"

"It was the first thing she said when you two got back, yeah. She comes across as this mature, put-together woman, doesn't she? But really she's a massive gossip."

"Don't tell Arzak stuff. Noted," I said. "I think you misunderstood me, though. I wasn't asking why they'd send someone over to see how you were. I was asking why they'd send specifically *me* over for that. Surely any of them have known you longer."

Val looked at me with a slightly stunned expression on her face. "Well, you know, because—"

I crashed across the deck as the ship suddenly collided with something, bashing my nose against the wood hard enough that blood poured forth and my health bar drained some. "What in the hells was *that?*" I cried to Val. "We hit something?"

Val narrowed her eyes. "Out here in the Iron Sea? There's no land to hit."

"Then what . . ."

An earsplitting screech erupted as a beast burst forth from the water, several pink appendages—each covered in suckers the size of my face—sprouting around the ship.

"What in the—" Val started, and then one of these giant, thirty-foot-or-so appendages slammed toward us.

I dove for my friend, opening a portal below us, and gestured open its partner somewhere behind and above me.

We fell through the portal just as the suckered arm slammed into the deck, splintering it, and found ourselves . . . in midair. Oops.

I reached out for the closest thing I could find, grabbing at the cloth of the mainsail while Val did the same thing at my side. From up here, near the top of the mainmast, I could see the monstrosity for what it was: a squid, the size of which would rival most inns.

"Cephalopor!" the captain roared below. "Cephalopor!"

It was the stuff of legends. The sort of beast that featured in horror stories, used to keep naughty children in line. A creature that was so often suggested as the cause of so many missing ships over the years.

And we had no choice but to fight it.

CHAPTER FIVE

Suckers

The sail ripped, sending Val and I hurtling toward the deck once more, just as a huge tentacle swept across the ship. Stifling a yelp, I grabbed Val and pushed the pair of us to the deck just in time to avoid it, the wet suckers sliding overhead.

The captain, however, wasn't so lucky. The tentacle caught her by the torso, flinging her across the ship and crashing her into a splintered wooden wall. She coughed up blood.

"Val!" I shouted at her.

"What?" came the response—also a shout.

"You want *Healing* experience?" I asked, pointing to the injured captain. "Get to it!"

Val nodded, then sprinted across the deck, leaving me to spin my head around to pick out the rest of the team amidst the chaos.

Between screaming passengers, I saw Corminar staggering to his feet, nursing cuts down one side of his body. The elf pulled his bow up, ready to nock an arrow in it, and then found . . . that it had been snapped in two. He groaned, threw the bow to the floor, then armed himself instead with an arrow in each hand.

"Corminar!" I shouted, trying to get his attention, but the elf's was fixed on the monstrosity—as mine should have been. A tentacle crashed across the deck once again, and while Corminar leaped deftly over it, it forced me to drain my mana some and fall through a portal, landing clumsily on my feet at the elf's side.

"Cormin—" I tried again, but the elf charged into the fight. Following his line of sight, I saw Arzak and Lore standing back-to-back, swords raised, ready to strike. Not a second behind the elf, I charged across the deck toward my fellow party members, racking my brain for a plan to deal with a creature as large as this. It certainly wouldn't fit through one of my portals, at least not as they currently were, not without—

A crashing at my rear announced another sweeping tentacle just in time for me to know what was coming, but *without* enough time to react to it. The great, five-foot-thick limb crashed into both me and Corminar, knocking us from our feet and sending us careening through the air. While I crashed into the deck near Val, Corminar had been hit harder, and so he was high in the air when another of the cephalopor's limbs caught him.

"Hi," I said to Val.

"Going well?"

"No." I pulled myself back to my feet and watched my elven friend struggling against the smaller tentacle that was wrapping itself around him. A great maw rose from the water below—a circle of teeth, something that should really have been reserved for the deepest circles of Tartarus—and . . . opened.

"Ugh! Disgusting!" Corminar shouted, apparently more concerned with the gooey liquid that coated the tentacle than the fact that he was about to be eaten.

The tentacle released him over the cephalopor's mouth, and I flicked a hand forward to open a portal between the elf and his death, causing him to crash into the deck instead.

"What do you say?" I asked him.

"I did not enjoy any part of that."

"The correct answer was 'thank you,'" I replied.

Across the deck, Arzak—still standing back-to-back with Lore—shouted "This side!" just as a tentacle came sweeping at them. The barbarian pivoted to face the same way as Arzak, and together they planted their legs strong and swung down their weapons as hard as possible. The three blades met the tentacle in the same spot, cleaving their way through about half of the limb. The damage dealt to the enemy beast caused it to scream—or howl? It was somewhere between the two—and the rest of its visible appendages quivered.

Corminar, as ever seizing the advantage, ran and leaped at the damaged tentacle, burying his—presumably poison-tipped—arrows into the cut. If I wasn't mistaken, this act made the enemy screech some more.

The cephalopor pulled its injured tentacle from the deck, flailing it around in the air until it smashed into one of the masts, cleaving the wood in two. A great wooden beam plummeted toward the deck, causing Lore and Arzak to dive to one side. A rope from the fallen mast wrapped itself around Arzak's leg in the process, and as the mast began to fall over the side, the rope dragged Arzak across the deck and toward the deep blue below.

"Arzak!" Lore shouted, just as I opened a portal in front of him, its partner at the edge of the ship where the mast had gone over. He understood immediately—nobody had taken to the portals quite like him—and he hopped through the portal, blade swinging. He brought the Bane Sword down toward the deck, slicing the taut rope in two and saving Arzak from a horrific end.

Distracted by the portals and the rope, I didn't notice when the cephalopor swept the deck once more, this time with more force behind the attack. I opened a portal beneath me to avoid the attack, but was too slow, being only halfway through when the tentacle collided with my head and shoulders.

I spun through the portal, landing once again beside Val and the captain, who was now looking a lot less likely to die.

"I'd ask again if it was going well, but . . ." Val gestured generally toward me.

"Thanks," I said, then charged into the fray once more, where Arzak and Lore were back-to-back again, ready for another strike.

"We must do more!" Corminar shouted from across the ship. "Our approach is too—" We didn't hear the rest as he ran for cover to avoid another of the leviathan's attacks.

"Land ahoy!" Val shouted from behind me.

"What?" I cried back.

"Land a—It's what sailors say! It means, like, 'Look! There's some land over there!'"

I pulled a face. "OK? And how is that useful right now?"

"Because . . ." Val said, throwing me the captain's spyglass. "This is a *sea* beast."

"Ah." I understood well and truly where she was going with this, but there was still one problem: this creature wasn't getting through one of my portals. At least, not without a great force squidging its soft flesh through.

. . . Ah.

I ran across the ship, the captain's spyglass firmly in my grasp, dodging as a tentacle smashed atop the deck in front of me, ducking and weaving to avoid splintering wood and injured passengers, until I arrived at the edge of the boat at Arzak and Lore's side. "The rope!" I shouted to the orc.

"The rope?"

"Get the rope!"

As Arzak ran after the rope that had caused her trouble earlier, I pressed the spyglass to my eye, squinting the land into focus. By now, Val knew my *Worldbending* abilities very well—and she knew the specific wording of their restrictions.

> **Local Portal II (Worldbending):** Create a portal to another location within current range of sight or within a ten-yard radius. Uses mana/second.

The restriction of this one? "Within current range of sight." No part of that said I couldn't improve my vision beforehand. Staring down the spyglass, I gestured open a portal high above the distant land, its partner opened above me temporarily, just to hold it in place.

Arzak hurried back to me, a pile of rope in hand. I snatched it from her—there was no time for politeness—and hurriedly searched for the end.

"What doing?" the orc asked.

I ignored her, finally finding one of the rope's two ends. In my haste, I dropped it, and had to pluck it from the deck once more before tying it firmly around my belt. "You and Lore? Drop your weapons. Find the other end. Hold it tight—it's going to pull hard."

"What are—"

I eyed my mana bar, which was rapidly draining with every second I held the portals open. "Just do it, Arzak. There's no time."

The orc nodded, unraveling the rope behind me as I turned to face the cephalopor on the right-hand side of the ship—whether that was port or starboard I didn't know, and frankly, didn't care.

I glanced back to see Arzak holding the rope tight and Lore plunging his Bane Sword into the deck to do the same. With one nod to the orc, and one deep sigh, I ran.

I charged toward the leviathan, leaping over the side of the ship, remembering to hold my nose shut only moments before I plunged into the freezing water below.

My eyes stung when I opened them, but the salt water wasn't the most disturbing thing in the surrounding sea. The body of the creature hovered in front of me, its fleshy pink surface so terrifyingly different to that of any monster I'd faced down before.

In this moment, I fought the urge to panic, shaking my head to rid myself of questions like "And just why in the hells did you think *this* was a good idea?" Rather than surrendering to my fears, I reached a hand forward and shifted the portal above the ship.

I opened it just behind the creature, illuminating the murky depths with the midday sun.

I felt the current shift immediately as torrents of water flowed through the portal and toward the land below, pulling anything that was currently *in* the sea along with it. It was only at this moment that I realized there could well have been people underneath where I'd opened the portal, but it was too late to worry about that right at this moment.

I lurched forward, the rope jerking taut behind me, and—thankfully—not splitting from the force. The cephalopor, however, had no such security. It flailed its tentacles desperately toward the ship, failing to get much purchase, as the waters pulled it backward. Soon it reached the portal, and the rear of its horrifying form, for a moment . . . plugged it.

I thought, then, that my usual plan of "dropping things from a great height" had let me down. I thought that before long, the beast would notice me, that it would send a tentacle to wrap itself around me and fling me into that terrible maw.

But then it slipped.

It was just a little at first, the water pressure in front and the gravity behind overcoming the creature in some minuscule way. But then it slipped again, more so this time. And again. Then, suddenly, daylight streamed into the water once more as the leviathan fell through my portal toward either its death or, at the very least, to a place far away from us.

I breathed a sigh of relief as I closed my portal and pulled at the rope to drag myself back to the surface, where I gasped for breath just as the notification came in.

Level ? Cephalopor defeated!

Worldbending: +4,200XP
Worldbending increased to Level 25!
Base Points Gained: +2 INT, +2 Free Points (INT/WIS/CHA)
Ability Selection Unlocked

. . .

CHAPTER SIX

Sisyphus Rewards

My ability selection was delayed by the fact that the ferry was taking on water. Honestly, I couldn't fault the ship build too much—it had, after all, survived a cephalopor attack—but that didn't mean I fancied drowning anytime soon. It was Arzak—no surprises there—who hurried to organize a means of keeping us afloat.

Not two minutes after we'd beaten the cephalopor—no time for celebrations, even—Arzak had us and the rest of the passengers standing in a line, stretching from the bottom deck to the top. Each of us had a bucket or similar container in hand, and between us we kept the ship afloat long enough for the remaining crew to mend the cracks in the hull.

When the ferry finally made it to the Goldmarch town of Last Soil, I breathed a sigh of relief that we'd encountered no more trouble. If I'd had my way, I wouldn't be setting sail again anytime soon, but that did pose the question of how I intended to get back to the Tundras without adding literal weeks of travel to my journey.

As we passed through the small town, we noticed several residents hurrying eastward, many dragging small carts behind them. Lore grabbed one such man by the arm and asked him what all the fuss was about.

The local blinked at him, eyes wide in amazement, and replied, "You wouldn't believe it—a cephalopor has appeared out of nowhere, down the road! It fell from the sky!" Without sparing another moment, and likely not wanting to be beaten to the creature, he turned and continued on running.

"Was anyone hurt?" I called after him.

"Who cares?" the man cried back. "The ink will be worth a small fortune!"

I watched the man go before turning to the rest of my party. "A small fortune? Why didn't any of you tell me that?"

Arzak shrugged. "Our reward is we are alive."

"We could've had *two* rewards!"

This only elicited another shrug from the orc; she didn't seem to care much for coin beyond it putting food on the table.

As matters moved on for all but the most coin-hungry of us—Corminar and me, who were still grumbling about it—Arzak led us on the road south, toward Tarenthe, where our contact was waiting for us.

I turned my attention instead to the notifications I had queued up: notifications of growth in power.

Ability Selection Unlocked
Select an ability from the list below:

Option 1: Warped Shield (Worldbending)—*Passive*. If an enemy strikes you with a low-level melee weapon, Warped Shield automatically activates to open a portal that deflects this attack. You must not have any portals currently active. Uses mana on activation.

OK. So now we are talking.

It took me a moment after reading this option to fully comprehend its real value, and that value was . . . game-changing. So far, I'd been pouring all my points into Intelligence, wherever possible, and as a result, I'd been skimping on Vitality. My mana reserves might be growing fast, but my health bar on the other hand . . . well, let's just say a particular severe strain of the flu could still knock me out. The build I was rapidly growing into was one that so many called the "glass arrow"—able to deal some pretty hefty damage, but likely to run out of health after just one or two decent hits.

I'd known this going in—Val and I had discussed this at depth—and I'd decided that this was a price worth paying for ample mana, at least in the short-term. But with this new *Warped Shield* ability . . . maybe that low health wasn't so much of an issue. After all, this basically worked as a mana-powered health bar. If I picked this, not only would I not have to worry about stamina for my melee attacks, due to my *Mana-Fueled* ability, but I'd be able to not worry about health, either. I could just keep investing my points into Intelligence . . . forever?

Obviously, this didn't account for the downsides, namely the part about being hit by a "low-level melee weapon." I interpreted this as meaning that spells wouldn't be covered, for a start, and then any meaningful melee attack wouldn't be, either. But I knew what ability upgrades were like, and this ability had the makings of one that would increase in coverage very quickly.

Though my heart was already shouting for this particular ability, I forced myself to read the others with an open mind.

Hidden condition met! Alternative ability choice unlocked.
Option 2: Cloth Storage II (Worldbending) [Requires: *Needlework* skill unlocked]—Open a portal to an inventory space, wherein you can store up to ten distinct *Needlework* supplies.

The synergistic—was that a word?—abilities that required you to progress in other skill trees were always powerful, and I could see this was the case for this one, too. If I was fully invested in leveling up my new *Needlework* skill, then this would have been a great one; I could drop this thread and cloth that I'd been lumbering around in my knapsack, and I'd have a larger range of items on hand at any time.

I also noticed this was a level 2 ability. Presumably, I'd already long since achieved the *Worldbending* requirements for the level 1 equivalent, and so the system was jumping me straight to the next.

A recent memory tickled my mind—that of Elandor "sheep-napping" Lore's animals, putting them in a so-called pocket world. Did this not share some of those qualities? Was Elandor's ability not, at the end of the day, a storage ability? With this new information, I had to applaud the old elf's creative use of his abilities—he'd turned a storage one into, essentially, an attack in its own right.

Elandor's ability was far more advanced than mine, of course. Surely storing a good twenty or so sheep required a much higher level than one that stored essentially ten bits of cloth. But it was a start, and if I picked this one, I might unlock new, more interesting versions in the future . . .

As always, these decisions came with an opportunity cost. If I selected this *Cloth Storage* ability, then I was missing out on *Warped Shield*, and there was no way of knowing when I'd next be able to pick this ability or its higher-level equivalent. Not that I was considering picking the storage ability over the one that might keep me alive, of course.

But there was one notification remaining; I still had another possible choice.

Option 3: Local Portal III (Worldbending)—*Upgrade to Local Portal II.* Create a portal to another location within current range of sight or within a thirty-yard radius. Uses mana/second.

Now, maybe I'd been spoiled recently by all this quick progression, but my understanding of ability selections was as follows.

You'd normally get between three or four choices. The first one or two would be pretty decent, but not Alterra-shattering, and you'd force yourself to consider them properly, weighing up all their pros and cons and use cases. And then you'd . . . move on.

The next ability choice would be, inevitably, much better. You'd spend a decent amount of time thinking this one through—much more than the previous ones—and you'd actually get excited about this one. You'd think *Yes, this is it. Surely the last choice couldn't possibly beat this.*

And then it does. The last ability choice is the best, as though the system were sentient. As though it understood drama, and knew to save the best until last.

So maybe I'd been, subconsciously, expecting that again. And then it was *Local Portal III.* Don't get me wrong, it was a strong enough upgrade, increasing the radius of my portals some decent amount. I could think of plenty of use cases for it—robbing a bank came to mind, though maybe I was spending too much time around Val—and yet . . . this upgrade just wasn't as exciting.

What's more, I had the lower-level version of this ability already. From my previous experience, I knew this meant I'd see upgrades for this ability quite regularly, unlike the choices for any new abilities that I passed over. *Looking at you,* Cloth Storage.

Now that I'd muttered that ability name aloud—resulting in a peculiar glance from Corminar—I realized that it really wasn't a very good name.

"Styk, dear friend, are you feeling yourself?" Corminar asked.

Before I could reply, Val piped up from the road behind us. "If he's doing the face that looks like he's thinking so hard that his head is about to explode—"

"He is," the elf confirmed.

"Then he's got himself an ability upgrade," Val finished.

"I do."

"Ooh!" Lore said, turning around on the road in front of me. "Need any help?"

I shook my head. "You know what? Not this time. I think I know *exactly* what I'm about to pick. And then, when I do, I'd like you to poke me with your worst weapon."

Lore furrowed his brow, absolutely perplexed by this suggestion, and I made my ability selection.

Ability Unlocked: Warped Shield

Warped Shield (Worldbending)—*Passive.* If an enemy strikes you with a low-level melee weapon, Warped Shield automatically activates to open a portal that deflects this attack. You must not have any portals currently active. Uses mana on activation.

Immediately, I felt a strange sensation ripple over me—the same one that I got when stepping through a portal. The ability was in place. That was good to know; I didn't need to remember to switch it on every morning, or anything.

Feeling a strange confidence wash over me, I slowed my pace a tad and started walking at Val's side.

"You here to show off?" she asked.

"A bit."

"Fine. Tell me about this new ability."

But I shook my head. "No, it's not that, it's . . . With this quest we're on, there's got to be some stuff to fight, hasn't there? And with the artifact's upgrade, I could progress even faster if I really—"

"Faster? Styk, you've been progressing at whiplash speeds."

"And yet not fast enough, is it? I'm done messing around, Val," I told her. "You know my biggest mistake in all that pyroknight stuff?"

"You mean other than making a near-godlike figure want to kill you?"

I ignored the jab. "It was not spending enough time gathering experience. If I'd done that—if I'd done that *properly*—then maybe I wouldn't have had to die in the process of killing him."

"Die *again*," Val corrected me.

Again, I ignored her, my mind's eye instead fixed on a man I'd never thought I could be. I saw myself, blazing daggers in hand, a glowing portal open behind me, crowds of admirers throwing themselves at my feet.

With the power of the Sisyphus Artifact behind me, I realized, I could be a hero. A real one.

CHAPTER SEVEN

Answers Under Lock & Key

Corminar knocked a very precise seven times on the dark green door.

We were by this point in the middle of the large town of Tarenthe, one of the many key stopping points on the east–west Goldmarch road—that which connected the Badlands in the east to the Beached Armada in the west. It was a vibrant town, without an ounce of poverty to go around—or at least, nothing that I could see, and I didn't think something like that would escape my notice. The people seemed happier as a result, some of them smiling, even greeting strangers in the street. It took me a moment to get my head around it, though Lore had been eagerly returning their greetings from the second we'd stepped foot in town.

Val had made the case for stopping at a tavern to try out the local craft, but Arzak and Lore had focused us—the sheep were on the line here, and the sooner we resolved all of this, the better. And so Corminar brought us to this address, to an almost intentionally average-looking home, with common vines stretching up the walls and a clean, vibrant, emerald door.

"Yes?" a voice called out from inside the house.

"Corminar Cladenor," my elven friend said. "Here for Aiwin Pelayor."

There was a moment of pause. "On what business?"

"Information. We can pay handsomely."

"Information on their crimes?" came the response from the man inside.

It was Corminar's turn to pause. "I am not sure I understand, sir."

"Are you asking for information *from* Aiwin, or asking for information *on* Aiwin? Not that I can help all that much with both, you understand."

"He just said he didn't understand, no," Val called out. "And neither do I."

Corminar hushed our big-mouthed friend with a held-out hand. "We have no intention of asking for information on Aiwin, I assure you. It would not . . . *suit* me for many of their crimes to be uncovered."

At this, a bolt slid back, and the green door opened to reveal an elderly man, his hair graying, wearing a necklace with elven text engraved thereon—text that he, as a human, surely couldn't read. "You are a friend," he said, looking up at Corminar.

"From times long past," Corminar agreed with a nod.

The older man gestured us all to hurry into the large house, then spent a moment on the boundary looking up and down the street. Satisfied that nobody had seen us—which was probably not true; we were a pretty ragtag group of adventurers and likely to stand out in these parts—he closed the door behind him, and turned to face us.

"Aiwin?" Corminar prompted him. "I would like to see them as soon as is possible. Do they not reside at this address any longer?"

"In a matter of speaking . . ." the old man said. "Before I say any more, I have to know: are you truly a friend to Aiwin? Can I really trust you?"

"How would you have me prove it?" Corminar asked.

The old man considered this for a moment. "I would have you answer a question: where does Aiwin consider home?"

Val balked at this. "I thought *this* was their—"

This time, it was up to me to shut her up, which I did by putting my index finger on her lips. She made a show of moving to bite it.

"Their home? Like me, Aiwin has no home. Not exiled from the Woods— we are not Red Thorn—but both of us guilty of enough that we are no longer welcome there. I assure you, sir, whatever you think we might be, we are not. We are here on unrelated work."

The old man met Corminar's eyes, as though judging whether the elf was speaking truth or regurgitating someone else's. Finally, he nodded. "You wish to see Aiwin? Then I have bad news, I'm afraid. Aiwin was caught up in some rather nasty smuggling business. Seeds from the Dawnwood, you see—a matter that the Goldmarch government takes rather seriously, considering their shaky diplomatic relationship with the elves."

"Birth seeds?" Corminar asked, eyebrow raised. So rare was it that he volunteered expressions like this.

But the man shook his head. "No, no, nothing like that. Regular old seeds, but enough, perhaps, to dilute the magicks of the Dawnwood. Not that Aiwin was directly involved, of course—they act only to put interested parties together—but the subsequent clampdown has been broad."

"Has Aiwin fled?" I asked. "Where are they? We just—"

"Tarenthe general prison," the old man said. "Awaiting trial. Queen Amira has broadened legal powers, however—for matters such as these, they can be held indefinitely. And until they secure any meaningful evidence, the authorities might just do that."

"Sorry, just to be clear," Val cut in, "the only person who knows the whereabouts of this depth-raider is currently in . . . *prison?*"

"If it is information you're after, I can check the notes," the old man said. "If the information is anywhere outside Aiwin's mind, then it'd be there. Though these notes are not the most thorough, I am afraid."

Corminar shook his head. "Anything Aiwin writes down will be encoded, and half of what they have written will be a lie, intended to fool anyone who pries. If we want the information, we will have to retrieve it directly from Aiwin."

"Does prison have visiting hours?" Arzak asked. "We go speak them."

"Visiting hours?" the old man replied, blinking at the orc. "No. No, dear, it doesn't. Things are changing in the Goldmarch. It might not look like it, but they are. Queen Amira is tightening her grip on her subjects. The law is just a part of it, even, but it's where you're most likely to notice the change. No visitation, holding without charge . . . all of that is new. Soon enough we'll lose the right to a jury of our peers. After that . . . I do not believe there will be a trial at all."

Out of the corner of my eye, I could see Val trying to suppress a smile. Never a good sign.

"Tell me about this prison," she said.

The man furrowed his brow, but complied nonetheless. "Built thirty years ago with the expansion of the new kingdom under Amira's father's reign. It sits on the old site of a human cemetery, and—"

"Yes, yes," Val said, waving the man down. "I'm not after its history. I want to know what it's like now. Tell me about the defenses. What's keeping Aiwin from breaking out? Sounds like they're resourceful enough, after all."

The man laughed, then strolled across the room to take a seat in a plush armchair. "'Resourceful' will only get you so far, dear. The prison is guarded by the finest of Goldmarch soldiers, trained in the ways of the sword and the bow. There will be a sorcerer on staff, as well—"

"Was that a pun?" I asked. This question went unanswered.

"—who will be responsible for enchanted traps at every conceivable entrance, as well as being able to rain magicks down on any escapees. And that's before we even talk about the building itself. There is an outer wall, high enough to be near unscalable, and even if you *were* to scale it, that would only take you to the guards' sleeping and living quarters. The actual cells are behind *another* wall, just as high, patrolled day and night by soldiers in golden armor. If none of this is enough to deter you from attempting escape, then perhaps the artifact at the center of this building *is.*"

Before Lore could ask the obvious question, Aiwin's friend—housemate? Lover? I realized I didn't quite know the relationship here—continued.

"When a new prisoner arrives, their personal effects are taken away, and they are forced to wear a belt. Upon equipping this belt, it becomes locked—you cannot take it off. This would not in itself be a problem, beyond it being unfashionable, however that is where the aforementioned artifact comes into play.

"Built into the very structure, at the center of the complex, is a cube—one powered by an enchanted gem. When one of the linked belts moves far enough away from the cube—that is, somewhere between the inner and outer walls— then the cube activates the belt."

I licked my lips, resisting the urge to ask—

"What happens when it activates?" Val asked.

"It tightens. It tightens until it can tighten no more—and few forces in Alterra can stop it."

The sorcerer nodded. "OK. OK, that's interesting. We can—"

"Val, why are you asking all this?" Lore asked.

"Because we need to break them out," Val replied with a wide, toothy grin on her face.

"I thought it was a bank heist that you wanted to do," I said.

"Yeah, but do you know the only thing better than a bank heist? A prison break—and it seems we have no choice but to do one." She flung her hands in the air in celebration. "How great is that!"

CHAPTER EIGHT

Large, Stealthy Barbarian

Lore and I stood with our backs against the prison's outer wall, pipes in hand. Lore puffed away happily, but I—with alcohol always being my vice of choice—struggled to resist the urge to cough.

"Did we really need to be smoking for this to work?" I asked Lore.

The man shrugged, and between puffs said, "Smoking always makes you look more casual."

"What, so you're saying if we were stood up against this wall without anything in our hands, people would be suspicious, but because we're smoking, nobody cares?"

Lore gestured to the people passing by, two of them wearing the gold—well, mustard really—surcoats of Goldmarch soldiers. None of them gave us a second look.

I tried puffing again. "Well, I still don't like it."

The barbarian didn't comment, instead nodding down the road to our right, where Arzak and Corminar had their wrists bound together, and were being led toward the prison entrance by a Goldmarch soldier.

Not the *real* Goldmarch soldier, of course. No, she was currently unconscious, bound and gagged in the plush armchair of Aiwin's elderly housemate. If she regained consciousness, it was unlikely to be for very long, considering the very specific type of poison that Corminar had left the old man with.

But this left Val free to take the soldier's place, without rousing any suspicions, and I couldn't help but remind her that she should be making use of her changeling abilities more often—an idea that caused her to stick her tongue out at me.

"You ready?" Lore asked as I pressed one hand flat against the wall behind me.

"Are we *sure* we're standing next to the supply closet? I don't wanna end up standing in the middle of . . . of . . . I dunno, a training yard or something."

The barbarian shrugged. "Old guy said so. He seemed to know what he was all about, though, didn't he?"

I wasn't sure I was quite as convinced by Aiwin's friend as Lore was, but the disguised Val and her two "prisoners" had now reached the arch. Val was talking their way inside—new intake, by order of the captain—and so we were already committed to our plan.

"As soon as they go through . . ." Lore said.

"I remember the plan, Lore."

The barbarian held up his hands in surrender. "Sorry, just checking!"

I placed my other hand on the stone outer wall of the prison.

"Ready . . ." Lore said, and I prepared myself to activate the spell. ". . . Go!"

In a flash, I opened one half of the portal ten yards behind me—as far as I could open a portal without the aid of sight—and another underneath our feet. As soon as our heads passed through it, I closed it again, and hoped nobody on the street we'd left behind had noticed my magicks.

Lore and I stood, as the old man had said, in a large supply closet, one filled with buckets and mops and various other contraptions I didn't quite understand. Most importantly, we stood in this supply closet alone.

Neither of us breathed, trying to be as stealthy as possible, one of us more adept than the other. And considering *I* was the more adept at stealth, being at level 6, this really wasn't that stealthy on the whole. But it was the best we had.

As far as we could tell from this side of the thick outer wall, nobody on the street had seen us—at least, there was no shouting, no metal armor clinking as guards rushed toward our position. The first part of the plan was complete.

"One wall down . . ." I said.

". . . one to go," Lore finished, though it hadn't been necessary. "You got any thoughts on *how* exactly we're gonna deactivate this cube thing?"

Like the last time he'd asked me, I shrugged. "I'll think of something. This is what I do." It was what I *had* done, at least, though admittedly that had been with a whole different build.

Keeping low, Lore and I approached the exit to the supply closet and opened the door a crack, me poking my head through the gap low, and Lore poking through high. We saw this would take us onto the open space between walls, illuminated by pole lanterns every five paces. This wasn't necessarily a problem— I could portal us across fairly easily—but unless we remained hidden, any of the dozens of guards might spot us.

"You think the others have found Aiwin yet?" Lore asked, a bit too loudly.

"Lore, keep quiet."

"Sorry."

I closed the door gently. "They might have, sure. I imagine they're being taken to the same cells. But that doesn't help anyone if we don't deactivate this artifact first, so . . ."

Lore mimed zipping his lips shut, then immediately said, "Got it."

I looked across the gap between the walls, scanning for signs of trouble. There were a few guards atop the inner wall, but if we portaled to the base of that wall quickly enough, they wouldn't notice. It was those roaming the grounds between the walls that were going to cause trouble. They patrolled in pairs, moving slowly but deliberately, spaced apart but not so much that any part of the ground was out of sight at any one time. If we were going to reach the base of the inner wall, and then open another pair of portals to get us inside, then we were going to need a distraction.

"Distraction," I said to Lore. "Any ideas?"

"I could juggle!" the man replied.

"Any ideas that don't get you spotted and captured?"

Lore bit his lip. "Oh, right, yeah. Sorry, I just never get to juggle with a captive audience."

I blinked at the man; sometimes it was hard to know whether he was joking or not. "If we had Corminar here, he could distract the guards with his arrows somehow. But—"

"I could throw something. I've got a good arm."

I waited for the final part of this thought, knowing exactly what was coming.

". . . From all the juggling."

"Not from swinging a massive sword around?"

Lore considered this. "Maybe a little of both."

I nodded as Lore disappeared back into the closet proper. "Right. There's an armor stand next to that empty training area to our right. If we can hit it, making enough noise, or maybe even knock it over, then—"

Lore suddenly reappeared at my side, heavy wooden brush in hand. "Throw brush at armor, yeah?"

Before I could respond, he shoved the door open enough to get his arm out, then lobbed the brush toward the stand of armor. It crashed to the ground. Turning back to face me, Lore asked, "Wait, you were ready, right?"

I responded by opening a portal beneath us, pairing it with one at the base of the inner wall. We fell through it, and before I could worry that we'd been spotted, I placed my hands on the wall behind me. Opening another portal ten yards back, and one on the wall behind us, we fell through it and out of sight.

Well . . . not *quite* out of sight.

As Lore and I turned to take in our new surroundings, we found ourselves in very close proximity to a woman in a gold surcoat, her mouth open, a sandwich in a hand that had frozen on its way to her face.

Lore and I stood deathly still, as though if we didn't move, then the guard wouldn't see us—despite the fact that we were standing no more than two feet directly in front of her.

"I can . . . explain?" I said.

The guard narrowed her eyes.

I reached for my blade.

Lore hit her with the butt of his sword.

In just one hit, the woman fell to the ground unconscious, and I turned to blink up at Lore in surprise.

"What?" he asked.

"How'd you do that?"

The barbarian shrugged. "Special ability. *Two-Handed* ain't just killing people."

"Not the way *you* do it, perhaps," I said, which I supposed I meant as an insult, but judging by Lore's smile, he understood it as a great compliment.

"We should . . ." He gestured to the unconscious body.

"Yeah." I looked around for a place to stuff her, and saw a low cupboard that might hold her if we pushed her in just right. I nodded to it, and between Lore and I we succeeded in the spatial-awareness puzzle put before us.

"That was the hardest part of the whole thing," Lore said.

"The hardest part *so far*," I corrected him, ever the optimist.

With this, we made our way to the door of the room, and slowly inched it open. The door gave way to reveal a corridor—one which, we had been told, would lead to the innermost chamber, above the dungeons and cells, and where the binding artifact would be located.

"You know," I whispered to Lore, "did you ever wonder how that old guy knew all this?"

Lore shrugged. "Figured it was cos he was a soldier."

I raised an eyebrow.

"What?" the barbarian replied. "You didn't notice the tattoo on his hand? It's an army one."

"Huh." Even having known Lore for a few months at this point, I still didn't quite know what to make of him. One moment you could think he was the dumbest—if kindest—soul you'd ever met, and the next he'd completely out-smart you.

We crept down the corridor to the wooden door at the end, and Lore readied his sword. There was a reason it couldn't just be me sneaking in, of course—at this point, reaching the warden's chamber, we could well run into trouble. And I fancied my chances much more with Lore at my side.

I took in a deep breath, nodded to Lore, and flung the door open.

The room was empty.

"Oh . . ." Lore said as we pressed inside and I closed the door behind us. "Problem?"

"No problem! Just thought that'd be harder."

I laughed. "Well, it's not over yet."

Stealth: +1,300XP

Stealth increased to Level 7!

Stealth increased to Level 8!

Base Points Gained: +2 DEX, +2 WIS, +4 Free Points (DEX/WIS)

"Nice," I muttered, already excited for my next ability choice, which would be in just two more levels. For now, though, there was another priority.

In front of us, a square stone pillar rose from the ground in the center of the room. In the very middle, the stone gave way to a brass-like frame, and in the center of *that*, floated a giant purple gem.

"Alright, Styk," Lore said, "do your thing."

I had no idea quite what "my thing" was going to be, but there was a single focusing factor. Right now, Corminar and Arzak would be in the cells—likely alongside Aiwin, yes, but with belts of their own in place. If I failed here, they were doomed. They'd never be able to escape.

I took a deep breath, and I got to work.

CHAPTER NINE

Crimes Against Fashion

"Styk?" Lore asked while I stood in front of the pillar in which the binding artifact was embedded.

"Yeah?" I answered, my hands hovering in the air at my sides, as though about to spring into action.

"Is this it? Are you doing your thing?"

"Yes," I replied.

"Nice."

Still, I didn't move. Staring at the gem in front of me, I had nothing. All I could think of was brute force—ripping the gem from the pillar. But I knew from the experience of a past life that such simple solutions were often doomed to fail. There would be a trap or an enchantment or an enchanted trap that stopped us from doing so. Without a better plan, though . . .

"Help me with this thing, will you?" I asked Lore.

Together, we reached out and put our hands on the gem—*no ill effects so far, so that was good*—and began trying to wrench it free of its frame. By myself, I might not have expected to pull it out, but Lore was about the strongest man I'd ever met. Even with him helping, however, the gem didn't budge. Not an inch.

"I don't think it's gonna work," said the barbarian helpfully.

With a sigh, I released the gem and went back to scratching my head. "Nope." At that moment, another idea occurred to me, and I tried to *Portal Slice* my way through the brass frame. Again . . . nothing doing. The frame itself was enchanted, then, and likely why we couldn't wrench the gem free with hands alone.

"Alright, OK, OK," I said, wondering if my deficiency in this situation was more down to no longer having thievery-based abilities or having an audience for the first time ever. "Could you go keep watch?" I asked Lore, and found myself relieved when he smiled, nodded, and left me to it.

OK. What do I know?

I knew that brute force wasn't going to pull the gem from its frame, and I knew that, likewise, I wasn't going to be able to pull the frame from the pillar, considering that it was enchanted. More and more, it seemed like removing the binding gem wasn't an option—nobody said prison break was going to be easy, after all.

A vision of Corminar and Arzak, sitting in the cells, belts around them, flashed through my mind. Where before, a botched thievery attempt would just cost me a payday, it would now cost my friends their lives. This really wasn't the time to come up short.

I couldn't remove the gem, then. But that didn't mean I couldn't destroy it.

"Lore," I said, and the barbarian peered around from his position at the door. "I don't expect this is going to work, but just in case . . . could you attack it?"

"Attack what?"

"The gem."

Lore nodded furiously. "Right, yes."

I took a few steps back—knowing better than to get between Bane Sword and its target—and watched as Lore swung his weapon through the air with almighty force. The blade clattered against the gem and reverberated away from it, not even leaving a scratch.

"You were right," Lore said, inspecting the gem, "that didn't work."

"Worth trying, I guess. But I think we're gonna need something even stronger than your sword if we're going to destroy it."

Lore raised his eyebrows. "You got something in mind? What're we gonna find in the middle of a prison that's gonna be more powerful?"

I couldn't help but smile at my idea—there was a simple elegance to it, using the prison's own magicks against them. "We're gonna check out these belts."

"Great!" Lore replied, ". . . where are they?"

"No idea. Want to go find out?"

We crept out of the central chamber, blades—Lore's big, mine small—at the ready, and kept our breathing quiet. This central chamber was much less protected than the outer walls, which made a certain sort of sense, I supposed—anyone trying to get out of the prison would head, you know, *outward*. At least, unless they knew what their fancy new belts did.

We tried room after room after room—three rooms, yes—looking for these belts, but we found nothing. One was a meeting room, with flies buzzing around half-eaten pastries. One was a storage closet, which contained—in addition to the usual—a scented candle, a limp rose, and the suggestion that two of the guards had recently been a tad frisky in there. And the last door we tried led to a plain old corridor, which Lore and I crept along, the big man in front.

> **Stealth**: +1,300XP
> *Stealth increased to Level 9!*
> **Base Points Gained**: +1 DEX, +1 WIS, +2 Free Points (DEX/WIS)

I blinked. That I was gathering experience for *Stealth* was no surprise—we were, after all . . . sneaking. But I didn't typically get *Stealth* experience until the stealthing was over. Which meant—

A black belt swept over my head.

"Lore!" I cried, at the same moment that I sank to the floor, trying to avoid being caught by the belt. As I sank, I turned and saw a woman in a freshly pressed golden surcoat standing over me, her eyes wide. She pressed the belt down toward me, and I held up my hands to force it back. It was already over my neck by this point, though.

"Her mouth!" I shouted to Lore. "Don't let her shout!"

Lore did exactly as I suggested, and I mean *exactly*. He jumped along the corridor, his hand shooting for the woman's mouth, and for some reason he dropped his sword in the process.

I scrambled for my Blade of Samal, allowing the prison belt to droop over my shoulder for just a second, and readied myself to *stab*. The guard cried—the noise muffled by Lore's hand—as blade plunged into her flesh.

"You'll survive this," I told her. "If you're quiet, you'll survive. If you make noise, well, I'll have to stab you some more, won't I?"

The woman frantically nodded her understanding, reaching a hand into her pocket.

"Lore, you'll have to knock her out. We'll cover the wound and—"

The guard pulled a small purple crystal from her pocket.

I glanced at it. "What's—" I started, and then realized at the same moment that the woman crushed it in her hand. The nearby belt—the one currently slumped over my right shoulder and left arm—hummed for a second, and I made the incredibly quick decision to open a portal beneath me.

I tumbled through it, pushing the belt away from me in the same moment, and it snapped from belt into disc in a flash. If I'd still had it over me, I would have been in two distinct pieces. I didn't suspect my health bar could handle *that*.

Lore glanced down the other end of the corridor to where I'd landed, made sure I was OK, and then nodded for his Bane Sword. I portaled it over to him, the man snatched it out of the air, and then before the woman could make another play, he hit her square in the forehead with the butt of the sword.

> *Level 18 Guard defeated!*

Worldbending: +400XP
Worldbending increased to Level 26!
Base Points Gained: +2 INT, +2 Free Points (INT/WIS/CHA)
Knifework: +1,850XP

"We'll go find another cupboard?" the barbarian asked, standing over the body.

"Yes," I said. "Wait—first of all . . ." I hurried over to the unconscious woman's side, and I rummaged through her pockets until I found what I was looking for—two more purple gems. They had to be linked to the central gem, that much was obvious, and if I could use one of them to close a belt, then . . . All I needed was the belt.

The answer to this part of the situation came quickly. As we located another room in which to stuff our unconscious attacker, we found spare uniforms. And part of spare uniforms, it turned out, was a spare belt. There was a logic to this—if a belt ever went wrong, or their wearers managed to find a way to overcome the binding spell and removed them, the guards would want a fresh one on hand. And it explained why the guard we'd encountered a moment ago had been ready with one.

Belt in one hand, tiny purple gems in the other, I hurried back to the central chamber, Lore following at my heels and ready to strike at any more guards who came across us. Fortunately, we encountered none.

Wasting no time, I plunged the gems into my pocket for a moment and unclasped the belt, wrapping it around the pillar and the central gem therein. As soon as I touched the two ends of the belt together, it fused, becoming one solid circle that shrunk gently to the size of the object it was holding.

In this case, that was the pillar.

"You ready?" I asked Lore. "I'm about to 'do my thing.'"

"Exciting!"

I pulled one of the purple gems from my pocket and smashed it against the floor.

Nothing happened at first, or at least nothing *seemed* to. There was a faint straining sound, like leather stretched too far, as the belt tried its best to contract against the magically reinforced brass frame. It was the proverbial unstoppable force against the proverbial immovable object.

I considered checking with Lore if I was using the word *proverbial* correctly, before deciding he probably didn't know.

And then . . . it happened. The brass frame buckled under the pressure of the closing belt, and once that had gone, the purple gem followed soon after.

As the crystal disintegrated, so too did the belt. This belt, yes, but also every other belt that was magically linked to this pillar. Mine and Lore's part of the job was done, and all we needed to do now was—

A noise erupted around us. No, multiple noises. From all around the prison complex.

Of course, we'd known we were releasing the belts on every single prisoner. I, personally, had thought these objects were cruel; they were already prisoners, so there was no need for such a barbaric device on them. What *hadn't* occurred to me was the real impact of releasing all belts at once. It was, to the prisoners, an opportunity.

Guards shouted and screamed, magick attacks screeched, and footsteps belonging to both guard and prisoner alike echoed around the prison.

The prisoners knew full well what those belts did, then. And they knew full well that this was their one and only chance to be without them.

It wasn't just Corminar, Arzak, and Aiwin trying to escape.

It was everyone.

CHAPTER TEN

Free-Range Prisoners

"Err . . ." Lore mumbled.

"Yep. I know."

"You think that makes getting out easier or harder?"

I ran toward the door, holding it open for him. "Only one way to find out."

We charged down the corridor and out into the central building's main atrium, just at the same time that several freshly risen guards charged down the stairs. They hurriedly pulled their uniforms on, blades still in scabbards, their eyes on the door and not on the two fleeing saboteurs—us.

"Fight?" Lore asked.

"Nope!" I said, flinging open a portal in front of us and opening another through the crack in the opening door. I jumped through, followed by Lore, completely bypassing the fight against the five new guards running out to help.

Outside, in the space between the inner and outer walls, the prison was . . . chaos. Dozens of guards in gold uniforms fought with prisoners, balls of fire and lightning, poison-tipped arrows, and throwing knives all flying through the air. There was a chorus of metal against metal, the smartest of the prisoners having rushed to retrieve weapons rather than heading straight for the outer wall.

I scurried for cover, Lore close behind me, but quickly found there was no cover to be had. "Alright, portal time," I told my barbarian friend.

Lore grabbed me by the arm. "What about the others? Shouldn't we help them?"

"If you can find them in this mess, sure. Otherwise, I think it's time we got the hells out of here."

Lore said nothing, frantically searching the skirmish for signs of our fellow party members, while I reached a hand up to the top of the outer wall to open a portal.

But just as I was about to open, a great wall of misty light—no, not a wall, a *bubble*—encapsulated the prison at the outside boundary of the outer wall. This magick-summoned wall was apparently enough to stop bodies passing through—as evidence by a fleeing prisoner bouncing off it rather comically at the main gate—but also enough to stop me opening a portal beyond it. That was it; our escape plan gone.

"Styk?" Lore asked as one of the guards spotted us and he was forced to bat the resulting arrow out of the way with the flat of his sword. "Styk? What's going on?"

"We're trapped," I replied. "We need to find . . . We need to find their sorcerer. Knock them out."

"There!" Lore shouted, pointing across the grounds to a spot near the supply closet where we'd entered the complex.

"The sorcerer?"

"No! Corminar!" Lore was already running at the point, so I opened up a portal in front of him to carry him across the grounds as quickly as possible, minimizing the risk of him being hit by a stray arrow or spell. I, too, charged toward it and jumped through, landing with a stumble at the feet of my elven friend.

"Styk," Corminar said, catching me.

"Good to see you, too."

At his rear, Lore pushed open the door to the supply rooms, then Corminar and I charged inside.

"I assumed I would find you here," the elf said. "This was your entrance route, after all."

"Where's Val?" I asked. "And Arzak?"

Corminar frowned. "We were separated in the confusion. Val was preoccupied by orders from a ranking soldier, while Arzak had already joined a prison gang."

"A . . ." I started.

"Yes. The *Reach Fiends*. She attempted to acquire me an invitation as well, though alas I was not Orcish enough for their tastes. Or, indeed, Orcish at all."

Lore held the door nearly closed, one eye peeking out through a crack. "I don't see either of them. They're alright though, you reckon, yeah?"

The elf shrugged. "It is a mistake to worry too much about either of them, in my experience. They are perfectly capable of survival, even in such chaotic circumstances as these."

"Yeah," I said, "I didn't really expect this."

"Seems rather obvious in hindsight, though, one supposes."

I almost stuck my tongue out at him, then remembered he wasn't Val, and therefore was unlikely to take such a childish response in the same spirit. "What's the plan, then?"

"It's my understanding that *you* are the planner of the group," Corminar replied. "Why did you think we brought you on board?"

"I thought it was the portal stuff," Lore suggested.

"That as well."

I blinked, but now wasn't the time to question the two guys on all of this.

"Guys . . ." Lore said.

I turned to Corminar. "OK, whether or not we're looking for the others, we need to find this sorcerer, get this magick wall thing down."

"Guys . . ."

"Agreed. Our initial intelligence suggested she would be atop the wall. A view of the battlefield, if you will."

"Yeah, so we head up there, we move quick—"

"Portals," the elf suggested.

"—and we eliminate her as quickly as possible."

"I must ask: are we killing or rendering unconscious? I do not think I agree with killing someone who is only doing their—"

Lore slammed the door closed just before a heavy *something* crashed into it, making the very room shake. Corminar and I turned to blink at him.

"I tried to tell you: I think we've been spotted."

"Ah."

"Yeah."

"How many?"

"Nine coming this way," Lore replied.

"Ah."

"Yeah," Lore said again. "Too many."

"How high do you think the wall is?"

"More than ten yards, I am afraid to say," Corminar said, seeing where I was going with this line of questioning. "You cannot do this blind. Is there another exit?"

I shook my head. "None."

"Ideas," the elf said. "Quickly."

There was only one that came to me. "Lore," I said. "Open the door."

The barbarian knew better than to delay on following instructions in the middle of a fight—act first, ask questions later, and all that. He flung the door open and I charged straight through it, at the group of nine soldiers who were advancing on us. I bared my teeth at them for a moment, thinking for some reason that would make me look a lot scarier than I was, but in hindsight it maybe just made me look like an idiot.

The nine soldiers didn't slow their advance at the sight of a thief charging at them, even if I was now being followed by a huge barbarian and a ranger who admittedly looked more like a talented hairdresser than a mercenary. One soldier with a bow nocked it once more, preparing to fire, and in that moment I spun around, midstep.

I flung one hand back and the other gesturing up to the top of the wall, and I opened the pair of portals just in time. I fell through it backward, landing hard on the solid stone wall and knocking my head, Lore and Corminar jumping through behind me. In the daze that followed from me hitting my head, I forgot for a moment to close the portal, and in that time, one of the soldiers slipped through.

"Lore!" I said, alerting my barbarian friend to the danger close at hand.

The barbarian, alarmed, swiveled on the spot, and in doing so knocked the soldier from both his feet and the top of the wall. He landed with a *thud*. "Oops," Lore mumbled, and the three of us peeked over the side of the wall. "You think he's . . . ?"

"They probably got a good healer on hand," I told him, very keenly aware that this could be a lie. "He'll be fine."

Lore either believed it or he chose to believe it—the end result was the same—and the three of us turned our attention to the few soldiers on the wall.

The gold-cloaked guards were dotted every thirty or so yards along the wall, each of them armed with a crossbow, and unbothered by the prisoners below, who had no way of reaching them. None of the prisoners, of course, except us.

"I see Val!" Lore said, pointing to a woman in a very loose-fitting uniform. She was at the bottom of the wall, by the entrance to the inner gate, and something—likely magicks—had forced her to drop her disguise. And the guards around her were just starting to notice.

I eyed up my mana bar—drained a good way by this point—before ultimately realizing I had no choice here; only I could pluck her from trouble. I heard Val yelp as the portal appeared beneath her feet, and for a second she scrambled to avoid falling through it, before apparently realizing what was going on.

She fell to the top of the wall at my side and managed to avoid hitting her head like I had. "Took you long enough," she said, punching me on the shoulder.

"Is that your version of 'thank you for saving my life'?"

"Yes," Corminar and Lore both said in unison.

". . . Fine."

"Bit of a mess, all this," Val said, quickly switching the subject.

"Yes, I know, I didn't account for it."

"Guess it seems pretty obvious in hindsight, though."

"Yes, thank you, Val. You happen to know where this sorcerer is?"

A huge fireball exploded down below, and the four of us crept back from the edge of the wall.

"One of this lot," Val said, nodding to the soldiers on the wall. "What's-his-face back at Aiwin's was right. She's up here."

"These are all rangers."

"Nope," Val said, nodding to our right. "Look. The one four spots down. Not really firing, and anything she *does* fire . . ." The ranger released a shot that soared far over its presumed target's head.

As though her ears were burning, the soldier in question turned toward us. Her eyes widened when she saw that four "prisoners" had made it atop the wall.

"Styk?" Lore asked.

"Yeah?"

"How much mana you got left? How much portal?"

I checked my mana reserves. "About . . . ten seconds? Not much. What are you thinking?"

The sorcerer shouted, her fellow rangers snapping from their focus on the prisoners below, and following the sorcerer's gesture to, and I quote, "Look the hell over there!"

"Don't need to kill them, do we?" Lore said. "Just gotta make them unconscious."

I didn't quite know what it was, but Lore and I seemed to always be on the same page. We operated on one strategic wavelength more so than any of the others—except for perhaps between me and Val when it came to whether or not to have another pint. In this case, with ten or more crossbows being suddenly pointed toward us, this aspect of our relationship was vital; we didn't have more than a few seconds before we were all speared.

Lore charged.

I flashed open a portal in front of him, opening its pair just in front of the nearest ranger. As soon as Lore was through it—not quite, even—I closed it, preserving mana. The barbarian, instead of attacking, simply . . . ran through the ranger, knocking him from the wall and causing him to scream as he plummeted toward the floor below—and then, silence.

Level 20 Guard defeated!

Worldbending: +650XP

Lore charged on, not slowing for a moment, and perhaps even gaining in speed. The next ranger released a bolt from his crossbow, and I blinked open a portal just in time to save Lore from being hit. The burly barbarian bashed the guard in the shoulder, sending them, too, toward the ground far below.

Level 18 Guard defeated!

> **Worldbending**: +500XP

"I haven't bowled for a while," Val mused as she watched the events unfold in front of us.

"My thoughts as well," Corminar agreed.

Once again, I flashed open a pair of portals in front of Lore, my mana now dwindling, and closed the gap between him and the next ranger. (I think you know, dear reader, what happened next.)

> *Level 22 Gambling Enthusiast defeated!*

> **Worldbending**: +650XP

I noted this guard having a different class; it was good to see that not *all* of them lived to work, and at least one of them worked to live instead.

The next ranger ahead of Lore was the one we were after—if we eliminated them, then the shining white wall spell would be broken. We'd be free.

As I opened up one last portal, my mana reserves draining to a mere sliver, Lore jumped, swinging his Bane Sword pommel-first. He passed through the portal, and his target's eyes widened. The very beginnings of a new spell—flames, from the looks of it—formed in the guard's hands, but it was too late.

The pommel of the Bane Sword collided with the woman's head, just between the eyes, and she staggered. It didn't knock her out in one go, like the guard back in the central chambers, but it was enough to cancel the fire spell and give Lore the chance to bash her from the wall.

> *Level 25 Sorcerer Captain defeated!*

> **Worldbending**: +900XP
> *Worldbending increased to Level 27!*
> **Base Points Gained**: +2 INT, +2 Free Points (INT/WIS/CHA)

The shimmering white wall faded away, and it didn't take long for the remaining prisoners down in the grounds below to notice, many of them cheering at this apparent victory.

Lore turned around, a good fifty paces down the wall, and gave us a thumbs-up, a goofy smile on his face.

"Alright, nice," Val said. She nodded to the ground below, outside the prison wall. "Styk, you wanna portal us down there?"

"I . . . err . . ." I replied, one eye on the barest sliver of mana supply left in my power bar.

"... Styk?"

Someone down below shouted, "People!"

"What?" I replied.

"Are you seriously about to tell me that you're out of mana?" Val asked. Before I could either confirm or deny it, she continued, "And how in the *hells* are we supposed to get out of here, then?"

"We could jump," Lore said, appearing at our side once more. When Val and I raised an eyebrow at him, he clarified, "Sorry. Was a joke."

"People!" the voice down below said again, and in that moment, both Corminar and I realized this voice belonged to Arzak. We poked our heads over the side of the wall to see the orc standing with a beautiful elf at her side, apparently having already long since escaped the prison complex. I could only assume that this slender elf was Aiwin. If I had been a better man, I would have picked up my jaw from the floor more quickly.

"Finally," Arzak grumbled.

"You could have . . . used our names?" I replied.

The orc shook her head. "Then they know your names. Breaking prison? Crime too great. Best nobody know."

I sighed. "Yeah, I'm sorry about the confusion. I didn't think it would happen."

"I did," Arzak shouted back up. "Was obvious."

"See?" Val muttered.

"You not portal down?"

"I'm out of mana!" I replied.

"I thought always pick Intelligence?"

"I do!"

"Hmm," Arzak said. "Then need level up faster."

"That doesn't help us right about now!" I replied, at the same moment that an arrow caught Lore in the back, making him furrow his brow but otherwise not even complain about it.

Down below, Aiwin eyed the gate, a good way down the street, where guards were still doing their best to keep the prisoners contained. "Might we move this along a little?" the new elf asked.

"Is OK," the orc said with a shrug. "I catch." She held out her hands in front of her, and I was completely unconvinced.

"You sure?" I asked. "It's quite a fall, and I—"

At that moment, Val gave me a quick, sharp shove, and only seconds later I was cradled in Arzak's arms.

"See? I catch."

I looked back at the woman currently carrying me. "This is very emasculating."

Arzak smiled. "Yes," she said.

CHAPTER ELEVEN

In the Absence of the Trees

We accompanied Aiwin back to their home on the south side of town, the two elves striding far ahead of us and engaging in a conversation the rest of the team weren't privy to. Aiwin's hand, I noticed, often touched against Corminar's arm, and made it down to his bottom a couple of times, too.

"Do you think those two—" Lore started.

"Yep," I replied at the same time as Arzak grunted her agreement.

"When Cor's involved, is it ever really a doubt?" Val asked.

"S'pose not."

The kettle was boiling over a magick-induced flame when we entered Aiwin's home, and the old man and the young elf hurried to embrace one another.

"You succeeded!" the man said to Corminar, once the embrace was over, and he then moved to hug the ranger as well.

"I don't suppose you really thought we would fail?" Corminar replied. "Being that you *do* have the kettle on, ready for us."

The old man smiled. "Always plan for the best outcome, I do."

Lore nodded. "Me, too!"

We settled in various spots around the room—Corminar and Aiwin on the sofa, Lore leaning against the wall, Arzak on the floor with legs crossed, and Val in one of the armchairs scowling at me for perching on one of the armrests. A few moments later, the old man—who, it had turned out, was just an old friend of Aiwin's—returned with a tray full of cups on saucers, each of them clattering slightly in his shaky hands. He passed them out one by one, and when I took my own, a pungent wood smell filled my nostrils.

"What is it?" Val asked, staring into the red-brown liquid.

"The bark of the saltash tree," Aiwin replied. "It is no surprise that you haven't come across it before; there is little demand for it outside of the Dawnwood. But for me, it is a taste of home."

Corminar murmured his agreement.

"My birth seed was a saltash, you know," Aiwin said.

Arzak leaned forward, tiny teacup in giant green hands, pinky finger pointing out stiffly. "What is birth seed? Corminar not tell us this."

"It was no secret," Corminar clarified. "Only a matter I did not share."

"And why not, Cladenor?" Aiwin said, knocking at Corminar playfully with the back of their hand. "Always so secretive, this one." They turned their head to the orc. "Arzak, was it?"

Arzak nodded, her face betraying no emotion—as ever.

"For an elf, a birth seed is a seed plucked from the land where you were born. If planted in the Dawnwood, the wood of the resulting tree will be enchanted with properties tailored toward your class. Supposedly, it is intervention from Gaia herself, plucking at the strings of reality, that enchants the plant in this way."

"Is powerful?" Arzak asked, her eyes on Corminar. "Why never plant it?"

"To plant it . . . to nurture it . . . this would require me to reside in the Dawnwood. You know I do not return there."

"You never say why."

Aiwin gasped. "Cladenor! Have you really changed so little?" The elf turned their attention to the rest of the room. "This man will simply not talk about his demons. When we were together—"

Lore gasped. "You were together?"

Aiwin and Corminar both shot the barbarian a curious expression, and then the former shook their head and got back to their story. "When we were together, this man would not tell you if he had so much as a headache. Ever the lieutenant, always seeking to lead his men by appearing untouchable."

"Wait, what? You were a lieutenant?" I asked.

Val elbowed me in the side. Hard. "Styk."

"What?" I replied, upturning my hands. "What did I do?"

"I assume your friend knows Corminar does not much like to talk about it," Aiwin said, which earned a nod from Val. "Unless . . ."

Corminar shook his head, and an awkward silence fell over the room. To fill it, I sipped at my tea and took a slightly too pointed breath afterward.

"I never asked," Aiwin said, turning to Corminar. "I suppose you are here to . . . reconnect?" Though they'd phrased it carefully, I think everyone in the room—except maybe Lore—knew exactly what they'd meant. "I've never had a man put together a team to save me before . . ." Aiwin's hand stroked Corminar's long hair—and yet only the second most luscious head of hair in the room.

The ranger smiled at them. "As much as I'd like to . . . reconnect, my dear, I am afraid we sought you out on rather urgent business."

Aiwin's hand paused midstroke, then surreptitiously moved away from Corminar's head. "Oh?"

"Difficulty with the Thorn," Corminar explained. "A matter of an unpaid debt. We seek the depth-raider that you mentioned in your letters."

"The Thorn?" Aiwin asked, raising an eyebrow. "I was under the impression that you had sworn off all affiliation with our fellow emigrated kind?" There was a pointed look that accompanied this question. Aiwin knew something about Corminar that we didn't. A great many things, perhaps.

"I assure you, no affiliation was intended. For all their great many sins, the Red Thorn do pay rather well."

Aiwin held the ranger's gaze, as though silence might break him. They couldn't know him *that* well, then, if they thought that was going to work.

"Corminar . . ." I said, able to hold back the question no longer. "Have you been . . . exiled . . . from the Dawnwood? Like the Thorn?"

The elf glanced over at me. "Exiled? No. Do not categorize me with those criminals. I am only . . ." He searched for the word. "I am *discouraged* from returning. They could not exile me—certainly not after all that I did for them."

"I don't suppose you have told them?" Aiwin asked.

Corminar shook his head—a single, definitive movement.

It was Val, of all people, who saved Corminar from what was clearly an uncomfortable conversation for him. She turned to Aiwin. "You can tell us where the depth-raider is?"

"Certainly. The depth-raider is no complicated matter; it is being kept as a pet by a young family not two days' travel from here."

"As a pet?" Lore asked. "Is that safe?"

Aiwin nodded. "The depth-raider is a small beast—one that many mistake for being harmless. *Cute,* I believe is the word most often used. In most situations they *are harmless,* at least. It is only once the raider moves into the vicinity of someone with immense power that the trouble begins, for it will use this power. It will adopt immense power as its own, if only for a short time, but a creature such as this only requires a moment to reap great destruction. But you know all this." Aiwin glanced at Corminar, who gave no indication of his own feelings about the matter. "Or at least Corminar does."

"Good," Arzak said, putting the empty teacup down as carefully as she could manage. "We get your hair out, then."

"'Get out of your hair,'" Lore whispered to her.

"We get out of your hair, then," Arzak corrected herself. "Tell us where is. We pay."

"Pretty sure getting you out of prison is payment enough," Val added.

Aiwin glanced at the sorcerer, and if I wasn't mistaken, a flicker of annoyance flashed across her eyes.

Val, sitting on the chair next to me, tensed slightly—she'd noticed it, too.

But Aiwin didn't refute Val's statement, instead saying, "The depth-raider is the least of your concerns. Simple, in fact, is the retrieval of such a beast. The true value exists in knowing how to control it, and for that, you will require—"

"A witchfinder's clasp," Val said, voice low.

Aiwin turned to Corminar. "Oh, so *that* you have told them? Just which of our platoon's excursions have you spoken about, and which have you not? I will need to know, if I am to travel with you."

The ranger remained silent for a moment. "They knew of the clasp regardless of context—context that I had not shared."

"And what makes you think you're traveling with us?" Val asked.

"You want a witchfinder's clasp?" Aiwin replied. "This is no small feat. The witchfinders know their value—the blood of a witch is oh so rare, these days—and they will not part with one for just anybody. Fortunately for you all, I have contacts in the Goldmarch. The right word in the right ear, and anything can be yours." They turned to Corminar. "I learned that from the best."

Val opened her mouth to speak, but Arzak suddenly—wisely?—broke in to speak before she could. "OK. You come with. We get clasp first."

Ted

Three weeks earlier

"Raspberry bonbons—five for a bronze!" Ted shouted over the murmur of the marketgoers as they strolled past his stall. "Rose cubes—four for a bronze! Get 'em while they're . . . a normal temperature."

He sighed; business was slow today.

There'd been maybe ten serious browsers at his stall, and only two of them had actually purchased anything. And, what's more, one of them had bought only five sweets, which was barely worth the trouble of bagging them up.

It was no wonder, then, that Ted had needed to pivot his business over the last few months. Creating and selling sweets—that had been his dream, back from when he was a young boy, but now that he was actually doing it, he realized just what a cutthroat world it was.

There were narrow profit margins, high time investments required for actually cooking the sweets, and enough competition in the relatively small Tundran market that every so often merchants would sabotage one another. Ted had been the victim of such a crime twice, and the perpetrator of such a crime around eight times.

"Raspberry bonbons, sir? For the partner, sir?" Ted tried, doing his best attempt at a smile as he shook a bag in the general direction of a passing gentleman.

The man didn't so much as glance at him. Customers held all the power in this relationship; with this power came a complete disregard for social norms. Norms like being polite.

But then Ted saw a woman he recognized—or, at least, a hood that he recognized; he never saw the woman's face. The small woman approached casually, looking down at the stock atop the stall as though browsing, before whispering, "Do you have what I came for?"

Ted nodded, meeting the woman's lack of gaze and rifling through the boxes underneath the stall. This side business—the aforementioned "pivot"—was where the real money came from. Perhaps the term *real money* overstated how much revenue it was pulling in; it was still few and far between.

"Here," Ted said, pulling an identical paper bag up from beneath the stall, this one filled with blueberry bonbons. The difference with these ones, however, was that they were enchanted.

"Stamina drain?" the woman asked, her voice raspy.

"That's the one." Ted handed the sweets over, taking the decent amount of coin from the woman in return. "Could I ask what they're for, madam? I imagined a competition, perhaps, or—"

"It wouldn't be good business to make a habit of it," the customer replied. "Asking, I mean. Patrons of your industry . . . I cannot imagine they much want to advertise their deeds."

Ted held up his hands in apology. "Please. Forget I asked."

The woman nodded, took the enchanted—some might say "cursed"—sweets, and then turned away. When she'd taken a few paces, she turned back to Ted. "I intend to challenge someone to a duel. One that I would not naturally win."

Ted smiled. "For love or for honor?"

The woman turned away once more, without replying.

And so, Ted filled in the rest of the story for himself. He daydreamed this duel—a hooded woman storming into a grand castle, throwing down her disguise and revealing her beauty before challenging a duke to fight for the death. It was for both love and honor, in Ted's mind—to win back the hand of the duchess, to whom the hooded woman had always intended to be married.

"You got duprica?" a passing old woman said.

Ted snapped from his daydream, pulling himself from the top of the cart and hearing it creak as a result. "Duprica?"

"Fabric," the old woman clarified.

"Yes, I know, madam, but . . ." Ted gestured toward the sign that read Ted's Confectionary. There was still an arrow hole in it.

The woman looked at the sign, blinked, and then looked back to Ted. "Duprica?" she asked again.

"I sell sweets, madam."

"No fabrics, then?"

"No, madam."

The woman said no more, and she turned away.

Ted couldn't help but eyeball his swinging sign once more. Specifically, he couldn't help but eyeball the damage those adventurers had done to it. He was trying to run a business here, and he didn't need adventurers hiding from soldiers behind his stall!

At least fate had seen fit to allow him some revenge. Those cursed sweets had been meant for a customer—one who had been very angry that Ted had gotten rid of them already—but it was worth it. He couldn't help but smile at the thought of that dumb rogue vomiting conjured water and not understanding where it was coming from. He only hoped that the pretty sorcerer hadn't gotten caught in the crossfire—she seemed the type to like sweets, too.

Ted sighed and got back to work, shouting about his wares and getting only momentary glances in his direction in return. It was feeling like an increasingly futile business, all of this. The customers of the Tundras didn't know good produce when it was displayed in front of them, and they damned well didn't have the money to pay a fair price for it. If only he was able to—

Suddenly, a notification flashed before his eyes. A boost to *Enchanting* experience—the skill he used to create those cursed sweets.

It wasn't uncommon that he got notifications like these, as these enchantments were so often used in resolving a fight. Like all magick and combat skills, experience was rewarded at the close of battle, based on your contribution to the fight.

What set this particular notification apart was the amount of experience—it was in the tens of thousands.

Level up notification after *level up* notification came flooding in, boosting his Intelligence and Dexterity with every moment that passed.

Someone out there—some genius of a person—had used his cursed sweets to take down someone or something of an *incredibly* high level. A rare monster, or a hero, or . . . a god.

Ted sank to his knees, closing his eyes in silent gratitude to whoever it had been that had helped him so. This amount of experience was game-changing. This increased his skill to a level that put him among the best enchanters in the land.

"Sir, could I get—" a passing customer said.

"No," Ted replied, batting the man away.

The Gentle Tundras were beneath Ted now. At this level of skill, he could be one of the finest enchantment merchants in the land. And he could take his business to somewhere rich, where the customers would hand over decent coin for his services.

"But I—" the attempted customer tried again.

"I'm closed," Ted replied, and finally the man got the message.

There was only one thing for it—it was time to head to more prosperous lands. It was time to head for the Goldmarch.

Fame and fortune awaited.

CHAPTER TWELVE

No Obvious Sign of Trouble

The further east we traveled down the main merchant road, the more aged the population seemed to get. By the time we were only a day out from our destination—a village that the witchfinders used as an informal base of operations—everyone in the inn with us looked like they could drop dead at any moment.

Apparently this was normal, at least to a degree. For towns on the Goldmarch's famous trade routes, the young population so often went off to find fame and fortune, either as working merchants or through gainful employment in the prosperous Goldmarch cities.

Recently though, there was another factor at play. Apparently no longer satisfied by dominating land trade, the government of the Goldmarch was now expanding into sea trade as well. But the geography of this part of the world didn't exactly make this easy, with all the major ports being on seas that were entirely separated from one another.

This, the Goldmarch were looking to change. A decade or so ago, the town of Lenktra, on the Tundran border, had created a small canal system that connected the Coldwater in the northwest to the Iron Sea in the northeast. Building on this, there was a new canal project, not two days' ride from where we were—a so-called Great Golden Canal Project, which the locals thought was intentionally fancy-sounding to convince all the young'uns to offer their services. This canal was a far more ambitious project, stretching over a good amount of land, but would—upon completion—connect the Iron Sea with the Sea of Roots, the elven sea.

Sea trade would stretch from the Beached Armada to the Dawnwood, and the Goldmarch would be able to collect taxes on all of this.

(Now, I know what you're thinking, reader. You're thinking "why in the hells are you telling me this?" My reasoning is twofold. Firstly, as we all know, all great stories have substantial and detailed descriptions of trade deals between various factions, often as inciting incidents. Secondly, I tell you this because Arzak was completely enchanted by the concept.)

"Make money for go through land? Why?" the orc demanded of an old local.

The local man seemed stunned by this response; clearly, he'd just been mouthing off about it all, rather than expecting any follow-up questions. "Amira's in charge of this land, so she gets to say what goes on in it, right?"

"I don't think this right, no."

The rest of our team, tired from many days of travel, watched this conversation at the bar from a corner booth, where we'd all finished our beers but none of us could be bothered to buy any more. I considered trying to portal some beer from within the kegs into my glass, but I didn't really want to get kicked out, either.

"I ain't saying it's right," the increasingly perplexed local said. "Only that she can do it. And besides, walking down a toll road is one thing, sure, but using a canal that the queen's spent thousands, tens of thousands, whatever amount of gold on . . . well maybe she deserves to get paid back for it?"

"So you for this canal now?" Arzak asked.

"No, of course not. But what I think is moral isn't the same as what is legal."

"Why not? In Reaches, no law. We just do right things."

The old man opened his mouth to reply, then thought better of it. He turned to the barmaid. "Better call it a night, I think." He tossed a bronze coin onto the bar. "A drink for my friend here," he said.

"What about my friends?" Arzak asked, nodding to us in the booth.

The man left without saying another word.

The witchfinder base was a few hours away from the main merchant road, taking us on a well-worn track through the beech forest, which we were forced to trudge down single file. It had been quite a long few days of travel—we really needed to buy some horses at some point—and conversation had grown quiet. In fact, I'd spent some of the evenings barely participating in conversation, instead focusing on leveling up my new *Needlework* skill. This effort had gotten the skill up to level 7, which had the added benefit of putting me up to level 12 overall—more and more, my profile wasn't incredibly embarrassing.

As I'd passed level 5 in *Needlework*, I'd had the choice of new abilities, and my decision was an easy one; I chose the ability most useful for myself.

> **Ability Unlocked**: Basic Cloth Armor
> **Basic Cloth Armor (Needlework)**: Craft a basic cloth armor, quality dependent on materials, time, and skill level.

I'd not been able to, you know, use this ability yet, considering that all I was working with was a large piece of increasingly busy fabric and a spool of thread that Arzak had loaned me. Next time we passed through a town with a suitable shop, however, I was going to stock up on materials.

We came suddenly upon our destination, a secluded village formed of wooden buildings, some newer than others, based on the amount of moss present on their walls. It was a surprise that we'd stumbled upon a place like this without knowing well in advance that it was ahead of us—and it took me a moment to realize that this stemmed from the village being eerily quiet.

"Huh," I mumbled to myself, then turned to the rest of the team at my side, everyone peeking through the bushes at the town like I had been. Everyone except Val and Arzak, at least.

I turned back to see Val and Arzak a few dozen paces back down the path, muttering something inaudible to one another. Val shifted from foot to foot, glancing nervously at the rest of us.

"You coming?" I called back to them, and the cry made Val flinch.

She turned to glare at me.

"What?" I asked, accompanying the question with a shrug.

"Well, there goes the element of surprise," Val mumbled as she and Arzak cautiously approached.

"Element of surprise?" I repeated, then pointed to Aiwin. "They know Aiwin. We're just here to talk, right?"

Val raised her eyebrows, but made no further comment.

"Shall we?" Aiwin asked the group, their gaze flicking to Val. Without waiting for an answer, they stepped through the growth and out into the open of the secluded village, the rest of the group following close behind.

Nobody in the village stirred, and nobody came to meet us.

"Hello?" Lore called out cheerily. "Witchfinders? We've come to buy something from you!"

We waited. Still, there was nothing. No signs of life.

"I don't like this," Val said, already inching away from the village.

"This certainly isn't right," Aiwin added. "There should always be someone here. There was a woman in charge—a monster hunter of sorts; witches, demons, and the like—who should be here, or an assistant in her place. That neither of them are present is . . ."

"Unsettling," I said.

Aiwin nodded.

"Blood," Arzak said suddenly, staring around the village.

"What?" I asked, doing the same. "Where?"

"Nowhere. No blood."

"Well, you could have said—"

"No blood, and no discarded weapons. No sign of a fight at all," Corminar said. "It is as though they have moved on."

Aiwin shook their head. "Impossible. I am told they had work here."

"Could be that they finished it?" Lore asked.

"It was impossible work, never to be completed."

"Our job feel like that sometimes," Arzak mused.

We all fell silent, the only sound being the rustling of leaves in the wind and the cries of distant birds.

"So . . . what do we do?" Val finally asked, shattering the silence.

"I suppose we look for information as to where they have gone," Aiwin said. "I am sure there will be a clue or two inside."

Val nodded. "Great. Go ahead. I'll keep a lookout."

Arzak glanced at Val, and Val returned the look. Even though I couldn't translate it, I knew there was a whole conversation happening in the way they stared at one another.

I turned to Lore, glancing at him, trying to do the same silent method of communication.

"What?" he asked.

I sighed. "Shall we go inside?"

"Oh! Yes."

While Arzak ambled inside a small building to our right, and Corminar and Aiwin took a new, freshly constructed building to our left, Lore and I made for another structure. This looked to be the largest of the buildings here—three floors, and a wider floor plan than most taverns, almost as if this had been here first and then built around.

The village was no less creepy when you were *inside* the old abandoned structures, though maybe I should have seen that one coming. Ancient floorboards squeaked below Lore's heavy feet, and the sound of the wind billowing through cracks in the walls made an eerie whistling noise. I tried to ignore it as we searched the building, looking for anything that might give us a clue to our next move.

I finally found it in a grand study at the rear of the building—a room with an impressively ornate old desk with stacks of disorganized paperwork sitting on top of it. Most of these documents were meaningless to me, or at least not at all useful—records of witchfinding reports, and the like. But one piece of paper caught my eye because of a familiar coat of arms printed at the head of the thick, posh paper—that of the kingdom of the Goldmarch.

Lots of it was meaningless to me, but a few parts stood out. For one, the woman who had been in charge of this operation—apparently installed by some-one in the capital—had been reassigned, and would not be returning. This, I could only assume, was the monster hunter that Aiwin had mentioned earlier. The other key piece of information, however, was more crucial.

The instruction given to the witchfinders was to remain put, and to, under no circumstances, continue with their experiments.

Just as I looked up to ask Lore what he made of all this, I heard a distant scream.

CHAPTER THIRTEEN

Playing Our Hands

Lore and I sprinted through the building, floorboards creaking underneath our feet, the big man's elbows knocking at the doorframes as he passed through them. We spilled out into the center of the witchfinder's encampment. Across the way, Corminar and Aiwin spilled out of their building, too, alarm plain on their faces. Val stood in the center, spinning around, as though searching for the source of the scream.

"Who is it? What was that?" I asked.

Before I could wonder if it was Arzak who had somehow produced that strange, high-pitched shriek, she too stumbled out of her building, apparently safe and sound.

"It wasn't you?" Val asked.

"That was a *woman* screaming."

"What, men can't squeal?"

"We can," Lore said. "Mostly around spiders."

"Who scream?" Arzak asked, hurrying over to the rest of us. "Styk?"

I blinked at her. "No, it wasn't—"

"It would appear that it wasn't any of us," Aiwin cut in, their eyes scanning the dark trees that surrounded the secluded village.

"So, someone's here?" Val asked. "Did any of you find anyone?"

There was a round of unsure headshaking.

"Nobody," I said. "The place is deserted."

"Then . . ." Val gestured to the surrounding woods.

We each remained still, silent, barely daring to breathe, our ears open for sounds of movement, or . . . further shrieks. But nothing came.

"Is anyone there?" Lore—sometimes the bravest of us—cried out.

We heard nothing but the rustling of leaves and the cries of the distant birds.

"Perhaps it was a fellhawk," Corminar suggested. "Rather odd for one to be this far from the Dawnwood, yet . . . They are said to have cries that resemble human screams."

There was a moment of pause before Arzak finally nodded. "Fellhawk. Must be screaming bird. Yes."

Others in the team nodded. I didn't know whether this was just because they *wanted* to believe the source of the noise was a bird, or because this was actually *likely*, but it was a convenient enough truth for me to leap on board. I clapped my hands together. "Alright," I said. "Shall we make camp?"

"Here?" Val asked.

"Might as well. At least we'd have a roof over our heads."

"Ladies and gentlemen," Aiwin said, dealing out the playing cards, "the game is six card twist. Buy-in is two bronze, or one item of clothing."

"Just coin," Arzak grumbled.

Aiwin shrugged, but continued dealing.

All six of us were sitting around the largest table we could find in the secluded village, which had been in the building that Lore and I had checked out earlier. We'd made it to this table to discuss what I'd found: the instructions for the witchfinders to remain here, an order that they clearly hadn't followed. There was one worrying moment where Val suggested the witchfinders *were* still here, and that the scream was the bait in a trap designed to snap shut around us, but this fear was quickly put to bed when we realized this was a completely bonkers idea.

And so it was that we'd settled into a game of cards, which was precisely the sort of activity that would distract Val from any fears, whether justified or otherwise.

We each put our ante in the center of the table, Corminar trying to buy in with his trousers until Arzak quickly put a stop to that, and picked up the cards.

"Wait, how does this work, again?" Lore asked.

"Three rounds of betting," Val explained, "a chance to draw between each one, and the best hand wins."

"Oh right, yeah. And what's the best hand again?"

Val sighed, and Aiwin leaned in to offer Lore some help.

"I fold," Arzak said, immediately throwing her cards into the middle of the table.

"Nobody has bet yet," I pointed out.

"I fold," Arzak said again.

"You have a chance to draw different cards," Val reminded her.

The orc grunted. "I fold."

"OK," Aiwin said. "Moving on. Corminar?"

"I raise two socks."

"We play with coin," Arzak reminded him.

"And what would that matter to you?" the elf asked. "You are already out of this round."

"Nobody want see your jollies," the orc said, which caused Corminar to pull a face, remove his socks from the table, and throw in two bronze coins instead.

"Lore?" Aiwin asked. "I assume you now understand how the hand rankings—"

"All in," Lore said, pushing all his coins into the center of the table.

Aiwin did their best not to wince.

"I can change cards still, right?" Lore added.

Val, next in order, immediately pushed all her coins into the center to match Lore's bet, taking full advantage of the barbarian's lack of understanding of the rules.

"Styk?"

"I fold." Going up against Lore's presumably terrible hand was one thing, but I didn't want to go up against Val's hand, too.

Corminar, apparently thinking the same thing, threw in his cards.

"OK," Aiwin said. "Lore, you are to trade in your hand first. How many cards?"

"Six," he said.

Aiwin blinked at him. "That is your whole hand, yes?"

Lore nodded. "Yes. Six cards; I counted."

I tried to resist the urge to put my head in my hands, and ultimately, I failed.

Val, already laughing and counting the money in the center of the table, traded in just two cards. Lore responded by sticking with his hand this time, while Val traded in one more card again.

"A rather interesting first hand," Aiwin said. "If you will please reveal your hands?"

Val threw her hand down on the table—three sparrow cards, three blade cards—and moved to take all the staked coin before Aiwin put a hand out to stop her.

"Usually we see all hands on the table before claiming victory," they said.

Lore placed down his hand hesitantly.

Around the table, three jaws dropped upon sight of the barbarian's cards, all of which were crowns.

"This is good, right?" he asked.

Val visibly slumped in her seat. "How in Tartarus did . . ." she muttered, before shaking her head and rising from the table. "I'm gonna go drink my wine."

Corminar's head poked up. "You brought wine?"

The rounds continued in much the same fashion, with Lore's somehow incredible luck winning more hands for him than he lost, and the stack of bronze coins in front of him was growing much larger than anyone else's.

While we played, Aiwin and Corminar reminisced about times long past, and though the latter was initially hesitant to speak of these events in front of the rest of the Slayers, Aiwin eventually brought him around. It wasn't long before Corminar was speaking almost in sonnets about his home, the capital city of the Dawnwood.

"Oh, 'twas a beautiful sight, those towers that reached for the heavens, the great trees which stood taller still. Orange, not green, was the color of Sunalor, both for the ash-fed clay and the leaves of autumn for which the Dawnwood is so famous . . ."

Arzak had gone out of the game next, but remained at the table to analyze it and work out where she'd gone wrong. After that, a particularly tense final round of betting between me and Corminar had ended with Corminar's hand just about beating mine, and I sought commiseration in Val's bottle of wine.

I found her back outside, sitting on a moss-covered bench that faced only the dense woodlands. On the ground in front of her was a pile of sticks in the rough shape of a fire, with the one important distinction being that they . . . weren't on fire.

"Cold?" I asked, sitting next to her.

"No."

"OK," I said, then left for a moment to amble over to my knapsack and retrieve a spare jacket for her. I offered it to Val silently, and she took it immediately, barely mumbling a thanks in response.

We sat side by side without saying a word for a few moments, passing the already half-drunk bottle of orange wine between us, before I—not Val, surprisingly—shattered the silence. For some reason—one which eludes me even to this day—I'd suddenly found the confidence to have *that* conversation. "You're not liking it here, are you?"

Val said nothing, but the next swig of wine was a lot larger than the one previous.

"I don't suppose you wanna tell me why?" I prompted her.

Another swig of wine preceded any more words from Val. And then, finally, she sighed. "I guess there's . . . there's something I haven't told you. About who . . . About *what* I am."

I tried to catch Val's gaze, but her eyes were fixed squarely on the dirt. As the pause extended into a silence, I realized she was going to need some help here. "That you're a witch?" I asked.

Val flinched. "What?"

Even though I knew damn well what kind of "what" this was, I repeated myself. "That you're a witch. I'm not *completely* clueless, Val, as much as you think I am."

Now Val turned to look at me, though her expression wasn't what I'd been expecting—it was one of fear. "How . . . long have you known?"

I shrugged. "I had my suspicions back when you set those wolves on me. Quite witchy behavior, if you ask me."

"That was like the day after we met."

"Well, yeah," I replied. "And then it's not like you've done much since then to really dissuade me from that idea, is it? Control over plants, over air . . . That's all nature magicks, right? *Witchcraft*? It wasn't exactly the hardest thing to work out."

(Maybe I'd been expecting relief from Val, or even perhaps a smile. I don't quite know now, in retrospect, what I'd been expecting, but I'd thought this was going to be a more positive interaction than it had so far turned out to be.)

I could tell from the way Val was looking at me that her brain was working overtime on figuring out the precise best words to follow up with. "And this doesn't change . . . how you feel about me? We're still friends, I mean?"

I resisted the urge to laugh. If only Val knew the truth about me, about who—or "what"—I really was. Would she be as generous if she knew about my own Player ancestry? I could only hope she would, but I definitely didn't want to find out. "You are who you are. *What* you are doesn't change that."

The relief broke on Val's face then, at last. Something brushed my hand, and I was surprised to see Val giving it a short, gentle squeeze of gratitude.

"You know," she started, but I never found out quite what it was she knew, because Lore suddenly burst out into the courtyard.

"Quick!" he shouted, and the high pitch reminded me of the shriek we'd heard a few hours earlier. "Come quick! Trouble!"

CHAPTER FOURTEEN

Spooked

Val and I charged after Lore back into the main building of the witchfinder village, back to where we'd been spending the evening playing cards. When we spilled into the room, I was surprised to find both that the table had been upturned, and that there was no trouble in sight.

"What?" I asked, my head whipping around the room. "What is it? What's going on?"

"Yeah, couldn't you have chosen a different moment to—" Val began.

"They are here," Corminar said. "The witchfinders. They remain."

Val's face paled. "Where?"

"Just here!" Lore said. "In the room!"

Everyone went quiet as Val and I looked around. ". . . Where?" I asked, repeating Val's earlier question.

"You no listen. They here."

I blinked at Arzak, still completely lost. "Was it me and Val drinking, or was it you lot?"

Val waved the empty wine bottle to show support in this line of questioning, though her expression remained concerned.

"They weren't . . . *here*," Aiwin suddenly said.

"You all just said the exact opposite," Val retorted.

A dark look flashed across Aiwin's face. "If you would listen for a moment . . ."

"Listen, it's a simple enough question: was there or wasn't there a witchfinder in here?"

"Yes," Arzak, Corminar, and Lore said, at the very same moment that Aiwin said, "Almost."

"Almost?" Val repeated. "What in the hells does that mean, *almost?*"

"It was as though they were here, and they weren't," Aiwin explained. They turned to the other three. "Did you not see?"

"Was dark," Arzak said.

"I saw only a silhouette," Corminar agreed with the orc. "Wearing a long coat, as the witchfinders do, but a silhouette nonetheless."

"Are you telling me you all got spooked by a shadow?" I asked. "I know we're in a creepy old building and all that, but I thought you lot would know better."

"There was figure! In corner!" Arzak protested, pointing to a doorway at the other side of the room—one which led into a hallway into which the light of the full moon spilled through a window.

"You're seeing things," I said. "There's nobody here; we would've found them by now if there was. Seriously, you lot, I thought you'd not get frightened by a bit of darkness here, a squeaky floorboard there . . . You probably just saw me or Val outside."

Lore shook his head. "No, you two were sitting together. This person was standing. Alone."

"A tree, then, or a bird, I dunno." I cast a glance at the still-pale Val, hoping my words would reassure her, being a witch in a witchfinder's den, and all that. "There are no witchfinders here, alright? Get back to your game."

Lore looked down at the upturned table, and the cards and coins scattered across the floor. "But how will we know who was winning?"

"You were," Arzak and Corminar said at the same time.

"Oh, really?" Lore replied, scratching at the back of his head, apparently slowly coming around to the idea that we weren't under attack after all. "I just thought—"

Another shriek cut through the quiet.

Upon hearing it for a second time, I realized there was no mistaking it. This was no fellhawk. This was, without a doubt, human.

It was my turn to have my face grow pale.

"Nobody here?" Aiwin repeated, eyes on me. "Are you sure?"

Val took a step closer to me, her gaze fixed on the door.

"Mm," Arzak said. "Was elf."

"It was human, darling," Corminar corrected her. "Elves do not shriek."

"Not often . . ." Aiwin muttered.

Nobody moved for a moment, and nobody said a word until Lore finally gathered the courage. "Should we . . . ?"

"We have two options presented to us," Corminar replied. "Either we confront our fears and understand the nature of the scream, or we cower here and we wonder. I believe I know which option I prefer." He stepped toward the door, but Aiwin reached out to grab his arm.

"Together," the other elf said.

Lore and Arzak pursued the pair of elves out of the room, leaving just me and Val alone. I moved to follow, but spared a glance at Val that stopped me in my tracks.

I'd always seen Val as this incredibly resilient woman, someone who could rarely be touched by either word or blade. In this moment, though, I saw her pale face and her hands clasped tightly together, as though to stop them from shaking. The loudmouth wasn't here right now; all I saw in front of me was a terrified young woman.

"What if it's them?" she asked. "What if they're back? What if they realize what I am?"

"Val . . ."

"No, don't say it like that," the witch replied. "Don't say it like it's irrational, or something not worth thinking about. You know what they do to us, don't you? They don't just *kill*, they *exterminate*. And they take great glee in it."

"That wasn't what I was going to say," I told her, meeting her eyes. "I was going to say that there isn't one of us who wouldn't die keeping the others safe. They might pretend otherwise, but—"

"Aiwin would sell me out at the first opportunity," Val cut in. "I think they know what I am. You've seen the way they look at—"

More noise erupted from outside, this more of the shouty "we're under attack" kind than the terrified shriek we'd heard previously. At this, the sound of our friend in trouble, Val and I turned and bolted for the door.

We charged out into the center of the encampment, where we saw our four friends staring at the dark tree line.

"What is it?" I cried out as we ran to approach.

"Witch!" Aiwin shouted, pointing to a figure stepping out from between the trees.

Val stumbled almost imperceptibly. Her wide eyes shot to the approaching figure, before hardening. "That's no witch. That's a hag."

"Same thing," Aiwin responded, their mouth warping into a snarl. "Both use *Witchcraft*. Both are—"

"Aiwin," Corminar said, cutting the other elf off. "We must concentrate."

The hag stepped into the light of the moon. It was a strange creature, humanoid but definitely not human, being that its limbs were scrawny and bulbous in all the wrong places. It had covered itself in drooping moss, which blended in with its long black hair to give an overall slimy impression. That Val wouldn't want to be compared to one of these was completely understandable.

The hag twitched its head to one side as it set its eyes upon each of us in turn, and then it growled, its voice deep. Up until this moment, it had crossed my mind that this hag was the source of the shriek, but now that I'd heard its voice . . . there was no way. Whoever had shrieked was still out there.

"Do you think she is going to . . ." Aiwin started, staring the creature down.

"It," Val corrected them, resulting in a raised eyebrow from the elf. "Not 'she.'"

"Is that *really* your concern in this moment?" the elf retorted.

"I just think it's important to be accurate with our—"

"Enough," Arzak barked at the pair of them. "Be quiet. Noise make it angry."

I looked over at the hag again, the creature still lurking at the edge of the tree line, its black eyes stabbing at us. "How intelligent are they?" I asked.

"They're not witches," Val said again, "they're—"

"Hags, yes, I know. How intelligent are hags?"

Val shrugged. "Some smart, some dumb, just like any creatures. This one could be as smart as me, or they could be as smart as you." I didn't need to ask which end of the spectrum I'd landed on in this scenario. "Why?"

I nodded to the hag again. "Cos I think that one is working out how to attack us." I glanced at Lore, checking he had his sword in his hands. "Big guy?"

"Yeah?" the barbarian replied.

"We're gonna strike first. You ready?"

Lore adjusted his grip on the Bane Sword. "Ready."

I nodded. Then, with the flick of two wrists—one hand pointing to the ground at Lore's feet, the other to the air above the hag—I opened a portal.

The barbarian swung his greatsword downward as he fell toward the beast, this move already having proven to do enough damage to injure all but the strongest people. He roared as he did so—Lore couldn't resist a good roar when he was swinging his sword; I think he found extra strength in it—and the hag looked upward just in time to see the blade shooting toward it.

And then it blinked out of existence.

The six of us fell silent.

"Err . . ." I said.

"Val?" Corminar prompted her.

She shrugged. "It's a hag."

"Which means . . ."

"Which means it can travel between the material and aethereal planes?" she replied, her tone seeming to imply that we were stupid. "Did you not go to school?"

OK, maybe her words were implying we were stupid, too.

"So it's gone?"

Val made a show of looking over my shoulder. "No. It just means it's behind you."

I spun around just in time to see two long-clawed hands swiping toward me.

At last—another worthy opponent.

CHAPTER FIFTEEN

Be Witching

Arzak whipped up her swords to slice at the hag's outstretched claws, and the creature disappeared from the material plane in the second before blade met flesh. An arrow, released by Corminar, soared through the air where it had been standing, and then buried itself in the exterior wall of a nearby building.

I pulled my Blade of Samal free of its sheath and each of us slowly edged around, looking for where the hag would next reappear.

"You seem to understand these hags, Valerie," Aiwin said. "Perhaps you can tell us how to fight it?"

"Her name is not Valerie," Corminar replied.

"I don't think that's really what we need to discuss right about—" Val started, but I cut her off.

"What? Val isn't short for Valerie? What's it short for, then?"

Val gestured to a nearby building. "I think it's over there."

"Equivalence," Corminar said, answering my question.

"Equivalence?" I repeated. "*Equivalence?*"

"After her changeling grandfather, I believe."

"Can we concentrate on the thing trying to kill us, please?" Val said, glaring at Corminar, clearly not wanting to get into this conversation.

For whatever reason, I took enough pity on her to mumble, "My real name wasn't Styk, either," which resulted in raised eyebrows from many members of the group.

"Insult Val later. Fight now," Arzak said, just as the hag reappeared.

As before, the creature rematerialized in the throes of an attack, wrapping its clawed hands around Lore's neck. The barbarian, choking and with the beginnings of blood dripping down his shoulder blades, tried to attack it with his greatsword, but failed to get an angle.

Being closest, I charged first, jumping atop the hag's back with my blade drawn, *stabbing* it toward the creature's own neck. But again, just before the knife met the creature's flesh, it faded away from existence and I collapsed into the injured Lore's back.

"Equivalence, *heal* him," I said, pointing to Lore.

Val screwed up her face. "Don't do that, 'Styk.'"

"May I inquire just what 'Styk' is short for, then?" Corminar asked.

"It's not *short for* anything, it's just—"

A screech announced the hag taking form once more, this time at my side—apparently reacting to my attempted *stab*. I fell backward through a portal to avoid the hag's attacks, using the gravity of my fall to land back on my feet on the other side. I appeared, by design, at Val's side.

"This is annoying," she said as the hag disappeared once more.

"You've gotta know a way to stop it, surely, *Equivalence*."

"How soon before that gets old, do you think?"

"Three or four years," I replied.

"Great." Val whipped her head around to look for signs of the hag, but like me, she saw nothing.

"How stop it?" Arzak repeated, having heard my earlier question.

Val furrowed her brow. "Witchfinder tactics. Iron, spilled with the blood of . . ." She trailed off, her eyes darting anywhere but at Aiwin. "Magick user's blood. It won't be as powerful as one of their clasps, but it might just stop the hag from using its *witchcraft* for long enough that we can kill it. Corminar?"

"Iron-headed," the elven ranger said, throwing Val an arrow.

The hag, apparently more intelligent than we'd given it credit for, appeared in the space between them, snatching the arrow out of the air. With a glance at Val, it disappeared from this plane once more, the arrow going with it.

I held up my blade—the one I'd borrowed from Corminar all those months ago. "Iron, right?"

"Styk, I swear to all the gods, if you stab me, then I'll . . ." Val said.

I flipped the blade in my hand, taking it by the pointy end and handing it to Val. "Do what you gotta do, Equivalence."

Val took the blade. "And just what *is* your real name, Styk?"

I mumbled the answer under my breath.

"What?" Val replied. Even she, closest to me, hadn't heard what I'd said.

I changed tack. "It doesn't matter. It's the name I was born with, not the one I chose. That man doesn't exist anymore."

Val said nothing, staring back at me completely unimpressed.

"Besides," I added, "it was still better than 'Equivalence.'"

Lore, still with small streams of blood flowing down the sides of his neck, laughed at this.

Val blinked at him. "And what's the deal with *you*, then? Or do we all think his *real* name is Lore?" She sliced at the back of her arm, drawing blood onto my blade, and I noticed the obscurem around her neck glow a subtle green color.

The hag appeared in the blink of an eye, standing over Val. I dove at her, flinging her and myself to the ground, opening a portal beneath us that would save us from the hag's attacks. As I fell through, I felt something wrap around my ankle.

"Err, Styk?" Val said from beneath me, looking down at my feet.

"Don't tell me," I replied, just before the hag's bony hand yanked me back through the not-quite-closed portal. I turned, kicking against the scraggly arm with my free foot, but it didn't seem to bother the creature.

An arrow, released quickly by the ever-opportunistic Corminar, buried itself in the hag's side, causing it to screech. But it didn't let go, and it didn't dematerialize; it was set on seeing this attack through.

Arzak charged, twin blades held out at her side, but she was too far away— she wouldn't get here in the next few moments. I needed to act fast; my health reserves were forever low, and I didn't trust that the hag's claws would qualify as the "low-level melee weapon" that my *Warped Shield* ability would repel. I turned back, meaning to open a portal in front of Arzak to help close the distance, but as I did so, Val made a sudden move. She threw the dagger to me, and the blade arced through the air the few feet toward me.

I snatched it by the wrong end. "Ouch."

"Sorry," Val said, cringing slightly.

I flicked the blade around in my hand, ignoring the stinging pain of the deep flesh wound and the drain to my health reserves, and I swung around to *stab* at the hag. Once again, with my blade just half an inch away, the creature disappeared into the aether, releasing me.

"How does it *know?*" I cried.

"It is," Lore said.

"What?"

"Lore. It is my real name."

"Seriously?" Val asked.

Lore smiled. "Lore. Yes. Seriously!"

"So it's your last name that sucks, is it?"

The barbarian shrugged. "Yeah, it sucks."

"Aha!" Val cried out in victory, in the same moment that the hag reappeared at Corminar's side, digging its claws into his skin. The elf cried out in pain as the hag pulled its arms away from his shoulder, a horrific amount of flesh coming with it. The ranger fell to the ground at once, and Aiwin rushed to his side, clutching at his wounds.

Where before the hag had seemed like a nuisance, like a small problem to solve, now I realized that even with claws alone, it posed a real danger. What's more, short of Corminar's one arrow, we hadn't been able to deal it any damage; it seemed to sense strikes before we could hit it. So if I needed to strike it with my blade in order to stop it shifting to the aethereal plane, and it shifted to the aethereal plane before being hit, then . . . we were caught in a cycle.

The hag appeared at my side, and I moved to strike it before it could strike me. Again, as soon as my arcing blade was a fraction of an inch away from hitting the beast's flesh, it was gone again.

"Styk," Arzak said. "You need hit it."

"I'm trying!"

As I spun on the spot, the hag appeared in front of me once more, and a hurrying Lore released an uncharacteristically inaccurate attack—his thrown greatsword not landing anywhere near the hag and almost slicing off my leg in the process. But there wasn't time to complain, and I feigned a strike with my blade, dropping the knife midattack and catching it with my other hand. The hag didn't disappear; it seemed to know somehow that it wouldn't be struck, or had some kind of *Witchcraft* ability that automatically activated, like my *Warped Shield*. I prayed to gods I'd lost faith in that it would think my second strike—with my left hand—was a fake out, too, and I pushed almost all of my stamina into a powerful *stab*.

My bloodstained blade met air.

"Gods *damn* it!" I cried as Arzak arrived at my side swinging her swords a moment too late.

"It move fast," she noted, though it really hadn't needed to be said. This was just how the orc expressed frustration—through a frank and reasoned accounting of events.

At least this fight stretching on—and my dwindling stamina reserves—gave me a chance to try out an ability I'd unlocked over the past few weeks. One that I hadn't had any excuse to use just yet: *Mana-Fueled*.

As the hag appeared once more, I struck with my knife again, this time pulling on my mana reserves to *slice* at the creature. Not that this made much difference, my blade still meeting air, but it at least kept me useful for longer.

"I fear this creature means to exhaust us," Corminar said, his voice strained as he and Aiwin clutched at his wound.

"Val," Arzak said, nodding to the elf's injury.

"On it," the witch replied, and hurried over to Corminar and Aiwin's side.

"We can't keep doing this. We can't—" I started, and then cut myself off when the solution finally occurred to me. It was an old ability—one I hadn't found much use of recently—and the very first *Worldbending*-adjacent ability that I'd unlocked.

"Styk?" Lore asked, clutching at his wounds as he made his way over to his tossed Bane Sword. "Have you . . ."

I nodded.

The hag next materialized beside Arzak, its clawed hands wrapping themselves around the orc's wrists, squeezing tight enough that it forced her to drop her blades to the floor, grunting with pain as she did so.

But I didn't waste any time, jumping into a sprint and closing the distance between the hag and me even further with the use of a pair of portals. Before the hag could disappear once more, I made to *stab* at its torso, but ceased the movement a mere three inches away from its flesh. As I hadn't gotten any closer, the hag remained present, and screeched as it further tightened its grip on Arzak's wrists.

And then I activated *Closed Reach*.

As reality bent on itself, the bloodstained blade pierced the beast's flesh instantly, not giving the hag a chance to disappear. I'd landed a blow. I'd temporarily extinguished the creature's *Witchcraft* abilities. But we needed to strike fast.

"Lore!" I shouted, throwing the injured barbarian through a portal to land at the side of his discarded blade. "Throw!"

Lore, ever the good soldier, picked up his blade without a moment's hesitation, and he threw it. He had the power, but again, not the accuracy—but that didn't matter. I opened a portal in front of the soaring greatsword, redirecting it squarely toward the hag's chest.

The barbarian buried the Bane Sword deep.

> *Level 17 Forest Hag defeated!*

> **Worldbending**: +1,000XP
> **Knifework**: +3,600XP
> *Knifework increased to Level 24!*
> *Knifework increased to Level 25!*
> **Base Points Gained**: +2 DEX, +2 STR, +4 Free Points (VIT/DEX/STR)
> **Ability Selection Unlocked**
>
> . . .

In the aftermath of the fight, after Val had successfully healed him—leveling up pretty substantially in the process, according to her—Lore approached my side.

"Thunder," he mumbled to me.

"Sorry?"

"Thunder. That's my last name."

"Your name is Lore . . . Thunder?" I replied.

The barbarian nodded.

"*Gods*, that's cool."

Lore's forever-grin grew wider. "I know!"

As the barbarian strolled away happily, I turned my attention to my notifications; it was ability-unlocking time.

CHAPTER SIXTEEN

Notions of Heroism

I took a seat on the bench that Val and I had sat on earlier in the evening while the rest of the team saw to healing their wounds. Or getting Val to heal them, as the case may have been.

> **Ability Selection Unlocked**
> *Select an ability from the list below:*
> **Option 1: Slice III (Knifework)**—*Upgrade to Slice.* Slice the enemy for physical damage [+50 percent] worth weapon's base damage and additional damage scaling on [STR].

So it was an upgrade first, and not a bad one at all. I'd never invested in the upgrade to *Slice II*, only having chosen to upgrade my *Stab* ability, and yet now I had progressed enough to skip that level of ability entirely. The rest of the team had reminded me again and again that upgrades were often the most powerful—if least exciting—choices, so I forced myself to truly consider this option. That 50 percent increase percent to physical damage was now quite the modifier, and would mean I'd start dealing pretty decent damage even without any imaginative trickery.

> **Option 2: Execution II (Knifework)**—Attack a target while undetected for +200 percent damage.

This was an upgrade to an ability I'd not selected, though I'd given it pretty substantial consideration. And if 50 percent damage boost on *Slice III* was tempting, then it was nothing compared to the 200 percent boost—up from 100 percent—that I got here. The only difference, of course, being that I'd have to remain undetected for this to work.

I was doing well to level up *Stealth*, even though it hadn't been my focus. Already at level 9—and very close to turning level 10, I believed—then maybe a return to the *Stealth*-oriented build of a past life could pay some dividends. And who knew what level 10's ability selection might offer?

I turned my attention to the third and last of my ability selection options.

> **Option 3: Parlor Tricks (Knifework)**—Impress others with a wide variety of knife-related parlor tricks, including five-finger fillet and blind throws. Chance of success scales with [CHA].

Every fiber of my being wanted me to select this option.

I supposed it was a side effect of the *Needlework* skill tree leveling up my Charisma that I got this ability as an option. That is, a *Knifework* ability that wasn't combat-related. It was certainly the coolest of the three choices, and I had made good use of this precise skill in a previous life to pick up a certain type of woman, but . . . my priorities were different now.

I looked up at the rest of the group, at Val helping Corminar to his feet, and at Arzak trying to get the red stain of blood out of the collar of Lore's tunic.

This team was well on the way to being heroes, not just the slayers of fake ones. If we just tried a little harder—if we were just a *little* less dysfunctional— then maybe we could be great. And part of that was *me* being great, too.

I ruled out option three, and returned to options one and two.

I knew I'd probably get the choice of both of these skills—or more likely, their upgraded versions—down the line, but what if that wasn't the case? Which would I regret not taking more? I already had a decent basic offensive attack in *Stab II*, and so it was *Execution II*, really, that gave me more breadth of options.

"Alright!" Val cheered. "Level up!"

"Yeah, I—" I started to reply, before realizing that she was talking about herself.

"And an ability selection at that."

"What you picking?" Lore asked.

Val shrugged. "Don't know. Gonna think on it while we figure out what happened here."

Aiwin looked up at that. "What do you mean? We know what happened here; hags attacked. Perhaps as vengeance for fallen siblings."

Val, without looking back at Aiwin, shook her head. "This hag? It only came cos of the noise we were making. And there was no sign of a fight, remember? There's no bodies. And—"

"It wasn't the hag that screamed," I called across the open space.

Val pointed an index finger in my direction. "Exactly."

Aiwin continued to stare down Val. "And just how is it that you know so much about hags?"

"I studied at an academy," Val said. "Managlass Academy. Where did you study, Aiwin?"

The elf remained quiet.

"Hags, they don't have notions of vengeance," Val continued. "They're not human. It's a stretch to even call them humanoid; they've just adopted this form cos they've spent so long trying to hide from us, trying to blend in."

"Then we not know what happen here," Arzak said. "The hag not answer anything."

"No," Val agreed.

I watched as the team fell into silence, considering their next steps, and I predicted exactly how the conversation would go next.

"One might argue that it does not matter," Corminar said. "We arrived at this location in search of a witchfinder's clasp—let us not forget that this is all that ties us to here. Perhaps we simply locate this clasp and leave, fulfill the terms of our deal with the Red Thorn, and retrieve Lore's sheep from Elandor?"

Lore nodded his agreement.

"Are you scared, Corminar?" I called out, causing all heads to swivel to face me.

"Corminar Cladenor does not feel fear," Corminar Cladenor said.

"Then why are you in such a rush to get out of here? We don't know what's happened here, true, but I think it's pretty clear that something terrible did."

"He's right, Styk," Val said. "There's no reason for us to—"

"What do you call yourselves?" I asked them.

Everyone remained quiet, some of them casting confused glances to one another.

"I call myself Arzak," Arzak said.

"I meant collectively. What do you call yourselves?"

"The Slayers," Corminar replied, one of them finally giving me the answer I was looking for.

"Exactly. And that name should carry some weight. People should know what you've done for them, by killing those evil Players. You lot are heroes, don't you see?"

Val chuckled. "Heroes? Styk, we're just—"

"You're doing the right thing in the face of overwhelming odds. Without any chance of people being grateful and without expectation of being paid for it. What is that, if not the definition of heroes?"

"Styk, if this is more about you wanting to be some big hero, worshipped by—"

"This isn't about *wanting* to be anything. This is about *being* it!" I resisted the urge to put my head in my hands. "Don't you see? You're heroes already. And people have gone missing here. Maybe they've been kidnapped, or killed. Do you all really think you can leave without figuring out what happened to them? Do you think you won't regret trying to help them?"

Quiet passed across the village once more, and Corminar seemed suddenly very interested in the ground.

"You want us to stay?" Val asked. "Here? Really?"

"I want you to help the people who were here." I saw Val's eye twitch. "And if some of them were guilty of other crimes, we punish them proportionately."

After another pause, Arzak piped up, "You want be new leader?"

"I don't want us to have a leader. I just want us to do the right thing."

Lore, after another moment of consideration, put his hand into the air.

"Yes?" I asked him.

He blinked back at me.

"Was there a question?"

"Oh no," the barbarian said, "I was just saying I'm in. I agree. Let's be heroes."

Val stared at me. "I'm trusting you," she said, before raising her hand.

Arzak and Corminar, perhaps due to peer pressure, followed suit, before the latter turned to his elven friend.

"I'm not a part of this," Aiwin said. "It's your choice."

I nodded. "Good."

When there was silence, and no movement, I realized I was going to need to take charge in this particular scenario—it was my idea to stay, after all.

"We start by searching the village. More thoroughly, this time. We know there's something here—we've heard the screaming—so let's find it. Look for signs of life, yes, but also look for anything else that might offer a clue as to what's going on. OK?"

The team nodded, and then everyone but Val and I paired off and began searching the buildings once more. Instead, I ambled over to the witch's side, who was standing over the body of the beast we'd just slain, nudging it with her foot.

"I hate hags," Val muttered to me. "They've got so much to do with why witches are so hated. It's just a magick type, *Witchcraft*. If hags hadn't hurt so many people over the years, people wouldn't be so scared of it. And I'd be . . ." She stared into space.

"People shouldn't judge you for your class."

"Yeah, well, thanks for stating the obvious," Val replied, her tone bitter. Then, she seemed to catch herself, and she turned to me, offering me a small smile. "But thanks for saying it, too."

I nodded, and for a moment we fell into silence.

"Upgrade my *Slice* or get *Execution*?" I asked her.

"What?"

"I leveled up *Knifework*," I said, then proceeded to explain what each choice did. Val gave a pretty definitive answer, and I did exactly as she chose.

Ability Unlocked: Execution II

Execution II (Knifework): Attack a target while undetected for +200 percent damage.

CHAPTER SEVENTEEN

Disturbed

Eventually, we had to sleep.

(I don't want you, reader, to think we all just made a token effort on the search of the witchfinders' village before calling it a night; it was the early hours of the morning before we finally decided we might have better luck with rested and functioning brains. We'd even been spurred on by a stray murmur from Lore that "whatever happened before might happen again"—not a comforting thought—but even then, we'd had to rest eventually.)

Or, we'd had to *try* to rest, in my case.

Everyone else was asleep on their bedrolls in the main hallway of the main building, as this was the only space large enough to sleep the lot of us, and nobody was keen on the idea of splitting up in the current circumstances. The light was low, the one lit torch dying a slow death at my side, and I fiddled with needle, thread, and cloth in the gentle glow.

Since I'd woken from the lightest sleep of my life drenched in sweat, I'd tossed and turned—resulting in a half-asleep grunt of annoyance from Val, who was nearest me—until I'd finally realized that dreams just weren't going to take me tonight. Instead, I'd retrieved my crafting materials and sewn, in an effort to make full use of all my waking hours to gather experience. I'd leveled up *Needlework* to level 8, but progress was slow. I needed new materials if I was going to take full advantage of my recently unlocked *Basic Cloth Armor* ability, which I could only assume would get me leveling up faster.

When I could take sewing no more, I gathered my energy—and my courage, I'm afraid to say—and rose from my bedroll to explore the village some more.

I knew that splitting up from the rest of the team was a foolish idea, considering all the disembodied screaming we'd heard, but I could stay in that room no longer. Besides, I had my trusty Blade of Samal on me, and I had my shiny new *Execution* ability to go along with it. I moved slowly and silently, just in case I had to use it.

Floorboards creaked beneath my feet, and the wind rustling through the trees made an eerie whistling sound, but both noises were—in regular circumstances—completely normal. It was just the environment, the absence of people in man-made structures, that had made us feel that something wasn't right. It was only the silence that made the few penetrating noises seem terrifying.

Except . . . I was coming around to the idea that this wasn't entirely true. The presence of the hag was real enough, and Val seemed to think that something had drawn it here. And then there were the witchfinders, who so many of my friends seemed to think were still here, at least in some capacity—and Corminar was not the type to scare easily.

I adjusted my grip on my blade, held out in front of me, as I stepped onward through the building. I didn't quite know what I'd been looking for, but my feet had taken me back toward the study I'd been in earlier—where I'd found the letters about the monster hunter being reassigned. Perhaps, subconsciously, I thought this was the place best suited to finding answers. As I turned the corner into the room, I nearly jumped out of my skin—one of our party was already in there, standing over the desk.

I couldn't make out their face in the shadows, but from their size I thought it must have been Corminar, Val, or Aiwin. Whoever it was, they had their hands on the top of the desk, and were staring down, tensed, as if frustrated by our lack of progress—a feeling I shared. "Find anything?" I asked them.

The figure didn't move, and I wondered if any among us had the ability to fall asleep standing up, as knackered as we were.

"I scoured the room pretty thoroughly before," I continued, "but didn't find anything else." I stepped further into the room, not ten feet from my shrouded friend, but still I couldn't see who it was.

"Who's there, anyway? Gets so dark in these buildings at night that—" I cut myself off when I noticed the shape of the figure's coat, of all things. It was long, a straight cut, and completely unlike any of the clothes any of my party my friends wore. What it *did* remind me of, however, was the supposed traditional uniform of the . . .

"Witchfinder," I breathed.

The figure snapped its head up at this word, and though I couldn't see its eyes, I knew with utter certainty that it was staring straight at me.

I took an unconscious step backward. "So they were right," I said, forcing my voice to be steady. "You *are* still here. Where are you hiding? Where are you—"

The figure took a single step around the desk, as if to mirror mine, and I realized that it wasn't cloaked in shadow. It *was* shadow.

A being formed of . . . of nothing. Of the absence of light. Of an absence of reality, its shape defined only by the lack of anything else.

"Witchfinder . . ." a breathy voice, so quiet it was almost silent, said—a delayed echo of my earlier realization.

I stepped back, and the shape took another pace forward, toward me. I held my blade high. Would I even be able to attack such a being? Would my knife hit flesh? Would my blade, too, fade from reality?

The figure's mouth opened wide in a silent scream.

I whipped my hand to my mouth, to stop myself from compulsively echoing this noise of fear.

The witchfinder slowly raised its arm, stretching toward me as I stumbled backward, hitting wall rather than doorway. I whipped my hands behind me, searching frantically for the edge of the door, its location lost to me in my fright, in the room starting to spin, in the horror of the sight in front of me, the figure reaching forward, forward, forward, almost touching flesh, almost unleashing its—

The figure faded.

Its form disintegrated, billowing away like a cloud of smoke, there one moment and then gone the next, leaving no sign that it had ever been there but for my pounding heart.

There was only one thing to do next. I turned, shouted for help, and ran.

I passed through the doorway, out of the study, charging down a long hallway back toward the chamber we'd been sleeping in. I reached the end, turning the corner, and—

Halfway down the corridor, illuminated only by the low, flickering light of a dying torch around the corner, was another figure. Another figure of shadow, and one that I was this time quick to identify as an enemy. It stood, staring me down, and my feet seemed to stop working, planting me on the spot.

I reached both hands forward, my blade in one, preparation of a portal in the other, and I waited for it to move. To attack. But it only stood, staring me down, its outline a threshold between reality and the unreality. And that outline was not firm.

At its shoulders, and at its elbows, wisps of nothing-smoke drifted into the surrounding hallway, bleeding slowly into reality. It spread, gradually at first, but growing faster with each second that the unreality was allowed to fester. The surrounding hallway faded away, replacing itself with the ghostly, dark outline of a cobbled courtyard—one that could not have been part of the witchfinders' village. One that had the architecture of some faraway land, unknown to me.

There was no time to take it in, though, because the figure started to move.

It took a step forward, then another, then another, its mouth opening in a wide scream that I never heard, and before long it was charging at me, the border of reality between the building and the courtyard following just behind.

I flicked my hand to open a portal behind it, meaning to get my blade on its throat before it could turn, but the portal . . . never materialized. This shadowland that it had summoned was impenetrable to my magicks, a place that I could not portal to. I searched for another plan of attack, panicking like I'd never panicked before, raising my blade to *stab* the creature, if nothing else, and it drew closer, closer, five feet away, two feet away, and . . . faded away again, a cloud of smoke of the unreal passing over me, completely without scent.

I regained control of my feet—though whether this was an ability of the witchfinder or simply my terror, I didn't know—and I turned on the spot. Again, I ran. (If you judge me for this, just remember that you weren't there, and you didn't see what I'd seen. You, too, would have fled.)

I charged back down the corridor, then around the corner. I collided, heavily, with firm flesh.

CHAPTER EIGHTEEN

I Ain't Afraid of Not-Ghosts

I pulled my head up slowly to get a look at the being I'd just crashed into, countless thoughts running through my head, most of them along the lines of *Is this a monster?* or *Can shadows have form?* or *Am I about to die a horrible and painless death, possibly with none of my friends ever knowing where I got to?* Fortunately, the first and last of these questions were answered when I saw a face frowning down at me.

"You no sleep?" Arzak asked.

I took a moment to gather myself, trying to calm down my very rapid breathing, before finally being able to answer. "No. No, I . . ." I looked over my shoulder at the hallway behind me. There was nothing there but shadows. Shadows of the regular kind, that was—though could I trust myself to know for sure? Were any of them about to move?

"Hmm?" Arzak prompted me.

". . . Ghosts."

The orc stared at me blankly, her face barely illuminated in the light of the dwindling torches. "No such thing."

"Wanna bet? Cos up until five minutes ago, I would've said the same thing. And yet . . ."

Arzak's face remained neutral—just why was she so bad at poker, with this ability?—as she considered what I'd just told her. "No such thing," she said again. "Is mistake."

"No mistake," I assured her. "It was made of shadows."

"Ghosts not made of shadows."

"You just said they weren't real, so how do you know what they're made of? What *are* they made of, then?"

"Ectoplasmic matter," Arzak said, with no hint at all that she was joking.

I blinked. "Ecto-what?"

"Ectoplasmic—"

I turned past her. "We should wake the others. There's danger out there."

The orc followed me down the hallway back into the central chamber, where the rest of our group were sleeping. "We tell you this already. Witchfinders out there. Not ghosts."

"Alright!" I shouted, clapping my hands together as loudly as possible. "Alright, wake up, everyone!"

Val sat bolt upright, eyes wide for a moment before realizing it was me waking her, which caused her to glare nastily in my direction. Corminar gently shook Aiwin awake by the shoulders, and Lore continued to snore. We all looked at him.

"Seriously?" I asked—the question rhetorical. "We haven't got time for this. I saw a ghost. *Two* ghosts, actually. Maybe three!"

"I believe we could defeat three ghosts. Four or five is perhaps our limit," Corminar said.

"Ghosts not real," Arzak said again, but her words were drowned out by Lore's snoring.

I opened a portal beneath his bedroll and spilled him out onto the floor, eliciting a high-pitched yelp from the barbarian in the process. He blinked up at me, confused for a moment, then grinned. "You got me!"

"What?"

Confusion blinked across Lore's face again. "This was a prank, wasn't it?"

"No! This was a 'we're under attack' wake-up!"

"Oh. From what?"

"Ghosts," Corminar murmured, at the same time that Arzak said, "Not ghosts."

Lore scrambled to his feet, reaching for his sword. "How many? Not more than three or four, is it? Think we'd struggle against more than that."

Corminar nodded his agreement.

"Not ghosts," Arzak said again. "Must be witchfinders. Using magicks on you?"

"They were ghosts, Arzak. I don't know how many times I've gotta tell you. It was a person—wearing a long witchfinder coat, sure—but one made of shadows." Before Arzak could remind me that ghosts weren't made of shadows, I continued, "And the shadows spread. They ate up some of the building. In them, I saw . . . I don't know, another place? I couldn't open a portal in them, that's all I know, and . . ." I stumbled on my words when I realized I hadn't taken a breath in far too long.

"Some of the building's gone?" Val asked. "Where?"

"It came back."

"What did?"

"The building," I replied. "Look, I don't know what's going on, I just know what I saw. Something's here! The ghosts of the witchfinders, I think, or if Arzak's right and they're not ghosts, then it's what's left of them."

The room fell silent for a second, before Val—of course—opened her mouth. "Do you know what I'm thinking?"

"Yes," Aiwin said, beginning to pack their stuff, "we leave immediately."

"No. I'm thinking we need to look into these experiments these witchfinders were doing. It's clear what's happened here, right? These . . . *people* didn't just leave, did they? Something happened to them. And I think we'd be idiots not to suspect whatever these experiments were."

Arzak nodded. "We search for information. We look for people before, now we look for parchment. We look for paper." She nodded to the elves. "You two, go building over—"

"No," I said. "We're not splitting up when there's ghosts around. You've read the stories; you know what happens when people split up in these situations."

Corminar nodded. "Disembowelment."

"Besides, you want information on the experiments? I saw some. I know where it is." With my friend group behind me, I led the way through the building once more, weapons raised, but this time I encountered no ghosts/not-ghosts. Of course, seeing one might have made the others a little more inclined to believe me.

"I saw something . . ." I said, leafing through the papers atop the desk, discarding the letters about the monster hunter being reassigned elsewhere, until I saw it: strange sketches of strange devices. Three small towers, almost. Metal columns with gem-filled orbs every few inches up their height. Placed—according to the diagram—in a perfect triangle.

Val leaned in as soon as she saw what I was looking at. "You found *this* and you didn't think to mention it?"

"I didn't know it was relevant!"

"You don't even know what it *is*; how are you supposed to know if it's relevant or not?"

"Oh, so you *do* know what it is, then, do you?" I retorted.

"Please, you two, if you will cease flirting for one moment," Corminar said. "If there are truly dangers still around, then the sooner we understand their meaning, the better."

"*Flirting?*" Val replied, mouth agape, and I was about to do much the same before I saw Lore trying to hold back a grin.

"What this, Val?" Arzak said, tapping the parchment with the devices sketched on. "What you know?"

Val's eyes remained on Corminar for a moment, who met her gaze, before finally looking up at the orc. "I don't know what they *do*, exactly, but I know what they channel."

"What?"

"Witchcraft."

Aiwin raised their eyebrows. "It cannot be. You do not know these folk; they would not dare gamble with such—"

"Oh, so you think they were killing these witches for the fun of it, do you?" Val replied. "Well, yes, maybe they were. But they were getting something in return, clearly." Val traced her fingertip over the document as she skimmed it. "Look, they were using *witchcraft* to power the devices, and then . . ."

"Then?" I prompted her.

"Then . . . something else. It says only 'the creature.'"

"OK. So they build these devices?" our orc friend asked.

"How am I supposed to—"

"Yeah, they built them," Lore chimed in, matter-of-factly. All eyes turned to him. "What?"

"Lore?" Val asked.

"Yeah?"

"How do you know they built them?"

"Cos they're in the basement, aren't they?" He paused. "Did none of you go in the basement?"

"Did I go in the basement of a creepy—possibly haunted—old building?" Val replied. "Let me think. Hmm."

"Where is the basement, Lore?" I asked, trying my best to steer this investigation back on track.

We followed the barbarian through the building to a small storage room behind the kitchen, where there was an unassuming trapdoor in the floor. He paused before reaching down to open it, hesitating, and though he eventually opened the way for us, I could see he was gripping his sword tight, as though about to use it.

"You alright there, big guy?" Val asked.

Lore remained still at the top of the staircase revealed by the now open trapdoor. "It's like you said: dark basement in a creepy house. I only poked my head in before."

"Scared?"

"Sensible."

Val raised her eyebrows in acknowledgement, then led the way down into the dingy room.

After she went, I looked up at Lore, but he only gestured for me to go next. "Fair enough, mate. Fair enough."

Val's torch flickered ahead of me, silhouetting her and casting a dim orange light around the surprisingly large basement. As she crept forward, me not far behind her, the rest of the team slightly further behind me, the first of the seven-foot-tall devices came into view. Unlike in the drawings, this real version was scarred, its metal fixings somehow charred, some of its magical gems shattered, or missing entirely. And unlike the diagrams, this one had a body chained to it.

"The witchfinders?" I asked Val.

"No," Val replied, her voice quiet, small. "Hags." She raised her torch in the air, and the other two devices—each complete with their own chained bodies—became visible. Though they were rotting, I could see that Val was right; the witchfinders had used hags for the sources of power. For their sources of *witchcraft*.

"I suppose this explains the one we saw earlier," Aiwin said, nodding to the nearest of the beasts. "Getting vengeance after all. I did say."

Val, for her part, didn't rise to the elf's bait, letting this dig slide. She came to a stop a few paces away from the nearest device, in its triangular formation, and I and the rest of the group arrived at her side. The flickering torches—one in Val's hand, one in Arzak's—were enough for us to get far too good a view of the hags, in fact, and their flames illuminated the walls of the room.

Something on one wall caught my eye. A shape. A humanoid shape. My heart skipped a beat, as I thought one of the ghosts had made it down here, that a shadow creature was about to attack, but then I saw it for what it was. The shape was etched into the wall, or rather, the wall was etched away *around* this humanoid shape. It was as though something to do with the devices had eaten away at the walls, except for where some clueless onlooker had blocked its view.

Val stepped forward again, her eyes fixed on the hag at the nearest tower.

"Err, Val?" Lore asked. "What're you doing?"

"Trying to get a better look," the witch replied. "You want to find out what happened here or not?"

"Well, don't touch them," I added.

This made Val stop, slouch her shoulders, and turn to flash me an irritable glare. "Oh yeah, Styk, I was going to touch the things that etched people into the walls."

"You noticed."

"Rather hard to miss," Corminar said, his eyes sweeping across the room's perimeter. It wasn't until that moment that I realized there was a good dozen or so of the same shapes.

"Well, don't—"

And then, as Val grew close, as though sensing her magicks, one of the devices stirred.

CHAPTER NINETEEN

Fleeing Shadows

Lightning arced between the three towering devices, stray sparks crackling in the surrounding air, causing the lot of us to stumble backward. Before our eyes, we watched as the raw magical energy—green, to my eye—grew greater, a power that made the hairs on the back of my neck stand on end. And in the space the power left behind, I saw shadows.

This time, I knew for certain that these were the same shadows as before—the ends of reality, burned into existence by these strange devices. From strands, the shadows grew, until the flickering torches did nothing to illuminate the space before us.

"This time," Aiwin said, their eyes wide, "might I suggest we run?"

There wasn't a single soul among us who wanted to argue this particular point—even Val seemed to agree—and so all six of us turned on the spot and charged for the stairwell.

And just in time, too.

Figures of unreality stepped forward out of the darkness, out of the power, out of the walls themselves. Eyes of nothing stared upon us, and though their gazes gave me surely nothing to feel, I felt chilled down my spine nonetheless.

"Ghosts!" Arzak shouted.

"I bloody well *told you*!" I cried back from the rear of the group alongside Corminar as we reached the stairs.

"I dunno . . ." Val started, apparently now unsure that these really *were* ghosts, but now was not the time for any follow-up questions.

As I sprinted up the stairs, something caught my leg. I tripped, my mouth colliding with the edge of a step and a splatter of my blood spraying over the dusty wood. I looked down to see two things: Corminar behind me, growing pale, and a ghostly hand, reached out from the wall, wrapped around my left ankle.

They have form after all.

I kicked at the unreal hand with my other foot, and Corminar drew his bow in this confined space to loose an arrow into it. His shot passed right through, but in the moment that the arrow would have hit, the hand's form faded, and I was able to slip out.

Corminar helped me to stagger back to my feet, and we continued onward and upward, back into the house proper, and toward the screams of our friends up ahead. We burst out of the pantry, back into the kitchen, and saw as the rest of the team dodged similar reaching arms emerging from the walls of the corridor. But where, before, Corminar and I had only had to deal with a hand and wrist, now these arms were taking more shape, up to the shoulders, even.

I opened up a pair of portals for Corminar and I to hop through, to catch up to the rest of the team. When we got to the other side, I immediately had to open another portal beneath us, to avoid the reach of the ghostly arms. We fell through the portals and stumbled out the other side, with the enemy hands snatching the air above our heads.

Looking back at the hallway, I could now see shoulders, torsos, and legs emerging from the walls, the silhouettes of the witchfinders taking shape just as they had before, when I'd been roaming the walls overnight. The difference now? There were dozens of them.

"Faster!" I shouted, opening a portal for the team to leap through. "Faster!"

"*We know!*" Val cried back as she fell out of a portal at my side.

Lore and Arzak leaped through next, but Aiwin—still new to my portal magicks—hesitated. And in that moment of hesitation, a shadow reached out.

"No!" Corminar shouted, reaching toward his . . . whatever Aiwin was to him; I still wasn't entirely clear on that.

The arms yanked Aiwin into the wall, the impact knocking the wind out of them, and then the shadows began to spread. Just as I'd seen before, the shadows spread across the wall, fading it away from reality, and building a whole new shadow reality—for lack of a better phrase—in its place. And before Corminar could reach Aiwin, they were pulled through.

The elf faded from this reality, yanked into the other—if, indeed, it was even real, and not a Tokas-esque illusion.

"Styk!" Corminar shouted, pointing at the spot where Aiwin had disappeared. "A portal!"

"I can't!"

"Then I shall press through myself."

"You do no such thing," Arzak shouted back at him, and flashed me a nod.

I opened a portal in the corridor, between Corminar and the other reality, and the elf fell through—saving him from his own notions of heroism.

"Aiwin!" he cried, looking frantically up at me.

"We not know we can get back from there," Arzak said, grabbing the elf by the upper arm and wrenching him backward despite his desperate, flailing limbs. One of the elf's stray legs kicked me—likely unintentionally, though I wouldn't put it past him—and I stumbled backward into the wall.

A ghostly being grabbed me, yanking me to the floor by my ankle.

I looked down, seeing the creature without a face somehow staring back at me, and pulled against the creature's firm grasp. Of course it wouldn't budge, but this time I had some idea of how to get out of it. "Val!" I cried. "Help! Attack it!"

My witch friend grabbed an arrow from Corminar's quiver, apparently meaning to use it as a weapon of her own—without a bow.

I glanced from her to the creature of shadows, and I realized the ghost wasn't trying to pull me away. In fact, it only reached its other hand forward, and in that hand, a small leather notebook faded from unreality into reality, taking shape and form with every second that passed.

I pulled again against the creature's grip, trying to free myself, but it was hopeless. I was trapped.

The ghost pushed the small notebook into my chest, crushing against my ribs as though it didn't know how hard it was pressing—or perhaps this was its strange form of attack. Either way, I had no option but to bash the notebook, now fully out of this shadowland, away, freeing myself from the attack just as I felt a rib crack.

As I screamed out with pain, my fairly insignificant health reserves draining a good way, Val tossed the borrowed arrow into the air with one hand, and summoned a strong gust of wind with the other. It was enough to propel the arrow down the corridor, it landing squarely in the space that the ghostly arm had been until only a fraction of a second earlier. As the arm faded from reality to avoid being hit—if this was, as I suspected, a conscious move—I wriggled my leg free once more.

I wasted no time in stumbling back to my feet, still clutching the notebook in my hand. Before the shadow-arm could grab me again, I opened a portal. The struggling Corminar, Arzak, and I fell through it, pouring out the other side, just through the exterior door.

Corminar moved to charge back inside again, but Lore and Val, who were just now reaching the doorway, blocked him. I say it was both of them—both of them certainly tried—but it was the broad Lore who did most of the heavy lifting here.

"They got Aiwin!" Corminar shouted. "We must—"

Arzak grabbed him again by the shoulders. "We—"

"We leave no one behind, is that not true?"

"We do not know can return!"

The ranger grimaced. "And yet we will not learn until we—"

Aiwin tumbled back into reality from an exterior wall of the building. They took form slowly at first, but with every second that passed, it seemed more and more that they had their feet planted firmly in this reality.

Corminar shot Arzak a glare that I interpreted roughly as meaning, "Well, not a one-way trip, then, is it?" even though Aiwin's reappearance meant they didn't actually need saving anyway. The elf hurried to catch Aiwin as their trembling legs gave way, and though Corminar asked them what had happened, they did not respond.

I glanced back to the building, where the shadows were beginning to fade. Whatever we'd done to activate the devices, its power was now waning again. The worst of it, it seemed, was over.

Worldbending: +1,100XP

It wasn't a bad amount of experience considering we'd only fled, and I hadn't defeated a damn thing. But this wasn't the top priority right now.

"Aiwin," Arzak said, "what you see?"

The elf blinked, then turned their head to look up at Arzak, gazing at the orc with blurred eyes.

"Please, Aiwin," Corminar said at their side. "Tell us: what did you see?"

Still, Aiwin remained quiet, shaking their head, and I think the interrogation might have continued if not for the notebook in my hands beginning to crackle with the same lightning energy as the devices.

"Styk . . ." Val said. "Just what in the hells is that?"

Though the sound of the magicks were almost frightening, it didn't seem to do me any damage, the lightning passing through my hands as though they weren't there. I looked down at the notebook, glanced up at Val, and then opened it.

"Huh," I said.

"What? What is it?"

"I think it's . . . answers."

CHAPTER TWENTY

Seeing Enemies Where There Are None

The lightning slowly subsided as I stared down at the opening page of the notebook.

If found, please return to Witchfinder Colonel Hara Teramura, it read.

"What do you mean, 'answers'?" Val asked.

"I mean . . . it's one of the witchfinder's journals. A senior one, from the sounds of it."

"And how'd you get that?"

"A ghost handed it to me."

Lore blinked. "Ghosts give people presents now?"

"I don't think it was a present; it attacked me with it."

"A peculiar choice of weapon," Corminar commented, walking over to my side and peering at the book over my shoulder.

"I guess maybe their swords and whatever didn't get ghostified with them?" I suggested.

"And their books did?" Val replied. "What kinda logic is that?"

I shrugged. "Fair point." With that, I returned my attention to the book and turned the page. Inside was an inordinate amount of scribblings, the quality of which—I discovered as I flicked through—got worse with time. The handwriting, the inkblots, and the word choices all seemed to grow more manic, crazed, as though the owner of the journal was under ever-increasing pressure.

I read it aloud to the team—as well as the slowly recovering Aiwin—and they listened in silence. The notebook told of the witchfinders' tale, of their journey from hunting Val's kind to being adopted by a group of powerful people in Auricia.

It started with a good deal of money, as all things do. One of these powerful people had donated a large amount of coin to support the witchfinders in their "valuable" efforts—Val rolled her eyes at this bit. The donations kept coming, every month, but more and more they came with requests. Then instructions. Then . . . orders.

And soon it was that the great monster hunter had arrived—the woman who had taken charge, who we'd seen mentioned in other documentation about the village. Their efforts were torn away from witchfinding, and focused instead on a new goal: breaking through.

"Breaking through?" I said again, pulling my gaze from the book and looking at the rest of the team. Most of them looked just as clueless as me, except . . .

"Reality," Aiwin said. "Breaking through reality. Into another."

The courtyard fell silent as the implications of what Aiwin had just said sunk in.

"There are . . . other realities?" Lore finally asked.

"No, there aren't," Val replied. "Aiwin must be mistaken."

"The old scriptures do imply that our world is not the only one out there," Corminar said. "The word of the ancient Architects—"

"You believe the words of Players now?" Val cut in. "Cos that's what they were, at the end of the day, weren't they? The Architects are Players."

"They create this world," Arzak said. "Why not others?"

"Are you so arrogant as to think yours is the only world that can be?" Aiwin asked Val—a question to which the witch did not react to. "I *saw* it. If you will take nothing else as proof, take *my* word."

I continued to read aloud from the notebook once more, as much to drown out the inevitable argument as anything else. I read Hara's increasingly mad scribblings about their progress with the experiments. They were slow at first, excruciatingly so, but just as it seemed they might scrap the whole project, they would advance. These advances grew more frequent as the benefactor funded more time and resources for the project, and with new sources of power tested, they zeroed in more and more on success. They went through beasts of all kinds—rockrats, hags, graybacks, and finally one they would not dare name, calling it only The Creature. It was with this last beast that they, eventually, breached the walls in reality.

It was only for a second, for less than a second, and yet it was encouraging to all involved. This project had potential—up until this point, they hadn't been sure—and focus redoubled. That is, until the monster hunter's mysterious superiors reassigned her elsewhere. It was the monster hunter's extreme capabilities, Hara speculated, that was to blame for this—there was another more desperate situation that needed seeing to.

This left the witchfinders twiddling their metaphorical thumbs, until Hara, who was by default in charge, allowed her eyes to wander to the devices once more. *Why not continue the tests without oversight*, she thought. Would their new benefactors not appreciate this act of initiative? Did they really need the monster hunter to make such progress?

Hara left the Creature caged; she would not dare release it onto the world. But they'd had success with hags, too, and their forest baits meant they had no short supply. They would use more of them—as many as it took—to replicate the successes of their earlier experiments, and they would do so without incurring the risks associated with provoking the Creature.

As I read on, the scribblings grew less and less legible, and from both this and the few words I could make out, I could tell that Hara was growing desperate. The hags weren't enough. No matter how many they drained, it was not enough.

And then the journal abruptly ended.

"That's it?" Val asked. "I thought we'd get answers."

"What, that wasn't enough for you? We know what they were doing, and we know—"

"We know what happened to them," Aiwin said, cutting me off. "Arzak was correct; those are not ghosts."

"See," the orc said, then frowned and turned to Aiwin. "What they then? They not dead?"

"They're not dead, no. The witchfinders are as alive as they ever were, in some ways," Aiwin replied, sparing a glance to watch Val shift uncomfortably on her feet. "They are alive, but they are trapped. Trapped between realities."

"Not totally trapped, though, are they?" Val replied. "Otherwise, we wouldn't have seen them."

"No. But perhaps we should ask ourselves: what does that mean?"

"Nothing good," Val said.

"Well, *of course* nothing good," Aiwin retorted. "I meant beyond this."

From how Val's face paled next, I could see that the two of them were finally on the same page about something. "We didn't just see them."

Aiwin nodded. "We saw another reality."

"What?" Lore asked. "What's that mean? Do we need to worry?"

"I would say so," the elf said.

"It means the borders between realities are disintegrating. It means our world is bleeding into another. The consequences could be . . ." Val trailed off before finishing the sentence, though in my head I was choosing between *terrible* and *catastrophic*.

"We must power down these devices," Aiwin said.

"How?"

I closed the notebook gently, the next few words getting lodged in my throat for a second—I didn't want to say them aloud. "There's only one magick source we know they even had some success with before." I glanced toward Val. "*Witchcraft.*"

If Val's face was pale before, it was paler still now.

Everyone remained silent but for Aiwin, who only said, "Then it is hopeless; we will never wrangle the hag beasts enough to direct their magicks in—"

Corminar coughed pointedly, glancing from Aiwin to Val, and at that moment I realized something. I wasn't the only one who knew the truth about Val; the others did, too. She'd already confided in them, and she'd only recently come to trust me enough to tell me the same. I didn't like the way this revelation weighed heavily in my stomach.

"What do you—" Aiwin started, but Corminar cut them off.

"Go."

They raised their eyebrows, a confused smirk crossing their face. "What do you mean, 'go'? We need every capable mind here if we are to . . ." Aiwin trailed off, and the truth dawned upon them. "Oh."

The other five of us remained artificially still, painfully quiet.

"Which of you is it?" Aiwin asked. "Which of you . . ." Their eyes landed on Val.

The witch among us took a step back, but with a foot in midair, she paused, then placed it gently back down where it had been.

"I could have you exterminated," Aiwin spat. "I *should.*"

"I would not give you the chance," Corminar said before anyone else could respond. His voice carried a weight I'd rarely heard in it before.

"You would kill me? For *her*?" Aiwin glared at Val. "Why? Is she another of your conquests? Is that why?"

Val, this time, did step backward, though this time it seemed more out of surprise than fear. "Him? No. No, he's . . ." Val licked her lips as though to stifle a laugh. "He's not my type."

"Then why?"

"Because it would not be just." Corminar paused. "Go, Aiwin."

The other elf met his gaze for a moment, before tearing it away. Aiwin turned away from us, without another word spoken, and without another glance in our direction. We watched the elf leave. After a few seconds, Corminar ran after them.

I thought, at first, that Corminar meant to apologize. But in the conversation that followed, the body language was stiff—there was no love there. Whatever he told the elf, it had them hurrying away much faster than before.

"I am sorry about that," the elf said, looking everywhere but at Val. "I knew about Aiwin's temperament. About Aiwin's values. And yet I saw to overlook it in order to have someone warm my bedroll. There was no real need for Aiwin to come, and for that . . ." He finally managed to look Val in the eye. "I apologize."

The witch nodded and flashed him a sad smile that was returned in kind. "Styk?" she said, thrusting out an upturned hand.

"Yeah?"

"The book. If I'm going to deal with these devices, then I've got to figure out *how*."

I handed Val the book, then watched her walk away. Just when she was almost out of sight, into the building furthest from the horrors from earlier, I hurried after her. Because I wasn't using my *Stealth*, she heard me coming.

"Leave me alone," she snapped.

"No."

"Why?"

"Cos I want to know if you're OK," I replied.

Val scoffed. "Of course I'm not. Styk, I'm *never* OK. I'm forced to hide what I am from everyone, forced to worry in every moment that someone will catch me. You saw Aiwin—an otherwise intelligent . . . ish elf—and even they would've had me exterminated and think it was nothing more than justice."

I didn't know what to say. I couldn't know what she was going through with this—I couldn't imagine what it was like. So instead, I moved forward to put a hand on her shoulder.

Val pulled herself away. "If you'll excuse me, Styk, I have some thinking to do."

I watched her walk away into the darkness, her eyes on the notebook.

CHAPTER TWENTY-ONE

Patching Reality

"Are we all clear on the plan?" Val asked, her voice raised even though we could all hear her perfectly fine—perhaps in an effort to rally us.

We stood outside the main building of the witchfinders' village, our eyes on the door and the shadows that lurked inside. Dawn was just beginning to break on the other side of the building, silhouetting it, illuminating the dewdrops on the grass beneath our feet.

"Fight," Arzak summarized. "Get you to basement."

"And then what do you do, Val?" Lore asked.

"You just let me worry about that," the witch replied. It was refreshing to think of her as a witch, rather than having to pretend to myself that I still thought she was a sorcerer, in case my tongue slipped. Though when there were other— less open-minded—people around, I would still need to be careful. "Styk?" she prompted me.

"I'm all mana-ed up," I said, raising the empty potion vial to Corminar in toast. "Will portal you all the way. As much as I can, at least."

Val nodded, turning her attention back to the building.

"What do you think?" I asked her, and everyone, really. "Doing the heroic thing? Makes you feel good, doesn't it?"

"I'm doing this because I don't want my world to fade away, Styk. Not cos I'm a hero."

I shrugged. "Still, though."

"Ready?" Arzak asked.

Four heads nodded.

"Alright . . ." Val started. "Go."

We charged into the building in our usual formation: Arzak and Lore at the front, their great health reserves meaning they could take the brunt of any damage; then Val and I, offering support and healing where necessary; and finally, Corminar, who was able to pick enemies off with his bow from afar. We stumbled into the building, into the shadows, and . . .

"Nothing here," Arzak said.

"Do we think it fixed itself?" Lore asked. "Maybe we can just go back to finding that clasp and then get out of here."

"These things," the orc said, shaking her head, "they not fix selves. They get worse."

Lore tilted his head to one side in acknowledgement of this. "Had to ask, though. Just in case we—" Movement up ahead caught my eye, and from the sudden pause, Lore's, too.

"They're still here," I said.

Val snorted. "Surprised?"

"I guess Lore had me hoping. He's an optimistic guy." I saw Lore smile at this, though I wasn't sure I'd intended it wholly as a compliment. "Better get moving."

Arzak nodded, and began walking down the corridor toward the kitchen at the rear of the building, her dual swords held high. Lore followed close behind, creeping, but I had a suspicion the shadows already knew we were there. I followed soon after, keeping Val close, but I didn't hear Corminar behind us.

"Erm . . ." the elf said, and I turned to see a hand reaching out of the floor, grabbing him by the ankle.

"Yes?" Val said as she turned, then her eyes bulged.

"Run," Corminar said. While he nocked and fired an arrow toward the clasping hand, I took Val by the arm and threw her into a portal, narrowly avoiding the shapes that suddenly sprang out of the walls. We landed at Arzak's side, Lore at our rear.

"Didn't you hear him?" I shouted. "Run!"

Arzak chopped at the hands, arms, heads, and shoulders that protruded from the walls, their shapes an absence of reality. Her blades passed right through them, but as we knew from our earlier encounter, it stopped the shadows taking form enough to grab us. It wouldn't work forever, but it might just work for long enough to get Val into the basement.

I spun, flinging another hand forward and down the next hallway, opening a portal within the kitchen at the other end. I hopped through first, followed by Val, followed by Arzak. It took me poking a head back through the portal to realize that Lore wasn't following because there were five ghostly hands gripping him tightly, holding him to the wall.

"Go!" he shouted. "Quickly, though!" He slammed the butt of his blade toward one of the hands, but it passed through. The shadow regained form in a second—they were getting faster at reshaping every time we attacked.

I turned back to the kitchen to see Arzak and Val standing at the trapdoor, standing next to the pitch-black basement. "What are you waiting for?" I cried. "We gotta move quick! Get a torch down there!"

"There is," Arzak replied.

"What?"

"There *is* a torch down there," Val said.

"Ah." I realized then why the pair of women were so hesitant to step down; there was a torch down there, and yet it was impenetrably dark. ". . . We gotta go anyway, haven't we?"

Arzak looked at me, nodded, and then jumped down the length of the staircase in one stride. She should've landed heavily at the bottom, but I heard nothing.

"Arzak?" Val called into the darkness.

"Is . . . on the . . . need to . . ." Arzak's words came and went, fading into and out of reality. It didn't take a genius to work out what that meant.

I looked up at Val. "What if someone gets trapped on the other side when you destroy the devices?"

"We'll have to make sure that doesn't happen."

"OK, but how? How are we going to—"

Val leaped into the darkness, and I had no choice but to follow after her.

I landed on grass. Looking down at my feet, I could just about make them out through the shadows, which were so thick here that they made me feel a bit claustrophobic. I stood upon grass—not the grass of our reality, but the other— and this grass was gray. For a moment I thought this was just the usual grass color of this new world, but when I looked up at a farmhouse in the distance, I could see that it, and the mountain scenery, all existed in a shade of gray. Perhaps I simply wasn't enough a part of this world to see it for what it truly was.

"Styk?" a familiar voice shouted, and for whatever reason it took me a second to place it as Val's. I made toward it, stumbling through the sometimes patchy, sometimes intense shadows, doing my best to find any sign of the basement that I really *should* still have been in.

I collided with Val after a few paces, and I hadn't been able to see her until I was completely upon her, which caused me to step on her foot. Though I couldn't make out her expression in the shadows, I knew she'd be scowling at me.

"I can't find them," she said. "I can't find the towers. Can't *see* them, can't—"

She suddenly tumbled to the ground, and I instinctively reached down to grab her. I gripped tightly onto her arms as something in the shadows sought to tear her away. The opposing force grew stronger with every passing second, and soon it was all I could do just to keep Val's arms in my hands.

"Can you portal?" she asked, voice straining.

"I can try, but I'd need to let you go."

For a moment, the shadows gave way enough for me to see her face, and one of sheer terror stared back at me. "OK," she said, voice quiet. "Let me try something."

I gave it as long as I could before prompting her. "Are you doing it?"

"I'm *trying*. My magicks seem be struggling. I . . ." She paused for a moment. "Wait." Val screwed up her face, then suddenly ripped her hands from my grasp. She thrust them toward the shadows that were pulling at her, and she shouted as she released a gust of her wind magicks. It was enough to make the shadows all drop form at once, and she wriggled free. Not only that, but she cleared a line of sight between us and one of the strange devices. "There!"

"I got it!" I said, and even as I was speaking did I open a portal below us. Val and I dropped through, both of us slamming against the device in midair before tumbling to the floor. There hadn't been time to aim properly.

Val pushed herself to her feet using the device for support, then placed one hand on the device before pushing the other down her shirt—revealing her obscurem, which was already glowing a vivid green as she drew upon her *Witchcraft* magicks.

Lightning formed around both her and the devices, the other two of the latter illuminating in the distance. Val's hand on the device trembled as the power surged through her, her body slowly lifting off the ground, the obscurem glowing brighter and brighter.

A hand wrapped itself around my right foot, then another hand around the other, and suddenly I was hurtling through the darkness away from my friend. "Val!" I shouted, stretching out a hand in desperation. But she was already too far into the process; all I could do was try to survive long enough for her to fix reality.

I whipped a hand down toward my knife, but another shadow—this one fully formed—stepped out of the darkness and grabbed my arm, stopping me from arming myself. I tried the other hand, but that, too, was snatched by those trapped between realities. "Val!" I shouted. "Val, hurry!"

I wrenched my head upward to see Val floating, the lightning turning green around her, the obscurem glowing so brightly that it pierced even the thick darkness.

The shadows pulled on each of my four limbs, stretching me in different directions, the joints beginning to crack, the muscles beginning to strain, my health reserves beginning to drain.

"Val!" I shouted again. "Val, hur—"

The witch screamed, and the obscurem exploded. A great wave of green lightning blasted out from each of the devices, passing over me without harm, but wiping the shadows away like extinguishing flames. There was a second of silence before the same wave of lightning returned again, pouring back into the devices that had returned it.

Val dropped to the floor.

> *Level 24 Witchfinder Private defeated!*
> *Level 26 Witchfinder Private defeated!*
> *Level 29 Witchfinder Sergeant defeated!*
> *Level 32 Witchfinder Colonel defeated!*
> . . .

The list went on, every person who had been trapped between realities considered now defeated—because we'd broken free of combat.

> **Worldbending**: +7,100XP
> *Worldbending increased to Level 28!*
> *Worldbending increased to Level 29!*
> *Worldbending increased to Level 30!*
> **Base Points Gained**: +6 INT, +6 Free Points (INT/WIS/CHA)
> **Ability Selection Unlocked**
> . . .

"Woah," I heard Val say, her form becoming clear once more as the intensity of the darkness softened.

"You OK?"

"More than. Just leveled up *Witchcraft*, and let me tell you: these ability choices are incredible."

"Don't you think we should check on the others before doing that?"

"Is OK," Arzak said, stumbling weakly to her feet and brushing the dust off her shoulders. "I here." She turned and cupped a hand to her mouth. "Other friends? You alive?"

Lore popped his smiling head down the trapdoor. "I'm alive. You did it?"

"No, Lore, it just ended by itself, as if by magick," Val replied.

"Well, it *was* by magick, wasn't it?"

"Is Corminar still with us?" I asked him.

As if in answer, Corminar's elven hand waved his bow through the trapdoor. "This bow is *completely* inadequate. I must insist that we replace this 'borrowed' bow with one of my usual caliber at the earliest opportunity."

"So you're unhurt, then," I replied.

Val snorted, and in the silence that followed, all five of us found our breaths.

"Right, then," I said. "Heroic work, done. How about we go find what we came here for?"

CHAPTER TWENTY-TWO

What We Came Here For

With the shadows eliminated, and some peace and quiet at last, it took only thirty minutes of the team poring over Witchfinder Colonel Hara's notebook to work out where they kept the witchfinder's clasp. After all that had happened, I'd almost forgotten what we'd been looking for, and if I was honest, I was very thankful to put this all behind us.

I wasn't as thankful as Val, however, who I'd never seen so cheery as when we finally began trudging down the road that would put the village behind us. She'd unlocked a new ability, too—one which she simply *would not* shut up about, not that I'd have ever asked her to. This ability was available to her only because shutting down the devices was categorized as her defeating a lightning-wielding enemy, which met a hidden condition for her *Witchcraft* skill tree. All in all, this meant Val was now the proud owner of an ability that allowed her to temporarily imbue objects with lightning effects. It wasn't the classic *Lightning Ball* ability that a Sorcerer might have, but it definitely made Val more useful in a fight.

And then there had been my ability selection, too—one that I'd discussed in great detail with Val in between her picking up sticks and making them crackle with lightning.

> **Ability Selection Unlocked**
> *Select an ability from the list below:*
> **Option 1: Soften Dirt II (Worldbending)**—Your magicks alters the form of earth, making it soft, pliable, and significantly more vulnerable to digging.

Both Val and I had ruled this one out very early on—that is, without even seeing the rest of the choices—for the same reason: that it was boring. Arzak, who overheard, was not particularly impressed with this, telling us that "Boring is good sometime. Should think about boring," but already both of us were over this choice.

> **Option 2: Ash Husk II (Worldbending)**—*Upgrade to Ash Husk.* Convert your flesh to ash, strengthening it against flame for 10 minutes. Gain 60 percent resistance to fire attacks, and deal fire damage whenever you are hit while this ability is active.

This was an update to an ability that I really didn't make enough use of, mostly because it had only really been useful when we were fighting down the Player. Come to think of it, we hadn't so much as *met* a fire-magick wielder since. But with this upgrade, the ability would have a broader appeal—dealing damage to anyone who attacked me. Though Val had sort of shrugged this one off, I was more keen, and kept it in my back pocket going into the last two choices.

> *Hidden condition met! Alternative ability choice unlocked.*
> **Option 3: Tamed Portals (Worldbending)** [Requires: *Stealth* level 5]—*Passive.* Increased efficiency of portal magicks means that your portal glow is reduced by 50 percent, making them less likely to be detected by enemies.

This was another good one. If I was really going to continue rebuilding my *Stealth* skill tree—and I really was intending to, even though opportunities to level it up had been fairly few and far between—then this offered great . . .

I'd failed to find the word, and described it to Val.

"Synergy," she'd told me.

This was one of those ability choices that could become one core to my build, if indeed "stealth portaler" was the way I wanted to go. Synergy.

But there was one more choice, for a massive total of four choices this time around.

> *Hidden condition met! Alternative ability choice unlocked.*
> **Option 4: Saved Portal (Worldbending)** [Requires: *Local Portal*]—Select a location to "save" for future portals. Until your save point is moved, you may always open a portal here, even if it is beyond your current *Local Portal* range. Uses significant mana to save new location.

This final choice was very tempting, particularly if I wanted to create a home somewhere. It would mean I'd be able to return home in the blink of an eye, without all the days—or weeks, or months—of travel in between.

But the combat application was somewhat lacking, not just because I couldn't figure out a good use for it, but also because of the "significant mana" required to save the location. Even though I was dumping most free stats into Intelligence—because my *Warped Shield* helped prevent damage using mana rather than losing health, and because *Mana-Fueled* let me use mana instead of stamina to melee attack—I still couldn't go around draining my whole mana reserve for things like this.

But then, if the team was all going to use Lore's farm as a base, then this would have a positive impact for all of them, not just me. After much discussion with Val, we decided the selfless thing to do would be to pick *Saved Portal*, even though it wasn't quite as fun. Yet . . .

Ability Unlocked: Tamed Portals
Tamed Portals (Worldbending): *Passive*. Increased efficiency of portal magicks means that your portal glow is reduced by 50 percent, making them less likely to be detected by enemies.

Sometimes you've got to be a little selfish. As a treat.

Looking at my profile, my list of abilities was getting to be pretty hefty, and it was no wonder that I didn't always think to use them all in the heat of battle. I'd have to spend some time meditating on them, I figured—so I would know better whilst in the middle of a fight what to do next.

As we continued down the path back to the main traveler's road, the witch-finders' village not far behind us, Lore—occasionally the most philosophical of the lot of us, surprisingly—piped up with a thought that I think the rest of us had been repressing. "Why'd they give you the book, then?"

I came to a halt.

"The notebook, I mean. If it was going to tell you how to shut down those devices, and trap them between worlds, why did they give it to you?"

"Because we were their only chance for salvation," Val replied. "I think the witchfinders thought we might use the knowledge to get them back."

"May I ask," Corminar said, "might that have been possible?"

There was a moment of hesitation before Val responded. "No. No, I don't think so." My thoughts dwelled more on the hesitation than the words—was Val the kind to convict the witchfinders to being trapped for, potentially, eternity, as punishment for their crimes? For all the fellow witches they would have tortured, and killed? I, in the end, decided I was better off not knowing, and didn't ask the question.

"This why they attack us," Arzak said. "On way out, not attack, just try give notebook. When we go back in . . ."

"Their efforts were certainly doubled," Corminar continued for her. "Perhaps because they knew what we were planning."

"Mm."

"Do you think we'll ever wholly understand what happened there?" I asked the group. From the silence that followed, the answer was clear.

As we finally reached the main road, the muddy overgrown path giving way to well-worn hard-packed earth, a figure approached from the other side. Aiwin's eyes remained fixed on Val, not Corminar, as they drew near. I drew my hand toward my blade, anticipating trouble—Aiwin had seemed the sort to see that Val got the justice they deemed was necessary.

But what they said was nothing of the sort. "I won't tell anyone what you are."

Val remained quiet for a second before replying. "How can I trust you?"

Only at this did Aiwin's gaze blink, just for a second, in Corminar's direction. "Because Corminar does not speak any idle threats. I have seen firsthand just what that man is capable of. I served with him, remember. One day, ask him what he did in the Honey Wars. You'll have to ask him why he can never go home. Then you'll understand."

Aiwin's eyes remained on Val a moment longer, before finally—and seemingly with great effort—turning to Corminar. "Perhaps this will placate you. A peace offering, of sorts; a piece of information that I know you value greatly. The identity of the woman in charge, the great monster hunter? The one that was reassigned?"

"Tell me," Corminar said, his voice quiet.

"She was a Player." With that, Aiwin turned and walked back into the shadows of the trees.

Witchfinder Colonel Hara Teramura

The great Monster Hunter had departed many days prior, and still there was no sign of her replacement. In the basement of headquarters main building, the three world-punchers stood, gathering dust, calling out to be switched on once more. And Witchfinder Colonel Hara Teramura heard them calling.

She awoke from dreams of her celebration, of the riches rewarded to her for her successes, and of the life she might have once she completed these experiments. When she awoke, there was none of the moment where you exist between the unconscious and the conscious worlds; her mind was already functional, and working at maximum capacity.

"Orla!" she cried out, and a young woman, barely of age, hurried into the room.

"Yes, colonel?" the private asked.

"Fetch the Creature," Hara said. "We go again in an hour. Ensure that all parties are present."

"Yes, colonel," Private Orla said, and disappeared from the room once more.

Hara ambled over to the window that overlooked the courtyard. Though the witchfinder village had existed at the start of Hara's leadership, it had been a humble affair. The village she looked onto now had grown—two new buildings constructed since her elevation, each housing a new generation of privates. With this number of witchfinders under her command, they may yet rid the western continents of witches forever. Oh, what a delightful thought that was.

Another private—a new recruit, new enough that Hara had not yet thought to learn his name—brought her breakfast, and she ate it at her desk while leafing through the latest correspondence. The few notes or required actions she jotted down in an old leather journal—one that her father had given her when she had been initially accepted as a witchfinder. The years had long passed, of course, and her father was not still of this world, but she treasured this notebook, her last remaining reminder of her loving father.

As Hara rose, meaning to head to the basement in time for the next stage of testing, a knock on the door announced the arrival of a more senior employee. "Walk with me," Hara told them, and together they strode down the long corridors of witchfinder headquarters.

"You seek to use the Creature?" Witchfinder Sergeant Alti asked as they walked, his hands clasped behind his back, as he so often did when uncertain. "Would it not be more prudent to continue to use the hags? If we were to *kill* the Creature by accident, then I'm not certain our benefactors would forgive us . . ."

"Must you always be so negative, Alti? Perhaps they would appreciate a little initiative on our part, hmm?"

"But what about Ni—"

"Our last supervisor was many things, but perhaps a little too cautious, a little too considered in her approach. After all, it takes a great deal of courage to make history, wouldn't you agree?"

By the time Hara arrived in the basement, she was pleased to discover that the requisite witchfinders were present, and the heavy wooden crate in the center of the triangle signified that the Creature, too, was in attendance. A witchfinder sorcerer stood at each side of the triangle, each of their hands clasped in front of them, their eyes closed, preparing themselves for the task ahead.

"The Creature is awake?" Hara asked, wasting no time on pleasantries.

"If not, it will be soon," Alti murmured. The man had a point; for all his flaws, he rarely spoke that which was not true.

Hara nodded, then took the one seat available in the room. She hadn't instructed Orla to provide it, but the woman had learned quickly. The witchfinder colonel gestured to the other seven witchfinders present in the room. "Whenever you are ready."

"Such haste, Hara?" Alti asked, and Hara noted both his familiarity and lack of correct address.

"I intend to conduct several such tests today," Hara said, and had considered expanding on this point further, but soon realized that it would not do to explain herself to her underlings; it might encourage them to question her more often. "Please, begin. Release the Creature."

Three witchfinders—not the three sorcerers—stepped forth from the darkness, and gripped the edges of the crate. On the muttered count of three from the one in charge, they moved in one practiced, fluid motion, allowing the box to unfold, revealing the Creature inside. The mala.

The sorcerers released their spells, three lightning-based magicks that met around the Creature to trap it in a cage of a new making. Hara tensed for a moment as the mala tested the boundaries of the trap, pushing against the sheets of lightning before eventually settling once more.

She breathed a sigh of release; it was a tamer one.

Their suppliers of the malae—a rather unsavory group of elves, so unlike the typical elven stereotypes—had been inconsistent with their deliveries. A failed shipment many moons ago meant this was the last such creature available to the witchfinders. Their experiments would need to be successful.

"Is anyone compromised?" Hara shouted over the noise of the spells. "Does anyone feel fear?" When none of her soldiers replied, the colonel nodded once more.

"Press!" Witchfinder Sergeant Alti commanded, and the sorcerers intensified their magicks. The Creature began to squeal and began to push against its confines once more. Hara, at that moment, saw one of the sorcerers twitch, and she knew then that the trouble was beginning.

"Replacement sorcerer required on side—" Hera began, but at that moment, the faltering sorcerer screamed, her hands slamming at her face, as though patting out flames that weren't there.

One of the backup sorcerers stepped forward to replace her in the triangle, but the mala was already pushing against its now-weakened bindings.

"Faster!" she shouted, but it was too late—the inky surface of the mala protruded through a vulnerability in the spells, and with a grotesque wet sound, it squeezed through the gap and flopped onto the floor. The sorcerers rushed to redirect their spells and recapture it once more, but it was slippery, sliding through the lightning until finally it squelched onto one of the world-punchers.

Hara's heart dropped as she realized what was about to happen. "No!" she screamed, reaching a hand forward. But it was too late. One sorcerer, in their haste to contain the fear-inducing creature, allowed their lightning magicks to touch one of the devices.

A wave of dark light erupted from the three world-punchers, sending the present witchfinders soaring into the wall, hitting them hard. Hara, winded against the staircase and with several cracked ribs, tried to sit up, but another wave of dark light hit her again. And then another, and another, each with increasing frequency. She watched as Witchfinder Private Orla, pressed against a wall to her left, began to fade away.

"N-no . . ." Hara managed to breathe.

Soon, the very walls faded, being replaced by a courtyard of stone, a tall wooden structure towering above them, the blazing flames of a signal fire at its crest. Hara, understanding but not quite comprehending that which was happening, tried to stand. She pressed her hand against the wooden steps, and it passed right through.

Orla, falling backward through the wall, screamed.

CHAPTER TWENTY-THREE

Big City Fun Time

In the days that followed, we split the team in two. Corminar and Lore would go after the depth-raider with the witchfinder's clasp in their possession, while Val, Arzak, and I would begin investigating this Player.

It hadn't taken us long to realize that we needed to act on Aiwin's information. The presence of a Player set off alarm bells at the best of times, but to know that one was involved with such dangerous schemes as the witchfinder experiments meant they were definitely not up to anything good. Our solution to this problem of not having any more information than that was to find more information, naturally. Without any other semblance of a lead, we decided to head to Auricia, the capital of the Goldmarch. After all, there was only one place where someone with enough coin to bankroll the witchfinders could be from. Surely, all the wealth of that description had to come from Auricia in some capacity.

We said our goodbyes to Lore and Corminar, watched them walk away, then turn and mutter to one another before Lore jogged back over to us. "Forgot the clasp," he explained, then hurried off once more.

"Lore?" I called after him.

The barbarian turned. "Yeah?"

"Sword."

He patted his back where his sword should be, then realized it was still on the floor in the camp that Val, Arzak, and I were sitting around. He hurried back again. "Whoops!" After that, Lore finally had everything, and the three of us were left to our own devices.

We'd continued along the merchant road for many days until the taverns grew more frequent and the dirt more well-trodden. Soon, we were passing through Auricia's peripheral towns, and not long after that, we caught our first sight of the capital itself.

I had thought some of the peripheral towns were big, so it hadn't really prepared me for the sheer size of Auricia. Huge stone towers seemed to pierce the heavens themselves. The walls of the city, as high as any building I'd ever seen before, seemed to stretch for miles in either direction, and still the buildings sprawled out of the gates. A giant spiraling brass dome in the center of the capital announced the seat of the Goldmarch, Queen Amira's Golden Palace.

"Why's it brass, though?" I asked, nodding to the spiraling dome.

"Even queen not have *that* much gold," Arzak responded.

Fair enough; it was a bloody big dome, after all.

We walked into town through the—apparently "poor," though it seemed pretty much in line with the Tundras—outer town, then had to queue at the gates to get inside the city proper. The guards waved those citizens with specific paperwork right through, but for the rest of us, we had to brave interrogation by the soldiers in mustard surcoats.

When the guards finally allowed us through, it was early afternoon, and the people of Auricia were out in their masses. I put to Val and Arzak that it must be some kind of festival, but both of them replied that they thought this was just what Auricia was like. Neither of them seemed entirely sure, though.

"OK," Arzak said as we strolled up one of the capital's main roads toward the center. "Straight to tax office. Find out about Player."

As she was saying that, though, the lovingly illustrated sign of a nearby shop caught my eye. I came to an abrupt halt, and it took Arzak and Val a moment to realize I wasn't walking alongside them.

"What this?" the orc asked.

I nodded toward the shop—Needle & Felt.

"You want do shopping?" Arzak said.

"You can get your sewing stuff later, Styk," Val added. "We've got stuff to do."

I shrugged. "Lore and Corminar are going to be a few days, aren't they? I think we can spare ten minutes. Especially if it means I can start leveling up my *Needlework*."

"You're really that into sewing?"

"I'm into getting Dexterity and Charisma points every time I level up, if that's what you mean. And if I get some decent armor out of it . . ."

Val glanced to Arzak, who shrugged.

"We wait outside," Arzak said.

When I left the shop once more, fifteen—not ten, admittedly—minutes later, I carried a fresh batch of thread and some thick dark green cloth that the shopkeeper had said I could layer into a very basic armor. It wouldn't be something that would fend off a blade, but would keep me from the odd graze here and there, and that was a good start. My knapsack hung heavy on my back, and I was regretting picking *Warped Shield* over *Cloth Storage II* purely because I didn't want to have to carry all this stuff, though I did know, really, that *Warped Shield* was still the better pick.

Anyway, I was distracted by noticing both Arzak and Val were missing.

I spun around, searching the milling crowds, the striding workers, and the ambling tourists, and spotted them a minute or two later inside a women's clothing store. With a sigh, I adjusted the straps of my knapsack and followed them inside.

"What are you doing?" I asked Val, craning over her shoulder as she held a red dress up to her body, studying it in the mirror.

The witch blinked back at me. "What does it look like I'm doing?"

"It looks like you're—"

"What do you think of this? Would it suit me? Blue has always been more of my color."

"I thought—"

"Yes or no? Pretty?" Val prompted me.

"As pretty in red as in blue," I replied. "Where's Arzak?"

Val didn't reply for a moment, instead tilting her head as she studied the dress in the mirror. "Changing."

"Changing what?"

The witch scoffed and put the dress back on a nearby rack. "Clothes? Gods, you really are dim sometimes."

Before I could reply, a nearby curtain swung open, revealing Arzak in a ballgown, one clearly made for the orcish frame.

"So, me getting a few pieces of cloth was wasting time, but you two—" I started, but cooing from Val interrupted me. I waited patiently as the two women analyzed the dress and its fit in minute detail.

Behind me, an older, dapper gentleman coughed pointedly, then gestured me toward a small stool. "The boyfriend seat, darling," he said, then strode confidently across the floor to join Val in encouraging Arzak to buy the dress.

Many, many moons later, Arzak made the purchase, and the older gentleman wrapped it in a box and far too many ribbons. As we walked out, I couldn't help but voice a question I knew, really, that I shouldn't. "And just when are you gonna wear that? It's not like we go to many balls, do we?"

Val punched me on the shoulder, and didn't follow it up with the usual cheeky grin. "You're not funny."

"Are you joking?" I replied, finding myself more offended than I'd expected. "I'm the funniest of the lot of us."

"Am *I* joking? Are *you* joking?" Val responded. "It's clearly me or Lore who is the funniest. Though I don't know how often Lore intends to be funny, and how often—"

"It me," Arzak said confidently.

Val and I turned to her, faces blank.

"With orcs," Arzak clarified. "They say I hilarious."

Val and I remained silent, not sure whether this was an example of her humor. "Right . . ." Val finally said, and at that point we dropped the entire conversation. Instead, we focused once more on tracking down the information we'd come all this way to find.

Auricia's tax office was an enormous building not too far from the center of town and the Golden Palace. It was manned by hundreds, if not *thousands*, of people with ancestry from all parts of the world. This was a very serious affair, I realized, and that made sense: the Goldmarch had prospered from customs and import taxes. Without buildings like this, the treasury—and kingdom itself, I guessed—could crumble.

Val eloquently lied to a man behind a desk on the ground floor, telling them we were here to retrieve public tax records. A little palm-greasing to merchants in the travelers' inn had given us some information: those people and businesses who had contracts with the monarchy had to publish their records publicly—a matter of keeping these wealthy people under control, we suspected. So, it's those records we claimed we were after, and not those of a private individual who had nothing to do with Queen Amira, and everything to do with punching holes in reality.

The attendant led us up to the third floor, where they gave us a ticket number and forced us to wait—for literally *hours*—on uncomfortable wooden benches. I had to suspect they'd made these benches as uncomfortable as possible to convince people to give up waiting, and to make the lives of these civil servants an ounce less painful. But we had a job to do, and it was the three most stubborn members of the Slayers who were here to do it.

When our number was finally called, we were led to a booth manned by an orc. A good few paces away, Arzak paused and turned to us. "Let me handle this," she said.

"Err, don't you think—"

"I handle this," Arzak said, her tone making this sound more like an instruction than a suggestion, this time around.

Before either Val or I could argue this point—both of us surely itching to point out that we needed to be smooth and charming here if we were going to get the documents we were after—Arzak turned away.

I watched Arzak go. "Is this a good idea?"

"Probably not," Val replied, then after a moment shrugged her shoulders and took a seat on a nearby bench. I joined her.

It was a minute later, when I heard the orc behind the counter laugh his head off, that Val and I turned, eyebrows raised, to look over at Arzak.

"And then said . . . that not my sheep!" our friend said.

The orc behind the counter laughed again, this time violently, and had to wipe away tears from his eyes.

I looked at Val, who looked back at me blankly. "I don't—"

"No," Val agreed.

Eventually, Arzak returned to us with not only the information that we required, but also the offer of a date the next evening. When we asked whether she was going to follow up on the latter, she only shrugged and said, "If have time." We turned our attention next to the information on the witchfinder experiments, only for Arzak to tell us something that made our hearts sink: the people funding these experiments were from the palace itself.

If we were going to find out more, we'd need to break inside the palace vaults.

Val raised her hands in a cheer. "Bank heist!" she cried.

CHAPTER TWENTY-FOUR

Lemon Sherbets of Lightfoot

The palace, as well as its various grounds and peripheral buildings, would have alone been larger than any town I had ever seen. It wasn't so much that there were a huge number of buildings—though between the stables, the lauded merchants, the armorers, and the various servants' quarters, there *was* a huge number—but that the buildings themselves were larger than any of those I'd seen before. The sheer scale came with a substantial benefit, however: with so many people hurrying or milling about the palace grounds, we were more likely to blend in. This was what we decided: we would hide in plain sight.

Already, Arzak gloated her ball gown would come in handy; if we were going to look like the sorts of folk who belonged in a palace, then we'd need to look the part. This led to Val buying a dress of her own—a blue number, her professed color of choice—as well as buying me a waistcoat, shirt, and dress pants. These clothes didn't seem to fit me at all, but the man in the shop told me "that is the style," and my friends forced me to go along with it.

After Val handed over the money to pay for all this stuff, I realized I'd one day need to ask her where all the coin had come from. More and more I was wondering whether she was so keen on heists not for the novelty, but because they were a way of life for her.

As we strolled back toward the palace, Val finding her slim dress as confining as my waistcoat, we made an effort to walk as though we had a lot of money. To my mind—and Arzak agreed with me on this—I thought that looking rich was more to do with having a straight back and holding your head high, though Val was more of the opinion that it meant scowling at everyone. We settled for doing both.

Obviously we were doing a good job, because the crowds of locals sometimes parted before us, the working classes of Auricia so conditioned to make way for their supposed "betters" that they almost jumped to one side when they saw my waistcoat.

Val stopped at the side of a main road not too far from the palace and suddenly turned to me. She licked her thumbs pretty substantially and then started fussing with my hair.

"Oi, what are you—"

"Your mop is giving us away," Val said, wrenching the hair back. "We need you looking like you have servants to tend to this kind of thing."

"Are you offering to be my servant?"

The witch kicked me gently in the shins.

"Oi!" I said again—this apparently being my word of the day—but when I looked up at Val, I realized she was staring at something over my shoulder. "What?" I asked, following her line of sight.

I turned to see a shop with a queue of a few dozen people formed outside, many of them craning their heads to see if they'd be getting inside anytime soon. But it wasn't this that Val was staring at, I realized. She was staring at the banner above the shop, which read: Grand Opening: Ted's Confectionary Emporium.

"Oh no . . ." I mumbled.

"You don't think . . . ?" Val said.

Arzak looked at us, then at the shop, then back at us again. "What wrong? Hungry?"

"You remember those cursed sweets we had?" Val asked her. "It was a guy named Ted who gave them to us. Blamed us for his stall getting beat up. But surely he wouldn't be here, would he? How could he be? How could he have the money for all of *that*?" She nodded at the store.

I remained silent, having no answer for her. And then, against my better judgement, I made for the store. Val and Arzak followed at my heel.

A tiefling man dressed in black stopped me at the door by placing a hand on my chest. "You not see the queue, pumpkin?" he asked, the "pumpkin" bit delivered in a particularly sarcastic tone.

"We're old friends of Ted's," I told him. "Here to wish him well. And spend some coin on his big day."

"Oh yeah? And how many times do you reckon I've heard that today? You want in, then you get in line, alright?"

"If you know Ted as well as I do, then you'll know—"

"I don't," the tiefling said.

"Sorry?"

"Don't be."

"No, I mean, you don't know him?"

The man sighed. "I'm hired by the day. Just met the guy this morning, so—"

I groaned. "Oh, screw this." Turning to Val and Arzak, I asked, "You both ready?"

They responded by taking a step to stand in closer to me.

"What are you—" the tiefling started as I raised a hand to gesture to the busy shop behind him. I didn't hear the end of the sentence because I opened a portal beneath us, and Arzak, Val, and I fell through it, landing in the store proper. Though the *Tamed Portals* passive meant that my portals' glows were only 50 percent reduced, this was enough that three people appearing out of nowhere didn't seem to attract the attention of many of the shoppers. But perhaps that was due to the colorful and eclectic array of sweets piled in stacks on tables in front of them.

"Wow," Arzak said. "Pretty. I think Lore like this."

"He would," Val said, plucking a sweet from a nearby stall and moving to plop it into her mouth. I slapped it out of her hand. "What was *that* for?"

"He enchants them, remember?"

"Some of them, yeah. I don't think he's putting the black market enchanted ones out on display, though, is he?"

I raised my eyebrows. "You really wanna take that chance?"

Val, midway into reaching out for another sweet, reluctantly pulled her hand away. "Fine."

"So," Arzak asked, looking around the room. "Where this—"

"*You,*" a familiar voice cried out.

Val and I turned slowly to see him standing there. Ted. The Ted we knew.

"*You!*" Ted cried out. "How did you . . . How did you find me? How did you track me all this way? How did you . . ." He blinked. "Guard! Guard, chuck them out!" But over the din of the shop being absolutely packed with customers, the tiefling could neither see nor hear Ted.

"*We* didn't track you anywhere," Val said. "We just came across you. How can you be here, anyway? Last time we saw you—just a few months back—you only had a cart."

"A damaged cart," I reminded him.

The young Ted glared at me. "Are you here to do the same to my shop? Cos I got spells built in, you know. Came with the lease agreement. If you—"

"We're not going to attack your shop," I said. "Look, we've *never* attacked you or your stuff. Lambkin attacked your cart—"

"Attacked my cart trying to get to *you!*"

"And I seem to remember you immediately selling me out to him, yeah? *And* you poisoned us!"

Ted rolled his eyes. "Oh, a bit of watery vomit, big deal. You'll get over it."

"Wolves were attacking us when the effects hit," Val said.

The shopkeeper glanced at Val, his cheeks flushing, and then his gaze dropped to the floor. "Well . . . I'm sorry about that. But you're here now, you're alive, and you need to get out of my shop."

"No," I said, "you gotta tell us. How did you get here? Did you steal?"

"No, I didn't *steal!*" Ted retorted.

I held up my hands in surrender—a mannerism I'd picked up from Val. "No judgements here, alright? I just—"

"If you really have to know, I got a lot of experience a few months back. One of my enchanted sweets. Someone must have used it to off someone powerful, cos the amount of experience changed my life."

I eyed Val, who was pressing her lips together to suppress a laugh.

"And then, suddenly I can make the best sweets in the Tundras. So I figure why not go where the money is? And obviously the money is in the Goldmarch, cos . . ." Ted trailed off when he caught sight of Val trying not to laugh. "What?"

Val pointed a thumb at me. "Him."

"What about him?"

"It was him."

"Him what? Him who . . ." Ted paled when he realized what Val was talking about. "No. No, I refuse to believe that. Can't be *him*. Anyone but *him*."

"It him," my orc friend offered. "I Arzak, by the way. It nice to—"

"Go on then," Ted said, cutting Arzak off. "Who did you kill? A baron? A duke?"

"A Player." I thought I'd said it quietly, but apparently not, because a good dozen heads swiveled to look at me. Open a portal at their side, and they don't care, but talk about killing a Player . . .

Ted turned to soothe the crowd, waving them down with a sheepish smile on his face. "He's joking! He's joking, everyone!" He turned back to me. "You can't make those kinds of jokes. Not in the Goldmarch. You'll scare off my customers. No, worse—it's treason, so you'll get killed." He hesitated on this point for a moment. "Worse for you, I mean. I don't care if you get killed."

"Who's joking?" I replied, this time actually making sure to talk quietly.

Ted, incredibly finding it within him to grow paler still, paused for a moment before waving us through a door at the back of the shop. Passing through the threshold, we found ourselves in a stockroom, the walls lined with jars of sweets and confectionary ingredients. While Ted fussed with closing a jar he'd left open, Arzak leaned in close to my ear.

"He handsome," she whispered. "Maybe young, but handsome."

"OK?"

"He handsome and he like *Val*."

"Why are you telling me this?" I asked.

"Is competition."

I blinked at her. "Arzak? Shut up."

The orc smiled a knowing smile, but let the matter drop.

"I'm handsome, too," I mumbled, and immediately recognized how pathetic that was, so I was glad when Arzak didn't seem to hear it.

Finally, Ted turned around, glancing at the door to make sure Arzak had shut it behind her. "So you're telling me . . . All this, my entire fortune . . . it's built on the death of a Player?"

"Afraid so, buddy," Val said.

Ted gulped.

"Player's not good, though. He not innocent. He—"

Again, Ted interrupted Arzak. "I don't care about that. I care about my life."

"We aren't going to go about advertising it," Val said. "It's not like anyone's gonna find out."

"Well, hold on a minute," I said, cutting in with a raised finger, sensing the opportunity for a little light extortion. "We won't tell anyone, as long as . . ."

"Oh no," Ted mumbled.

"As long as you help us break into the palace record office," I finished.

"Oh, that's even worse than I was expecting. More treason? Double the treason?"

"Can they double-kill us?" I asked. "No. So it's still just the regular single treason, when it comes to sentencing."

Ted glared at me as though this didn't reassure him in the slightest. "I will do no such thing."

In answer, Val strode over to the door, flung it open, then cupped her hand to her mouth as though she was about to shout something.

"Wait!" the shopkeeper cried out. "For the love of the Architects, *wait.*"

Val, with a quick smirk in my direction, closed the door again.

"I don't know how I'm supposed to help you," Ted said, turning away and placing his hands on the edge of a countertop, one that was covered in a dusting of sugar.

"You can start by telling us about the palace," Val suggested.

"What would I know about the palace? I've only been here a couple of weeks, and it's not like I'm rich enough—yet—to be hanging about with royalty, am I?"

The witch pointed to the door, which seemed to make Ted rapidly reconsider.

"*But* . . . I know Amira isn't back until tomorrow, or the day after. She's out on some diplomatic mission, overseeing some deal with some Tundran lords or something, I don't know. But this helps you—it means that if you go today, you're not gonna see so many guards. Better for sneaking, right?"

"Right," I agreed with a nod.

"Good, so you can be on your way, and—"

"No. No, that's not helping us. We need more than that."

Ted cast his head up to the ceiling and muttered a silent prayer. "Alright.

Alright! You want me to help, then I'll help." He reached down into a cupboard and plucked from it a bag of sweets.

"This isn't—"

"You're holding, there, hundreds of gold. Some of the best enchantments in the city, and in confectionary form. Lemon sherbets of *lightfoot*, rosy apples of *voice throw*, tintdrop, *invisibility* sticks—those taste like licorice, they're good—and a good deal more. All the information is in the pack." He gestured toward the door. "And now, I think, we're even."

CHAPTER TWENTY-FIVE

Finally, Some Good Stealth Abilities

Val, Arzak, and I stood leaning against the exterior of the palace walls. We were smoking a pipe as though we were simply enjoying the dazzling afternoon sun—a tip in blending in I'd learned from Lore. In reality, Val was looking left, and Arzak was looking right, searching for the moment that nobody was looking this way.

"Clear left," Val finally said.

"Wait," the orc replied. "Wait . . ."

"Still clear."

"OK, we go."

I opened a portal on the wall behind us, and we toppled through it. I'd positioned the other side of the portal behind us in the palace grounds at the perfect angle that we would fall back into a standing position once more. As I closed the portal—now with 50 percent less glow!—we each looked around for signs that anyone had spotted us. But we'd been quick enough that nobody seemed to have noticed.

And now we were just three rich folks, in their fancy clothes, taking a stroll about the palace grounds. Val took my arm while Arzak walked ahead, and we made a conscious decision to stroll at the pace of the rich. That is, painfully slow, like we had nowhere better to be. Val made a show of pointing at the flowers, talking about them and stopping to sniff them—but if anyone had listened to her commentary on them, they'd have realized she had absolutely no idea what she was on about. Fortunately, nobody seemed keen to get too close to what appeared to be a young couple having a simple stroll.

Even the guards barely looked at us, though perhaps that had more to do with the surprising number of merchants, dignitaries, and the like allowed inside the palace grounds. We were just three of many, and blended in just enough that we didn't appear to require any special attention.

"OK, cool it with the flowers," I said. "Queen's back tomorrow, and at this rate we'll still be sniffing roses."

Val kept a relaxed smile on her face and replied, "Chill out, will you?" Still, she pulled on my arm a tad harder from there on, and we got moving more quickly.

As we exited one of the palace's many gardens, coming onto one of the inner city's few roads, I caught one guard monitoring us. It was just one—nothing, necessarily, to worry about—but he'd definitely seen something that he knew was wrong, on some level.

"Guard by the tower," I muttered, still smiling. "Got an eye on us." I glanced at Arzak up ahead; she'd evaded notice.

"Probably you having a go at me about the flowers that did it."

"I imagine we're not the first 'couple' to have a little tiff in the gardens, Val," I replied, then lifted her hand from my arm.

"Where are you . . ." she started, while I made straight for the guard, my eyes fixed on his.

The man moved a hand toward the hilt of his sword, but didn't yet draw it.

"Excuse me, sir?" I asked.

At this question, the man relaxed once more. "Yes?"

"Might you point me toward the records office? My wife and I . . . we have an appointment."

The guard cast his eyes toward Val, and they lingered for a moment. "Straight up this road, and it's on the corner at the end. But you'll need a guard to accompany you; it's policy." He cast his eyes to Val once more, who was approaching slowly. "I could do so, if you—"

"We'll be fine, thank you." I turned away, and I accepted Val's hand on my arm once more.

"What was all that about? He could've seen right through you. You don't exactly hold up to scrutiny up—"

"The best way to avoid suspicion, in my experience, is to walk straight up to it. Why would someone who shouldn't be here talk to a guard?"

"This is the thief in you talking, is it?" Val asked.

"Do you disapprove?"

"I didn't say that."

Up ahead, Arzak stood gazing at a bird in a tree, but I knew she was allowing Val and I to take the lead, having noticed me talking to a guard. I led her toward the record office at the end of the road, but on our way I noticed something more useful: a barracks.

I pulled Val to a halt. "Fancy being a guard?"

"I feel that's all we use my changeling abilities for, impersonating guards."

"I'm going to take that as a yes."

I turned, signaled to Arzak with a nod of my head, and we disappeared off the road around the back of the barracks. There was no entry at the back of the building, but with my portal abilities, this didn't exactly matter.

"What it?" Arzak asked when she appeared around the corner in this dusty back alley.

"We need a guard to get into the records office," I said. "Gonna get—"

Arzak pointed to Val.

"Is this all that you think I'm good for?" the witch asked.

Arzak, like me, ignored her. "OK. Sneaky inside?"

"Sneaky inside," I agreed with a nod, thinking we were on the same page, then, that Arzak would need to stay outside. I took a deep breath, opened a portal to get us through the wall, and moved to step through it.

But so did Arzak.

I closed the portal and looked at her. "What're you doing?"

"I can be stealthy," Arzak proclaimed. "I work on it. Level 3 now."

I looked to Val, who shrugged, then ultimately decided this wasn't a fight I could be bothered with. I opened the portal inside once more, and we all hurried through. As before, there had been nobody around to spot my only semiglowing portal.

At least, nobody *awake*.

Val, Arzak, and I found ourselves in the sleeping quarters, about a third of the beds currently occupied by dozing soldiers. Hanging above the bunks were fresh uniforms, the mustard-gold surcoats and the thin leather armor.

"This easy," Arzak said, and I hushed her.

"*Stealthy!*" I whispered, then turned to Val. "Quick, pick one."

Val took a quick look around, then crept over to a bed about halfway down the room. A woman was sleeping there—one with roughly the same build as Val. The size didn't matter, of course—Val's changeling abilities would see to that— but I suspected she didn't want to be caught out by the armor if she was forced to change back for any reason.

The witch picked up the armor, started stripping, and then hesitated. She cast a glance in our direction. "Turn around," she hissed.

I held my hands up to protest my innocence, but turned away alongside Arzak, finding ourselves staring at a large wooden wardrobe.

"Why they need wardrobe if uniforms out?" Arzak murmured.

I hushed her again.

"I quiet."

A bell chimed through the building, making the floor itself seem to shake. No, not a bell, I realized—a gong.

Arzak and I snapped our heads toward one another. Then, thinking quickly, we jumped inside the wardrobe, pushing aside unmarked brown and black armor. Just as I pulled the doors closed behind us, the soldiers in the beds stirred, and Val—with her new face—hurried over to the corner of the room, busying herself by studying a bookcase.

Stealth: +1,300XP
Stealth increased to Level 10!
Base Points Gained: +1 DEX, +1 WIS, +2 Free Points (DEX/WIS)
Ability Selection Unlocked

. . .

"Cozy," Arzak whispered, and slowly adjusted her legs so they weren't quite as uncomfortably close to my crotch.

I poked my eye up to the wardrobe's empty keyhole, to see the soldiers stretch as they awoke, grumbling as they pulled off their pajamas—any semblance of not wanting to be naked in front of their colleague notably missing—and wrenched on their uniforms. One of them, the woman who Val was copying, cried out, "Alright! Who took it? Who took my bloody armor again?"

"Maybe servants forget?" an orc soldier suggested with a shrug.

The woman grumbled something unintelligible—though I suspected it contained a lot of swearing—and hurried from the room in her pajamas, causing the rest of the soldiers to laugh.

While the soldiers changed, I considered trying to portal Arzak and I outside again, but the wardrobe was simply too small. Even with the *Tamed Portals* passive, someone was sure to notice the purple glow, and the last thing I wanted to do was to alert them to trouble. So I contented myself to take a look at my *Stealth* ability options instead.

There were only two, this time.

Ability Selection Unlocked
Select an ability from the list below:
Option 1: Danger-Sense II (Stealth)—*Passive*. Your senses grow keener; you are 50 percent more likely to notice traps and ambushes.

I knew this ability choice from a past life—well, two lives ago, now—and so I wasn't in too much of a rush to pick it. It wasn't that it wasn't useful, because it definitely was. My hesitation came only from the knowledge that this particular skill had several levels, and so I would likely have lots of opportunities to pick it, or an upgraded version, at a later level.

The other choice, however, was a little rarer.

> **Option 2: In Plain Sight (Stealth)**—When activated, you have a heightened ability to hide in plain sight, and are able to spot opportunities to break from combat at a higher rate. Scales with [WIS].

I could see so many situations where this one was handy, and it was only making poor choices that meant I hadn't selected this in the previous life—a matter that I'd, on occasion, come to regret.

I took another look through the keyhole, at the two dozen or so soldiers preparing themselves for the day ahead, then decided my instinct was correct.

> **Ability Unlocked**—In Plain Sight
> **In Plain Sight (Stealth)**: When activated, you have a heightened ability to hide in plain sight, and are able to spot opportunities to break from combat at a higher rate. Scales on [WIS].

I put my free points from the level up into Wisdom, and made a mental note: between this and *Identification*, there was value in upgrading this particular base stat.

Outside our cozy hiding spot, footsteps announced the departure—at last—of the soldiers. I poked my eye to the hole once more to get a look and saw everyone but Val moving toward the door. The witch adjusted her hair to cover her face and continued pretending to study the bookcase.

But the last two guards hesitated at the threshold of the room, spotting Val still in the corner.

"You'll be late for breakfast, mate! Don't wanna get stuck with Cook's porridge, do ya?" one of them cried to her.

When Val didn't reply, the soldier left his colleague at the door and walked back toward Val.

"Oi, didn't you hear me?"

Val, realizing she had no choice, slowly turned away from the bookcase, putting on her best innocent face.

It wasn't very good.

CHAPTER TWENTY-SIX

The Humble Lives of Soldiers

"Scril?" the soldier asked Val, who was wearing the borrowed face. "Ain't realize you came back. You got your uniform sorted, then?"

There was a brief moment of hesitation from Val, which I hoped that the two soldiers hadn't noticed. There was no sign that they did. "No thanks to you two," Val replied. "One of you, was it?"

The male soldier, from what I could see through the keyhole, looked genuinely upset by this accusation. "Us? You know we'd never, Scril. Probably Myrc; you know he's got a thing for you. Doesn't know how to express it, I reckon."

The other soldier, the woman, walked back into my view. "Yeah, well, he better know she's all ours."

"You try telling Myrc that. It'll be Calton Street all over again."

Val snorted knowingly, even though she definitely didn't know what they were talking about; she was easing into the role. *Maybe it's worth me recommending she work on getting the* Performance *skill—might do her some good in these situations.*

"Wait," the female soldier said. "Myrc's gone, anyway, ain't he? Went up north with Amira."

The other soldier shrugged. "Well, I dunno then. Maybe just the servants doing their usual standard of work—missed you. By accident, like."

"You gonna teach 'em a lesson, Soll, or am I?"

"I don't think we gotta be hurting people for a simple mistake like that," Val tried, maybe saying a little more than she should have, considering how risky it was.

"You've changed your tune," Soll said, laughing. "I've seen you cut off a merchant's thumb cos you thought he shortchanged you."

"And he hadn't!" the other guard added.

Val laughed along, but said nothing, apparently having realized she'd gambled a little too much with that last remark.

Arzak slowly pulled a cramped leg out from the corner of the wardrobe, succeeding without making any substantial noise. I shot her a glare—we were both uncomfortable, wedged in here—which she ignored. I turned my attention back to the keyhole, hoping Val would wrap up this conversation soon and see these last two guards on their way.

"Hey, speaking of," Soll said, "Ela got a letter from the guys up north." He flicked his head to the other soldier. "You tell her?"

"Nah, not yet. Only just got it last night." The soldier known as Ela raised her eyebrows enticingly at Val. "You wanna know what it says?"

"Well, you know me," Val said, then trailed off without finishing that sentence; it was up to the other two to decide whether Scril would normally want to know.

"Yeah, little gossip, ain't you?" Ela replied with a toothy grin, and my heart sank. We were going to be in here for a while, then. Arzak, apparently realizing the same thing, began adjusting her leg once more, but a glare from me brought that to a stop.

"Says they's killed a lord's husband," Ela continued. "A *lord's husband*! Don't get that kinda action in Auricia, do you?"

Val, for her part, nodded along encouragingly, not quite sure where Scril would stand on this whole murder thing.

Soll shook his head. "When it's our turn, we gotta do 'em one better."

"What's better than a lord's husband?"

"Err, I dunno, a *lord*, maybe? Or a duchess, or something, I dunno."

"And, erm . . ." Val started, voice hesitant. I knew exactly where she was going with this, cos I had the same follow-up question for these murder-happy soldiers as well—but now *really* wasn't the time. "Why are we killing lords' families, again? We aren't . . . We ain't at war, are we?"

Soll's eyes flicked to Ela, and he paused for a moment longer than Val's hesitation earlier. "You feeling alright, Scril?"

But Ela waved the question down. "She's just daft sometimes, ain't she? That's why we love her." She turned back to "Scril." "They ain't up there as Goldmarch soldiers, remember? Ain't think Queenie would like us killing lords and little lordlings while wearing gold. They're up there as bandits."

Val gulped down any sign that this was news to her. "Oh yeah. Course. One of them mornings, I reckon. Don't know my arse from my tit."

"Could show you, if you like," Soll responded.

"Anyway, there's always next time, ain't there? Amira'll need more bandits soon, I reckon, cos rumor is it ain't moving fast enough. So we get up there, put some pressure on them prissy local lords, get some killing in, and Queenie gets her way. Gets these Tundran folk to let her soldiers in. Everyone's a winner."

I glanced at Arzak, whose eyes were narrowing. She mouthed an outraged question at me, but what with her fangs and slightly different syntax, I couldn't work out what it was. After the third try of mouthing it, the orc gave up.

"Oh, and, er . . ." Val was saying.

A moment later, it occurred to me that *we'd* faced bandits in the Tundras. In the southwest of the Tundras, in fact, in the area nearest to the Goldmarch. The roads had been full of them around Aptleed, and we'd almost not been able to add Tokas to our party because so many bandits had attacked us—not that this would have been a bad thing, necessarily, considering what we'd learned later.

And there had been soldiers there, too. Goldmarch soldiers, wearing their mustard—definitely not gold, no matter what they told you—surcoats, and saying they were under strict instructions not to intervene with the bandits unless the local leader gave the order.

Queen Amira was manipulating the disparate powers of the Gentle Tundras, but to what end? These soldiers said they were not at war, but were they sure? This seemed like a conquest of sorts, one so insipid that I wasn't sure the Tundrans even knew they were being invaded. But then, if the mighty power of the Goldmarch was going to conquer anywhere, why the Tundras? There was nothing there of note, lots of the land barely workable, and no real industry beyond the basics. If the Goldmarch wanted to expand their territory, surely they'd look south, to the realms of the Sundorn families, or to the Dawnwood in the east, or to the Beached Armada in the west. Not the Tundras. Nobody ever wanted the Tundras, not since the fall of the old empire.

"You alright, mate?" Ela asked Val. "You been acting weird all morning. Not yourself, like."

"Sick of the pranks, is all," the witch gambled—one that seemed to pay off.

Soll looked to Scril again, then sighed. "Come on," he said, gesturing for the door. "Guess we better get to breakfast. Gonna be oats for us, as late as we'll be. But if we leave it much longer, we ain't even gonna have that, are we?"

Scril snickered. "Speak for yourself. I got a hookup with the cook. Thinks there's something between us. Don't worry, I ain't adding anyone to what we got going on."

But Soll didn't respond, instead moving to the door. I waited eagerly for them to pass through it, desperate by now to stretch my cramped legs. I could only imagine Arzak was feeling that temptation much, much more than me, considering her size, and I forgave her for her earlier fidgeting.

"Say," the soldier finally said, pausing halfway to the door. He turned to Val. "Remember that last guy we added in. That was *your* idea, wasn't it, Scril?"

Ela opened her mouth to answer for the other soldier, but Val—who had a problem with keeping her mouth shut even in situations like these—was quicker. "Yeah, that was me. I—"

Soll drew his blade, Ela quickly catching on and following suit.

In the wardrobe, I sighed. For now, I still made an effort to keep it quiet; I had stealth on my side at the moment, after all.

"You ain't Scril," Soll said. "You ain't her."

"I . . ." Val started, then sighed when she realized the jig was up. "What was it that gave it away?"

"There weren't no other guy," Ela answered.

I pulled my eye away from the wardrobe's keyhole and looked at Arzak. "Guess we're fighting," I whispered. "You ready?"

CHAPTER TWENTY-SEVEN

Executing, Plan A

At the flick of my wrist, a portal opened beneath us, and Arzak and I tumbled through onto the floor at the other side of the room. It seemed that my blind aim had gotten better, because the pair of us landed just where I'd intended. And I'd intended this spot because it was behind the two soldiers—I was still undetected.

It was time to find out if the damage bonuses from *Stealth Attack* and *Execution II* stacked.

I gestured for Arzak to keep quiet, rather than scramble clumsily to her feet, and I turned my attention to the two soldiers who were at this very moment staring Val down.

"I can explain," Val said, doing her best to avoid looking at me or Arzak, though she clearly knew we were there. After all, why else would she be trying to distract our enemies?

I approached slowly, using my innate *Stealth* abilities to keep the noise of my footsteps to a minimum. The soldier who'd realized the truth, Soll, was closer to me, and so it was to him I crept first, knife drawn.

"Oh yeah? You gonna explain why you're using our friend's face, are you?" Ela asked. "Cos that's treason in these parts."

Val raised her new face's eyebrows. "Maybe it is, but I got good reason." Her eyes flickered, just for a moment, toward me. The two enemies didn't seem to notice.

I stepped closer still, the man's unwashed stench filling my nostrils. *And this guy has not one but* two *lovers?*

"That I'd like to hear," Soll said. "Give us one good reason we don't kill you where you stand."

I swung my blade around in front of the enemy, activated my *Execution*

II ability—my *Stealth Attack* being a passive, and therefore always active—and *sliced* the soldier across the throat.

> *Level 19 Soldier of the Golden Kingdom defeated!*

> **Stealth**: +1,200XP
> *Stealth increased to Level 11!*
> **Base Points Gained**: +1 DEX, +1 WIS, +2 Free Points (DEX/WIS)
> **Worldbending**: +500XP
> **Knifework**: +1,000XP

He dropped.

I grabbed the man by one arm to stop him thudding to the ground and attracting the other enemy's attention. This had been a kill in one, and so, surely, the effects of the abilities had stacked? Or else otherwise the man hadn't really ever invested in Vitality—there was no real way of knowing. I internally cursed myself for not *identifying* the man before I'd killed him, as any information might have given me a clue.

The other soldier began to turn.

I stifled a cry, opening another portal beneath my feet, this time opening myself above the other enemy, readying myself for another *Execution*. But I hadn't moved quickly enough; even before the soldier was in reach of my knife-point, she was shouting.

"Intruders!" she cried. "Intru—"

I put an end to this second shout by *stabbing* her. It wasn't enough to kill her, considering I'd lost all my *Stealth* buffs, but there was nothing like a knife wound to stop you shouting.

The soldier staggered backward, and I moved to *stab* once more. In the same moment, Val pushed both hands forward and summoned a gust of wind to propel the woman toward me. Between the force of my *stab* attack and the movement toward me, I was able to pierce her armor, right where her heart would have been.

> *Level 18 Soldier of the Golden Kingdom defeated!*

> **Worldbending**: +700XP
> **Knifework**: +1,000XP
> *Knifework increased to Level 26!*
> **Base Points Gained**: +1 DEX, +1 STR, +2 Free Points (VIT/DEX/STR)

She, too, dropped to the ground, and I staggered backward before I could stain my new clothes with blood. Not because I liked them, of course, but because it would ruin the disguise.

On any other day, I'd feel bad about killing two people who were just doing their jobs—even if it was in inevitable self-defense. But these two—what with all that apparent indiscriminate killing of my fellow Tundran countrymen that they'd confessed to a minute ago—they hadn't earned quite as much sympathy. Besides, if we'd let them live, then the palace would enter a state of alarm, looking out for intruders. It'd make our lives a lot more difficult.

I looked to the wardrobe, eyeing it up as a place to hide the bodies. "Close—" I started, and then footsteps announced the appearance of more guards charging toward the room. "Uh-oh."

I moved to open a portal beneath Val to bring her to my side, while Arzak charged across the room. The witch fell through clumsily, not having expected it, and she grabbed a bedpost to stable herself. I then opened another portal to get us out of here, but remembered I couldn't do that without hiding the bodies first, or the whole palace grounds—or city, perhaps—would be on lockdown. So instead, I opened a portal beneath the two bodies, its partner inside the wardrobe, and they fell through it with a heavy clunk. But before I could magick the three of us out of here, four guards burst through the door to check out what all the commotion was about.

We froze. "Err . . ." I said. "Hi?"

Nobody said "hi" back. Instead, they started attacking.

Three of them drew their standard-issue blades, while another, in slightly different uniform, raised her hands. This gesture was familiar to me, because I was currently doing roughly the same thing—she was a spellcaster.

Arzak rushed to stand in front of me and Val, protecting us with her brawn and drawn blades.

"Quick and quiet," Val hissed. She was right, of course; we couldn't let anyone else know there was a fight in here or we'd be in big trouble. I cursed myself; picking *Silence* as a *Worldbending* ability all those months ago would finally have come in handy, especially with my *Stealth* focus now. But that was the nature of leveling up; no matter how prepared you were, there was always an opportunity cost.

So I did the next best thing; I portaled myself through the floor to the other side of the room, and I closed the door. Turning back to face the rear of our attackers, I realized something. With how broad Arzak was, the soldiers hadn't been able to see me. And with the *Tamed Portal* ability reducing the glow of my portals, they hadn't known I'd gone anywhere.

I was, surely, the very definition of *unnoticed by an enemy*.

I drew my dagger once more and moved to attack before the four soldiers could figure out what was going on. As the spellcaster released a fireball—why was it always fire magicks? What was it about the allure of fire that always made people specialize this way?—I realized there was another approach I might have taken, in activating *Ash Husk*, but this way was safer.

Arzak suffered the brunt of the fire attack on her shoulder, damaging the new clothes she'd spent, presumably, a lot of money on. And she seemed more annoyed about that than the hit to her health bar.

Before the spellcaster could release another magick attack, I charged at her, thankful that she was standing at the rear of her group. I went straight in for another *Execution* boosted by my *Stealth Attack* passive, and because this woman had presumably put more points into Intelligence than Vitality—mana over health—I downed her in one hit. This was despite me attacking her with the pommel of my knife rather than the blade. After all, neither ability said I actually needed to stab anyone, just "attack," and I couldn't say for sure whether this woman shared the horrific values of the first two soldiers.

Level 24 Fire Mage of the Golden Kingdom defeated!

Worldbending: +700XP
Knifework: +1,400XP

I moved quickly, not even letting the spellcaster hit the floor before I sprang—assisted by a quick pair of portals—to the next soldier. As I soared through the air, pommel of my knife arcing toward the soldier's temple, Val again summoned a blast of air that sent the man stumbling backward. The movement toward me increased the impact, allowing me to fell this man, too, in one hit.

Level 18 Soldier of the Golden Kingdom defeated!

Worldbending: +100XP
Knifework: +1,000XP
Knifework increased to Level 27!
Base Points Gained: +1 DEX, +1 STR, +2 Free Points (VIT/DEX/STR)

But it also alerted the other two soldiers to my presence at their rear. I was noticed once more. Now that I didn't have the 350 percent—by my count; I wasn't exactly adept at math, though—boost to damage, I had no chance of taking out either of the others with one hit.

Fortunately, Arzak took full advantage of the distraction I'd created, reaching out and bashing one soldier over the head with the end of one of her swords. When he didn't go down, she hit him again in the same place, and then again and again until he finally dropped.

This left only one.

I ran toward her, hoping I'd be able to at least do enough damage to cause a distraction, and allow Arzak to swoop in. I charged, weapon raised, point-first this time as I knew I'd not inflict more than a light injury—one that Val could heal, if necessary—when the woman suddenly shifted. She hopped to one side, free arm stretched out, and she grabbed me with it.

Before I knew it, I had one arm around my neck, squeezing tight enough that I went lightheaded, and sword point in my face.

"Drop the swords," the tiefling soldier told Arzak.

"No," the orc replied.

There was a moment of silence. "But I have a sword to your friend's neck."

"I not drop swords. They make loud *clatter* and then more soldiers come. I not do that."

"OK . . ." the soldier said. "But—"

Val stepped out from behind Arzak, a soldier's sword in her hands. "Think fast!" she said, throwing the sword toward the soldier and me. As it left her hands, lightning magicks crackled around it.

The tiefling, surprised by this sudden turn of events, loosened her grasp on me just enough that I could wriggle free. I portaled myself to Val's side, not wanting to risk ending up in the same state all over again. The soldier caught the blade with her free hand, and all the muscles in her body went stiff as the lightning shocked her.

Arzak ambled over to the incapacitated woman's side and knocked her over the head with both weapons at once. She fell to the ground, dropping the lightning-imbued sword, and the shocks slowly faded.

"Nice," I said to Val.

The witch smiled. "Not a bad new ability, huh?"

Silence swept over the room as we listened for any more advancing assailants, but none came. Only when we'd remained still for a couple of minutes, listening, did we finally relax, and I surprised myself with a long sigh of relief.

"Hmm," Arzak said, weapons sheathed, hands on hips, looking down at the four unconscious bodies. She glanced over at where we'd stuffed the first two soldiers. "Going to be full wardrobe."

CHAPTER TWENTY-EIGHT

The Records Office

I'd portaled us back outside the rear of the barracks, and all three of us had hurried into the street, away from the scene of the crime. Or, well, *crimes*. We quickly remembered that our whole strategy here was to blend in, and three people walking quickly around a palace—like they actually had places to be—didn't scream "wealthy and privileged."

Now back at a walking pace, Arzak grabbed my arm much like Val had done earlier, and we began walking like a couple, which had the added benefit of hiding the burn to the shoulder of her dress. I had to admit I preferred this pretense when I was doing it with Val, particularly because the witch had allowed me to lead, whereas Arzak did not.

Val, still in her borrowed soldier's uniform and—more importantly—borrowed soldier's *face*, led us toward the record office at the end of the street. The sheer scale of the palace still struck awe in me; these roads within the palace walls were like a city in and of themselves, if with the notable difference of it being fancy, clean, and with well-maintained paintwork on the towering buildings.

When we reached the records office, just where the soldier from earlier had told us it would be, Val kept her head held high and led us inside. "Two for the records, on order of Her Majesty. I am required to accompany them."

The woman behind the desk, an old orc roughly Arzak's age, didn't look up from her paperwork, which she stared at through half-moon spectacles. She held out her hand. "Form Crescent-E."

I looked at the doorway behind the woman's desk. It was a solid metal door—no problem in and of itself for portaling through—and had glowing metal symbols around it. I'd spent enough time in the thievery game to know exactly what those were—the markings of a trap, and a trap that they wanted visitors to know was there. That could mean one of two things: either it was a bluff and there was no trap, or it was a trap so nasty that they didn't want to deal with the cleanup. In a place like this, I had no doubt that it was the latter. I couldn't portal us inside. This meant that both Plan A—Val escorting us inside as a soldier—and Plan B—us using my portals—were both out.

"It is an order direct from Her Majesty, Queen Amira," Val the "soldier" said.

"Then must have right paperwork," the orc said, pulling herself upright. When she saw Arzak, she did a double take. "Oh," she said. "Orc! Not many orc here. Only workers." She gestured to herself.

Arzak smiled, releasing my arm and stepping forward. "Not in Goldmarch much. On holiday. Honeymoon."

The recordkeeper leaned to one side to get a better look at me, then raised an eyebrow. I smiled as naturally as I could manage.

"He good at swordplay," Arzak said, and from the knowing nod she received from the other orc, I realized this wasn't meant literally.

At my side, I could see Val's body shaking slightly as she struggled to suppress a laugh.

"You help us? We look for Player records."

The new smile that was crossing the civil servant's face faded as quickly as it had come. "Oh. *Oh.*"

"We help with Player death in Tundras. Wrap up. Orders of queen."

The orcish recordkeeper kept quiet for a moment, studying Arzak and the burn on her dress. "Need more forms for this. Much more forms."

"We no have."

"Maybe when colleague gets here, I go check?" the orc suggested.

Arzak nodded. "OK." She returned to mine and Val's side.

"Why did you say OK to that?" the witch whispered. "As soon as she checks, she'll know we're lying."

"I got plan. I charm her."

"Arzak . . ."

"I charming with orcs!" Arzak insisted.

"Sure, but charming her is one thing, charming her so much that she lets us go *look at highly sensitive documents* is a whole other thing."

The orc shook her head. "No. You not understand. I distract her. And you . . ."

I reached into my pocket and pulled out a paper bag. One filled with a load of enchanted sweets. "Sneak in."

Arzak nodded, then returned to the recordkeeper's side to chat. The orc behind the desk looked curiously over at me and Val for a moment before Arzak began complimenting her glasses in a very rigid and overstated manner, which the other orc fell for completely.

"I don't get orcs," Val said.

I raised my eyebrows in agreement, then turned my attention to the sweets inside. I'd already studied what each of them did, so it was just a case of pulling out the right ones. When I finally located the three I'd been looking for, I looked Val in the eye.

"I'd rather have my saliva in your mouth than yours in mine," I said.

"Gross."

"What, you never kissed anyone before?"

"*Obviously*, I have. It's you putting it like that that's gross, not—"

"So you don't have any problem with it, then. Good." I tossed the first of the sweets into my mouth, sucking into it a good chunk before wrenching it out and offering it, sodden, to Val. She groaned, sighed, then tossed it into her own mouth.

"I hate you sometimes."

"That's an improvement on 'all the time,'" I replied.

Active Effect: Lightfoot
Minutes remaining: 29 / 30
Footsteps silenced.

"You sure we should be wasting all these immediately?"

I shrugged. "It's like good wine; you get a nice bottle, and then you spend years waiting for an excuse to open it. By the time you do, it's corked."

"Like you know about 'good wine,'" Val said, taking the next of the wet sweets and putting it into her mouth.

"I used to make it."

"You used to *try*, maybe."

Active Effect: Eyeslide
Minutes remaining: 29 / 30
Dramatically reduces chance of being noticed.

"Might wanna stop bickering with me," I said. "We're trying not to draw attention."

Val stuck her tongue out at me, quickly enough that the woman behind the desk didn't notice. Or perhaps that was the *Eyeslide* effect doing its job, I didn't know for sure.

Active Effect: Invisibility
Minutes remaining: 29 / 30
Renders you and all currently equipped items near-invisible.

"You not think this is overkill?" Val asked.

"You want a whole kingdom hunting you down for this?" I retorted.

"Fair point."

Armed with the three active effects, I grabbed the now invisible Val by the hand and strolled casually over to the door. As I put my hand on the handle, I prayed that these effects weren't considered magick abilities for purposes of the trap. I considered letting Val go first, but that was a terrible instinct for me to have. With a deep inhale, I opened the door and stepped inside.

I faced a human man the size of which I'd never seen. He'd have made Lore seem minute in comparison, and there was definitely something magick going on to make him so táll. He carried an ornate greatsword, engraved with runes that I didn't understand, but made me realize I absolutely did *not* want to mess with him. One swing of the sword would render me completely and utterly dead—this was something I knew for sure.

But the guard's eyes remained glazed as Val and I stepped inside the room, and after a moment he furrowed his brow, walked over to the open door, looked about, and closed it again. Moments later he had returned to his original position.

Val and I turned away from the guard to face the records room, and I felt a tug on my hand as the witch staggered backward. From the number of bookshelves in front of us, twenty-nine minutes was clearly not going to be enough time. There were a thousand, two thousand, maybe more boxes of records in here. I was never that good at estimations.

When we were far enough away from the guard, Val whispered to me, "Knight of the Realm." Her mouth was a bit closer to my ear than I'd have liked, though I supposed it was hard to judge when you were both invisible.

"What?"

"Knight of the—"

"Yes, I heard you, I meant . . ."

"The man at the door. Big boy. We don't wanna mess with him."

"Yeah, I figured," I said. "I'm not entirely stupid."

"I know. Just mostly."

I shook my head in exasperation even though I knew Val wouldn't be able to see it. "We should split up."

"Yes." Immediately I felt Val move to unlink hands.

"Wait." I pulled a freshly purchased spool of thread from my pocket, felt for the end of it, and handed it to Val. "Tie this around yourself. It'll help you find me."

"And the documents that'll be floating in the air won't be enough of a giveaway?"

"Just do it, will you?"

We parted ways, me still holding the end of the spool, and I hurried down one row of bookcases, glancing up at the helpful labels every few units announcing the section. The minutes faded faster than I'd have liked, and we grew close to being *very* visible indeed. What's more, the spool was rapidly running out of thread, and soon enough I wouldn't have been able to find Val until the minutes were up anyway.

So it was probably a good thing that, at the very end of the room, on a case of its own, I saw a sign that said, simply: The Records of the Architects.

CHAPTER TWENTY-NINE

How Gods Touch the World

I pulled down the first of the boxes, wasting not a moment of the eight minutes of *Invisibility, Eyeslide,* and *Lightfoot* that we had left. Within the boxes were dozens of folders, some thicker than others, each of which concerned one particular Player. My heart skipped a beat as my subconscious did the math. There were twenty-four boxes here. And in the box I had, there were maybe sixty folders. If they all contained the same, then that meant . . .

There were over a thousand Players in this world.

Maybe more. Maybe the ones here were just the ones the Golden Kingdom had noticed. Or just the ones they cared about.

Each, or at least almost all, of the files had a sketch attached—that of the Player in question's appearance. I supposed this would come in handy if the kingdom of the Goldmarch ever needed to track any of them down, whether to hire them, or to inflict justice. Not that justice ever seemed to be served upon these descendants of the Architects.

I pulled box after box from the shelf, skimming through the files for the name Aiwin had given us—Niamh. With the time on our active effects fading away, I searched quickly, desperately, almost so haphazardly that I became worried I'd missed her. And then something gut-wrenching happened.

I saw a sketch of a woman I recognized.

The drawing wasn't quite right—the nose was larger than it had been, and the hair was different than what I'd remembered—but otherwise . . . It was the same woman that Dad had kept a portrait of all those years.

It was my mother.

I staggered backward, the record of my mother in hand, and I stared down at it for a moment, urging myself to open it. But my hands didn't move. Couldn't move. I gulped, trying to ground myself, trying to force my body to truly realize: this was one of those moments that could change the course of your life. I stared down at the sketch of the woman who had abandoned me all those years ago, abandoned me on a doorstep without even checking if my father had still lived there. A woman who had abandoned me. My own mother.

But I realized she had given me one gift. Her blood, the blood of the Architects, ran through my veins. It was that very blood that had enabled me to use the Sisyphus Artifact. Without that blood, it would have been just a useless trinket to me. And I would have been dead.

I flipped the folder open.

Her name, the name that my father had never uttered, was Cleo. And Cleo was alive.

According to the file, as a member of a *Council*—a term I'd heard a few times now, which worried me—Amira's spies kept a close eye on her. She'd spent a good few years in the Badlands after my birth on a mission that was redacted from the files. But she'd been back to the Goldmarch since then, and more importantly, she'd even been to the Gentle Tundras. Yet she'd never bothered to check in on her child. I found my stomach churning, my eyes on the edge of watering, trauma falling free that I hadn't even known was there. It was as if—

"What you got there?" Val asked, appearing at my side. Not that I could have noticed, what with her footsteps silenced and her body invisible. Before I could reply, Val suddenly pulled the folder from my hands. "You found it? Why didn't you say anything? We have"—she paused, presumably to check her active effects—"five minutes left."

"I got distracted. It was . . . an engrossing read," I said.

There must have been something in my voice, because Val hesitated before replying. "You OK, Styk?"

"Not feeling so good. Must have been something I ate."

"You reckon Ted has poisoned us again?"

"No, I . . . It's nothing. I'm fine. Let's find this record."

Boxes flew out of the bookshelf at my left as the invisible Val wrenched them free. I considered keeping my mother's record, but something deep within me was repulsed by the idea. Maybe I'd never been supposed to learn this. Maybe I would have been happier if I never had. But then, that Player blood in me had to have come from somewhere, and it definitely wasn't going to have come from Dad. I pushed the record back in the box, finished leafing through the rest of it, then moved on to the next.

Niamh was one of the first names within.

"Val," I said.

A box, halfway out of the bookcase, slid back in again. "Yeah?"

"Found it."

I opened the file and began skimming through. From the gentle breath on my neck, I could tell that Val was reading over my shoulder.

"Alright," I said, reading aloud. "Niamh. Another member of this Council. Don't suppose that means anything good, does it? The Council."

"Very foreboding," Val agreed. "And if the pyroknight was a part of it, then I can only imagine everyone else in it is evil, too."

I tried to stop myself from dwelling on the fact that my mother was another member. And if she was evil, what did that make me? I forced myself to continue reading aloud. "Ah, look here: she was in charge of the Council's relationship with the witchfinders. So it's definitely her. Good performance review from someone named Tana—whoever that is—and that's what got her pulled away. Reassigned elsewhere. Reassigned to replace a man called Jacob. In the . . . Tundras . . ."

I paused, and Val remained quiet, too. At least, just for a moment. "*Told* you the pyroknight was called Jake," she said.

"Lucky guess." Before Val could say anything, I continued, "This means he wasn't just in the Tundras for no reason. He was doing something. On behalf of the Council. We've interrupted their plans, and I can't imagine an organization as mysterious as this is going to let that go unchecked."

"You think they'll be hunting us?"

"I reckon it's safer to assume they are and be wrong than the other way around."

From Val's lack of response, I inferred that she agreed.

"So she's in the Tundras, picking up from where the pyroknight left off. Did we ever get the idea that he was working on anything?"

"Just trying to kill you, I think."

"You reckon this whole Council is set up to kill me?"

"What? No!" She slapped me around the back of the head—an impressive feat considering we were invisible. "How is your ego this big?"

"Pretty rich, coming from you." I read on, scanning the text for a place name, a location in which we might find her, or at least pick up the trail. "Lenktra," Val and I said at the same time, reaching that point in the text simultaneously.

"Let's get going," Val said. "If she's still there, we can make this quick."

"What do you mean?" I asked. "We still got to wait for Corminar and Lore, and we've still got to deliver this depth-raider to—"

"Well, we gotta find her before we can kill her, don't we? And the longer we wait, the greater the risk of the trail going cold."

"Kill her? We don't know that she's done anything wrong."

"She's a *Player*," Val said. "Of course she's done something wrong. And do you not remember the witchfinder village? That in itself is—"

"Potentially a science experiment gone wrong? We can't assume she's guilty just cos she's a Player, otherwise . . ." I didn't say the end of that sentence, but it would have been "Otherwise you'd have to kill me, too."

Val sighed. "Fine. We'll get some evidence of something she's done wrong; I'm sure that won't be hard."

With a nod, I closed the folder. "OK. Fine. Good. We know where to find her. We might not know what she's up to, but we can head north. We—"

"No," Val breathed.

"Sorry?"

"No, that's . . ." If my voice had sounded pained earlier, then it was nothing compared to Val's now.

"Val? Are you OK?" I moved my hand out to grab her shoulder, but missed; the witch had staggered backward.

"The sketch. On the front of the folder. I . . . I know that face." I could tell Val was fighting back tears. "That's . . . She survived the . . . How could she have survived the bogspawn?"

"Val, what are you . . ." I started, but trailed off when I realized exactly what she meant.

"She's the Hunter. The one who tried to kill me. The one who exposed me as a witch, the one who ruined my life. It's her. Niamh is her. I can't . . . I don't think I can . . ."

I reached out, found Val, and wrapped my arms around her. "It's OK. It's OK, Val. We're here. We'll—"

But the sudden ringing of alarm bells all around the palace grounds interrupted the rest of my reassurance.

They'd found the soldiers.

And we only had one minute left on our active effects.

It was time to run.

CHAPTER THIRTY

A Welcome Overstayed

Grasping Val's hand tightly, I sprinted back down the row of bookshelves, opening a portal with my free hand to shorten the distance. I had one eye on my active effects—already our *Lightfoot* had worn off, as evidenced by the footsteps echoing around the chamber. In a few moments, *Eyeslide* would wear off, too, and then it would be the big one.

At the door, the guard—the so-called Knight of the Realm, as Val had said—began to turn, eyebrow raised, looking for the source of the noise. As the *Eyeslide* active effect ran out of time, my witch friend thought quickly, summoning a great gust of wind to blow a couple dozen boxes off the nearby shelf. The knight ran to investigate, shifting away from the door, and I opened another portal behind him.

And then *Invisibility*, too, faded away, and I saw Val's pale face, her eye makeup having run down her cheeks. My stomach lurched when I noticed the dried tears, and I hesitated just for a moment before swinging the door open.

"Arzak," I said, leading Val through. "Time to—"

"Stop there!" the knight roared. "Stop right there, on the order of—"

I didn't hear the rest of that sentence because I slammed the door shut behind me.

"Goodbye!" Arzak said to the civil servant, whose eyes were wide at the sight of Val and I leaving the records office, and together we moved for the exterior door.

"Wait," Val protested, tugging on my hand.

"Val, now's not the—" I started, releasing her grasp when I realized there was no need for it; we weren't invisible anymore.

"Wait!" she said again, and grasped the handle of the door to the records office, imbuing it with lightning magick. "This oughta slow them down a little."

As we ran out of the shop, I heard the crash of a door slammed off its frame, and I realized that Val's lightning magicks had, in this case, not been of much help.

"OK, keep running!" I cried. Portals really should have been good in situations such as these—that is, running away from people, but there were a couple of problems with that. Firstly, I could only portal far away if I could actually see the intended location, which was tricky when the buildings were so close to one another. Secondly, and much more importantly, the orcish civil servant had just charged out from behind her desk and casted a strange spell upon me—one that resulted in a glowing sigil on my chest and resulted in a not-so-fun new active effect.

Active Effect: Mana-Halted
Minutes remaining: 59 / 60
Prevents marked person from using their own magick abilities.

"Styk?" Val asked. "What're you waiting for?"

"I . . . can't . . ." I said.

"Seriously, Styk, now is *not* the time to not be able to perform."

"I can think of worse times." We charged down the main street, Arzak leading the way. If I wasn't mistaken, she was leading us to the nearest gate in the palace walls. What we'd do about all the guards when we got there was something I hadn't yet figured out.

"Any ideas?" I asked Val, who was at my side.

She shook her head and very wisely focused on running. Behind us, I could hear the heavy footsteps of the giantlike Knight of the Realm gaining on us, and my instinct again was to open up portals to get away from him. That this was still my instinct meant I was probably over-relying on my *Worldbending* magicks in fights; I wasn't exactly a well-rounded combatant without it. What with my recent growths in *Knifework* and *Stealth*, among other things, I was at least working on it, but that didn't exactly help me in this moment.

We rounded a corner and saw the gate up ahead. I scoured my mind for a plan, desperate, but came up short of anything that didn't involve opening a bloody portal. But Arzak, it seemed, had at least *part* of a plan. She ran up to the guards ahead of us, not trying to stay out of sight, but instead doing the exact opposite. She waved her hands in the air to get their attention, and cried out, "Guards! Guards!" The Goldmarch soldiers all turned, alarmed, apparently expecting any danger to come from *outside* the palace grounds. "Dragon! Dragon in palace!" As Arzak grew closer, Val and I hot on her heels, she pulled at her singed dress. "It already got pretty dress! Might next get me! Or you!"

A particularly alarmed soldier began pulling the great wooden gates open, allowing us—as fleeing, well-respected citizens—a way out. But among the crowd of soldiers, one or two weren't distracted by Arzak enough to miss the Knight of the Realm running after us, shouting, "Arrest them!"

"Close the gate!" a quick-thinking guard cried out, but the three of us were already close to squeezing through. A well-placed blast of air from Val knocked one of the gate's guards to his arse, and we slipped through the remaining gap.

But that didn't mean it was over, of course. We still needed to lose them.

At this point, Arzak faltered, and I took the lead in our running. I directed us back the way we'd come. This was partially out of habit and partially because it was at least an area of the city we'd seen before, and had some knowledge of. I risked a glance over my shoulder to get an idea for the number of soldiers that were following us, and I wished I hadn't. To our three, there were seven soldiers following—more than two for every one of us, *and* one of them was that huge Knight of the Realm fellow.

At least I, then, had an idea. "Maybe Ted can help us," I said aloud, and Val nodded frantically as we charged down the street. I pulled the paper bag of enchanted confectionary from my pocket and scrambled around as best I could while running. One of the sweets fell out as I thrust my hand into the bag, and I prayed I hadn't just lost the one I was looking for.

Val took the lead in the running as my frantic search for the white sweet with two red bands around it slowed me down. Finally, I found it: the rhubarb drop of *copycat*. As I unwrapped it, Val suddenly veered left—into a familiar building.

The queue outside Ted's Confectionary Emporium still stretched down the road, though it had at least shrunk slightly. I suspected this was in part due to the security guard no longer being at his post—a few people had "snuck" in, in much the same way that Val, Arzak, and I had just done. That is, we'd just run in with no regard for social decency.

"What are we doing in *here?*" I shouted to Val over the din of the crowded shop, customers browsing the many display stands chock-full of nonenchanted sweets.

"I thought you said maybe Ted could—"

I pushed the unwrapped rhubarb drop in her face. "I meant the sweets!"

"No time for bicker!" Arzak shouted, and grabbed both Val and I under her arms then pushed through the crowd toward the rear of the shop.

Even from this position, hanging from Arzak's arms, Val managed to stick her tongue out at me. I ignored her and instead pushed the sweet into my mouth, sucking enough of the—admittedly pleasantly flavored; good work, Ted—candy that I'd get some of its active effect. I could only hope that my *Mana-Halted* magick-prevention wouldn't prevent me from using *Ted's* magick, too. The answer to this doubt came quickly, just as Arzak turned a corner and hit my dangling head into someone's arse.

> **Active Effect: Copycat**
> Minutes remaining: 19 / 20
> *Creates formless copies of the user that distract and confuse any opposition.*

I spat the sweet back onto my palm and handed it to Val. "You know the drill."

"I'm using the sweet first next time," the witch replied, but didn't give me any more sass than that. While she sucked, I looked around for signs of my copies, but couldn't see any of them—that I was hanging upside down in a very crowded place probably had a lot to do with that, though.

"Arzak?" Val said.

"Mm?"

"Let us down."

We were in the storage room where we'd been earlier when Val and I were finally allowed back on our feet, but Ted wasn't in sight. Presumably he was elsewhere, making a hard sale on his confectionary.

"Arzak," Val said, handing her a particularly soggy sweet.

The orc raised an eyebrow.

"Just eat it," Val said.

Outside, I could see copies of both me and Val dotted around the shop, seemingly browsing the stock, apparently copying what the other nearby people were doing. Upon closer inspection, I realized these illusions were copying a little *too* precisely—unnaturally so, if you gave them a proper look.

"Do you think they followed?" Val asked. "Do you think—"

The booming voice of the Knight of the Realm answered her question. "Would all customers please *freeze*; we have criminals to arrest."

". . . Great," Val said.

CHAPTER THIRTY-ONE

Collateral Damage

"Mm," Arzak said, crunching down on the last of the boiled sweet with enough noise that it made my teeth hurt. "Fruity." As copies of Arzak bloomed into existence around the shop, Val moved to peek around the doorframe.

"How many?"

"Seven. Big boy's here, too." Val whipped her head back around quickly, like she was almost spotted. "Got your portal magicks back yet? Not sure the three of us can take down that many."

"We don't have to take them down, just escape," I reminded her. "What crimes have they committed to warrant us killing them? Thought we were doing the hero thing these days."

"They probably have committed crimes, though, haven't they?"

"Yeah, probably."

The three of us shuffled back to the door, peering around it more subtly than Val had been doing before.

"How long until you can magick again?" Val asked.

I checked. "Forty-eight minutes. You reckon we can hide for that long?" I meant it as a sarcastic comment, but Val glared at me like I was stupid. "Alright, it's going to have to be *Stealth* time, I reckon."

"I not have *Stealth*," Arzak said.

"Might be a good time to get it. Give it a go, and if it doesn't work out . . . barge through?"

"Mm. I do that."

I poked my head around the corner, just at the same moment that the Knight of the Realm—who was most familiar with what the three of us looked like—pointed at one of my copies. He thought he'd found me. "Alright, time to shine."

We dropped to a crouch and began creeping through the store while the soldiers concentrated their attention on a figure they'd soon realize wasn't real. I thanked the Architects—probably a bad habit, at this point—that Ted had drawn such an enormous crowd, as it made our navigating through the shop easier, being that it mostly shielded us from sight.

Up ahead, I spotted one of the soldiers in the crowd. This one wasn't closing in on the fake me with the rest of his colleagues. It was an ideal opportunity to eliminate him from the situation, and help to even the playing field a little. Realizing that a crouched man might draw unwanted attention, I rose slowly to a stand, and activated *In Plain Sight* to blend in with the crowd, which allowed me to draw in close to my target.

I removed my blade from its sheath as I approached, getting leers from various customers who seemed to wonder if they should just leave the store at this point, but thankfully none of them drew attention to me. When I reached the soldier, I grabbed him tight, holding the pommel of my dagger facing downward, and activated *Execution* not once, not twice, but three times. What with me not using the point of the blade, I wasn't going to do much damage—even with the boost applied by *Execution*—and I didn't want to risk leaving the soldier conscious.

Level 20 Soldier of the Golden Kingdom defeated!

Stealth: +1,200XP
Stealth increased to Level 12!
Base Points Gained: +1 DEX, +1 WIS, +2 Free Points (DEX/WIS)
Knifework: +1,000XP

"You ever notice we take out more people than monsters?" Val whispered.

"Not now, Val," I replied, easing the soldier to the floor. The nearby shoppers had noticed the attack—of course they had—and while, thankfully, none of them had screamed, they were now very noticeably moving away from me.

It drew another of the guards' attention.

"Arzak, stay here," Val said. "Styk, go right. I'll go left."

I nodded, and the witch and I left Arzak crouched in the center of the ring of empty space in the otherwise crowded store. Between Val and I, we had the next soldier flanked, and though Val hadn't said anything, I was pretty sure I knew by now what the plan was.

When the soldier in the mustard surcoat passed between us, their eyes widened. They spotted Arzak and realized that she was one of the so-called criminals who had fled through the gate. Not that I could really argue this label; if nothing else, we *were* criminals, even if we were currently committing crimes for good reason.

Val burst out of the crowd at the other side, flinging both hands forward and blasting the soldier with a blast of air. At the same moment, I pounced, bottom of my knife pointed toward the soldier, *Execution* well and truly activated. With the extra impact added by the blast of air, I could fell the soldier in one hit. I caught her as she dropped and placed her gently on the ground.

> *Level 21 Soldier of the Golden Kingdom defeated!*

> **Stealth**: +900XP
> **Knifework**: +900XP

The surrounding gap grew larger still, and it was only a matter of time before the rest of the soldiers spotted it. The only problem? The other five were still between us and the exit. There was *one* idea I was yet to try, and I pulled the paper bag of enchanting sweets from my pocket, beginning to rummage through them.

"What in the gods' green—" a familiar voice said, and I turned to see Ted emerge from the crowd. His eyes narrowed when he saw me. "Oh no. No. Not again. Not *again*."

It took me a moment to understand what he meant by 'again', but then it hit me. We'd damaged his place of work once before. And if this got out of control, we were about to do it again.

With this in mind, what he did next was absolutely the wrong decision.

"Guards!" Ted shouted, pointing down at me, snatching the bag of his enchanted sweets from my hand.

"Oh, Ted," Val murmured.

Cries erupted as soldiers barged through the crowd of customers, not caring for the wellbeing of those they cast aside.

"Scatter!" Val half whispered, half shouted, then me, her, and Arzak all ran our separate ways, preventing the five remaining soldiers from being able to surround us.

I soon realized I was hurrying *away* from the door, then took a hard left between two high display cases. Ted had arranged the jars of sweets in each case by color, which I thought was a nice touch. Up ahead, I saw one soldier getting distracted by a copy of Arzak—surely he would have known it wasn't her, as she'd been on the other side of the shop only seconds earlier?—and I swung left once more, past an elaborate alchemical display. This display featured two tanks of some kind of liquid, as well as complex-looking glassware down which colorful liquids ran. From the fact that it seemed to be a closed system, I figured it was just for show; Ted had really put his heart into the shop decor.

Moving on, I kept low, weaving through the thinning crowd. Two soldiers were up ahead, so I doubled back to the alchemical display, and risked poking my head up above the display cases to search for a route out. I saw Arzak—the real one, not a copy, based on her movement—getting close to the exit. What I *didn't* see, somehow, was the Knight of the Realm barreling straight toward me.

He hit me with a tackle rather than his sword, which was probably a good thing, considering I didn't think I'd survive a hit from his weapon. Not that he didn't do any damage; I felt a rib crack as I hit one of the two metal tanks of liquid, and involuntarily cried out with pain. I grit my teeth, pulling myself to my feet, desperately searching for a way out that didn't involve my portaling abilities. Through all of this, I completely failed to notice the tank wobbling on the table behind me.

The knight swung with his heavy sword, an attack just slow enough that I could leap to the floor to avoid it, and he hit the tank instead. At this point, it toppled.

I rolled out of the way as the heavy drum hit the floor with a clang, the top bursting off and its contents washing over both me and the storeroom floor. I couldn't help but taste the liquid as it washed over me, and I can't tell you how happy I was to discover it was just salt water.

The knight charged to swing his blade down at me, and I skittered backward across the wet floor. As the knight swung, he lost his footing on the now-slippery stone tiles, and had to grab the top of a desk to stabilize himself. I took advantage of this distraction to climb to my feet—also nearly sliding over in the process—and charged for the door. Clearly, we would not win this fight; our best bet was to keep running until my *Mana-Halted* active effect wore off, so I could portal us away. Which was just another . . . forty-one minutes. Great.

At least I still had plenty of mana, and through my *Mana-Fueled* ability, I could use that to power my *Knifework* attacks, if it came to that. As I arrived at the door, I skidded into someone and pushed my hands out to separate us before realizing it was Val. "Run!" she cried, and we hurried for the door, where Arzak had already arrived. The witch slipped on the wet ground, the salt water now having covered the entire shop floor, and I grabbed her arm to keep her upright. As we crossed the threshold to the outside, Val suddenly halted.

"What is it?" I asked as she turned back to the shop.

The witch gritted her teeth. "Sorry, everyone." She dropped to the floor, pressing her hands into the spilled salt water, and activated her newest ability. Lightning erupted all around the store, making everyone in it—soldier, owner, and customer alike—compulsively tense all their muscles, freezing them to the spot. As I caught sight of one of the display tables catching fire, the three of us fled.

> *4 x Soldiers of the Golden Kingdom escaped!*
> *Level 32 Knight of the Realm escaped!*
> **Stealth**: +2,200XP
> *Stealth increased to Level 13!*
> *Stealth increased to Level 14!*
> **Base Points Gained**: +2 DEX, +2 WIS, +4 Free Points (DEX/WIS)

CHAPTER THIRTY-TWO

Regrouping

Lore and Corminar arrived promptly to our arranged meeting point, a tavern just outside the Auricia perimeter. We'd been there a couple of days, killing time, and we'd been digesting both terrible tavern food and the information I'd found in the palace records office. That is, Arzak and Val had been processing the information about the Player—though Val hadn't shared the woman's true identity with the orc—while I'd been processing the information about my mother.

I still didn't know much about my Player heritage, even with the records we'd leafed through. But I knew she was out there, and a part of the same so-called Council that the pyroknight had been a member of. This definitely meant nothing good.

If my mother was evil, and her blood ran through my veins, what did that make me? Was I doomed to become just like the Players one day, if I ever grew strong enough?

Yet that wasn't the point that weighed most heavily on my mind. I dwelled instead on the revelation that my mother was both alive *and* had been in the Tundras. She'd known where I was, and she'd been in the area, but she'd never checked in. As a child, I'd always assumed there was some major reason my mother had never come back—the go-to had been that she'd died for some noble cause in the Badlands—but now I had the truth . . .

I didn't quite know what I felt, just that I had a heavy pit in my stomach.

When Lore and Corminar walked in, a thatched carrying case in the former's hands, I was relieved. I had a distraction now, and didn't have to dwell on the matter of my mother any further. We said our hellos, and Lore placed the carrying case atop one of the tavern's tables, before hurrying over to the barmaid to place an order for five ales and one large bowl of roasted carrots.

"It is the only food we can consistently get the depth-raider to eat," Corminar explained as Lore began pushing the carrots through the bars in the case.

I peered inside, expecting something horrific or otherworldly—there'd been so much of that kind of thing in my life recently—but inside, the creature looked only like a small rodent. It had two sharp, pointy ears, and large black eyes, and its two spindly hands gripped on the roasted carrot slices as it nibbled away. I caught sight of the small metal band of the witchfinder's clasp wrapped around its neck.

"That's it?" I asked. "I was expecting something . . ."

"Scarier?" Lore guessed. I nodded at this.

"Have you never heard the expression, 'One must not judge an elf by their visage'?" Corminar asked. "It is a being of immense power, you must remember, despite its gentle exterior. It might level the town were the right person—a *strong* person—to walk nearby. I keep reminding Lore of this, but, alas, it has not helped."

"I named him Oli," Lore explained.

"You know it boy?" Arzak asked.

"He has not gendered the beast, no," Corminar said. "He says only that—"

"It just *feels* like a boy, you know?" the barbarian broke in.

Corminar pursed his lips together, completely unimpressed.

"Not had any trouble, then?" Val asked. "Or I figure you probably wouldn't have named it."

"Him," Lore corrected her.

"We have not been unfortunate enough to encounter someone strong enough for it to latch upon. Apparently even I am not strong enough to gain its interest, though perhaps this is related to how useless my bow currently is." He placed the weapon on top of the table.

"That's a new one," Val pointed out.

"Indeed, yet it is still useless. Until I find another bow that is up to my usual standards, I'm afraid that I—"

Val piped up, "I don't think that's how it works. I think the depth-raider . . ." She trailed off when she caught sight of Arzak gently shaking her head; there was no point in telling Corminar this.

"The family were keeping it as a pet, you know," Lore said. "Thought it was a mouse. We had to pay quite a bit just to get it off them. Nice bunch, though. Said they were gonna use the money to go on holiday. I recommended the Tundras, but they said they wanted somewhere warmer. I told them they could go sledding, and the kids seemed quite excited by that, but no. No more Tundran friends for us just yet."

"Yes, thank you, Lore," Corminar said, then turned to the rest of us. "And may I ask how your task went? We have information on this Niamh, I trust?"

"She's gone north," I said. "Into the Tundras. More friends for you, Lore."

"I wish."

"Any ideas what she is doing up there?" the ranger asked. "I imagine something terrible."

"Almost certainly," Val grumbled.

"We know she's a member of the Council—the same one the pyroknight mentioned. The fact that a Council exists means there must be a purpose to what all these Players are up to; we don't think they're going around killing people for the fun of it, but—"

"I wouldn't put it past them," the witch added.

I pointed to her; that had been exactly what I'd been about to say. "The reason someone pulled her away from the witchfinders is because she was needed elsewhere. They needed her to replace the pyroknight."

Corminar raised his eyebrows. "So it was our doing that . . ."

I nodded. "Whatever the pyroknight was up to, she's now seeing it through. Up in Lenktra. So that's where we head, in the morning. And we go find out just what it is that she's up to."

The elf and the barbarian nodded. "Works for me. But my sheep . . ." Lore trailed off, leaving the question hanging in the air.

"Elandor said they're safe and sound in this portal dimension. Whether we rescue them now, or we rescue them later, they won't know the difference."

"No, it's not that," Lore said. "Or at least not just that. What if we're too late? What if he gets sick of waiting? What if he just . . . closes the dimension?"

"He will wait, Lore, I assure you," Corminar said, reaching up to place a comforting hand on the man's shoulder. "Elandor is smart enough to know that retrieving a creature to rival a mala will take time. We can afford the diversion."

"How sure are you?"

"Very sure," Corminar said. He turned away from Lore to face the rest of us, then mouthed, "*Not very sure at all, in fact.*" None of us said anything, though; as much as we liked Lore's sheep, we all knew that stopping this Player had to be our top priority.

"I think that's everything," I said, then made eye contact with Val. It wasn't everything, of course; the witch still hadn't told anyone else about her personal history with Niamh. "Unless I've forgotten anything, Val?"

The witch licked her lips a moment, considering, then said, "No. No, I think that's all."

I held her gaze and nodded; this would stay between us for the time being, at least until Val was comfortable sharing it with the wider group.

We drank until late into the night, allowing ourselves just one evening of downtime. As always, it was Arzak who called it a night first, followed sometime later by Corminar and then Lore, leaving just Val and I to finish off the last of the tavern's nice stout. When even I could drink no more, I stumbled up to the room I'd booked and collapsed into the bed almost fully clothed—I did at least have the good sense to remove my shoes.

Sleep took me quickly, and within moments of closing my eyes I began to drift from consciousness. At least, I did until I felt someone putting their weight on the bed. I opened my eyes just enough to see that it was not an enemy, but Val, slipping under the covers with me.

"What are you doing?" I mumbled, still half-asleep.

"I'm sick of pretending," the witch replied, "and I think you are, too."

At that, I wrapped one arm around her, pulled her close, and sank into the deepest sleep I'd had in a good long time.

Duke Cambelny

Of Duke Cambelny of Aptleed's three sons, only the youngest, Maximilian, was interested in his poetry. Timothy, James, and even his wife, Kimberley, entertained this desire to create with good manners, but only Xim asked questions, and only he began creating his own. The duke would spend hours upon the tower's balcony, the whole of his city stretched before him, parchment and quill in hand. He would fiddle with the words in front of him from dawn till dusk, scouring his mind for the precise, specific, perfect word to occupy each position in each line. That was the beauty of poetry, to his mind: that this form of art was so limited in length meant that he had to give ample consideration to each word—was it indeed the best word for this particular moment? Did it convey the emotion that the duke intended? Did it convey the imagery that he held, oh so vivid, in his mind?

But, as with all days of late, he found little joy in the process.

"Arnus?" he called out, and his aide arrived promptly at his side, looking down upon the parchment before him.

"You know, my lord, not *every* poem has to rhyme," he said.

Duke Cambelny ignored the cutting remark. "Tell me. What is the latest news on our new soldiers?"

Arnus hesitated. "All information will be presented at the morning briefing," he replied.

"Tell me now."

The prolonged silence that followed was almost answer enough; the duke knew, in his heart, the truth of the matter. Ever since he had accepted Queen Amira's aid in dealing with the recent bandit menace, the situation had devolved.

At the time, it had seemed to be the deal of a lifetime. The foreign queen had not demanded payment for the "borrowed" soldiers in coin, but in timber—and this was a resource that the Gentle Tundras had in plentiful supply. He would hand over this timber—a significant amount, to be sure—and the soldiers in gold would drive out the bandits that had seemed to emerge from nowhere over the past few months.

Yet the timber had not been the true payment. Now granted access to the city, the Goldmarch soldiers had taken certain . . . liberties. Crime was at an all-time low, or so the duke had been told in his morning briefings, but it seemed that the definition of *crime* had changed. That is, anything that the Goldmarch soldiers deemed necessary was by default legal in the city of Aptleed. It was legal only because their number was far greater than that of the local guards, and the duke's loyal men could do nothing without risk of injury or death.

And of that, there had been plenty.

With every day that passed, the duke found his authority eroded. Goldmarch soldiers hassled innocent locals, those simply going about their work. They stole, they attacked, they committed dreadful crimes of which Duke Cambelny would not permit himself to think about. For, of course, he was to blame.

"Any communication from my fellow statesmen?" the duke asked.

"No, sir. I . . ." Again, Arnus paused. "If you will excuse me, one of your guards is signaling that you have a visitor."

Duke Cambelny sighed; it had been so long since he had heard from any of his fellow Tundran rulers. The last letter, in fact, must have been over a week ago, and the Duchess of Lenktra had not sounded her usual self. "Very well, let them in," he told Arnus, then turned his attention back to his latest poem—one that, it was clear, possessed no heart.

"My lord," Arnus said at the duke's rear. "May I present to you— Oh, sword of Ares . . ."

The duke's heart sank in his chest, and he whipped himself from his city-facing chair just in time to avoid the coming attack. A woman stood at the threshold of the balcony in the fine clothes of the upper class, though there was an air about her of anything but. Arnus, who only put on the appearance of having come from a wealthy background, could not have noticed.

She released a dagger from her hand, throwing it forward. It stuttered forth, and with every foot that it passed away from her, it stopped, duplicated, and then continued on its path. The last of these copycat knives hovered in the air just where Duke Cambelny's head had been only a second earlier.

The woman ripped her hand back, and the furthest knife retreated, merging with the one before again and again until she had the full weapon back in her grasp.

Arnus roared something unintelligible, his words losing all the affected air of the upper middle class, and he threw himself at the would-be assassin.

They tumbled to the floor together while the duke drew his ceremonial sword. Ceremonial it may have been, and blunt as a result, but that did not mean it was useless. A local enchanter by name of Steven had imbued it with a powerful attack—one so powerful that it contained only the mana for a single use.

"Arnus, stand clear!" the duke commanded, but at the same moment, the aide's eyes bulged. The tip of a dagger emerged from his chest, then duplicated, shot forward, and then duplicated on as it soared toward the duke's head.

Duke Cambelny dove to one side, taking great care not to land on his own blade. Though it may have been dull, it could still do damage, and he would not want to activate the enchantment until the ideal moment. The last of the duplicating blades caught him by the ear, slicing through it but doing little enough damage that the duke's health reserves could manage.

He drew his blade, pointing it toward the assassin, and he couldn't help but smile.

"Do you really think—" the assassin began to ask, but the duke never heard the end of the question.

Duke Cambelny activated the enchantment, and magicks of all kinds shot forth. Fire attacks combined with frost attacks combined with lightning attacks, combined with the dark aura of magicks he really should not have possessed. As the magicks peppered the enemy, the blade risked slipping from his hand, and he gripped it with the other to steady himself.

When the enchantment finally ended, the woman sank to the floor, a hole in her lower abdomen and indeed in the wall behind her. The duke sank, too, exhausted, dismissing the resulting notifications for the time being, for there were other matters to attend to.

The duke then staggered over to the felled assassin, gritting his teeth together, and he ripped open the woman's shirt. The answer to a question he had not yet voiced was there in front of him—the ink of a Goldmarch prison. This woman was not a local, wasn't someone disgruntled by the terrible deal the duke had struck. She was the next stage in Amira's plan—the plan she had intended all along.

Duke Cambelny could not help but be impressed; in all his dealings with Amira, he had not thought she had such a strategic head upon her shoulders. Though, of course, the duke could not discount the possibility that this scheme had come from her impressive new aide.

The duke stood, then ran down the long corridors of the tower he called home, rushing for the room in which he might find his family. As he slammed open the door, he was relieved to find his wife and his three young boys were all together.

"Kim, Tim, Jim, Xim . . . pack your bags. We need to leave."

His beautiful wife rose from her chair, her face paling. "Darling? What is it?

Why must we—" She ceased her question when she saw the bloodstains on his hands.

"An attack on my life. And almost certainly not the last. We must leave. Now."

"Father?" Xim asked, still so, so young. "What are we packing for? When will we return?"

"My boy . . . I do not know that we ever will."

CHAPTER THIRTY-THREE

On Crossed Paths

I awoke from vivid dreams that I couldn't quite remember, of my childhood and my father, but also of war, and I was pretty sure Corminar—of all people—was there, too. There was something strangely lifelike about the dreams, even considering how weird some of their contents were—at least, what I could remember of them. I opened my eyes to find long black hair in my face, and it took me a moment to remember that I hadn't fallen asleep alone last night.

I pulled my face away from Val and spat out a couple of hairs that had made their way into my mouth. I removed my arm from around her as gently as I could, wanting her to continue sleeping, but then my heart skipped a beat when I realized there were three people standing over us.

"It certainly took you two long enough," Corminar said, a smirk on his face that put all previous classic Corminar smirks to shame.

At his side, Lore begrudging handed over a handful of coins into Arzak's upturned palm. "OK. You were right," he said.

Val, disturbed by the noise, crumpled up her face and turned around. "What . . . what's going on?" she mumbled, looking at me. When I nodded to the rest of the team, she was suddenly totally awake, scrambling backward.

"Oh, thanks for that," I said.

"This going cause issues?" Arzak asked.

"Might stop them bickering quite so much," Lore replied. "Could even be good for us."

Corminar nodded his head sagely. "Perhaps we might get fewer headaches without all such arguing."

"Who says we're not gonna argue?" Val asked, glancing in my direction.

The elf's shoulders slouched. "Ah."

"OK, maybe not," Lore added.

"Want us leave so you put clothes on?" Arzak asked.

In response, Val grabbed the sheet and whipped it back over us, to reveal that we'd both passed out fully clothed.

"Aha!" Lore said, at the same moment that Arzak grumbled, ". . . Oh," and then handed the coins back to the barbarian.

I nodded to the transaction. "Do I even want to know what—" I started, but was cut off by the woman next to me elbowing me in the ribs.

"Why are you lot even up so early?" Val asked, grasping her head and beginning to *heal her* hangover first, as evidenced by the yellow-white glow of her magicks.

"Why are *you* up so late?" Lore retorted. "It's past lunchtime. We were getting worried, especially when we found your room empty."

"Well, I—" Val started, but was interrupted by Arzak clapping to urge us out of bed.

"Up! Up! We have kill horrible Player."

"We don't know they're horrible," I replied, aware now that I was apparently going to have to convince not just Val of this.

"They Player. They horrible."

"What crimes has she committed? What does—"

"Might I remind you that she is a member of a so-called Council?" Corminar asked. "I have only encountered 'councils' when there is some evil afoot. Particularly when they capitalize the *C*."

Lore nodded knowingly.

"Up! Up!" the orc said again, once more clapping her hands together to spur us into action.

Lore thrust his hands forward, a package each wrapped in paper. "I packed you sandwiches for the road."

We traveled north, along the winding merchant road that connected the Goldmarch with the Gentle Tundras and, further north still, the orcish Reaches. With our foray into the palace records office revealing that Niamh was in Lenktra, we couldn't make use of a ferry to cut days off our journey. Instead, it was the good old-fashioned method of travel that consisted of putting one foot in front of the other.

As we journeyed, we occasionally passed through small towns on the merchant route, and I activated my *In Plain Sight* ability to acquire more *Stealth* experience, but without there being any real danger, I hadn't quite leveled it up from 14. Likewise, I made a habit of using *Shrill Perimeter* to make sure we were warned of any approaching enemies while the whole team slept, though there had been none of the sort. There probably *would* be none, too, or at least I'd thought so until Arzak had voiced something she'd apparently been pondering.

"So pyroknight work for Council?" she'd asked.

"Jacob. Yeah," I replied.

"Jacob work for Council, and we kill Jacob. Now Niamh do same Council work. I follow, yes?"

"You follow, yes."

"Think Niamh know about us?"

Lore, who'd been sitting at the campfire at my side, suddenly stopped slurping his stew to look up at us.

"Why would she—" I started, but Arzak interrupted.

"Council know Jacob dead. Council are powerful, so must know who kill Jacob. So . . ."

"Niamh might want to avoid the same fate," I finished for her.

"She knows we're coming?" Lore asked.

After a pause, the orc shrugged. "Eat stew," she said.

If the rest of the team had thought that Val might stop picking fights with me after what had happened—though admittedly they all thought I was just as guilty of fight-picking—they were dead wrong. If anything, the casual digs became more common than ever, and this forced me to return them in kind.

Once we'd spent one night too many under the stars for Arzak's back, the orc talked us into staying at a tavern overnight—on the condition that *some of us* didn't get carried away on the beer. I had no idea who that applied to.

Val and I were three pints deep when the vibe changed. Corminar had been nursing a glass of what he described as "swill" but was in fact wine—I mean, I don't know what he expected from wine served on the south Tundran border, to be honest—but paused as a group entered the tavern. At the sight of whoever had entered, his eyes widened, and I immediately wrenched myself around in my seat to get a look.

It was a group of elves that had arrived in the tavern. They were looking around with absolutely no expression on their faces, but I'd been around Corminar long enough to read elven eyes. They couldn't quite seem to believe they were entering a building such as this—a matter on which most of the patrons seemed to agree.

I turned back to Corminar. "Red Thorn?"

The ranger shook his head, but said nothing more, only continuing to study the group of elves as they ambled—though, *floated* might have been a better descriptor—over to the bar, and ordered more of the same wine that Corminar had described as "swill."

Corminar remained oddly silent for the next hour or so—not that he was typically the Slayer with the loudest mouth—his eyes trained on the elves at the bar. But he didn't move, nor did he comment on them. And, if I wasn't mistaken, one of them was glancing back. Knowing Corminar, there was only one possible answer to this question—the grizzled elf glancing back at him was a former lover. Though, that didn't exactly narrow it down.

"Marriage?" Arzak asked. "Babies? Grandbabies?"

"Arzak, shut up," Val replied.

"What are we talking about? I got distracted," I said, returning to the conversation.

"Arzak is interrogating me on my intent."

"Intent with what?"

"With you," Val replied.

"I defend your honor," Arzak explained. "Make sure she not break your heart."

"If anyone's getting their heart broken around here, it's—"

The sound of glass shattering against the floor interrupted me, and I looked around to find that Val had dropped her—nearly full—pint glass. Her face grew pale as she stared at an older gentleman sporting an old-style sorcerer's hat, who had just entered the tavern.

"Val?" I asked, placing a hand on her upper back. "Are you alright?"

"He . . ." Val's eyes remained on the older human as he hurried over to the elves at the bar and clapped a couple of them on the back.

"Sorry about that, old chaps," the man said. "Had to nip off. Academy business, you understand. How is the wine? Good, good . . ."

Val suddenly stood from the table. The witch swayed slightly, though I suspected that didn't have much to do with the beer, and she turned as if about to leave.

"Val, what are you . . . ?" As she moved toward the exit, I also rose from the table and hurried after her, grabbing her softly by the forearm. "Val, what's going on?"

"He knows," Val said. "He knows what I am."

"Equivalence Vignor," the voice of the sorcerer boomed across the tavern floor. "I did wonder if we would ever meet again . . ."

CHAPTER THIRTY-FOUR

Traveling Companions

Val raised her hands, moving her fingers in the way I'd seen before, when she'd been about to start weaving her magicks. But these days, ever since the incident with the witchfinder village, she wasn't carrying an obscurem to mask what would be the green glow of *Witchcraft.*

I grabbed her hands, lowering them. "Val, no. Not here. It isn't—"

"He already knows!" the witch hissed back at me.

"*He* might, but nobody else does. Let's keep it that way, yeah?"

"Equivalence?" the sorcerer called out again behind me. "Do you not recognize your old tutor?"

Val and I turned slowly, and I placed myself between her and the stranger, still expecting trouble.

"I recognize the man who expelled me," Val said after a moment of staring the man down.

"Yes, well . . . We all know what that was about."

By now, a good chunk of the tavern's patrons were staring at the interaction; the atmosphere had changed enough that they recognized that something could be about to go down.

"Do you intend to . . . seek further 'justice'?" Val asked, talking around the point to not clue the onlookers in on what was going on.

The older man's eyes shifted from her, to me, and then to the rest of the group. Of the others, all four—Arzak, Corminar, Lore, and the depth-raider, in its cage—stared back at him. The sorcerer's eyes lingered on the last of these. "Perhaps I . . . acted too swiftly, all those years ago. Without due consideration.

What you—" He cut himself off, also apparently keen to avoid using the word *witch*. "The disciplinary matter of which we speak perhaps was rooted in archaic rules. Rules that perhaps do not hold up to the evolving standards of the modern day."

I could feel Val remain tense, but she said nothing.

"Come," the sorcerer said, waving her over toward him and the group of elves he was apparently here with. "Allow me to buy you and your friends a drink. It would not be enough to make amends, but it would, perhaps, be a start."

Val stirred behind me, and I glanced over my shoulder at her. Though still tense, she had softened somewhat at the mention of free beer.

"He's making peace," I whispered to her. "Sometimes it's best to go with it."

After another moment of consideration, Val finally nodded, and walked—very slowly—over to the sorcerer and his elven friends.

"What will it be?" the sorcerer said, waving to the barkeep.

"Ale. Red," Val replied.

The barkeep nodded their acknowledgement of the order, and the sorcerer turned to me, raising his eyebrows as though to repeat the question.

"The same."

"Excellent," the sorcerer said, then pushed forward a hand to shake mine. He gripped it firmly. "Arnold Orellan. I'm sure you've heard of me."

I wasn't quite sure whether I was supposed to have heard of the man through Val or more generally, but either way, I had absolutely no idea who he was. I answered only with a polite smile and a nod.

Arnold turned back to Val. "And for your friends?"

"Three more of the same."

"Won't Corminar want—" I started.

Val shook her head. "He doesn't know what he wants. He'll prefer the beer to the wine; he just thinks he should be drinking wine."

"Wine *is* the preferred drink of his people," one of the elves—the man who had eyed up Corminar earlier—offered.

"He's not been one of 'his people' for a long time," Val said, almost snapping at the elf. I thought if she hadn't been so stressed in the current situation, she probably wouldn't have been so snippy about the matter.

As the night went on, Val began to relax, and the team mingled with the sorcerer and his elven friends. It took me asking to find out that the elves were low-level diplomats from the Dawnwood, and part of Queen Amira's ongoing efforts to bring their two countries closer together. All around the Goldmarch were other elven diplomats, being given tours around the land by locals in high standing—like Arnold Orellan here—and becoming experts in specific regions. The sorcerer was paired with a group of elves charged with becoming experts in the Goldmarch's trade with the Gentle Tundras to the north.

By the time the hour grew late, Val had relaxed some more. Enough even that when Arnold Orellan asked if we would consider traveling north with them, Val accepted the deal. The deal being that we would provide the group with protection on these bandit-infested roads and get paid in return. Well, to be honest, "accepted the deal" might have been overstating it; Arnold didn't seem to give us much of an option, but Val at least didn't push back on it.

And so it went that our group, for the time being, grew larger.

Over the next few days, we avoided any bandits, though we saw and heard that they were operating in these parts. Locals complained about them and sought to hire us to deliver justice. And there was no shortage of burnt buildings—those who had resisted the criminals. No bandits had attacked us, however, though I thought this was more to do with them preferring to pick on smaller groups, rather than the dozen or so of us.

As we traveled further north, near enough to Camp Claw, the landscape began to grow desolate. We were in a part of the world where the forest should have grown denser, but that was no longer the case. Instead, there were tree stumps as far as the eyes could see. Someone had harvested all the timber in this region, with no evidence of any reforestation efforts taking place.

But that was far from the only strange thing we saw on our travels. As we made our way along the coastal road, we encountered locals who complained about disturbances in the Iron Sea. Some recounted events so horrifying that they were abandoning their homes, and based on the evidence we saw firsthand, I was inclined to believe them. Some spoke of monsters rising from the depths, slaughtering livestock and lone travelers alike. I'd seen many animals ripped apart on the road, and at one point we came across a farmyard that contained two dozen cows in much the same state, none left alive. This sight horrified Lore in particular.

Other locals spoke about cephalopors making trips onto the land, too, and we'd witnessed this one for ourselves. We saw no sign of any other ones making the trip to the coast, thankfully, but I was very wary of the depth-raider sometimes stirring in its cage—were these beasts strong enough to engage the creature's powerful abilities?

Whether or not these tales were true, there were enough to form a trend, and one thing was clear: some new power was forcing these creatures from the Iron Sea. I sat one evening outside a tavern, doing my best not to overindulge after the headache I'd woken up with the night before—one that Val had refused to *heal*, saying it served me right—and worked on my *Needlework*. The gentle waves of the Iron Sea lapped the beach in front of me, though the night was dark enough that I could barely make them out, even with the torch planted in the sand next to me.

As I finished a stitch, a notification popped up in front of me.

> *Needlework increased to Level 10!*
> **Base Points Gained:** +1 DEX, +1 CHA, +1 Free Point (DEX/CHA)
> **Ability Selection Unlocked**
> *Select an ability from the list below:*
> **Option 1: Flamboyant Stitch (Needlework)**—*Upgrade to Stitch.* Create an artful stitch in common fabrics. Ability scales more significantly on [CHA].

It would have been a decent enough ability choice if my plan for *Needlework* had been to sell my wares; people—particularly wealthy people—paid substantially more for clothes with a flair of design beyond the usual functional elements. But my plan for this skill was more practical than that: I wanted to create armor that I could wear, that would assist *Warped Shield* in making up for underinvesting in Vitality. After all, I was going to continue to put points into Intelligence over Vitality at every opportunity, to boost my mana reserves.

Fortunately, I had another option.

> **Option 2: Cloth Armor (Needlework)**—*Upgrade to Basic Cloth Armor.* Craft a cloth armor of higher quality, dependent on materials, time, and skill level.

I didn't need to give it a second thought; this was the ability choice for me. Even removing the *Basic* from *Basic Cloth Armor* might not allow me to create armor that protected me too much, but it was a start, and it surely lent itself to more similar abilities as I continued to progress.

> **Ability** Upgraded: Cloth Armor
> **Cloth Armor (Needlework):** Craft a cloth armor of higher quality, dependent on materials, time, and skill level.

I put my crafting materials down for a moment and stared out at the dark sea. My thoughts returned to my dreams. Ever since we'd left Auricia, I'd started dreading sleep. Dreams had become . . . not quite nightmares, but definitely both manic and vivid enough that I wasn't exactly enjoying them. I couldn't even blame Val—she'd only returned to my bed a couple of times since Auricia—and I didn't think it was the beer, either, because that was hardly new.

The most common dream I'd had was one of being restrained, while Players stood over me and discussed me, considering me in a language I couldn't quite understand. They told me they would reveal who—what?—I was, and that bit I *could* understand. From my restraints, I could only watch as they told my friends, one by one, and one by one they turned against me.

Last night someone had shaken me awake. I regret to say that I'd hoped it had been Val joining me again, but instead it was Lore. He'd held the depth-raider's cage in his arms.

"Lore? What's . . . I don't think we'd both fit in this bed," I mumbled, still only half-awake.

"Someone tried to get in my room. Tried to break in."

I blinked up at him. "Probably a drunk. Probably *Val.* We're in an inn, after all."

Lore had looked down at me, considering this, then nodded and went back to his room.

Someone joined me on the beach, planting themselves down at my side and tearing me from my memories of the night before. I could sense who it was before they spoke.

"I've been drinking too much," Val said.

"Tonight, or this lifetime?"

"Last few days. Thought I'd try some of this 'fresh ocean air' you were talking about, instead." She nodded down at the *Needlework* supplies. "How's it going?"

"You really want to know? Thought you thought it was stupid."

"Tell me," she said.

I paused for a moment, waiting for a punch line that never came, and then told her all about the different techniques I'd been trying, and the new ability I'd just received. All the while, the witch remained quiet, listening intently.

It would have been nice if I hadn't had the sinking feeling that something was lurking in the Iron Sea.

And I hadn't known then just how right I was to fear it.

CHAPTER THIRTY-FIVE

Not the Bees

Val and I returned to the traveler's inn that night to find the downstairs empty but for Corminar and the elven diplomats. They were usually the first to go up for the night, but they'd discovered that this inn actually had decent wine, and they were making up for lost time.

We'd planned to head straight up to my room, but Corminar caught sight of us and waved us over, so there was nothing we could do to excuse ourselves that wouldn't have made our nighttime plans obvious. Corminar poured us each a rather healthy glass of wine when we joined them, and this shattered my promise to myself to not drink tonight.

They spoke of elven things—that is, things very specific to elvish culture—and Val and I largely kept silent, sipping our wine. But then the grizzled male elf suddenly snapped his head to Corminar, his eyes wide.

"I fancy that I know who you are," the elf said.

"Urlwan," one of the other elves warned him, but the elf was undeterred.

"You are the Champion of Iranir, are you not? Lieutenant . . . Cludelor?"

"Cladenor," Val said absentmindedly, and Corminar shot her the closest he ever achieved to a glare.

"It is a matter of which I would rather not discuss," Corminar responded to the elf.

"My brother served under you," Urlwan continued. "On many an occasion did he paint you to be the only reason he survived the Honey Wars. You may not wish to discuss it, yet I must offer you my utmost gratitude. You saved the life of my kin and the hearts of my parents."

"Yes, well—" Corminar started, but Urlwan, bolstered by the wine, continued some more.

"And yet I find you in such lands as the Goldmarch? Surely you should be home, leading the Rooted Guard or living the life of a hero?"

"*Urlwan*," the same elf from earlier said. She clearly knew the answer to this question, and knew why Corminar might not be comfortable answering it.

"Yes, quite," my ranger friend said. "Well, I assure you that I am here with purpose. We are looking for someone, in fact. A woman who dwells in powerful circles."

"Oh?" one of the elves asked. "Please, provide us with a name. Perhaps we know her. After all, we have spent the past six months in the presence of those who fit that description."

"Her name—"

"Corminar?" Val prodded him. "Are you sure this is a good idea?"

"My kind can be trusted, I assure you. We do not tend to gossip quite as much as humans, or tieflings, or Arzak. And perhaps we might learn some vital information." He turned back to the group of elves. "You may indeed know her. She is a Player. One by name of Niamh."

Many of the elves leaned back in awe, almost unconsciously. "We do indeed know Niamh, for she is on one of Queen Amira's councils."

There's that word again.

"And who are you, in these days, that you have business with the descendants of the Architects?"

"I can assure you that we mean only to assist her," Corminar lied. "Though in order to do so, we must first find her. I am afraid, alas, that we have only a physical description, and little information about class and skills that may aid in our location of her."

Urlwan leaned forward once more. "In this, I can aid you. Anything for the elf who saved my brother. The Player you are looking for . . . amazingly intelligent she is, particularly for a human—though I mean this in the social sense, rather than that of the system. Though she demonstrated little of her actual skills in our presence, I do at least have it on good authority that her class is in the Hunter line. Or perhaps Trapper, I do believe."

I glanced over at Val, who was doing a very good job of keeping her expression neutral.

"Thus, you might find her in the forests, though I believe she has risen to a station, these days, where she has attendants to see to any such hands-on work. As far as I am aware, she spends her days in Lenktra and the surrounding area."

Corminar nodded. "Good. This matches the information we already possess. I am grateful."

Urlwan smiled, which doesn't sound like an extreme reaction, but you've got to remember that elves don't express emotions very often. "Of course. Anytime."

"I think we should be getting up," I said, gulping down the last of my wine—an action that resulted in blank stares from all the elves but Corminar—and gesturing to the stairs.

Val nodded, and—oblivious to the elven glares—did the same thing with her wine. Corminar, who seemed less comfortable with the other elves now that they'd recognized him, made to do the same.

As we reached the landing, I stopped. "Corminar," I said, then pointed into my room.

The elf paused, looking at Val and me. "I always knew this day would come, though I didn't think your bedroom antics would grow dull so quickly."

"What?" I replied. "No. We need to talk."

Corminar nodded. "Of course. Perhaps next time, then."

I closed the door firmly behind him, then listened at it for signs that the elven contingent were coming up to bed. From the sounds of it, they were still happily drinking downstairs.

"She's a Trapper," I said, turning. "A Trapper. Do any of you get the impression that's exactly what we're walking into? A Trap?"

"I think you overstate how much these Players care about—" Corminar started.

"Do I? Don't you remember what Arzak said, a few days back? Niamh could know we're coming, especially if she was on this same 'Council' as the pyroknight."

Corminar paused, then shrugged. "I do not believe this changes anything. We still must do what we must do."

"We can be more careful about it, though. We don't have to go blundering in," Val said, and only now did she let her face pale.

The ranger paused when he saw her, immediately recognizing something was wrong. "You seem . . . nervous?" he asked.

"You should tell him," I told Val. "All of them, really. They have a right to know." I was right, of course, but that didn't change the fact that this was deeply traumatizing for Val. Having to relive it again wouldn't be easy.

The witch shook her head for an instant, and then . . . sighed. "Maybe."

The room fell silent, both Corminar and I allowing Val the space to process.

"I'll show you mine if you show me yours, Cor," the witch finally said. Before Corminar could inevitably start undressing, she clarified, "Tell me about the Honey Wars. Tell us what happened at Iranir."

The elf said nothing for a moment, licking his lips as though deliberating. "How much do you know about the Honey Wars?" he asked.

"I know they were bad," Val replied. "Killer bees infested the Dawnwood. Took lots of lives. But that's from what I read. I've never spoken about it with anyone who was there."

Corminar nodded. "There are no words to describe the horrors I witnessed, and so I will not attempt to. Know only this: times were desperate, and in the most desperate of times, you might find you have to bend otherwise firm moral codes. Do you know we still have treason written in law, in the Dawnwood? Even after the fall of the elven kings?"

"I didn't," I said. I knew little of elven affairs, if I was honest, particularly those of the Dawnwood.

"I would not say it was a crime worse than murder or the like, of course, but it is a crime treated equally by elven law. Now that there is no king to rebel against, you can commit treason in only one way: by burning the Dawnwood itself."

He trailed off there, leaving Val to fill the silence. "And at Iranir . . ."

"I was only a lieutenant in that battle, but so many of my kin had fallen that command rested on my shoulders. There was still a captain there, it would later turn out, but our soldiers were so scattered that we could not have known. The bees, they . . . there were too many of them. Our prospect of victory was nil, and yet my fellow elves looked to me to save them. And I did just that. By burning Iranir to the ground."

I felt a chill run down my back. I knew enough about elves at least that I could see burning the trees was truly a last resort for them. It was beyond a last resort, really, and yet Corminar had done so. "They couldn't charge a hero," I said.

The elf nodded. "Not formally. But they made it very clear: I had committed treason, and I would never be able to turn home."

The room fell to silence, everyone processing their thoughts. It was Corminar who recovered fastest—none of this being news to him, of course—and he looked up at Val. "Your turn," he said.

And so Val told him. She gave him little more detail than she'd given me, only that Niamh had hunted a changeling, and decided one changeling corpse was as good as another. There was only the one thing that she hadn't said before.

"I was a kid," Val croaked. "Just a kid. And when I survived, after the bog-spawn, people started to put things together. A month later, all of the northern Goldmarch knew I was a witch. Including my parents." Suddenly, she turned on me, almost snarling. "You say we can't be sure she deserves to be killed? We bloody well *can*."

I said nothing, but I nodded.

"Then you know more than you've said," Corminar said to Val. "Urlwan says she's a Trapper. Is that correct?"

"My information is years out of date, but . . ." The witch nodded. "Yeah. Yeah, that adds up. But if you think her traps and her tracking and her bow are what we need to watch out for . . . then, no, you're mistaken. The most danger-ous thing about Niamh is her mind."

CHAPTER THIRTY-SIX

From the Depths They Rise

Twilight cast red across the sky, punctuated only by long, fluffy clouds, as we made our way north along the coastal road accompanied by Arnold Orellan and his elven guests.

Lore, who did not share a single thing in common with any of our new elven friends, had been spending most of his time with the depth-raider. He'd decided it was definitely male, based on its "energy." You might not have known it was a beast capable of leveling cities from the way the barbarian kept tickling its belly. According to the information we had, the witchfinder's clasp *should* have kept it from gaining any power from any particularly strong people around him, but Val was nervous about it. "Those things only go so far," she said.

Corminar had grown distant from the other elves since their recognition of him last night. He seemed ashamed of his past, though these diplomats did not seem to see any reason why he would be, Urlwan in particular. With time, Corminar's uncharged crimes had been . . . if not forgotten, then at least they seemed less important.

We were running late for the stop that Arnold Orellan had planned for us, and if we didn't get there soon, then we were going to be traveling in darkness. It wouldn't matter how many of us there were, then—bandits would surely give robbing us a go.

Arnold hadn't really spoken to Val since the first night, and Val was starting to think his words about making amends had been just that—words. I'd suggested to her that maybe there were some nerves on his side, but she disagreed, saying he wasn't the kind of man to get nerves. Based on what I'd seen so far, I was inclined to agree. Maybe he really had just wanted protection through these increasingly dangerous lands, and was the type to say whatever he needed to secure it. It was always those sorts that became rich and powerful, after all.

Instead, Arnold Orellan had spent a lot of his time with Lore, interrogating him about the nature of the depth-raider—it being "one of those few creatures I've never had the pleasure of dissecting." Lore wasn't exactly *thrilled* to hear this, and he always kept his sword nearby just in case, though I couldn't believe this otherwise mild-mannered old man had anything but academic discussion in mind.

As we climbed over the crest of a sand dune, right on the beach, we finally spotted the inn we intended to stay at. And it was a good thing, too, because the red sky had grown dark, and the last of the sun's rays were just disappearing over the barren, deforested landscape to our left.

It was almost peaceful, the sound of the waves lapping against the beach, but again I had this sense of something being wrong with the sound, something about the way the waves swept in that wasn't quite right.

Val was walking slower, too, her eyes on the shoreline.

"What is it?" I asked. "Do you hear it?"

"Hear it? No. I feel something."

We stopped at the front of our party, causing the rest of the group to slow to a halt behind.

"Let's not dillydally, chaps," Arnold said, approaching us. "There will be dangers out on the road, this time of night. Bandits, and—"

Val shook her head. "No," she said, almost under her breath. "Not—"

We heard the unmistakable sound of something moving in the water. "Another cephalopor?" I asked.

The witch shook her head. "No, I don't think so. Something else. Something . . ."

We heard the sound again, and then a figure broke forth from beneath the surface. In the low light, I had to squint to make it out, and all I could see was the head and shoulders of—it seemed—a man. "Who . . ."

Another figure pierced the surface. A woman, it looked like. Staring at the lot of us.

"Not sure this good," Arzak said, joining Val, Arnold, and I at the front of the pack.

A third head, then a fourth, then three more, and more still all emerged from the water, each exactly the same distance from one another, all of them staring at us.

"Get to the inn," Val said softly.

Arnold did not need to be told twice, and he began running forward, incredibly agile for his age, without sparing a glance for the elves he was supposed to be guiding.

"Get to the inn!" I shouted, echoing Val, waving the elven diplomats onward, drawing my blade with the other hand.

The shapes in the Iron Sea charged at once, running through the water like it was air, not being slowed for a moment, their eyes fixed upon the members of the party who were standing their ground.

Corminar loosed an arrow, then another, then another, each of them embedding into one of the figures' chests, but not seeming to do any damage. "This *gods*-forsaken bow!" the ranger roared, but still he kept firing.

Val rushed forward, into the shallows of the sea before the creatures could reach her. She bent down, touching the water, and then summoned lightning magicks to ripple through it. The surface of the water sizzled from the spell, and Val was immediately shot backward into the air by the very same magicks, but still the figures were undeterred.

I flung a hand upward, opening a portal behind Val as she flew through the air, and opened another near me so I could catch her. "You OK?" I asked.

Val didn't reply, and she hopped free of my grasp, ready to launch more attacks on the encroaching enemies.

Meanwhile, Lore and Arzak were charging forth, weapons in hand. "Styk!" Arzak shouted, and I got the message, opening a portal in front of her and its partner in the air above the closest of the enemies. The orc brought two swords down upon the manlike creature—man*like* because it was clear, at this point, that they weren't men at all—and the blades . . . passed right through it. It wasn't like the specters of the witchfinders that we'd encountered before—the blades still hit flesh, and cut through it, it was just that the wounds sealed up again the moment the sword was clear.

"Guys? I think we might have a problem here!" Lore shouted, still running into battle anyway, the depth-raider's cage strapped to his back and the creature within bouncing around.

"The raider?" I cried back to him.

"*No!* The scary sea-people!"

"Oh, right."

"There are magicks in the air," Val shouted. "Not just mine and Styk's. Theirs, too."

"Idea what they are?" Arzak said, still swiping away with the blades but getting nowhere. One of the creatures flung the back of a limb into her, knocking the heavy woman into the air with ease.

"I've not seen anything like it," the witch replied. "I don't know!"

"Blade no work," Arzak grunted, lifting herself back to her feet. "Magicks no work. What left?"

"I don't—"

"Running away?" Lore suggested, then immediately took his own advice. He sprinted, sword in hand, down the beach.

The other four of us hesitated for a moment, before Arzak shouted "Regroup!"

and that gave us all permission to flee. We quickly put distance between us and the enemies, as they were slower on land than in water, and a year ago I might have used that simply to run away. But we were supposed to be heroes now, of a sort. Besides, the people currently in the tavern ahead of us had paid us good money to protect them.

I opened a portal in front of me and Val. We leaped through it, landing heavily on our feet at the door to the inn. The witch hurried inside, beginning to shout orders at whoever was there, while I turned back to open more portals, bringing the rest of the team to the building. Behind them, I could see the creatures creeping steadily toward me.

I heard a shrill, grumpy woman's voice behind me, and suddenly I was barged out of the doorway by a short, stout barmaid with her hand on her hip. "Scare my customers, will you?" she shouted at Val, back inside. "'Creatures attacking'? Good grief, there—" The barmaid immediately trailed off when she looked around at the dozen humanoid figures running toward her inn. She turned back inside. "Creatures attacking! Merfolk attacking!"

Merfolk, was it?

"Do what the weird woman says!" she continued. "Barricade the windows! Barricade the door."

"Not wait for us be inside?" Arzak asked the woman as she hurried past me into the building. The barmaid ignored her.

As soon as the last of our group was inside, I allowed the barmaid to slam the door closed, and Val and Urlwan were ready with an upturned table. They rammed it into place against the door.

"Think it'll hold?" Val asked.

Arzak responded by slamming one sword, then the other, into the floorboards just behind the table, helping to keep it in place. "It hold."

I nodded, then looked around at the other windows, where other customers were propping up tables in much the same way, or—in the case of a man in a cook's hat and an apron—were hammering loose floorboards across the windows. When we'd used the last nail, the inn suddenly turned silent.

"And now what?" I asked.

Nobody had an answer for me, and the enemy pounded on the door.

CHAPTER THIRTY-SEVEN

The Siege Begins

It was several hours before the merfolk stopped banging on the doors and walls. The fact that they'd surrounded us got no less terrifying for the patrons of The Net & Anchor. Even once the noise stopped, we were still incredibly aware that the merfolk were outside, because we could see movement through the gaps in the floorboards on the windows.

Rounds of beer, purchased by the elven diplomats for everyone trapped here, went some way to distract from the enemy outside, but it wasn't enough. Even for me, it wasn't enough. Normally I wouldn't have been too distressed by the promise of a fight, but we'd seen already that these merfolk were invulnerable to our attacks. Any fight that happened would surely end in our deaths. I turned back to my *Needlework* to keep my mind off things, but even growing it to level 12—the experience bolstered by the use of my new *Cloth Armor* ability—didn't settle me.

At my side, Arzak and Val discussed strategy, but the only feasible solution seemed to be waiting the enemies out. But how long would that be? It could be hours, or it could be days. And with the merfolk's invulnerability, there was little chance of any assistance.

With a sigh, I put my needle down and strolled over to the bar, where the previously disgruntled barmaid poured me a pint without charging me. Over here, I could hear Arnold Orellan still badgering Lore about letting him study the depth-raider, which was making the barbarian increasingly uncomfortable.

"Don't you have other things to worry about right now?" I called over to him.

The academic's easy smile faltered for a moment before he regained composure, and then he nodded. "Quite right; the merfolk are equally worthy of study."

It wasn't quite what I'd meant, but it took Arnold's attention away from the depth-raider, and for that, Lore smiled his gratitude. I raised my pint in mock cheers in response. The ale didn't taste as good as it should have.

The barbarian turned to the man in the apron and the chef's hat. "Are you—"

"Kitchen's closed," the cook replied, his arms crossed and his eyes trained on the barred door, as though wary that our besiegers could break through at any moment.

Lore pulled a sad face.

"I heard about 'em, you know," the barmaid said, and I turned back to see her polishing a notquiteclean glass with a dishrag.

"Depth-raiders?"

"Is that what we're calling merfolk these days? Ain't heard of them raiding before, but . . ." She gestured to the walls. "I guess you could call this that."

"Ah, no," I said. "Depth-raiders is something else. What have you heard? Anything that could help us?"

"I heard about them killing people."

"So no, then."

The barmaid shrugged, placed down the glass next to plenty more not-quite-clean ones, and picked up another. "Ain't saying it'd help, just that I'd heard of them. Last few months, like. Heard merchants, coming through here, saying something is forcing things out the Iron Sea. Magicks or something, I guess. It's always magicks, ain't it? How often when something big happens is it a woman with a sword behind it? Never."

"How'd these merchants escape, then?" I asked.

"Dunno that they did."

"Well, I mean, they came here, right? And told you about them? So they must have still been alive to do that, unless your husband's a necromancer or something."

The barmaid stared me down for a moment, then stared into the dirty glass instead. With a sigh, she placed it under the tap and poured a beer for herself. "Necromancers are another one, ain't they? Always up to trouble. At least that's outlawed. Not that it stops people. But these merchants . . . I dunno if they saw the merfolk for themselves, just heard rumors. That's what merchants sell as often as not—rumors, rather than knowledge."

"OK, well same question applies: how did the people they heard this from survive? Cos someone must have done at some point."

"Maybe they saw the bodies, then."

Val arrived at my side, clearly here for more beer but immediately distracted by the topic of conversation. "Bodies? What bodies?"

"You not heard about 'em? The bodies, all up and down the coast. Sucked dry."

"Of blood? That's vampires," I corrected her.

"Not vampires, you twit. They were sucked dry of . . . water, I guess. Moisture! That's the word: moisture."

"And you're saying these merfolk did it?" Val asked.

"Either that or fancy vampires." The barmaid shot me a glare that said she knew it wouldn't actually be "fancy vampires."

I heard some commotion coming from over my shoulder. It wasn't the first time there'd been any; an hour or so earlier, an older local had decided he'd go outside and take on the merfolk by himself. Free beer had a lot to do with that decision, I thought. Others, including Arzak, had needed to hold him back from pulling the floorboards off the windows and they'd distracted him with more beer instead. He was now dozing safely in an armchair in the corner of a room.

But I was surprised to find that Corminar was the source of the disruption this time. The group of elven diplomats cornered him on the far side of the room, though I couldn't hear what they were saying from over at the bar.

I jumped from the bar stool, started across the room, returned to the bar for my half-drunk pint of ale, and then joined the group of elves.

"You must," Urlwan was saying. "There is nobody else; it must be you."

"What's going on here?" I asked, butting in.

Urlwan pointed to Corminar. "Please, tell your colleague: only he can lead us to victory in this battle. He must take command."

"Corminar? A commander?" I asked, though of course I supposed he had been that once—if not now.

"Lieutenant Cladenor, the Hero of Iranir. *That* is who must take command if we are to survive."

I looked to Corminar, who shook his head at me. "I don't know what difference he can make right now. We can't hurt them. We could have the best commander in all the continents, but if we can't hurt them, there's no chance of victory."

Urlwan considered this, nodded, and then turned back to the Hero of Iranir once more. "You must identify a weakness. Tell us how we might defeat them."

"As I have already told you," Corminar said. "I do not have the answers you seek. I am no hero. I am no commander. Not anymore."

"Then we die," Urlwan responded.

It took everything I had not to roll my eyes. "I'm sure there are other options."

"By all means," the elf said, "tell us about these options. Or is the alternative only to be trapped in here until we starve?"

"We'll find a way."

"No. The Hero of Iranir will find a way. The Hero of—"

Corminar suddenly snapped, grabbing the other elf by the front of his shirt.

"If I'm such a bloody hero, then why am I not allowed home?" he shouted in Urlwan's face. He'd learned the word *bloody* from Val.

The other elf paled some, his otherwise typically elven stoic expression giving way to one of shock. "You were exiled? But you saved thousands!"

"Not exiled, but if you know that title—Hero of Iranir—then you know what I did. You know I committed treason."

"You were not charged. None have been charged with treason since the Old Kings fell."

"Yet you find me here, in the Tundras, where few who have any other choice choose to live."

"Hey!" I protested, but Corminar silenced me with an upheld hand begging my forgiveness. I gave it to him; I'd certainly not have grown up in these parts if I'd had a choice.

Urlwan said nothing, though I swore I saw him swallow some words.

"I am exiled in all but name," Corminar continued. "I am considered a traitor to my people. I am certainly *not* a leader."

I thought for a moment that Urlwan was going to continue to contest this, but his mouth opened and no words came out. Finally, the elf took a seat on an unused armchair and muttered, "Then all hope is lost."

As if to reinforce this point, the merfolk began thumping on the tavern once more, causing the walls to shake and the occupants to grow quiet. A chill ran over my spine. Though everyone else was distracted, their eyes on the walls—and the merfolk on the other side—I caught sight of a gentle green glow in the corner of the room. A glow around Val's hand. She was up to something. *Witchcraft.* And she was lucky that nobody else saw.

When Val caught my eye, she immediately released the spell, lowering her hand. It was just in time, too, because as soon as she ended her magicks, the banging stopped, and there was nothing to distract the other patrons. She turned and ambled over to my side. "Styk . . . I think I know how to defeat them," she said.

"How?"

"You're not gonna like it."

"When you're involved, I rarely do."

Val ignored the dig. "I've been testing. I can make them vulnerable. It's the moisture; that's the key. With moisture—moisture they've stolen from humanity—they gain strength, even on dry land. But without it, we can defeat them."

"OK, so how do we do that?"

"A ritual. Styk, I need to use *Witchcraft.* And I need to do it in front of everyone."

CHAPTER THIRTY-EIGHT

The Exile from Managlass

"In front of . . . everyone?" I repeated.

Val nodded. "I'll need to draw on their life forces for the ritual to work. It's one . . . I've only done it once or twice before."

I met Val's gaze, asking the inevitable question with my eyes.

"Trust me," she said.

I nodded. "I do. The others, though . . . Do they have to *let* you draw on their . . ."

"Life force," Val finished for me. "No. But anyone adept with magicks will know that it's happening."

I paused once more. "OK. Get ready. I'll warn the others; if need be, we'll protect you."

Val nodded her thanks, then hurried off around the room collecting supplies: dirt from a plant pot, cupped in her hands; a fallen leaf from the same plant; and a drop of her blood, sliced from the back of her forearm. She rubbed the blood upon the leaf, then took the pile of dirt and began scattering it in a loose circle around her.

"Gaia," she whispered, sitting in the middle of the circle, her eyes closed, "lend us your power. Gaia . . ."

By now, she'd started drawing the attention of others in the inn—making yourself bleed and rubbing mud around the floor generally had that result—but it wasn't until the sorcerer saw what was going on that anyone said anything.

"I recognize this," Arnold said. "This is precisely the kind of magicks that got you expelled from Managlass."

"Don't say that like you had nothing to do with it," Val muttered, her eyes fixed on the preparation of the ritual rather than the sorcerer. "You could have put a stop to it. You could have—"

"You think I could forgive *Witchcraft*?"

"I think you could forgive a young woman for just using the class bestowed upon her. And I think you could've made others forgive it, too. You had sway at the academy. You could've stepped in. At the very *least*, you could have not told my parents."

Arnold Orellan frowned. "They had a right to know. They had a witch in their house."

"They had a *daughter* in their house!" Val roared, snapping her attention away from the dirt lines and rising to meet his gaze. "You say you've changed. Do you really regret none of it?"

Arnold swallowed, his eyes shifting from the witch and scanning the room, lingering upon Lore and the depth-raider. "Like many, I have regrets. But I had a position to uphold—can you imagine I would still be a professor if I'd acted in the way you wanted? If I'd chosen to ignore your . . . If someone had found out that I had known?"

Val raised her arms as though to attack, but I could see her hands trembling.

"If you attack me, girl, there is only one way this will—" Arnold started, but was interrupted by a knife being placed gently upon his throat. I was as surprised as him to discover that it was *my* knife.

"Enough," I said in the man's ear, my voice barely above a whisper.

"Enough?" Arnold repeated, loudly enough that it was clear my threat hadn't landed. "I think everyone in this inn has the right to know what this is. It's *witchcraft*—magicks that will pull on your . . ."

I opened a portal beneath the sorcerer's feet and tossed him across the room, making sure to land him upside down.

But the damage was done; the others in the inn were already murmuring, and the barkeep's husband in particular was scowling like he might do something.

"You wanna know what the situation is?" I shouted, arms raised at my sides. "Alright, yeah: she's doing *witchcraft*. But you know what else she's doing? Saving all your bloody lives. So if any of you so much as step toward her, I'm going to have to do something about it."

The murmuring fell to a silence.

Lore put down the depth-raider atop the bar and stepped forward. "And so am I," he said.

Arzak and Corminar stepped forward, each of them recognizing that they didn't need to say anything; the message was clear.

"Anyone gonna try it?" I asked.

Nobody moved, and nobody said a word.

"Good," I said, then looked back to Val, who seemed to be trying to repress a smile. "Over to you, then."

Val nodded, then looked straight forward and closed her eyes. "Gaia, lend us your power. Gaia, your daughter beckons. Gaia, lend us your . . ." The prayer repeated over and over, Val's words beginning to echo as though her voice was joined by an unseen choir. It took me a moment to realize that *we* were the choir—those from whom Val drew life—but only myself, Arnold, and two of the elven diplomats seemed conscious enough to realize.

"She must stop," the sorcerer cried, but I whipped a hand up in front of him to stop him approaching. The older man looked at me, eyes wide. "She draws our souls! She will kill us all!"

"No, she—"

A blinding green light suddenly exploded from Val, a glow hovering in the air above her. Within it, I swore I could see a figure—one that the witch was talking to—but I couldn't focus enough to make her out.

I woke up on the inn's floor, stirring at apparently roughly the same time as everyone else. Humans, elves, and orcs alike murmured groggily as they stumbled back to their feet. Val grabbed me by the arm, helping me up. "How you feeling?"

"Weak. What did you—"

"It'll pass. Give it a moment."

I caught sight of my beer, still half-drunk, on the table next to me. I took a swig.

"Yes, that'll help," Val said, and I had no idea if she was being sarcastic or not.

"How long we were out?"

"About thirty seconds," she said, and I turned to look at her. I was surprised—funnily enough—to find her eyes had turned bright green, and a vivid green flame burned around her forearms. The flames didn't seem to hurt her, or me, for that matter.

"I assume it worked, then?"

"For now. Gaia granted me the strength we need, but . . . we only have a few minutes."

I turned to Lore and Corminar, the former helping the latter up. "You hear that? We—"

"We hear," Arzak said from another corner of the room. She took a deep breath, gathering and composing herself. "We ready." She moved over to the door and reached for her blades, which were still wedged in front of the upturned table.

"Are we?" I asked, still finding myself a tad weak, though it was fading with every moment that passed, as Val had said it would.

Corminar and Lore shuffled over to the door, taking deep breaths of their own, then looked to Val and me to join them.

"Alright, I guess we are."

"You're opening the door?" the barkeep called out. "But they'll—"

"It's now or never. We fight now, or we're trapped in here for good."

At Val's words, and her stony expression, the woman put up no more protest.

"Alright," I said, nodding to Arzak. "Do it."

The orcish woman pulled her swords free of the floor, and then—with Lore's help—picked up the table and tossed it into a corner.

Arzak turned next to Val, asking a question through the medium of raised eyebrows.

"Do it," Val said, and the flames engulfing her arms roared brighter.

The orc flung the door open, revealing the group of merfolk standing evenly spaced apart, their dark eyes reflecting the low light spilling out from the inn.

There was a moment of silence as each side of the inevitable fight stared one another down, and then Val roared. She charged toward the group of merfolk and whipped her glowing arms out, blasting them with her granted magicks. The creatures hissed and squealed as water evaporated from their skin like in a pan over a hot flame, but it didn't kill them. When Val's borrowed magicks was exhausted—as evidenced by the flames dying—all twelve of the merfolk were still standing.

"A little more than two each, by my count," Corminar said, and then he raised his bow. This time, when he fired, the arrow ripped flesh apart for good.

What followed was a web of chaos, and I could only just about follow my own role in this fight, let alone that of the others. But merfolk were dropping left, right, and center, and with the enemy in their weakened states, none of my friends seemed to take any meaningful damage.

When the first arrow hit, I hadn't wasted any time in launching an attack of my own. I portaled myself and Arzak into the air, and we tumbled down onto the merfolk at the rear—Arzak using her strength, me using the broken line of sight to activate my *Stealth Attack* passive. I didn't kill the first merfolk in one hit, but each *slice* that followed did ample enough damage that I could kill it before it hurt me. And what with my *Mana-Fueled* ability, I was draining Mana instead of Stamina to do it.

I hopped through a portal as this enemy fell and landed behind another. Val blasted it with her wind magicks as I *stabbed* it from behind, forcing my blade deeper than it would have gone otherwise. My knife got wedged in the creature's flesh, and I gave it a yank but still it didn't budge.

"Styk," Val said, nodding to the ground. I opened a portal beneath her feet and its partner above the enemy's head, and she landed with her feet on its shoulder. The force of the impact freed my blade and killed the creature in the same move, and I spun on the spot just in time to block the swipe of another enemy behind me.

I stumbled into Lore's back, and the merman charged in for another attack. I couldn't duck, because that would have made Lore vulnerable, so instead I portaled the both of us through the floor and three paces to one side. The two merfolk collided with one another, and Lore turned, swinging his heavy blade to cleave through the both of them in one hit.

"Styk!" Corminar cried out, and I turned just in time to avoid one of his arrows, which whizzed past my ear and into the head of another enemy at my side. The creature hissed but didn't die at this damage, and I launched it into the air with another portal. Corminar fired another arrow which hit the creature in the air, and the fading cry indicated it had been a fatal hit.

I turned to see Arzak surrounded by most of the remaining merfolk, and even with two blades, she couldn't kill all of them. Two of them pressed into her, their snarling, toothy mouths snapping at her face, and she couldn't swipe at them with her blades. I charged toward her, *stabbing* my knife into her back, and then at the last second activating my *Closed Reach* ability to make the blade pass through her. The creatures on the other side cried and hissed, stumbling backward from my blade and giving Arzak enough room to attack them with hers.

As those two merfolk fell, the orc and I turned to see Val and Lore finish off the last of them. It was over.

---

6 x Merfolk defeated!

Knifework: +3,750XP
Knifework increased to Level 28!
Base Points Gained: +1 DEX, +1 STR, +2 Free Points (VIT/DEX/STR)
Level up!
You increased to Level 14!
Worldbending: +5,200XP
Worldbending increased to Level 32!
Base Points Gained: +2 INT, +2 Free Points (INT/WIS/CHA)
Stealth: +950XP
Stealth increased to Level 15!
Base Points Gained: +1 DEX, +1 WIS, +2 Free Points (DEX/WIS)
Ability Selection Unlocked

. . .

"Nice," I said.

CHAPTER THIRTY-NINE

Academic Privilege

As the team ambled back into the inn to the applause of those who'd been cowering inside, I—naturally—turned my attention to the ability screen. It was one of those great days where you get to choose a new one. Was there ever anything better than that feeling? And that it was *Stealth*, too, was excellent, because I'd really been focusing on leveling up that skill of late.

> **Ability Selection Unlocked**
> *Select an ability from the list below:*
> **Option 1: Identify Traps (Stealth)**—Search for traps in an area—

Shouting erupting around me distracted me from the ability selection notifications, and it forced me to minimize them once more. It was Lore—a typically unfrazzled man—who was shouting, his hands on his head in distress.

"He's gone! He's *gone!*" he cried.

"Who's . . ." I started, and then my eyes darted to the spot on the bar where the depth-raider's cage had been.

"Where is it?" Corminar demanded. He turned his attention to Urlwan. "Who took it? You must have seen."

"I . . . I . . . My attention was on you. My attention was on the fight. Whoever stole your creature . . ."

"They must've taken advantage of the distraction," the barkeep said. "We was all watching you."

Arzak stepped forward, into the center of the room. "*Who?*" she shouted.

"Tell now and we not kill." Even under her snarl, the culprit didn't reveal themselves, and the inn went quieter than it had been even with the merfolk on the doorstep.

And in that quietness, we heard a gentle whimpering noise. A noise emerging from Arnold Orellan's robe. Countless faces turned to him.

The sorcerer held up his hands to protest his innocence. "Don't look at me, chaps, I . . ." he started, but trailed off when he realized the jig was up. "Aw hells," he muttered, and then he flung his hands to the wall behind him and summoned a tremendous blast of fire magicks to blow a hole in it.

"You," Val spat, stepping forward as the dust settled, finding Arnold halfway out the new exit he'd created. "You would sink so low as to steal?"

I thought about protesting that particular question; in a previous life, I'd made a decent career out of stealing.

"Is it stealing to take that which does not belong to you?" the professor of Managlass responded. "You should not have such a rare creature. It belongs with me. With the Academy. We must study it, for the benefit of future students, and future generations. *That* is what matters, not the schemes of a witch and her depraved friends."

"You never had any intentions of making amends, did you?" Val asked. "You lied, just so you could figure out a way to steal the—"

"At last she catches up." The professor smiled, or smirked, rather. "It takes a particular brand of naivete to have been convinced of my intentions so quickly. Did you really think that I, a high sorcerer at the great Managlass Academy, would lower myself to socialize with a witch? To forgive her of her sins? I could barely bring myself to *speak* with you, woman."

I took an unconscious step forward. "Oh yeah? And what sins are they?" I put a hand to my dagger and prepared to fling the other hand forward to open a portal behind him.

The professor took one look at me, and at my knife, then raised an eyebrow. "Please. Don't tell me you intend to fight *me*. What was it I saw, *Worldbending* magicks? And you intend to use those up against a Sorcerer? Do you really think you would stand a chance?"

"It ain't just *Worldbending*, though, is it?" Lore said, unsheathing his only recently sheathed greatsword.

"Oh, and a sword. Whatever will I do?"

Arzak stepped forward, raising her weapons. "Three sword."

Finally, it was Corminar's turn. "And a—" he started, but was cut off by Arnold suddenly raising a hand and sending a ball of ice magicks blasting into Corminar's chest. He flew across the room and landed hard on top of a table, with Urlwan and the other elves rushing to his aid.

Arnold Orellan turned and ran.

I opened a portal through which Val and I—and later the other three members of the Slayers—jumped onto the cold, hard mud of the desolate, deforested plains outside. Ahead, I saw Arnold summon a sheet of ice which floated ahead of him and slightly to one side, positioned so that the reflection gave him a clear view of his pursuers. Of *us*.

Glancing back—having no handy summoned ice sheet of my own—I checked that we were all through the portal. Satisfied, I closed it then opened another pair that would land us just in front of the sorcerer.

But as it opened, Arnold Orellan cast a spell with an elaborate flourish of his hands—a glowing light blue ball that floated in the air and immediately charged toward my portal. I'd thought for a moment that it meant to blast through it, hitting anyone who tried to use the portal, but instead it suddenly sprouted long, squid-like tendrils, which wrapped around the edges of the portal. Once latched on, it squeezed the portal shut, and it looked like—if any of the team had reached the portal—it might have sliced through them, not obeying by the usual rules.

And so we had no choice but to sprint faster, though with our enemy's advanced age, we closed on him quickly. At least, we would have done, if he hadn't started lobbing orbs of dark green liquid over his shoulder. Where these spells hit the ground, the remaining foliage and tree stumps fizzled, the magicks eating away at them. Though none of the spells hit us—it almost seemed like the high sorcerer didn't *want* to hit us, considering he was aiming so low—they did mean that we had to twist and turn in our pursuit to avoid the spells eating away at our flesh.

Still, we grew steadily closer, Arzak and Lore closing the gap out ahead of Corminar, Val, and me. I opened another portal to try to close the gap, hoping that Arnold Orellan wouldn't realize. The moment I cast my spell, another glowing orb sprang from the sorcerer, wrapping its tendrils around the portal before I—or anyone—had a chance to hop through. It was almost as though the sorcerer's spell automatically triggered when magicks was used nearby—I wasn't going to be able to portal anytime soon. It was time to change up my strategy.

Portals might have been out, but I had a whole array of *Worldbending* magicks in my arsenal, ones that I really didn't get enough use out of. Some of them really weren't useful right now—there was nothing nonsentient, or nonmagick-reinforced to *Portal Slice* through, and Arnold was hardly using enough fire magicks that *Ash Husk* was relevant, but then . . . there were other abilities that maybe just *seemed* irrelevant.

Like *Shrill Perimeter*.

I already knew there was an enemy nearby—the alarm itself wasn't exactly useful right now—but the noise was. I flung both hands forward and summoned a twenty-foot glowing circle around Arnold. Being adept in magicks, this circle would have been visible for him, but in this circumstance it didn't matter. Because the sorcerer had ill intent, the system immediately recognized him as an enemy, and the spell immediately triggered.

The shriek of a banshee echoed across this desolate plain of wood stumps and low hills, but nowhere would it have been louder than in its very center. Where Arnold Orellan was.

He whipped his hands to his ears in surprise, covering them, shielding them from the noise, and he stopped his casting. This allowed the charging Arzak and Lore to grow closer to him without risk of being hit by spells, but it had another consequence that I hadn't intended.

The depth-raider—apparently incensed by the noise—hopped from the pocket of Arnold's robe, landing on the hard, cool mud, and began to bounce away from him. Or rather, it bounced toward Lore.

I released the spell—it had done its job, and I got the impression that I needed to save mana, as this could be a long fight.

"No!" the high sorcerer shouted, turning to reach down and scoop the creature up once more. It squealed—an eerie, bone-shaking, spine-crawling noise. Arnold Orellan stopped, spinning on the spot, and the intensity of the rage of his face was enough to encourage Arzak and Lore to a halt, as though fearful of what he'd release next.

And, it would turn out, they were right to.

"Enough of this," the high sorcerer spat. "I fled so that I would not need to harm innocents, but I think we're well past that." The man pushed the depth-raider back into his coat pocket, then raised both hands at his sides.

As he floated in the air, balls of magick appeared from nothing, spinning around him. I began to wonder if we hadn't bitten off more than we could chew.

And then the pain began.

CHAPTER FORTY

Total Sorcery

Arnold Orellan shoved his hands forward.

The dozens of orbs—of all manner of colors, sizes, effects, and types—that had been spinning around him like a tornado suddenly stopped spiraling, and soared toward all five of us.

We had only a split second to react, and my instinct was to protect the most vulnerable among us. I flung a hand back toward Corminar, opening a portal underneath him which he fell through before the blue orb could close it. The elf tumbled to the ground at mine and Val's feet. I then opened up another portal just ahead of us, with no more than a second to spare. It caught most of the spells heading in our direction, sending them into the sea at our right—I'd not had enough time to think about where to aim them—but still a few slipped through after the portal was forcibly closed. One of these spells—a fire spell, naturally, considering I'd *decided not to spend mana on Ash Husk*—caught my arm, searing the skin from it.

Up ahead, the charging Arzak and Lore had caught most of the spells, but where I'd shielded three of us with portals, Arzak had chosen to use her own body. She'd spun around as the spells had shot off toward us, wrapping her giant arms around Lore and preventing him from getting hit even once—which was more than I had managed.

Unfortunately, this also caused the old orc to collapse onto the floor.

"Val!" I shouted, pointing to our severely injured friend.

"On it!"

I opened a portal to help Val close the distance, but Arnold's magicks threatened to slam it shut before she could step through. I let it close myself, deciding not to risk any injury to Val, in case Arnold's spell stopped the portals from not closing around living beings.

Arnold raised his hands again, summoning the same storm of all kinds of sorcery, but we knew what to expect this time. I opened another portal amidst the tornado of magicks, and each of the orbs soared through . . . straight into the Iron Sea, where the high sorcerer lost control of them.

In the meantime, Corminar launched arrow after arrow after arrow into the enemy, but the man knocked all but one away with invisible, fleeting wards. The one that hit caught Arnold in the shoulder, and I thought at first that it hadn't done much damage. But then I saw the telltale black growths on the sorcerer's skin that told me Corminar had seen fit to use a poisoned arrow—a decision I was fully on board with.

Lore, too, had been on the move. While we'd both charged toward Arnold, he had the advantage, being both closer and larger of build. The barbarian reached the enemy as the sorcerer finished healing the poison before it could take root proper. Lore swung his Bane Sword at Arnold, but the sorcerer raised his hands just in time to summon another ward to stop the blow. The barbarian pushed against the magical barrier, grunting as he put all his weight into it, but soon it became as clear to him as it was to me that he wasn't going to win this one. He spun like a ballerina—a strange sight on a man his size—and swung again with his sword. Arnold moved to summon a ward once more to stop it, but then we all realized that Lore was up to something else.

As he slammed sword into ward, Lore slipped his hand into the sorcerer's pocket, and the depthraider squealed as it ran up the barbarian's arm to perch on his shoulder.

With the enemy distracted by Lore's attack, Corminar was able to slip another arrow past Arnold's wards—this one also poison-coated. The sorcerer slapped a hand to his neck to wrench the arrow out, blood spraying, and he was fast enough that not much of the poison could take hold.

I pressed the attack, arriving at Lore's side with my admittedly much smaller blade in hand, and together we *sliced* and *stabbed* at the enemy. Even with blood trickling from his neck, Arnold could fend off melee attacks from the both of us, though it seemed to strain him to do so. When my knife hit the wards, it wasn't like hitting a solid surface. Instead, the blade seemed to slide slowly through them. I tried pressing my weight into the knife and activating *Closed Reach*, but the wards were effective against magicks, too—my ability didn't do anything.

When I thought we might have finally overwhelmed Arnold Orellan, he seemed to get a new lease on life. His eyes, once brown, turned blue, and the wards grew larger, pressing into mine and Lore's attacks, forcing us away from him. And behind them, he summoned his whirlwind of spells once more.

On Lore's shoulder, the depth-raider squeaked, apparently becoming enchanted by whatever abilities the sorcerer was making use of. I glanced at its large, dark eyes growing wide, staring at Arnold and the magicks he was conjuring. The squeaking grew ever more excited-sounding with every passing moment.

"Val . . . ?" I cried out as I tried to slip blade past ward once more. "How're you doing? We need a hand over here."

"It's bad!" came the reply. "It's going to take some time."

"Just get her stable, we—"

The wards suddenly merged and expanded, and a wall of magicks blasted out from the high sorcerer, sending Lore and I flying through the air to land with a heavy thunk, me on top of him. Arzak's unconscious body slid across the dirt, bashing up against a tree stump, and Val slid after her. Even Corminar, furthest away from the enemy, almost fell from his feet, though Urlwan and the other elves arrived at his side to steady him.

"I don't like this . . ." I muttered, staggering off Lore and back to my feet. I turned back to the enemy to see that his power was growing ever more so.

Arnold Orellan's newly summoned tornado of spells grew greater than we'd seen before. Far greater. It twirled far into the sky, the man floating in the air, his eyes glowing with the sheer blue light of absolute sorcery.

And the depth-raider, too, began to glow.

"Guys . . ." Lore said. "Guys . . . we gotta . . ."

"Soldiers!" Corminar cried out. "On my mark, release!" I whipped my head toward him to see the elven diplomats lined up behind Corminar. They each had a bow in hand, the arrow tips coated in a substance that could only be some kind of poison. Meanwhile, Lieutenant Cladenor's eyes were on me. "As with the pyroknight," he shouted to—no, *commanded*—me. "Into the sea."

I nodded my understanding as the elf turned to Val, but my witch friend was ahead of him. She nodded. "I see where you're going with this."

"Soldiers? Fire!"

Seven elves fired as one. Though many of the arrows were blocked by spinning orbs or summoned wards, two of them slipped through and met their mark. The sorcerer's spells began to flicker, and then fade away, and I glanced at Corminar just long enough to hear him explain. "Poison of Mana-Halting. Ted's ideas aren't all bad."

I didn't know how long the effect would last for—I couldn't imagine long, if Corminar was new to this poison—so I launched into action. I flung one hand forward and one toward the Iron Sea, and I opened a portal below where Arnold was falling.

As the sorcerer slipped through the portal, landing in the sea with a splash, the depth-raider crackled, radiating the same glow as Arnold's eyes had moments earlier. Lore dropped it to the ground, backing off slowly. "Hurry!" he roared.

Val jumped across the beach to the edge of the Iron Sea, and she pressed her hands in the water once more. Huge lightning magicks shot out from her hands, making her limbs tremble as she sucked up the pain of her spell rebounding upon her. And then all the storm energy suddenly shot toward the high sorcerer.

Without access to his mana reserves, Arnold could not defend himself, and more importantly . . . he couldn't heal. Only when we got the notification that we'd defeated him did Val stop her spell, and she staggered away from the water then tumbled to the ground.

Level 38 High Sorcerer of Managlass defeated!

Worldbending: +7,900XP
Worldbending increased to Level 33!
Worldbending increased to Level 34!
Worldbending increased to Level 35!
Base Points Gained: +6 INT, +6 Free Points (INT/WIS/CHA)
Ability Selection Unlocked

. . .

It was quite the victory, and quite the display of the team working as one, but there wasn't time to celebrate. All eyes turned to the depth-raider.

Had we just made a huge mistake, exposing it to that kind of power?

I drew my knife and readied myself.

CHAPTER FORTY-ONE

The Tundras, Reimagined

The depth-raider's squealing, crackling, and glowing grew more and more intense with every passing moment, and I got the terrifying idea that it was about to explode.

But Lore, finding within himself a new source of courage, edged closer to the beast once more, his hand held out, palm up, trembling. "Shh," he said gently. "It's all over now. Shh . . ."

Oddly, the creature seemed to respond to him. It turned to face Lore, its wide eyes staring up at him, and the crackling and glowing softened some.

"There's a good boy," the barbarian continued. "Come back to daddy. There's a good boy."

The depth-raider softened more still, still looking up at Lore. It squeaked at him.

"Good boy . . ." Lore said, stepping steadily closer until his outstretched hand was just in front of the creature. After another moment of consideration, the depth-raider released its growing power, and it hopped back onto Lore's arm, then crawled up to perch on his shoulder. The amassed crowd stared silently as Lore petted the beast and then turned to face us. "What?" he asked, a toothy grin on his face.

"Is that . . . safe?" Val asked, whose *Healing* magicks had returned Arzak to consciousness, though she was still looking worse for wear. Those remaining injuries would need some time, or a stronger healer.

"Maybe put it back in the cage?" I suggested.

Lore looked around at the creature on his shoulder, then back at me. "I don't think it's going anywhere?"

I met Val's gaze, but she—like me—didn't have the energy to fight Lore on this point any further.

Behind us, the elven diplomats approached Corminar, and I could just make out what they were saying.

"Perhaps it is best we return home," said one elf whose name I didn't know, "if this is to be expected of human regions—betrayal and aggression around every corner."

"Indeed," another agreed. "We have been away from home for long enough; it is time we return to our own kind."

But Corminar shook his head. "Do not judge entire regions by the actions of one man. You will notice that for one monstrous sorcerer, there were four non-elves putting their lives at stake to see him brought to justice. If you are to judge the Goldmarch and the Tundras by any standard, judge it by *theirs*." He turned around to gesture at the four of us as he said this last bit, and I responded with a nod of gratitude.

Corminar convinced the elves to continue the last leg of their planned journey, telling them they'd paid us to accompany them to Lenktra, and that was exactly what we would do. From there, they could return home via ship—though they would admittedly have a full day's ride as they crossed land from the Iron Sea to the Sea of Roots. At least, unless the Great Golden Canal Project was finally complete, and those seas connected.

As we journeyed north, I turned my attention back to the not one but *two* ability selection choices I had to make—*Stealth* from the battle with the merfolk, and *Worldbending* from our fight with Arnold Orellan. I'd thought Val might have been relieved in a sense to be rid of the high sorcerer, but having killed him—even if in self-defense—she had retreated into herself a little. She'd assured me she was fine, but just needed a little space. It was the ability selection choices I concerned myself with while I was doing so.

Ability Selection Unlocked
Select an ability from the list below:
Option 1: Identify Traps (Stealth)—Search for traps in an area limited to eyesight range and determine how to disarm. Scales with [WIS].

The first of my two *Stealth* ability options was a good one, and one I'd found ample use of in a previous life. Though, admittedly, I'd made a career out of stealing, and so this ability was likely to have come in handy more often. Since teaming up with the Hero Slayers, had I really encountered that many traps? The ones I could think of, I could count on one hand.

Still, it didn't mean we wouldn't encounter any in the future, and even a single trap had the potential to be deadly. I mentally put this choice in the *maybe* column.

> **Option 2: Stealth Attack II (Stealth)**—*Upgrade to Stealth Attack. Passive.* 80 percent boost to damage when unnoticed by an enemy.

Being an upgrade to an existing ability, picking this one wouldn't broaden my effectiveness, but it made my existing strategies a lot stronger—putting the damage boost up from 50 percent to 80 percent. This might, in many cases, be the difference between taking an unsuspecting party down in one hit, and them surviving to counterattack.

After much consideration, I decided there was only one real answer to the question of which I picked.

> **Ability** Upgraded: Stealth Attack II
> **Stealth Attack II (Stealth)**: *Upgrade to Stealth Attack. Passive.* 80 percent boost to damage when unnoticed by enemies.

I was happy with that. Very happy indeed. But that was only one of two ability selections I had to make on this journey. I also had what was increasingly my core skill tree: *Worldbending*.

> **Ability Selection Unlocked**
> *Select an ability from the list below:*
> **Option 1: Far Hands II (Worldbending)**—While active, your *Barehanded* attacks have a 50-yard range, extended through portals.

I won't lie, this first one was a disappointment. I'd already ruled out *Far Hands* as not being useful twenty levels ago; I didn't—and was never going to have—sufficient *barehanded* strength for this to be viable. If I'd been able to use the ability for things other than attacks, I could see some functionality for it, but . . . No. I ruled it out.

> *Hidden condition met! Alternative ability choice unlocked.*
> **Option 2: Silence II (Worldbending)** [Requires: *Stealth* level 10]—Create a bubble of 20-yard radius in which sound is eradicated. Uses mana/second.

This was another upgrade to a skill I'd passed on before, but this one I could get behind. In fact, I'd almost selected the first version back at level 5, if memory served. I'd had concern then that five yards wouldn't be enough for this to be useful, but now that bubble was twenty yards. This could have been really useful in preventing eavesdropping, and maybe in any sneaking around I was doing, which would pair well with my *Stealth* abilities.

However, as I was about to discover, the third and final option also had a synergy with a skill I was leveling up.

> *Hidden condition met! Alternative ability choice unlocked.*
> **Option 3: Cloth Storage III (Worldbending)** [Requires: *Needlework* level 10]—Open a portal to an inventory space, wherein you can store up to 30 distinct *Needlework* supplies.

This, the third version of the *Cloth Storage* ability, was getting pretty strong. Whereas the first two versions had allowed for five and ten items respectively, this new one increased the limit to thirty—pretty huge. If I was serious about leveling up my *Needlework* skill—and I definitely was—then this would allow me to carry around a range of materials and tools without them weighing me down. Plus, maybe I could get a little trade out of it, buying and selling these goods at local towns based on their pricing.

It was a tough decision, this one. *Really* tough. I would have liked to talk Val's ear off about it, but I'd heard her when she'd said she needed some space, so I turned to Arzak instead.

"Storage," she grunted.

"Why?"

"You soft feet anyway. Basically silent. Not big, strong man."

"Thanks, Arzak," I said, pressing my lips together.

"Was compliment! I enjoy little guy. I like know can snap."

I wasn't entirely convinced by Arzak's logic (can you blame me?) but it was just enough to push me from straddling the fence. Besides, maybe there would be a *Silence III* ability option down the line anyway.

> **Ability Unlocked**: Cloth Storage III
> **Cloth Storage III (Worldbending)**: Open a portal to an inventory space, wherein you can store up to 30 distinct *Needlework* supplies.

I sighed, enjoying the sensation of gaining new abilities, and I even closed my eyes for a moment. This was a mistake, because it caused me to trip slightly on an old tree root that poked through the dry dirt, but fortunately I was at the back of the group and so nobody could have seen.

"You trip?" Arzak called out ahead of me without turning.

OK, maybe not.

"Clumsy little guy."

"Please stop calling me little," I replied. "I'm average height."

"For *human*, maybe."

We continued on, and the sun grew lower and lower in the sky, casting a red glow that was obscured only by vibrant white clouds. As we'd grown closer to Lenktra, the devastation of the Great Tundran forests was even more prevalent—there wasn't a tree left alive in sight, and there was absolutely no sign of any efforts to reforest. Whatever Lenktra had needed so much timber for was clearly a desperate need indeed, and so I was almost dreading climbing the final crest of the low hills that put the city in sight.

When we finally did, I breathed a sigh of relief to find that Lenktra was still standing—and, in fact, didn't seem to be under attack at all. It hadn't been a defensive need for timber, but then . . . what other needs were there?

And then, up at the front of the group, Lore suddenly came to a halt.

"What is it?" Val asked—one of the first things she'd said today.

The barbarian remained very still and very quiet, and so I and the rest of the Slayers joined him at his side. I followed his line of sight, then realized what he'd seen.

The flags atop the towers on Lenktra's walls weren't those of the duchy of Lenk. Instead, the flags were red, featuring the golden sun of the Golden Kingdom. Of the Goldmarch. Of Queen Amira.

"It's a conquest," I said, surprising myself with the words. "She's conquering—"

"No," Corminar said glumly.

"No? Cos it bloody well looks like—"

"It is not a conquest, Styk, because it's already over."

Niamh

Niamh stood over a large wooden table, one she'd had intricately carved to display a map of the region known as the Gentle Tundras. It had been an expensive pursuit, but coin was no object when you worked with Amira, Queen of the Goldmarch and future Empress of the Golden Empire. Upon the table, too, were small cast-iron sculptures of the castles in each town that boasted significant nearby land as part of their domain. And, finally, small statuettes of Goldmarch soldiers were dotted around the map, largely in cities or in their vicinities.

"This is up to date?" Niamh asked her chief aide. She nodded at the army on the western coast. "I thought we were projected to capture Garnokk last week?"

Sulla licked her lips. "Is correct. Chancellor Orjkan put up more resistance than we think. But think she flee now."

Niamh nodded to the orc. "Increase the pressure. Shift some of our 'bandits' from Aptleed—any remaining government in Garnokk should surrender within the week. Understand?"

"It take five days to—" Sulla started, but a sharp glare from Niamh cut her off. "Within week. Yes. Understand."

"Good." Still, Niamh stood over the table, hands clasped at its side. She took in every possible piece of information until she knew it intuitively; as with all things, she did not know when and how information would prove useful, just that it would. Her System-assigned class considered her an Expert Trapper, and she was, in a way—though she considered her greatest skill not to be the traps she laid with her hands, but those she laid with her mind.

Though Tana and Amira had since forgotten, the Tundran venture had initially been her plan. That they had gifted oversight of the project to Jacob had hurt at first, but the experiments in the eastern Goldmarch had proven intriguing in their own right. Still, she was happy that Jacob had failed in delivering upon this plan, so that she might now see it to fruition. Amira would get her reward, the Council's terms of the arrangement would be fulfilled, and then Niamh would be once more involved with their own grandest of schemes.

Her mind might have been Niamh's greatest asset, but that was no excuse to forsake training her other skills—that had been an oversight of late. "Walk with me," she told Sulla, and began walking down the corridors of her makeshift fort on the coast near Aptleed.

"There is other thing," Sulla said, her voice dropping to a near whisper, so Niamh knew it could be about only one thing.

The Player turned off from her planned route into a small room, where four of her commanders were discussing troop placements. "Out," Niamh said, pointing to the door, and the soldiers hopped to obey her order.

Only when they were alone in the room did Sulla speak. "Yusef and Ascendency Cult not happy."

"Tell me."

Sulla sighed. "His spies say Jacob killers are back in Tundras. Say you should have killed them now."

"They do know we have larger concerns right now? I am not going to go out of my way to deal with a band of peasants who happen to have ideas of god-slaying. Either Jacob was a one-off, in which case we have little need to worry, or he wasn't, in which case they are coming for me. If that should prove to be the case, I'll deal with them then, but not before."

"Will not make happy."

Niamh resisted the urge to huff; so many of her colleagues not capable of operating on her level was so often a source of frustration. "Then please remind their *dear leader* that I know his identity. I could reveal his crimes to the world in a matter of minutes, and then his life would be forever changed. Remind him of that, and then let's see if the pressure stops."

Of course, Niamh didn't just have documentation on Yusef, leader of the Cult of Ascendency. This cult was a group of devout Player-worshippers who believed that with enough devotion, the Players might take them to the so-called Ascended World. Of course, none of them knew that the "Ascended World" was broken, that even Niamh and her fellow Players couldn't return there for any length of time without risking harm or even death. But none of the Players were going to tell them that, for the cultists were so often a useful resource.

Stored away in her quarters, Niamh also had documentation on every member of the Council, whether or not they had intentionally revealed their identities. They may have kept their faces hidden, but there were always clues: their handwriting, their gait, their dominant hand, the topics that interested them, and the timbre of their voice—to name but a few.

Should the need arise, Niamh would have no hesitation but to blackmail. She did it for a noble cause; nobody wanted more than her for their plans to be successful, though other members of the Council did so often pose obstacles. Yusef was no exception—far from it—and the day was growing steadily closer that Niamh would have to make use of his file.

Niamh continued down the corridors to the training room she'd had built for herself, complete with a range of bows, targets, mana potions, and trap equipment. While Sulla continued her update, Niamh set about disarming and dismantling the traps from her last training session, which had been under the last moon.

"Timber," Sulla said. "Up twenty-two percent."

"We need it up at least forty," Niamh replied as she delicately unbound the enchantment on one of the traps.

"I know this. This is Garnokk. Lot of forest near Garnokk."

"Within the week," Niamh reminded her.

"Within week, yes."

"And logistics?"

"We paying farmers now to use their carts. Is working. Up more than thought. Even with no Garnokk, target hit in eleven days."

Niamh nodded to herself, taking this on board as she disarmed a bear trap by touch, the process so familiar to her by now. "Our lost leaders?" she asked, and Sulla began leafing through the papers she carried. "Did we ever track down Duke Cambelny, or the Duchess of Lenktra . . . Duchess Yar, was it?"

"Yua."

Niamh cursed herself silently. Perhaps there was too much on her plate; she should not have forgotten a name. Who knew what that error might have brought, down the line? "Yua. Yes. Did we retrieve her? Execute her?"

Sulla shook her head. "No sign. We think she move north. To Aptleed."

"Then she doesn't know Aptleed has fallen, too?"

"Looks like this, yes."

The Player sighed. "No matter. What harm could a few fallen crowns truly reap? They are nothing without their cities."

Niamh extrapolated from all this information. They were nearly there; this was almost enough, and the Great Golden Canal Project had reached its completion. Soon, the next stage of the plan would need to be put in action. The trap—*her* trap—would spring.

She took no joy from the fact that so many would die.

CHAPTER FORTY-TWO

The Sun Rises

"Stay low," I told the rest of the team, "trouble ahead."

Since dropping off the elven diplomats in the city of Lenktra—Queen Amira's latest addition to her kingdom—we'd headed north. All the whispers on the street said that Lenktra was far from the new Goldmarch border, and the queen's influence stretched much further into the continent. From what we knew of Niamh and the Council's involvement with Queen Amira, we could only assume that she would be at the front line, long since departed from Lenktra.

Val and I had tried to sneak into the city anyway, on the basis that we might have been able to get a more precise location out of someone. But we'd fallen at the first hurdle; in the queue at the gates, Goldmarch soldiers roughed up all those trying to get in, extorting them, sometimes seeming to do it purely for enjoyment. We could have portaled our way inside, but as we peered in through the gates, we could see how many soldiers in mustard surcoats were already inside. Moving around in Lenktra—and trying to find information—was going to be difficult. Instead, we turned north, and hoped the density of Goldmarch soldiers wouldn't be quite what it had been in Lenktra.

We couldn't have been any more wrong.

Soldier presence actually seemed to *increase* on the roads leading north, particularly toward the eastern coast. Wherever you looked, there were people in the sun-marked armor of the Goldmarch, and they definitely didn't get any better behaved outside of Lenktra. All of them seemed keen—or perhaps even *briefed*—to take whatever they wanted and to hurt anyone who tried to stop them.

I'd made that mistake once in the past couple of days, stepping in to stop a half dozen soldiers from taking the crop of an elderly farmer. We'd won the battle, but they'd been stronger than I'd anticipated, and Val once again had the opportunity to level up her *Healing* magicks to fix injuries to Lore, Corminar, and myself. She *healed* me last, as I "was the one who got us into this mess." At least I'd leveled up *Knifework* and *Worldbending* some in the process.

But all of this hadn't even been the worst of it. The morning after Lenktra, the team still groggy, having just awoken, Corminar had barged into mine and Val's shared bedroom and slammed a stack of papers onto the chest. I'd wiped my eyes, trying to focus them, and then my stomach lurched when I saw what the elf had brought in.

"Wanted posters," he said. "One for each of us. They know not our names, but the sketched likeness is largely very accurate."

"Largely?" Val said, picking one of the papers up, raising her eyebrows.

"I am more handsome in person," Corminar clarified.

The bounty placed on our heads had been . . . large, but that wasn't the most surprising part. The bit that shocked me most was *who* had placed the bounty—not Niamh, or the Council, as I might have expected, but the Cult of Ascendency. I hadn't thought about them in a long, long time. Not since killing that cultist who had attacked Val and I in that tavern, from whom I unlocked the *Worldbending* skill tree. That they'd be interested in us threw me for a loop, at least until I realized why.

The cult members were Player worshippers. Somehow, they knew we'd killed one of them. And they were out for revenge.

All of this led, days later, to the five—or six, as Lore insisted on the depth-raider's behalf—trying to sneak into a small village just off the main road, hoping to grab some overdue food. My stomach was rumbling just thinking about it.

"I swear we didn't have to sneak around so much until we met you," Val said, glancing in my direction along the low stone wall we were crouched behind.

"Are you really blaming me for—"

"You have a suspicious-looking face."

"No time for bicker," Arzak said, slapping Val and I around the head. "Not eat in long time. Need food."

I gestured to the two dozen Goldmarch soldiers milling about the village in front of us—almost enough of them to outnumber the locals. "We got time. Gotta wait for an opportunity. Unless you want to start a fight that we *definitely* can't win."

"Reckon it's time for a Styk-Val snatch and swap?" Lore asked.

"A what?"

"You know, that thing you do."

Val and I looked to one another, both apparently equally lost.

"Styk opens a portal, grabs a soldier, pulls them here, we all knock 'em out, and then Val wears their armor and changes into them," Lore explained.

"Lore . . . that's happened *once*," I replied. "Why do you have a name for it?"

"And why do you expect us all to understand it?" Val added.

Lore shrugged. "Sorry, thought you smart folk would know what I meant."

"He has point," Arzak said, interrupting both Val and me before we could respond to this strange assertion. "Good way get food. Soldier can do what want, nobody stop them."

I sighed, preparing myself to summon a portal on one of the soldiers who was out of sight of the rest. "Alright," I said to Lore and Arzak, "get ready to knock them out."

"Ready," Lore said with a toothy grin.

I nodded, opened a portal just behind the lone soldier, put my arms around them, and then tumbled backward through the portal, spilling out onto the ground next to them. Just as the soldier was crying out, "You fools! The army will—" Lore hit them around the head with the butt of his sword. Due to his strength, they passed out in one hit.

Level 18 Soldier of the Goldmarch defeated!

Worldbending: +650XP

"You know, we've really gotta do that more often," I said.

Lore mumbled his agreement.

"What was this about an—" Val started, and then Corminar suddenly straightened, alert. Not that he didn't always possess perfect posture—he did—but suddenly he found an extra half an inch in his spine and peered around, eyes wide.

"We must flee. Immediately," the elf said.

"What? Why?" I asked, looking around. Whatever he could see, I definitely couldn't. Though elven eyes and ears were so often said to be better than human senses, and he had the hunting abilities to back that up.

"An army," he said. "It approaches from the south."

We attempted to hurry around the town without being spotted, but there were enough soldiers ahead that it wasn't going to be easy, even with my low-glow *Tamed Portals* ability up my metaphorical sleeve. So we instead turned east, toward the distant Iron Sea, running while keeping low as the sound of marching grew louder and louder behind us.

"If we continue going east, the army will soon be upon us," Corminar said.

"Then what do you suggest?" I asked.

"We find cover."

Val dropped to the ground, placing her hands on the dust, and closed her eyes. She breathed deeply, and when she opened her eyes again, they glowed a gentle green. "There's a cave. Not far from here." She began jogging northeast.

We wasted no time in following her, but I had to ask, "How do you know? *Witchcraft*, was it?"

"Worms," she said. "With my *Summoning* magicks, I can sense them, too. And there's none in a large cavern a little way under our feet."

I nodded, and I accidentally pulled a face that reflected how impressed I was. I couldn't really risk inflating Val's ego any further.

We soon came upon a river, and following it upstream led us to a small opening in one of the banks—one still large enough to fit through if you crouched slightly, but obscured so that anyone passing might not see it.

"I not want go in," Arzak said as Lore and Corminar hopped in first.

"Why not? There's no other option," Val replied as I slipped into the dark. It was roomier than it looked from the outside—a reasonably sized cavern that seemed to go further back in the form of a couple of tunnels, but they were dark enough that I wasn't about to hurry into them.

"I not like small spaces."

"Close your eyes, then," the witch said, then she, too, slipped inside.

When it became clear that Arzak—the largest and most noticeable of us—wasn't going to step inside, I poked my head out, summoned a portal under her feet, and tossed her inside the cave. She grabbed at the rims of the portal to stop herself falling through completely, but an irritated "Arzak . . ." from Corminar had her release her grasp.

I closed the portal, and the cave fell into darkness once more, no longer illuminated by the gentle purple glow of my portal.

And then we waited. It was hard to know how long we waited—it seemed like a long time, though I had a feeling it wasn't as long as I thought—before we heard the army marching over our heads. The rumbling noise of the footsteps of hundreds—could it really be *hundreds*?—passing overhead grew louder, then quieter, and I breathed a sigh of relief that we'd escaped undiscovered.

But that celebration was a moment too soon.

Two faces appeared at the mouth of the cave, and from what little I could make out of their torsos, they were in the uniform of Goldmarch soldiers.

"Your turn," one of them said.

"Nah, it's yours."

"I did the last one!"

"The last cave wasn't a cave, though. Just looked like one. You still owe me."

There was a pause as the first soldier considered this counterargument, and then he said, ". . . Doesn't matter. Still your turn."

"Nah, cos if I do it, my head will be bitten off by a cave spider or something, won't it, knowing my luck."

"*Cave spider?*" Lore repeated under his breath. Someone—I couldn't see who—hit him, presumably to get him to shut his mouth.

"Alright," the other soldier said. "How about this: neither of us go in, and we just report that we did? Say we swept the lands all thorough and that."

There was the barest hint of a pause, as though the woman was trying really hard to be in two minds about it. "Yeah, fine. Deal."

With that, the two soldiers left, and the next sigh from me was surely not celebrating too soon. Right?

But then rocks fell, somewhere deeper inside the cave, followed by the sound of something approaching. It was too soon after all.

Gods damn it, me.

Arzak and Lore hurried toward the cave mouth, but I rushed to stop them. "Not yet. You go out there, and you'll be spotted. We'll have a whole army on us."

"Better that than a cave spider," Lore replied, only half whispering.

"No, it isn't and you bloody well know it. Now stand your ground and . . ."

But then I noticed something about the approaching sound. It wasn't the pattering of animal legs on stone, but the steady *dun-dun* of footsteps. Of a thick-soled boot, in fact. Whoever was inside this cave with us was . . . human.

"Weapons ready," I said, and Arzak and Lore drew their blades, rushing toward the noise to stand between the enemy and the more fragile members of our party—me included.

A gentle yellow glow appeared around the bend in the cave tunnel—flickering, so it was flame, not magick. We stayed deathly still as the noise grew closer, praying that the potential enemies didn't know we were there, affording us the advantage we might so desperately need.

The figures that came into view were not what I'd expected. Their faces were graying, their movements weak, their body language saying they hadn't eaten in days. These weren't enemies; these were people in trouble. Yet their clothes said they should have been anything but. They wore the sorts of threads we'd seen in the palace at Auricia—definitely not clothes suitable for delving into caves. So what could they have been doing down here?

The woman at the front of the group—who carried herself with her head held high, despite her obvious tiredness—studied us with glossy eyes.

"Who are you?" Val asked, after a moment of the two groups staring one another down.

It was the woman who spoke. "You may put down your weapons. I have a feeling we share the same enemies."

"Not until you tell us who you are," the witch continued.

The pale woman sighed. "You have the honor of speaking to Duchess Yua of Lenktra. Now, please, put down your weapons. We must talk."

CHAPTER FORTY-THREE

Fallen Crowns

After the army had moved on—turning northeastward, from the sounds of it—we Slayers led Duchess Yua of Lenktra and her group out of the cave. I portaled them into an abandoned barn that Val and I spent an hour scouting out, shielding them from sight in a place that didn't have them worrying about cave spiders. Even better, the barn had a lock on it, presumably placed there by its absent owner, who might have been fleeing the conquering soldiers. This meant we didn't have to worry about anyone getting in easily.

Val, disguised as one of the soldiers, brought everyone some food, and the duchess and her group ate hungrily before finally committing to their previous promise to talk.

After some kind of nonverbal signal from Duchess Yua, she and another man rose to walk over to where I and the other Slayers were sitting, eating food that was long overdue for us, too.

"Duke Cambelny of Aptleed, at your service." The man at Duchess Yua's side bowed awkwardly, clearly not accustomed to bowing all that often. "Behind me are my wife, Kim, and my children, Tim, Jim, and—"

"How many of you *are* there?" Val interrupted. "Not in your family. Fallen leaders, I mean. Lenktra, Aptleed . . . where else has fallen to Amira?"

"We believe that every town of note west of Tanar has fallen," Duchess Yua answered. "Though reports do vary. The advancement of the Goldmarch has been swift; each of us struggled with the rising bandit problem and were eager for aid from someone we thought an ally. Of course, we did not know then what Amira intended, and her agent in the Tundras moved on all cities near simultaneously."

"Am I to assume you understand the nature of the bandits?" Corminar asked. "That they were the very same soldiers, out of uniform?"

The duchess nodded. "We understand that now, but of course 'now' is too late."

"You say all cities fall?" Arzak asked. "Where other leaders?"

"Many have passed on," Duchess Yua replied. "Not all, but only a handful of us were lucky enough to escape. Not all of us had sufficient escape strategies. Those who escaped number only myself, Duke Cambelny, and—or so the reports say—Chancellor Orjkan of Garnokk, with whom we are supposed to meet at Fort Tanil in two days. Of course, that will not happen; even if we were to depart this very moment, it would take three days to reach the fort by foot. This precludes, too, any chance of encountering Goldmarch soldiers on our journey—a chance that is more likely than not."

A moment of silent contemplation passed over the barn. I didn't like it.

"You're telling us a lot," I said. "Stuff that could get you killed."

"Do we not all hide in this building together? I think it likely that you, too, would lose your lives in any encounter with the Goldmarch."

"They might try, but they would not succeed," Corminar clarified, though if we encountered a whole bloody *army* then I wasn't so sure about that.

Val shifted from foot to foot at my side, and a quick glance over at her told me she was wrestling with saying something—caught between biting her tongue and speaking her mind.

"I much enjoy your confidence," Duchess Yua said, a twinkle in her eye as she glanced Corminar up and down, "though I suspect you underestimate our enemy. In ability, perhaps, they are middling, but they number enough to outweigh any such weakness. And of course, that is to say nothing of their leader in the Tundras, who—it seems—is of considerable intellect. Their capacity for strategy certainly cannot be overstated."

At my side, Val broke, her mouth opening compulsively, as it so often did. "They're a Player," she said. When Duchess Yua turned to her, eyebrow raised, Val continued, "The woman in charge. We believe she's a Player, operating on Queen Amira's behalf." The witch then went quiet, allowing this information to soak in the silence that followed.

"We know," the duchess finally replied, her tone glum. "A woman by name of Niamh. It is she with whom Duke Cambelny and Chancellor Orjkan negotiated their deal: Goldmarch soldiers would enter their cities in order to help deal with the bandit menace. I am ashamed to say it was a man named Jacob—a strange, frivolous man, but still wearing the title of *Player*—with whom I came to my own arrangement. In hindsight, so obvious a ploy, yet who would think to call into question the sincerity of a Player, of all people?"

"Then you know it is your trust of Players that cost you everything," Corminar said, holding Yua's gaze as it lingered on him.

The duchess nodded, though even this seemingly stoic woman could not help but blush. I supposed it was embarrassment rather than Corminar's gaze that did it, though I'd seen the latter have the same impact on many occasions. "Indeed."

"This is what Players are like, you know," Val said. "They're just people. Descendants of the Architects, sure, but just people. People with a good public image. You lot might think they're all heroes, but that's about as true for them as it is for the rest of us. And you know what? Maybe that's even *more* true for them—something about being lauded seems to go to their heads.

"You might think they're heroes. You might *still* think that, but they're not. They just do whatever gets them money. Or power. Or fame. They're just as mortal as the rest of us."

Throughout all of this, Duchess Yua met Val's gaze, not glancing away for a second. In that moment, I got the sense that she'd actually been a good leader—ready to listen, even if it challenged her dearly held beliefs. This was a woman who could keep an open mind. But still, she needed someone to tip her over the edge.

I put my hand on the small of Val's back to comfort her, the thought of Niamh—the woman who'd once tried to kill her—clearly having distressed her, but I kept my attention on the once leader of Lenktra. "One man's hero is another man's enemy," I said. "That's the nature of questing; there's always some-one suffering on the other end. It just so happens that it's *you doing the suffering* this time, not some criminal or murderer or someone who might deserve it."

Finally, the duchess's steady gaze broke, snapping down to the floor. She sighed, and with it, I got the impression that it was a sigh she'd been keeping in for a good long time. "I know," she said. "I know. I tell myself that all I can do now is mend that which I have broken, but . . ." She sighed once more, turning to the man at her side. "We should discuss."

Duke Cambelny replied to her with a nod. "If you will excuse us," he said, followed by another poorly practiced bow. The two once-leaders left me and the rest of the team alone in the corner of the abandoned barn.

"What make of them?" Arzak said, keeping her voice quiet, at least for her.

"They're desperate," Lore said, "but I guess I'd be desperate, too. I think we can trust 'em."

Val piped up next. "Trust is one thing, helping them is a whole other."

"Who said we help them?" Arzak asked.

"It'd be the heroic thing to do," I cut in. "I thought you were all on board with that? Killing heroes is just gonna make people hate us—even if those heroes aren't *actually* heroes. But if we can present ourselves as an alternative . . ."

"Even if we ain't heroes," Lore said, "the Tundras is still our home. If we do nothing, and Amira and her soldiers keep taking towns for her kingdom, then we ain't gonna have one. A home, I mean. It'll be gone."

"You believe we—a mere five people—could make a difference?" Corminar asked.

"Maybe not us, but . . ."

"They can," I finished for Lore, nodding to the exiled leaders. "You ever heard a bad word about them? You get all these stories about foreign lords and kings and such, and they sound tyrannical. But this lot? They're popular. They'll be able to bring people back to their cause."

Val looked up at me, her brown eyes dark in the low light, giving me the impression that she was studying me. She looked away when I met her gaze, and nodded. "Styk's right. This lot? They've gotta be around after we kill Niamh. They gotta be around to take back what they lost."

Lore nodded eagerly, though Corminar and Arzak hesitated in following suit. "Long as we not die in process," the orc said.

"Do we ever?" I asked.

"You have twice," Arzak pointed out.

"Oh, yeah." Maybe that wasn't quite as good an argument as it had originally seemed.

A few minutes later, Duchess Yua of Lenktra and Duke Cambelny of Aptleed returned to us, bringing their families and remaining personal guard with them this time. It seemed this was a conversation that all involved needed to be privy to.

"I can see that you are strong." The duchess glanced at me as if to say "except you," but I let it go. "You do not live so long as a duchess without a highly leveled *Identification* skill, believe me. Perhaps, then, we might pay you to escort us to Fort Tanil? There, alongside Chancellor Orjkan, we intend to scheme, to plan how we take back our cities from the invaders. We would pay handsomely—we conceal gold, gems, and artifacts on our person—and do not believe we would make it there alive without protection."

"You wish to add mercenaries to your revolution?" Corminar asked.

"I wish to *survive* our revolution. Will you help us?"

I stepped forward and reached out a hand. Duchess Yua took it.

CHAPTER FORTY-FOUR

Roots of Revolution

It took as many as five days to reach Fort Tanil, on the southwestern coast of the Tundras. It was a two to three day journey under normal circumstances, but we'd had to avoid Goldmarch platoons marching north, and we'd had to double back some to cover our tracks.

That wasn't to say we'd entirely avoided fighting, however. Sometimes, it had been quicker to deal with the smaller handfuls of soldiers than it had been to go around them—which had the added benefit of turning the war effort in our favor, in some small, small way.

There'd been another benefit, too, in fact. The few skirmishes we'd had on our way here had helped me level up *Worldbending* to level 38 and *Knifework* to level 31. Because the latter skill had passed another milestone level, the system had given me the opportunity to choose from a couple of abilities. There had been no *Execution* ability upgrades this time around, but I had upgraded *Stab* to level 3, which offered a 50 percent increase to damage. Because this ability had proven so useful lately, this was what I had opted for, though I was yet to use it in its upgraded state.

We'd come across areas of unpatched woodland on our journey west, but we'd lost hope of finding more landscape untouched as we grew nearer to the lands governed by Garnokk. Once more, the story was the same: trees that were decades—if not centuries—old, had been felled down to a stump. Wherever the wood had gone to wasn't clear, though I did on occasion see impressions in the dirt suggesting that laden carts had headed northeast. This sparse landscape had left little cover to hide behind, and so Corminar and Arzak had been on careful watch of the horizon; if they could see any enemies, then it was likely that they could see us, too.

But the last day of travel—our fastest day by far—was devoid of any enemies, who were concentrating in the east rather than the west. As such, we arrived at Fort Tanil at around dusk, and we arrived there to discover trouble brewing.

Lore and Corminar raced ahead the moment we first heard the shouting of battle, while Arzak, Val, and I remained with our defenseless party of exiled leaders and their families. Soon enough, Corminar returned, darting back and waving for us to hurry. Val, Arzak, and I charged ahead, deciding that any danger posed to Yua, Cambelny, and company was probably based in the tower ahead of us.

At the base of the tower was an orc woman, who managed to look glamorous despite wearing heavy armor and carrying a greatsword in a sheath over her shoulder. She and Lore were looking up at the tower, where the shouting was coming from.

"Chancellor Orjkan, I assume?" I asked the woman as we arrived at her side.

She nodded, her expression serious. "And personal guard. All that left, at least." Her way of speaking was less noticeable than some orcs I'd met—Arzak included—which suggested to me that she'd spent a good amount of time among humans, elves, and other races.

"Your guard are inside?" Val asked. "Who are they fighting?"

"Is not *who*. Is *what*. Forest spirits are inside. Dryads." As she said this, a worrying cry echoed out from the tower. "We try to clear out, but are outnumbered. If you get inside, maybe some of them survive. You can help?"

"We're pledged to," I replied, though the pledge in this case was a monetary transaction rather than the usual hero deal; I would work on that with the Slayers at a later date.

I reached a hand up at the tower and opened a portal inside, through a small arrow slit in the round stone building. Lore was through in an instant, having grown used to portal travel by now, and Arzak followed soon after, as she was the other part of the team that could take a few hits. After a few seconds passed, and when we were sure it was safe enough, Corminar, Val, and I followed them inside.

We stepped into chaos.

In the center of this floor of the tower, we joined three of Orjkan's soldiers, each of whom were covered in wounds. Down the adjoining corridor, I got my first look at the forest spirits—treelike beings that floated gently through the air. Petals dropped from their skin, and these shapes glided slowly around and toward us.

"Don't let petal touch you!" one of the soldiers roared at Lore and Arzak as they hurried to the door to protect the rest of our party.

"Why?" Lore asked, and then quickly had his question answered. One of the petals brushed against Lore's arm. Though it floated slowly and gently through the air, the edge of the petal sliced through his bracer as though it were butter, and moments later blood poured from the wound.

"Val?" I asked, turning to the witch.

But she was in a bit of a daze. "Yeah? What?"

"Lore! He needs healing."

"Right." She nodded and ran to his side, taking care to hide around the corner, where the dryads wouldn't be able to attack her.

While Lore clutched his bleeding arm, Arzak sliced at the floating petals with her dual blades. These petals moved slowly enough that hitting them was no trouble. Once she sliced them in two, they dropped limply to the ground, where they rotted at an accelerated pace. But there were enough of them that Arzak had to keep moving, with no opportunity to pause, otherwise she and Lore would be hit.

I opened a portal between us and the dryads to slow the advance of the petals, and though I could send the flowery attack back at our enemies, all of the petals turned around in midair to soar back at us once more. "Ah," I said.

Corminar poked up behind Arzak to fire an arrow at the dryads, landing the attack perfectly. It caused the enemy to stagger, the arrow wedged into its body—or trunk?—but not seeming to do enough damage to slow the attack. The elf turned to a soldier. "Please, a small cloth and a lit torch."

The soldier replied with a nod, then set about striking iron on flint next to an unlit wall torch.

"I don't . . ." Val started, but a heavy wave of petals forced everyone else's attention away from her.

"Fire!" the soldier said, hurrying back to Corminar's side with a torch, handing a piece of torn cloth—from his own tunic—to the elf, who wrapped it around the head of an arrow. I could see where he was going with this: wood and fire made a deadly combination. Corminar nocked the flaming arrow, aimed it, and—

"No!" Val roared, snapping her hand out toward Corminar.

It was too late. He fired.

Instinctively, some deep-rooted part of me recognized the fear in Val's voice and realized that she'd have very good reason for not wanting Corminar to launch the attack. So I stopped it. I reached out and opened a portal in the arrow's path, catching it and sending it slamming into the wall above our heads. Fortunately, there was no wall decoration or anything around it to catch fire, or then we might have been in trouble—we'd have spent a week traveling here only for me to burn the would-be revolution headquarters down at the earliest opportunity.

The elf turned on me, then Val, then looked back to me again, not quite sure who he blamed more for his failed attack. "Would one of you care to explain why—"

"How many of you are there?" Val asked, turning to the soldier at Corminar's side.

"Eight. Or was. Not sure how many now."

"Three of you here, so potentially five of your colleagues out there? *Killing* the dryads?"

Lore hesitated a moment at this, almost missing one of the petal attacks he was trying to take down. "Why'd you say it like that?"

Val gulped. "They're beings of *witchcraft*. I didn't know what I was sensing before, but it . . . it was their feelings. Their thoughts. They're one and the same I think, and . . ." She trailed off, then shook her head to get herself back to the heart of the matter. "Point is: the dryads, they're not evil. They're just . . . like us. Refugees. Trying to survive. Their homes torn down by the Golden Kingdom."

". . . The trees," I said.

Val nodded glumly. "We don't have to kill them," she said. "We have to *save* them."

CHAPTER FORTY-FIVE

Holding Back

"Save them?" one of Orjkan's personal guard repeated. "They try kill us!"

"Did they? Or were they just trying to defend themselves?" Val replied. "They find themselves a home, a place where they can escape their attackers, and—"

"We not their attackers!" the orcish soldier cried. "We not Goldmarch soldiers!"

"Do you think *they* know that? Do you think they see the difference in our kind? Or do you think they were lacking that nuance, just like you were?"

The soldier stared back at her, dumbfounded.

"Cos you saw them and immediately assumed they were monsters to be slain, didn't you? You didn't stop to ask yourself not just whether you *should*, but whether you *had to*."

"Guys . . ." Lore said, he and Arzak still frantically slashing at the forest spirits' petal attacks, which weren't slowing. If anything, the attacks seemed to be growing more frantic.

"Styk," Val said, ignoring the barbarian to look to me. "Portal."

I nodded, then ran over to the arrow slit so I could see the ground below, and I opened a portal down there that paired with one in the room.

"In," Val ordered the orcish soldiers. "Now."

"But this—"

"*Now*," the witch said again, and she did so with such force, and such a glare, that three orcs more than twice her size slumped their shoulders and did what she instructed.

Once the three soldiers were out of the way, I closed the portal behind them to conserve mana. Even with all the points I'd put into Intelligence these past few months, I still only had so much mana to use—and all the more recently acquired *Worldbending* abilities used more mana than the basic ones.

"You think you can get the dryads to stop attacking us?" Lore asked, sweat dripping down his forehead and chin.

"Maybe if those other soldiers stop attacking *them*!" Val turned to me. "Think you can portal us around until we find them?"

"I think if we can break off *this* attack then we might not need to search. We'll be able to hear them."

"Mm," Arzak agreed. "Attacking or screaming."

I hurried over to the other side of the tower, the arrow slits over here looking down onto the main courtyard of Fort Tanil, as well as onto the walls. I spied two of the soldiers down below, fighting off petal attacks in much the same way as Arzak and Lore were. The difference was that these soldiers were outnumbered. "I see two," I said. "Get ready to portal. At Lore and Arzak's side."

Corminar nodded, and he and Val ran behind the other two members of the party, standing just behind them and shielding themselves from any attacks. I opened a portal on top of a wall below and its partner just below the rest of the team's feet. They fell through, and suddenly dozens of petals turned toward me instead.

"Oh, right, yep," I said, then closed the portal and opened another pair, through which I fell to the top of the wall below.

The rest of the team were already fixing their attention on the battle below, doing their best to draw the attacks of the forest spirits so that the orcish soldiers wouldn't be so overwhelmed. But they could only defend against the dryad attacks, not wishing to do damage of their own.

"Styk? You gonna hurry up or what?"

"Hold your bloody horses," I replied to Val, and crept over to the edge of the wall to get a look at the soldiers below. Petal attacks rose up to meet my face, and I cowered backward just in time to avoid having my cheeks sliced.

Arzak swept in to deal with the rising attacks, dual blades sweeping rapidly through the air. "I say when clear," she said.

"But Val said—"

"No time for bicker," the orc interrupted, then added, "now go!"

Trusting in my party member, I peered again over the edge of the wall, one hand reaching forward. The two soldiers had become separated as the dryad attacks overwhelmed them, so I was forced to open a portal below one and throw him into the air above the other. The moment the soldier appeared, falling through the other side of the portal, I opened up another pair below the both of them to bring them up to the wall with us. They tumbled to the stone, clutching their heads and their wounds, and then one of the two soldiers vomited.

"I get *Worldbending* sickness," she explained.

"OK," I replied, not really sure what to do with this information.

"Where are the others?" Val demanded of the soldier who wasn't throwing up.

Looking up at her in a daze, dozens of cuts on his skin that were in dire need of *healing*, the soldier pointed back to the tower. "In there. At ground."

Val looked up to me, and I nodded once more. I stepped back from the two orcish soldiers to give my portal space and then sent the pair of them tumbling—and vomiting, probably—once more, landing them outside of the fort and out of trouble.

"Styk . . ." Lore said nervously as the petal attacks—now focused entirely on us—threatened to overwhelm him and Arzak.

One of the forest spirits, larger than the rest, with eyes glowing not just green, but blue, too, suddenly pressed its arms into the ground. The moment its body touched dirt, new roots suddenly shot through the ground, erupting from it in a line that rushed toward the wall.

"Time to go, I think!" Lore cried as the roots shot toward him at a frightening pace.

"Jump!" I shouted, and the whole team did as I'd suggested, leaping from the top of the wall. We fell through the air just before the dryad's attack reached where Arzak and Lore had been standing moments earlier, shattering the wall, and I reached down to open a portal beneath us.

The five of us fell out the portal at the other side, at the base of the tower, tumbling across the ground. Arzak—so often the most agile, surprisingly—was on her feet first, running for the doors and presumably about to tear them open to grant us entrance to the—

Arzak charged through the old, rotting doors, splitting them from their frames. *Or that. That works, too.*

The other four of us followed inside, bursting in on a fight between the last two soldiers of Orjkan's personal guard. But where the previous soldiers had been outnumbered, this time it was the orcs overwhelming a single dryad. A dryad on the verge of dying, it looked like.

Rotting petals littered the floor where a weakened forest spirit lay, raising a shaking arm in a pointless attempt to block the swinging blade of one of the orcish soldiers. I wasn't quick enough with my portals to stop him, but Val, fortunately, was.

She roared as she lit up with a green glow, and roots shot forth from the ground in much the same way as the dryad's had outside a moment earlier. The roots burst toward the soldier's sword arm, wrapping themselves around it in midswing, and stopping the blade before it could reach the dryad.

The soldier turned his head to Val, eyes wide. "They enemy! Not us!"

"No they bloody aren't!" she cried.

The other soldier, seeking to end this fight even despite the team's involvement, charged toward the fallen dryad, greatsword arching through the air. Val shot her hand forward to summon more roots, but they snapped against the soldier's running feet, unable to get purchase.

Corminar whipped an arrow from his quiver and shot it toward the charging soldier's foot, and . . . missed. Or, at least, that's what I initially thought. The arrow buried itself in the ground just ahead of the soldier's leading foot, doing no damage. But within a split second, the orc moved that foot again in his sprint toward the "enemy," and the arrow was so deeply embedded in the ground that he tripped on it, falling to the floor.

"They're *not* your bloody enemies!" Val shouted, summoning more roots that this time found purchase on the fallen orc, binding him to the ground. Only when it was clear that he wasn't getting out of his own accord did Val sigh.

"Err . . . guys?" Lore said, standing at the door and peering out. "It's good that you saved that one, but what about this lot?"

I turned to look outside and saw the other forest spirits floating menacingly toward us. Fast. "If you're gonna get them to stop attacking, Val, now might be a good time to do it."

The witch nodded and touched her hands to the ground once more. This was something she did a lot, I noticed, and I was starting to wonder if this wasn't about getting more in touch with nature—the heart of *Witchcraft* abilities. She glowed green once more as she activated her magicks, and veins of magical energy shot through the ground toward the strange creatures, but then . . . they faded.

"Doesn't look like it's working," I said.

"Yes, thank you," Val replied. She furrowed her brow, thinking deeply, and then turned back to me. "Styk—get me on top of them. The largest one. With the blue and green eyes."

I knew better than to argue—well, I didn't, but I decided not to on this particular occasion—and I opened a portal in front of Val, its partner in the space just above the space between the door and the dryads. "Get ready . . ." I waited until the largest spirits were directly under the portal. "Now!"

Val leaped through, appearing in the air above the creatures, and tumbled down onto the dryad. She grabbed at its shoulders and neck, steadying herself, and tried to climb onto its shoulders as it twisted and turned, trying to rid itself of this new attacker. The witch hung on for dear life, slowly getting to a point where she had her hands positioned on either side of the creature's head. When she activated her powers this time, both her eyes and the largest dryad's glowed a bright green.

Within a second, the dryad's advancement came to a halt.

"Did it work? Did you—" I started to ask.

8 x Forest Spirits defeated!

Worldbending: +4,900XP
Worldbending increased to Level 39!
Worldbending increased to Level 40!
Base Points Gained: +4 INT, +4 Free Points (INT/WIS/CHA)
Ability Selection Unlocked

. . .

Yes, then. It absolutely *did* work.

CHAPTER FORTY-SIX

A Legion Is Born

Only Val could communicate with the dryads, and so naturally she managed the peace talks between these strange creatures and the exiled leaders. As it turned out, peace talks weren't something that happened particularly quickly, so that left me, the rest of the Slayers, and the families and guards of the leaders kicking about a bit.

One soldier was showing Lore and Arzak a new orcish card game, and though it was new only to the human, he seemed to be consistently winning it, much to the annoyance of everyone else. Still, it was hard to be annoyed at Lore, particularly with his goofy smile and sincere excitement at having the best hands. Corminar, meanwhile, was busy making another batch of potions, me having used the last of his mana vials to replenish after the fight.

I, meanwhile, occupied myself by wandering around the now quiet fort and reviewing my ability selection choices. It really hadn't been long since my last *Worldbending* ability, I noted, though there'd been a fair few fights between then and now. Not to mention that Arnold Orellan had been of quite a high level, too. I supposed that at this rate, that 900 percent boost to experience points offered by the *Legacy of Sisyphus* effect really would bring me back in line with my peers, eventually. At least, it would if we kept getting into these sorts of scrapes.

Ability Selection Unlocked
Select an ability from the list below:
Option 1: Skinsmith III (Worldbending)—Toughen skin to act as natural armor. Strength of armor scales on [WIS]. Uses significantly less mana/second.

I knew deep down that I should pick a *Skinsmith* ability at some point, because I hadn't invested all that much in Vitality to increase the size of my health bar. But I already had my *Warped Shield* ability, which used mana to deflect any melee attacks—at least, low-level ones—and that meant the low investment in Vitality maybe didn't matter. Besides, I was sure to get an upgraded version of it at some point, and I could only assume this would increase its ability beyond "low-level."

With all this in mind, I was very much on the fence about picking this ability. I didn't want to rule it out entirely, but I had other options to review first.

> **Option 2: Ash Husk III (Worldbending)**—*Upgrade to Ash Husk.* Convert your flesh to ash, strengthening it against flame for ten minutes. Gain 90 percent resistance to fire attacks.

It was another upgrade—I'd had a lot of these sorts of options lately, it felt like—but this was a very encouraging one. The ability to have 90 percent resistance to fire attacks would greatly increase my strength . . . when fighting users who specialized in fire magicks. There were a lot of these, admittedly, which did make this choice a compelling one, but I had to admit it was more niche—if more powerful—than just picking the *Skinsmith* ability.

I kept this option in the running and opened up my third and final option.

> *Hidden condition met! Alternative ability choice unlocked.*
> **Option 3: Pocket Worlds (Worldbending)** [Requires: Any storage *Worldbending* ability]—*Replaces Cloth Storage III.* Open and access pocket dimensions. Storage capacity of summoned pocket worlds scales with [INT] of creator.

There was a lot to take in here. I'd only just gained *Cloth Storage III*—I hadn't even had a chance to use it yet, as we'd hardly been by any shops lately—and already I could replace it. Normally, I would have ruled it out immediately; I wanted to at least test how an ability might work in the real world before I upgraded or evolved it. But in this case . . . I could see *exactly* how it would change. I would no longer be restricted to just *Needlework* supplies, which I would still want to include, but would be able to carry just about anything.

I could carry *Alchemy* supplies for Corminar, or I could have an array of knives, each suited for a particular type of enemy. Or I could store Lore's sheep in there, if I ever became a weird elven crime lord, like Elandor. The possibilities were endless.

And that was before I even interrogated the wording. "Open and access pocket dimensions" didn't specify it had to be *my* pocket dimensions, did it? It was almost worded like I could access them in general.

The two health bar proxy abilities would have to wait to come around again; I knew exactly which one I wanted to pick.

> **Ability Unlocked**: Pocket Worlds
> **Pocket Worlds (Worldbending)**: Open and access pocket dimensions. Storage capacity of summoned pocket worlds scales with [INT] of creator.

And then, of course, I did exactly the same thing anyone would do in the situation of just having unlocked the *Pocket Worlds* ability—I tested it. I turned to find a weed at my side and decided it was probably as good a trial item as any. I ripped it from the ground and turned to find an empty patch in front of me. There, I opened my pocket world portal.

It came as naturally to me as opening any portal, and the portal itself even appeared largely the same. Though, there were two notable differences: the glow of the magicks of this portal were darker, and there was no partner to it. At least, not on this plane of existence. I resisted the urge to stick my head straight into the portal and instead pushed the weed inside, letting as little of my arm go into the portal as possible. I released the weed, pulled my hand out, and allowed the portal to close. There were no system messages or anything—nothing, in fact, to let me know how much of my pocket world's capacity the weed had used up. I supposed I would only find out that I was at capacity when I wasn't able to push anything else inside.

I gave the portal world another few moments before opening an access again, and I put my hand into it to find the weed. My fingertips touched . . . nothing. My stomach churned; was I not going to be able to retrieve things I put in here again? Was this ability pointless without some way of summoning the stored items once more? Was I not going to be able to pull this weed from the—

As soon as I thought of the weed, it seemed to shoot to my hand within the portal. I closed my grip around it and pulled it out, and the weed was just as it had been going in. If what Elandor had said about his version of this ability was true, then no time had passed for the weed—there had been no chance for anything to happen to it.

I took a deep breath, staring at the portal, and then stuck my head in. I simply had to know.

Inside, it was like how I imagined it would be to be inside a large, fluffy, purple cloud. Every way you looked, all you could see was the same purple glow that existed on the portals themselves, though it was speckled slightly in here with tiny dark dots, as though some other material was fighting to get in.

Well, now I knew, and it seemed pleasant enough. I pulled my head back out and allowed the portal world to close.

". . . What're you doing?" Val asked, appearing in front of me at the other side of the portal.

"New ability. Just testing it."

The witch raised an eyebrow, apparently unable to stop a smirk from crossing her face.

"You done with the dryads?"

Val nodded. "Yua is sipping tea with them as we speak."

"Ooh, tea?"

"I wouldn't. This isn't normal tea; it's nasty root stuff. Yua's being polite when she says it's nice, I reckon."

I slumped my shoulders; I'd been in the mood for a nice cup of tea.

"Turns out they have a lot in common after all. I didn't exactly have to do much." Val looked over at Yua, Cambelny, and the forest spirits, and I followed her line of sight. The cups of tea in their hands were glowing green, and suddenly I didn't have quite so much of a craving. "Yua and her lot want their cities back, and the dryads want their forests back. They have the same enemy, and want different things out of fighting them—there's never been such a good groundwork for a diplomatic relationship."

"You know a lot about diplomatic relationships, then?" I asked.

"I read." Val shook her head. "Anyway, I came to get you. We're all supposed to gather. Yua's gonna speak to us all."

I followed Val back to where the exiled leaders and the forest spirits had been talking, and found the rest of the team—as well as the soldiers and families—making their way there, too. I remained at the back of the milling crowd, leaning against a nearby wall, as Yua spoke.

"Thank you all for your patience," she started, pausing to sweep her eyes across the crowd, seeming to look at every single face. "We have discovered much in common with our new forest friends. So quick were we to fight that we did not realize that we shared an enemy. We have Equivalence to thank for reminding us of this." Yua nodded to Val, at my side.

Sometimes I forgot that Val's full name was Equivalence. That really was a terrible name.

"Still," the ex-Duchess of Lenktra continued, "we have much work ahead of us. Together with our dryad allies, we will take the battle to Amira's soldiers, and their general in the region: the woman known as Niamh. It will be long, and it will be grueling, and we have few soldiers in comparison to Amira's own legion.

"But we have something that she does not: loyalty that extends beyond coin. Her soldiers fight because they are paid, but the brave people of the Tundras will fight *because it is their home*. We will recruit where we can, and we will strike only where we can deal maximum damage to Amira's empire. We will need to be smart with our strategy—that goes without saying—but I do believe one thing above all else: we will triumph."

At this, a smattering of folk in the small crowd cheered, while others clapped.

Though the reaction was quiet, I sensed that those who heard Yua's speech were encouraged by it, that many of them also thought winning wasn't so impossible.

When the crowd dispersed, Yua locked eyes with Val and came striding through the amassed audience to take my friend—*friend* didn't feel like the right label for what we were now, but this wasn't the right moment to work that out— by the hands.

"In case I did not make it clear," the ex-duchess said. "I know now that I have misjudged witches. I will do better in future."

Val met the woman's gaze, and she nodded—a gesture that Yua returned in kind. When the witch turned to me, she smiled an easy smile. "So, Styk, are you ready to go to war?"

CHAPTER FORTY-SEVEN

Bread & Circuses

(Imagine, dear reader, that you sit upon a hard wooden stool, with a small, rickety desk in front of you. You hold a chewed pencil in hand, and upon the documents on the desk you doodle—perhaps flowers, perhaps dragons, perhaps rough impressions of male genitals. I ask you to imagine all of this because I am about to take you back to school.

The Gentle Tundras only received this name after the old kings fell. These were a cruel, tyrannical bunch, but I won't go into any more detail on these people because they don't deserve your time, and this isn't about them. What I want to talk to you about is what happened after the kingdoms fell. Some of this I knew already, and some of this I learned over the next few days from Yua, who—by virtue of her privileged position in society—had a far better education than I'd ever received. She was generous in sharing it.)

After the old kingdoms fell, there was talk of the orcs in the north, or the Goldmarch in the south—already established by this point—sweeping in to take over management of the region. But, of course, this never happened, and it happened because the new leaders—champions of the uprising—understood the Tundras like the kings never could.

They knew the Tundras could survive based on one resource alone: the ample, strong timber that grew in the region. Collectively, they set up trade routes with their neighbors to the north and south, and even with the elves, two seas away. They would trade this timber for the one thing they'd never be able to produce enough of: food. The soil simply didn't support wheat and other staple crops in the same way that it could support the old, established forests. Through these trade routes, the people of the broken kingdoms were able to support themselves. More than that: thanks to the food imports, they even flourished, at least for a few decades.

It was these very same food imports that we now attacked.

Over the past few weeks, we—that is, the Slayers, the dryads, and the few soldiers that Yua had already recruited—had been involved in skirmishes all across the southwestern Tundras. We'd fought Goldmarch soldiers, all of whom had been marching east, though in the last few days we'd barely encountered any. It had been good to not be outnumbered, for once, and so the battles had been fairly one-sided, and I'd been able to level up *Worldbending* and *Knifework* once each as a result.

When we'd finally arrived at the outskirts of Aptleed, Yua—the only ex-leader with us, who had insisted on traveling with us for recruitment purposes—had instructed us to scout out the city for a while. In particular, she wanted us to scout out any trade going in or out of the walled city. She was satisfied when Orjkan's soldiers reported "the usual" in terms of imports, which meant that Niamh had relied on Duke Cambelny's old methods of keeping the people fed.

If we interrupted that, then . . . well, Yua was pretty sure that the people of Aptleed would no longer be able to bear their new leader, and the revolution might have a chance of seizing one of the major cities back to their cause. From there, they could raise an army. But it would take time.

We crouched now in a wheat field, half of us on either side of the main road, awaiting our target. A few carts had passed us already, but they'd been heading out from the city rather than in, and besides, they'd carried timber rather than food. But if the scouts borrowed from Chancellor Orjkan were correct, one of the major trains of carts would pass by shortly.

I looked to Arzak and Corminar at my side. We had orcish soldiers here, too—Val and the dryads being on the other side of the road—but I was less interested in talking to them being that we'd found absolutely nothing in common. "Anyone else's thighs starting to ache?" I asked.

"It has been a long while since I crouched for so long," Corminar agreed. "It almost takes me back to my days in the Dawnwood. To the days of war." This was quite a change from the normal Corminar; he'd never mentioned the war before Aiwin and the elven diplomats had dragged it out of him, and now he seemed willing to bring up the subject of his own accord.

"Less talk," Arzak whispered. "More concentrate."

And she was right to call us out, because in the distance I heard wheels rumbling along the rocky road. Lots of them. This was it.

"Wait until Val give signal," Arzak reminded us, though I was pleased to see that she was addressing the trained, disciplined soldiers as much as she was the two men complaining about crouching.

The rumbling wheels grew louder and closer, and I couldn't help myself but open a portal next to me and in the sky above the convoy, so that I might get a look at what we were dealing with.

It was a good job that I did.

The food carts were just as expected—one or two drivers on each, a half dozen horses at their head, a full cart of vegetables and grains behind them. And enough of them, too, that it would affect Aptleed if they lost this batch. What we hadn't expected was the group of Goldmarch soldiers riding at the front and rear of the pack.

"Hm," Arzak grunted softly at my side, looking through the portal.

"They hadn't been protected before, right?"

"They had not," Corminar agreed. "Perhaps we must retreat and regroup?"

But the orc shook her head. "No time for this. Too close. And plan must go ahead anyway."

I closed the portal. The soldiers were getting close now, and I didn't want anything tipping them off to our presence. "Niamh," I said. "She must have anticipated this attack. Maybe she got reports of our presence, and figured this was the obvious weakness in her position? Cambelny and Yua did say she was smart."

Arzak raised her eyebrows in agreement, but kept her eyes fixed on the road. As she said, it changed nothing; we still had a job to do.

The convoy grew closer, and I gripped my knife with one hand. At my side, Corminar nocked an arrow in his bow.

It grew closer still, and Arzak and the orcish soldiers rose ever so slightly from their crouches.

Before long, it was upon us. On the other side of the road, Val stood up, shouting for us to attack, and Corminar released the first shot. As it hit the first soldier square in the chest, a soldier riding the first merchant carriage pushed a glowing stone into the air, and then something exploded.

Val dragged me back into the cover of the wheat, desperately *healing* my wounds. I could barely make her out, my vision blurry and black, the ringing in my ears drowning out whatever she was saying. I blinked down at my stomach, finding it covered in red, and it took me a moment to realize I was covered in blood. *My* blood.

"Hold still, idiot!" I just about made out, and I did as Val instructed, going limp against a low stone wall.

"What . . . happened?"

"Niamh was ready for us," Val said, a yellow-white glow flowing from her hands and into my body, making me feel all tingly. "Set a trap. They . . ."

I realized then that the fight was still going. I could hear the cries of soldiers and the *clink* of blade against blade. "Is everyone else . . . ?"

"Last I checked, they're fine. Left Lore lying somewhere in the field, but he was alive, and stable. Arzak and Corminar . . . they're still out there."

I moved to stand. "We should help."

"Woah, no. I'm going to make sure you don't *die* or anything, but you're not going to be fighting until we can get one of Corminar's health potions in you."

Val moved to leave, but I reached out to grab her arm. "Styk, I can't stay here to coddle—"

"No. Not that. Just . . ." I shook my head. "Go. I'll do it myself." As Val rushed off into the fray once more, I tried to pull myself up onto the low stone wall that demarcated the wheat field. As soon as I did so, a soaring pain erupted in my stomach and side, and I realized that it wasn't going to be possible.

So instead, I did what I always do, and I resorted to portals.

I placed a hand on the ground below me, then fell through the resulting portal onto the top of the wall, where I landed with enough force that I felt the searing pain once more, if only for a moment. Up from my new position, I had a view of the battlefield that lay before me.

On the left-hand side of the road, Arzak, Corminar, and the remaining orcish soldiers faced down Goldmarch soldiers, while the dryads continued to attack from the right. All of them looked worse for wear, and it was only because we were outflanking our enemy that we even stood a chance.

To turn the tide of the fight, I opened a portal below one of the soldiers, launching her into the air, and I turned away to avoid seeing the resulting *splat*. I flicked my hand around to the next, but these soldiers were clearly highly trained, because they'd seen what had just happened from their colleague and learned from it. The soldier I'd aimed at swiftly repositioned his body to grab at the nearest cart, stopping him from falling through and instead swinging himself onto the cart to avoid the portal completely.

Alright, then. Time to switch it up.

I opened another portal, but this time positioned it underneath one of the food transport carts, aiming to dump the cart on top of the soldiers. But of course . . . my portals weren't that big. All I managed was to put the back wheels halfway through the portal, sloping the back of the cart down, all its carried cabbages rolling to one side. I closed the portal again, *portal slicing* through the wheels—that cart wouldn't be going anywhere fast, at least—and one of the two wheel segments fell on top of one of the soldiers' heads. This distraction allowed the dryads to overwhelm them with their petal attacks, and they screamed as the nature magicks sliced them.

Right then, looking at the tilted carriage, I had an idea. "Corminar!" I shouted. "Corminar!" But he couldn't hear me over the noise of the fight. I opened up a portal at my side instead, paired with one near Corminar, and poked my head through it. "Corminar! The hinges on the back of the cart. For unloading. You think you can hit them?"

"May I ask your plan?" Corminar replied.

"Cabbages. Get the soldiers ready to charge."

"When?" the ranger asked, loosing an arrow into the carriage hinge.

"Now!" I closed the portals between us and instead opened another—at the back of the tilted carriage, just below where all the cabbages were rolling out of the cart. With the opening of another portal, I rained down cabbages upon the enemy.

Corminar and the orcs charged into battle, seizing the advantage of the enemies being pelted by heavy vegetable rain, and it wasn't long until the Tundran Resistance had its first meaningful victory.

9 x Goldmarch Soldiers defeated!

Worldbending: +4,600XP
Worldbending increased to Level 42!
Base Points Gained: +2 INT, +2 Free Points (INT/WIS/CHA)
Knifework: +3,750XP
Knifework increased to Level 33!
Base Points Gained: +1 DEX, +1 STR, +2 Free Points (VIT/DEX/STR)
Level up!
You increased to Level 15!

Cheers erupted around the street, the merchant—neutral in this—wondering what we might do to them. But there wasn't time to celebrate too much; there was still a lot of work to be done.

CHAPTER FORTY-EIGHT

Swords in the Hands of Farmers

The days went on like this. We led attacks—of varying levels of success—on transport convoys. We pushed out the remaining Goldmarch contingents from small outposts. We found allies in more dryads, communicating with them through Val, who was rapidly becoming Duchess Yua of Lenktra's closest ally in this campaign.

Back in Fort Tanil, Cambelny and Orjkan sent scouting reports to those of us in the front lines, identifying more weaknesses in the Goldmarch's presence in the Tundras. There were unprotected food carriages, small clusters of soldiers, and the like. We'd been in quite a few scrapes over the last week or so, and even with Val's rapidly improving *Healing* skill, we were feeling a bit sore. At least I'd picked up another couple of levels in *Stealth*, as well as one in *Knifework*, which was enough to make me feel this was all worth it. You know, in addition to saving my homeland from foreign invaders.

In fact, speaking of Yua, Arzak and I had been trying to convince her to leave the front lines for a few days now. There'd been a scrape before where a Goldmarch soldier had landed a bad blow on Yua, and it had only been Val's *healing*—along with some *healing* support from the dryads—that had saved her. She was better now, she said, but I still noticed her hobbling when she thought nobody was looking. It was her duty, she said, to be here, to convince potential loyalists to join the cause.

It was for this very reason that we were currently traveling to a small town not far from Aptleed, perhaps only a few hours' ride away. Duke Cambelny's scouting reports said that the people of this town were ripe for the picking. They'd grown dissatisfied with the new Goldmarch governance, and one of the enemy soldiers had turned up dead in the last few days. Nobody had stepped forward to claim responsibility, and not a single person had claimed to witness the incident.

When we'd reached the town borders, I'd been ready for a fight, if not exactly excited for one—I was really after a day off—and so was relieved to find that there wasn't a single soldier in a mustard-colored surcoat in sight. The Goldmarch had abandoned this town, and according to the tracks that Corminar had spotted, had headed east toward Aptleed. We must have come close to stumbling across them—another battle I was, frankly, happy to have avoided for now.

Our large group walked down the main road into the center of town, and though there were people around, it grew eerily quiet. The locals stopped in the streets and poked their heads out of windows to stare at us, but their expressions were neutral and they didn't say a word.

Finally, Yua came to a stop at the crossroads in the center of the town, and turned around slowly to look almost everyone in the eyes. The rest of her contingent—me included—stood uncomfortably, shifting from foot to foot, waiting for the duchess to take the lead. I caught sight of a few eyes set upon me, and I saw something in them. Not quite fear, not quite anger, but something in the neighborhood of both for sure. I couldn't blame them, I realized; they'd just rid themselves of occupying soldiers, and here were some more soldiers marching into town. Maybe it didn't matter that we didn't wear the same Goldmarch uniforms.

"People of Refton," the duchess finally said. "Fear not our presence here; we come in peace."

She'd noticed the same thing as me, then. Though, I supposed she'd told me already: her *Identification* skill was a very high level. She probably saw all that I saw and far more.

"If it is your will, I and my fellow peace seekers will leave your town immediately, never to return. But I ask this of you first: you listen to that which I have to say, and you give it due consideration. If, after such time, you still wish for us to leave, we will do so with no hard feelings, and without a moment's hesitation. Is there a mayor here who might represent you in such discussions?"

I'd heard this speech before, in other towns, though usually someone was quick to step forward at this part. In the town of Refton, nobody spoke, and nobody moved.

"I do not wish to harm them," Yua continued, "only to know who to direct—"

"Ain't no mayor," a woman poking her head out of the window of the first floor of a nearby building said.

The duchess nodded. "Very well. A council leader, or a—"

"Nah, we *had* a mayor," the same woman continued. "But they killed her, didn't they? Them soldiers."

"Yeah," another guy piped up, "and now *more* soldiers come in, asking to see a mayor. You're gonna have to forgive us if nobody be stepping forward."

"We are not with the Goldmarch," Yua said. "Forgive me for not properly introducing myself. I am Duchess Yua of Lenktra, to the south. I know I never had the pleasure of administrating your region—that duty fell to Duke Cambelny—but I assure you that—"

"Yeah, we figured you was something like that."

For the first time, I saw Duchess Yua look almost lost for words. Even then, she took only a half second to regather herself. "Then may I ask why you resist us so?"

"Cos none of you lot protected us, did you?" the woman in the window said. "You got your castles and your palaces and stuff, and yeah, maybe you rule *over* us with all the best intention in the world, but you still let them Goldmarch soldiers in, didn't you? And you ain't protected us for them. Tyll died cos of that."

"And Tyll was—"

"Our mayor! Proper good woman, she was. Never let any of us go hungry, always shamed those who hoarded crops. Paid to get food into the mouths of my nephew, she did, out of her own pocket. But she's dead now, and here you stand in your pretty dress and your silver necklace and all."

Duchess Yua unconsciously touched the pendant hanging down from her neck. I realized she'd never been forced to face her own inadequacies. Duchess Yua was a good woman—she'd proven that to me already—but even good women of her station didn't properly understand how the rest of us lived. There were . . . gaps in her visibility. Gaps that had cost Mayor Tyll her life.

I couldn't help myself here. There was something that needed to be done. Something *heroic*. I stepped forward. "Duchess Yua messed up, yes." Out of the corner of my eye, I noticed I was getting a stern stare and flared nostrils for my troubles here, but I continued nonetheless. "But she's been out here these past couple of weeks trying to put things right. She's put her life on the line, took a nearly mortal wound just a few days ago. With her help, we've disrupted supply lines, eliminated enemy soldiers, and recruited others to our cause. So she made a mistake, yes, but she's also our best hope of putting things right." I stepped back, handing the floor over to Yua once more.

I could see that her glare had softened, that she was no longer flaring her nostrils. She might well still have been annoyed at me, but I realized that there was something that even her high *Identification* skill didn't let her see. While in her usual role as duchess, she might never have been able to admit to mistakes. But commonfolk like me and those of Refton didn't respond in the same way to her peers. Making mistakes made you human—or orcish, or elven, or tiefling, and so on. They happened. Apparently they happened to leaders, too. But nothing was worse than not admitting to them. And nothing was better than putting your life on the line to try to fix them.

Duchess Yua nodded to me, then turned to the crowd of amassed locals. "I come to you with an offer: pick up your blades, and fight with me. Help us in repelling the southern invaders. Return the Gentle Tundras to Tundran rule. And in return, you will be rewarded. I will sell all my finery, my estates, everything down to the clothes on my back, and I will use the revenue for your benefit. Wells for every town. The latest in agricultural technology for each and every farmer. Reforestation efforts to undo the damage sown by Queen Amira and those under her command. I will do everything—and I certainly mean *everything*—not just to return the Gentle Tundras to the way they were, but to inspire a new golden age for its tough and loyal people."

The crowd of Refton remained silent for a moment, considering Yua, and then one man spoke up. "We ain't got no mayor. You speak to all of us. We all make our own decisions. But mine? I'll pick up a sword. I'll fight with you."

Another local stepped forward, and then another, nodding their agreement to Duchess Yua's terms. She had made quite the promise, forsaking all her riches, though based on what I'd seen of her over the past two weeks, I was inclined to believe that she meant it. From the masses of new soldiers now flocking to her cause, it seemed the people of Refton believed it, too.

This recruitment drive became the most productive yet, bolstering our number significantly. Once the people were settled, Yua returned to the Slayers and Orjkan's soldiers to tell us that we had enough people that we could split into squads, hitting Niamh all around the Tundras simultaneously. It would give us an advantage, and it would force Niamh to split her resources, to plug enough holes in this metaphorical bucket that she surely couldn't fill them all.

At least, that was what we'd believed until one of Cambelny's spies in the region tracked us down.

"Ma'am!" he said, riding fast for the duchess. "Ma'am!"

"What is it, soldier?" she asked.

"I came straight for you. News from Aptleed, ma'am. Niamh has new reinforcements from Auricia. Reinforcements that are here with the expressed purpose of shutting down the revolution. Amira has sent Knights of the Realm, ma'am."

Duchess Yua paled, and I met Val's wary gaze. Players might have been the strongest people in the world, but the Knights of the Realm were second to them. If we'd thought the tide of revolution was turning in our favor, we were wrong.

The true test was only just beginning.

CHAPTER FORTY-NINE

The Knights of the Realm

Over the next few hours, further scouting reports reached us. The Knights of the Realm weren't just heading out to put an end to the leaders of the resistance, but were also part of an effort to intimidate the people of the Gentle Tundras into forsaking the cause. Niamh knew what she was doing; she knew the people were the actual power in any region. At least, that was provided they had someone—or some*thing*—to spur them into action.

Duchess Yua wasn't happy to let these Knights of the Realm come to us, as there was no knowing what damage they might do to the cause before then. We'd have to go to them, and there were only so many of us with proper combat experience who even stood a chance. And that was including *me,* so we were really scraping the barrel.

This was how it was, then, that Yua gave each member of the Slayers a squadron of farmers, a bunch of light armor, and as many blades as they could carry. Our mission? Take down a Knight of the Realm.

Scouts had last reported our target knight heading southwest from Aptleed, Niamh's base of operations. Based on the most up-to-date maps, we could get a pretty good idea of where they were heading, assuming they were going to continue going from town to town. We'd set course for a point further along their journey, one far southwest enough that we were sure we'd be there first. After all, my plan depended on us catching the knight by surprise.

We arrived in the small town of Pelry to find that everything, so far, had gone according to plan. The residents hadn't yet seen a Knight of the Realm pass through, and we even shocked them when we said one was coming. We had a few hours to prepare, so I set about telling the locals to hide inside their homes, before Sir Claudia Fastus, Knight of the Realm, Second Order, could arrive. Because once she did, I said, there was a chance they'd all be in danger.

Ordering the locals about was one thing, but ordering around my battalion of armed farmers was another thing entirely.

"My *niece* has a higher level than you," one of them was saying. "Why should I be taking orders from you?"

"And I assume your niece has experience taking down heroes, then?" I asked. "Otherwise you wouldn't put her forward for the job, would you?"

"My *point* is," the farmer continued, undeterred, "you're level 15. I'm level 24. Maybe it's best I take this one."

"Yeah, but my level is all combat skills and magicks. What skill is it that most of your leveling has come from?"

". . . *Agriculture*," the man replied.

"*Agriculture*," agreed another farmer.

"*Necromancy*," said a third. Everyone looked at her.

"Seriously?" I asked.

"No, it's *Agriculture*."

"And that's why I'm in charge," I replied. "Levels? They're a vanity metric. I could be level 100, but if all I had was experience in, I dunno, *Wordsmithing*, then I wouldn't be much help, would I?"

"Maybe you could talk them to death?" one of the militants asked.

I ignored this suggestion. "Besides, if everything goes according to plan, then all you lot need to do is stand in a group with your swords raised in the air."

"How will that help?"

"You'll see."

The mutiny-in-progress now put to bed—was it still a mutiny when it wasn't on a ship? Probably not, but I wasn't going to let that stop me from calling it that—we took our positions around the town. The armed farmers took shelter in a barn that opened onto the main road, ready to charge out on my signal, whereas I stood in plain sight in the middle of the road. I had some doubts about the plan. These knights might attack first and ask questions later, in which case I was a goner, but it was still the best plan I had.

The Knight of the Realm came before long. She rode in on a huge brown stallion, galloping fast at first, but slowing as she entered the town. When she put her eyes upon me, in the middle of the road in the otherwise deserted town, she slowed to a stop. The knight stared at me through the visor of her heavy metal helmet, considering me for a moment, before stirring her steed into action once more.

"What is this?" she cried out to me.

I remained quiet, still, baiting her with my silence.

The Knight of the Realm's horse trotted closer. At this distance, I could make out the fine quality of her armor. A high-level blacksmith had crafted this, but still there were weaknesses in it—there had to be joints for the woman to move. I just had to hope that one of the many farmers' blades would find one of those cracks.

I glanced at the barn where my fellow soldiers were waiting to pounce. I couldn't help it. My glance happened before I really knew I was doing it, but the knight didn't seem to notice. For all her combat strength, she wasn't the most observant.

"I asked you what this was," the knight tried again. "I am a Knight of the Realm, and you will—"

"Not of *this* realm, you're not," I said, and I readied my hands. "Soldiers?" I cried out. "Now!"

The barn door burst open, distracting the Knight of the Realm in the same moment that I opened a portal below her horse's feet, paired with one high in the sky above. The horse cried as it fell through, clawing its front legs on the dirt road as it tried to stop itself from falling. This gave the knight just enough time to realize what was happening, and she swung her long sword to smash against the side of the portal. I thought for a moment that she'd meant to attack it—and figured she really *wasn't* the sharpest blade—but then something new happened.

The purple glow of my portal magicks crept onto the blade, as though being absorbed by it. The portals themselves closed as the Knight of the Realm extracted the magick from them, shutting around the horse without any regard for it still being in the way—I won't go into too much detail on that bit—and soon all of their magick flickered around the knight's blade like a raging purple flame.

Oh well, I figured, *I'll just open another one, then. She'll be falling onto raised swords before she knows what hit her.*

But when I raised my hands once more . . . nothing happened. I realized then what was going on. For the purposes of my *Worldbending* magicks, I still had a portal open. And I was only ever allowed *one* pair. My portal magicks was going to be useless while that sword remained enchanted.

"Is this part of the plan, *sir?*" the farmer who had questioned my orders earlier asked.

The situation forced me to improvise. "Attack!" I shouted.

To their credit, the farmers all charged, not a single one of them hesitating on the order for more than a second. They knew what they were getting in for, it seemed. Either that, or they didn't want to be shown up in front of their fellow villagers.

I charged the knight, too, my Blade of Samal in hand, very aware that even one good hit of the enemy's blade could be enough to kill me. After all, my *Warped Shield* currently only covered lowlevel melee weapons, and I suspected that a Knight of the Realm, of all people, would not be carrying a low-level blade. Besides, this ability used a portal to deflect the attack anyway, and I suspected for that reason it currently wouldn't work.

So it was a good thing—for me, at least—that the knight focused first on the swarm of armed farmers rather than the one guy with a knife. She swung her now-enchanted blade at the soaring farmers, and purple magicks flowed out of the sword. The magicks formed a circle as it passed through the air, splitting into two. As each of these circles formed portals, a good chunk of the charging farmers suddenly found themselves falling from the air. At least it was only a few feet.

Enough of the farmers remained charging—though admittedly they seemed a lot less enthused about the whole matter now that the knight's attention remained on them. I instinctively reached to open a portal between me and the enemy to close the gap, but of course that wasn't an option. I had to rely on plain old feet.

The knight sliced her blade through the air once more, this time having more of an idea of how to use its newly imbued powers. Some of the farmers dove out of the way of the purple magicks, but still a couple were caught, and this time they tumbled from a portal high above them. I heard bones snap as they landed on their arms and yelped from the pain.

But I was close enough now. The enemy was just in reach. I arched my dagger through the air toward them, activating *Execution*, hoping against hope that they'd been distracted enough that it would work, and that my *Stealth Attack* passive would kick in. I aimed for the gap in the armor at the woman's neck, between helmet and cuirass. The world seemed to slow. I was nearly there. I nearly had her. The blade tip was just inches away from its target.

And then the Knight of the Realm turned.

My knife slipped against the metal armor, clinking. I was at risk of dropping it from the impact, but I scrambled my fingers around it just as the woman's elbow came around to knock me in the stomach.

I fell backward, winded, my vision blurry from the knock.

I blinked my sight back into focus just in time to see the knight's *Worldbending*-imbued sword point squarely at my face.

CHAPTER FIFTY

The Siege of Aptleed

"Enough," the knight said, the tip of her blade half an inch from the ridge of my nose.

I mentally scrambled for a way out of this, racking my brain for abilities I could use. I still had my knife in hand, but even a decent *stab* wasn't going to take down a Knight of the Realm without *Stealth Attack* and *Execution* to back it up. And while the enemy's sword still had my portal magicks absorbed, I wasn't able to open any portals. Unless my *Needlework* abilities had an application I hadn't seen, then I was well and truly—

Wait.

There was still one ability I could use. One that specified explicitly "bending reality," not portal uses.

"Enough," the knight spat again. "Call off your peasants."

"No." I rolled to one side, away from the tip of the blade, and though I couldn't see the woman's face, I got the strange feeling that this amused her.

"You amuse me," she said.

Ah, that'll do it.

I took a step backward, facing down the knight with only a dagger in hand, compared to the woman's enormous sword. The farmers watched from a *painfully* safe distance.

"Don't suppose you're willing to drop the sword?" I asked. "Make this duel a bit fairer?"

"I assure you, you do not become a Knight of the Realm by fighting fair."

"So that's a no, then?" I replied, and without waiting for an answer I charged.

I ran straight for the woman's outstretched blade, then at the last second twisted to one side, ramming the tip of my blade into the woman's armored wrist.

There was a loud *clink* of blade against metal armor, and the knight laughed— a gentle snort at first, but then it grew with every brief moment that passed. "You really thought—" she began, but I cut it short by activating *Closed Reach*.

The woman screamed as I bent reality to push my knife into her wrist, and she dropped her magick-imbued blade. As she released it, the purple magicks suddenly rushed back into their owner—me—causing me to stumble backward from the impact.

Both the knight and I stared down at the disarmed blade for a moment before the woman leaped at it. I instead reached a hand down toward it, opening a portal underneath it.

But this wasn't just any portal. This was my *Pocket Worlds* ability coming in handy.

"I think I know someone who'd like that," I said. "I don't suppose you mind?"

Without her weapon, it didn't matter that the Knight of the Realm was armored. She was outnumbered, and that was enough.

If only that hadn't meant the experience points would be spread so thinly.

"This is best gift ever got," Arzak said, hugging the sword I'd pulled from my pocket world.

"You'll be able to carry it in one hand? The Knight of the Realm needed two."

"Knight is human. I orc. We stronger." To prove the point, Arzak shifted the weapon into her right hand and drew another sword from her back with her left. She waved them around in a half-arsed mock attempt at fighting. "See. One hand."

We had regrouped in the hills beyond Aptleed, just out of sight of the city. Corminar and I had been the first of the Slayers to return, much to the elf's surprise—surprise at me returning first, not him, I suspected—and the others followed suit within the day. Soon enough, it wasn't just Slayers and farmer accomplices in the camp, but Duchess Yua and a few hundred newly collected soldiers. Even Duke Cambelny had shown up on the front lines, and that gave a very clear signal to all involved what our next move would be. It was time to make some meaningful progress in this revolution.

It was time to take back Aptleed.

Duchess Yua spoke to us all on the dawn of the following day. "I ask you to remember these foreign invaders hold hostage your fellow countrymen. After the work we have done to seize food imports, they will be desperate. Some Tundran citizens may have been coerced to do that which they might later regret. When we take Aptleed, we must remember that we do not ourselves deal justice as we see fit. That is for the courts to decide. Any traitors—if indeed there are any—we will deal with at a later date. For now, we seek to remove those in golden armor from our city. From Aptleed, our revolution grows. We will be seen as a meaningful power, and we might tip the fence for those who have been too nervous to join our cause. Citizens of the Gentle Tundras: this is a turning point. This is the first step on a road to inevitable victory.

"Today, we take our positions outside of Aptleed's walls. Tomorrow, a week from now, or a month from now, we walk inside. We take back that which is ours!"

With this, we marched. There was an air of optimism—one which Val and her remaining dryads seemed most of all to emit. The forest spirits loosed their typical leaves and petals, but these were pink blossoms, and each petal healed sore muscles and minor wounds. Spirits were high when we marched over the crest of the hill, the walled city of Aptleed sprawling before us.

Our hastily cobbled together excuse for an army spread out wide. We may not have had many great warriors in our midst, but we definitely had numbers on our side. At least, that's what Duke Cambelny's spies had reported—our army numbered two for every one Goldmarch soldier within Aptleed. Our siege might take time, but it would work. There was just no telling how *much* time that would—

"Rider approaching!" a soldier at the front of the line roared, and Duchess Yua called her army to a halt. She looked around to us—well, Val, really—and summoned us over. "Is it her?" she asked. "Does Niamh ride out to speak with us?"

"Or fight, perhaps," Corminar suggested.

"It's not her," Val said, her eyes fixed on the woman on the horse rapidly approaching, charging for Duchess Yua.

"Lore," Arzak said, and motioned with her head for the pair of them to stand in front of Duchess Yua, to block her from any attack.

"Any scouting reports?" I asked the duchess. "Any super powerful people in there?"

"Only Niamh," Yua replied. "Perhaps one or two Knights of the Realm, though we believe we have eliminated all such threats already. This forces me to believe that this is not an attack, but a message. Though . . . of what kind?"

"There's only one way to find out . . ." Val murmured.

We remained quiet as the rider drew near, watching as the woman swerved to one side a good dozen yards from us. She called out, "Niamh wishes to speak with you. Now."

"We do not take orders from invaders," Duchess Yua replied, holding the woman's gaze.

"Do you speak for yourself, or for all?" the messenger asked.

"As their leader, I speak for all, as a united front."

The messenger held Yua's gaze, then nodded. "A shame. Because it's not you whom she wishes to speak with." The messenger turned away from the duchess and then looked Val in the eye. And then Lore. And then Arzak, Corminar. And then, finally . . . me. "She wishes to speak with Jacob Tailor's murderers."

This had me, Val, and Lore shifting uncomfortably from foot to foot, while Arzak and Corminar kept a neutral expression. With a poker face like that, it was a wonder that the orc was so bad at card games.

"I assume this man . . . *needed* elimination?" the duchess asked Val.

"As much as Niamh does."

Yua considered this response for a moment and then nodded. "There will be an opportunity for justice later. For now, I leave this decision to you: would you and your allies enter Aptleed? Would you negotiate their surrender?"

Val glanced to me, and I replied with a nod.

Yua's eyes flicked to me and then back to Val. "Very well. You have my blessing. But please, remember: you know what the invasion has cost us already. We do not wish it to cost us anything further."

"I know," Val said. If she'd replied to me with those words, I'd have thought she was being passive-aggressive, but to Yua they only sounded sincere.

The messenger, who had been silently following this conversation, turned her horse around to face the tall walls of Aptleed.

With one last look at Duchess Yua, formerly of Lenktra, I stepped out from the lines of soldiers and stood at the messenger's rear. Val followed soon after, then Arzak and Corminar. Lore followed suit only after handing the depth-raider over to Duchess Yua and extracting from her a promise to look after "him."

"Sure about this?" Arzak asked Val quietly.

The witch responded with a nod.

The deforested plains outside Aptleed's walls were eerily quiet as we began the walk toward the city bearing Goldmarch colors, the only sounds being the clip-clop of hooves on dirt and the gold flags flapping in the wind ahead. I could feel countless eyes on our backs—hundreds of Tundran citizens who risked everything to be here, who were counting on us to see their homes returned to them.

It was time. A few moments from now, we would stare Niamh in the eye.

And I could see no way that this didn't end in a fight.

CHAPTER FIFTY-ONE

What Matters is What's Real

The surroundings grew only a little louder as we passed through the main gate into the city. Soldiers wearing Goldmarch uniforms stood in even measures on both sides of the road, their gazes on us and the messenger. Few citizens were out and about despite the time of day, and those that were seemed to keep their heads down, trying to avoid notice. The invaders had quashed the renowned spirit of Aptleed.

We followed Niamh's messenger up the main road toward the central castle—where else would she be?—and the longer this went on, the more I wondered if we'd made a mistake coming in here alone. The siege would have been long and arduous, and many of Aptleed's citizens would likely have died, but . . . if we failed to negotiate surrender, then that would still be the case. That would be the case and we, probably, would also be dead. Even a team as dysfunctionally functional as us couldn't handle quite this many enemies.

Only when we reached the keep did I allow myself to breathe a sigh of relief; it didn't look like this was a trap for us, as we'd have been attacked by now. The gods knew there were enough soldiers out here to deal with us without any trouble. So this meant instead that Niamh really wanted to speak with us.

Some part of me thought that might even be worse.

Up the tower we went, my heart racing more and more with every step, my every instinct being to grab Val and the rest of them and get us out of there. My brain swam with thoughts of Val facing down the woman who'd once tried to kill her. This was a mistake. This couldn't end well. This—

"Come in," a woman said, standing on the other side of a long, dark wood table, one that looked to my untrained eye to be freshly polished. This woman was short, maybe three inches over five feet tall, and she didn't carry anything I could reasonably describe as a weapon. "Please, sit." She pointed to the chairs.

Corminar and Lore reluctantly did as suggested, but Arzak and I remained at Val's side. At the side of the woman who had paled like I'd never seen her pale before, whose arms were shaking, whose nostrils were flaring, and whose eyes were at risk of dealing real damage to the woman she glared at.

"Yes, I thought it might be you," Niamh said to Val. "Perhaps we can let bygones be bygones, for the sake of useful discussion?"

Lore and Corminar turned in their chairs, the former raising an eyebrow, to see who Niamh was speaking to—but neither of them commented on it.

"I'll stand," was Val's only reply. As an act of solidarity, I remained standing with her, and Arzak did the same.

Niamh shrugged, and she took a seat. An orc drifted from the corner of the room to stand at her side. "I don't wish to hurt anyone."

Val scoffed.

The Player begged for the witch's patience with the raising of her hand. "Once upon a time, I did. This, I concede. But are we not all capable of change? Of growth? Is that not what the System—so crude in its implementation—seeks to achieve in all of us?"

"We not here to speak philosophy," Arzak said.

The orcish aide at Niamh's side struggled to suppress a smirk.

"Very well," the Player said. "I suppose after all the unfortunate geopolitical tensions of the past two months, it is only right that you do not trust me. You would be a fool to, in fact. But allow me to say it again, nevertheless: I do not wish to hurt anyone. Unlike my colleagues in the Council, that is the last thing I want. But do not mistake that for me saying I will not do what has to be done. I will."

Niamh's eyes drifted over us, hovering over Lore, then me, then landing on Val.

"So you know about the Council. I suspected as much. Jacob's murder seemed too targeted. A commoner dies, and nobody bats so much as an eyelid. But when someone as powerful as him is murdered—even if he was the weakest of us—then there is a certain level of planning required. Someone who seeks to take down the Council."

All five of us remained quiet; Niamh had made a mistake here, and none of us were keen to correct it. We knew of the Council, yes, but our killing of Jacob was his own doing, really. We were happy to kill a Player, but we hadn't known of any greater schemes. Yet we all knew that if we kept quiet, we might learn more.

"But I talk too much," Niamh said, gesturing to the orc at her side, who disappeared into another room, leaving the Player alone. "This is to be a two-way street, as it were. Which of you speaks for the team as a whole?" She glanced at Val. "The changeling?"

"We all speak for ourselves," Val spat back at her.

Niamh nodded. "Then I shall address you all."

The orcish aide returned with a cup of steaming tea, which she placed in front of the Player and got precisely zero thanks for.

"I hope to make a deal. I address you, and not that duchess, because I think you are less . . . how shall we say it? Emotionally invested? And also because I think I know where I stand with you, and you with me. We understand each other."

Lore raised a hand. "I'm not sure I understand any of this," he said.

Niamh smiled at him like an exhausted mother might smile at one of her children. She turned back to address the lot of us. "You want Aptleed returned to Cambelny," she said.

"There seems to be a few Goldmarch soldiers standing in the way," Corminar said. "As well as a Council member. Unless you are happy to relinquish your grasp on—"

"I rode into town only to speak with you; my interest in Aptleed has passed," the Player said. "It has served its purpose. For all I care, you can claim it this afternoon. I will even ask Amira's soldiers to stand down—there will be no bloodshed."

"And in return?" Val asked, nostrils flaring.

"In return, I ask only that you return the favor. No bloodshed. You allow us to leave unharmed. We will leave Aptleed, and even the Gentle Tundras entirely, within the week."

The room fell quiet as I, and the rest of the team, digested this offer.

"You're giving it back to us? Just like that?" I asked.

"As I said, Aptleed is no longer useful to me. If I can return the Tundras to their previous status without another drop of blood spilled, then I will do just that. Duchess Yua has given you permission to negotiate on her behalf, yes?"

"She's given *me* permission," Val said, and I didn't much like that she didn't seem to trust the rest of the team to do it. Well, actually, I just didn't like that she didn't trust *me*.

"Very well," Niamh said, fixing her attention on Val. "Then answer this: do you wish to see more innocents killed in all of this? Or would you rather ride back to the duchess with news that we offer conditional surrender? I think I know which *she* would prefer."

The chamber fell quiet once more, Val and Niamh holding one another's glares.

"Of course, there is another alternative," Niamh continued. "I could activate the enchantment placed under this table. A rather complex trap, you see. Upon activation, it emits a poison gas—a cloud which will cover half of Aptleed before the enchantment fades."

"You'd kill yourself?" Lore asked.

"My dear, of course not. I just drank the antidote." Niamh turned to her aide. "Sulla, perhaps you should fix yourself a cup, too."

"And the Goldmarch soldiers?" I asked. "You'd kill them, too?"

Niamh waved a hand. "As I said, I will do what must be done. I just won't take any joy in doing it."

"You're a monster," Val said. It wasn't a shout, and she didn't spit it at the Player. In fact, it was worse; she said it with her voice level, calm, and matter-of-fact.

Niamh rolled her tongue around her mouth, chewing back her instinctual response. "You think I *want* this? You think anyone but children and man-children *wanted* to live in these worlds we created? No. If it were possible—if I could step outside without dying there—I would live in the real world. Not this excuse for one."

"Our world *is* real," Val replied.

"No, no," Niamh said, this now her turn to be matter-of-fact. "No, it's not. Do you think the food tastes the same here? Do you think the wind feels the same as it brushes along you skin? No. None of it is real. Not even . . ." She trailed off, gesturing to the team who sat opposite her. To me. To Val. To my friends.

"Oh, I assure you, I'm bloody real," I spat.

Val whipped out a hand to get me to back off—something I did after a moment's rebellion. "If we agree to your terms," the witch asked. "You'll disarm the trap? Everybody lives?"

"Everybody lives."

"We'd need proof that you've disarmed it."

"Val, you're really considering this?" I asked.

"Of course I'm bloody considering it!" she said. "If it saves lives, if it saves *innocents*, then . . . what kind of person would say no?"

"A hero would—"

"Please stop talking about what heroes do, Styk. You don't know, I don't know, none of us will *ever* know what it is to be a hero. We just do our best, and that has to be enough." Val turned back to Niamh. "On Duchess Yua's behalf, we accept your terms."

Niamh smiled.

The rest of the Slayers and I stood in silence as the Goldmarch soldiers—led by Niamh—marched out of Aptleed, heading to a camp in the north to regroup. Duchess Yua had been ecstatic when Val had delivered the news, going so far as to hug her before she remembered herself, at which point she apologized profusely. But us Slayers couldn't be so happy—part of the terms of the deal were that Niamh escaped unharmed, and that was our entire purpose: Player-killing.

"It cannot be this easy," Corminar said under his breath, and I—the only person to have heard him—nodded my agreement. It *was* too easy. The campaign had only been going a couple of weeks, and we'd been effective, sure, but Niamh hadn't seemed like someone who budged that easily. Whatever she'd wanted from Aptleed, she must have gotten it already.

"You don't really mean to let her escape," I said to Val. "After all that . . ." I considered spelling it out: after all that Niamh had done to Val. "After all that she's done?"

"Of course not," Val said. "They leave. Cambelny gets back Aptleed. And then we go after her."

"Her and her two-hundred-strong army?" I asked. "We were in a room with her. We could've taken her then."

"Maybe. We wouldn't have made it out of the city, though. We all know that."

"What next?" Arzak asked.

"We follow," Lore replied, with more confidence than we usually expected from the timid, if brawny, fellow. I turned to look at him, to see him staring into the depth-raider's cage. No, the depth-raider's *eyes*.

"What if we get spotted? You reckon Niamh will hesitate to set her army on us?"

"Trust me," Lore said, still meeting the creature's gaze. "They . . ." He paused for a moment. "It's about . . . it's about the timber. That's what she wanted from Aptleed, isn't it? That's what we've seen all around the Tundras. It . . ." He paused again while the depth-raider grew closer to him, within its cage. "We follow the timber; we find what Niamh's been planning."

We agreed, though I suspected I wasn't the only one wondering where this newfound wisdom had come from. Still, this would turn out to be the right move.

The answers that were coming soon would change everything.

Lore

"Quiet now, little thing," Lore said to the depth-raider squeaking in its cage as he carried it away from the camp, using the cover of darkness to stop any of the other Slayers from seeing.

Abstract images appeared in his mind's eye—an array of locations, the rest of the team fading away, the strange glossy tint to them that Lore had eventually realized meant the creature was asking a question.

"Away from them, little guy," Lore answered. "They won't understand this next bit."

The depth-raider squeaked, and Lore cast a glance back over his shoulder. But the team didn't stir from their sleep, only Styk moving, and only to put an arm around Val. The barbarian continued on, away from the road, wishing there were still trees around to hide behind.

Lore wished he was asleep, too, if only to get one more night to interpret the messages he'd been receiving.

All the Slayers had complained of strange, lifelike dreams over the past couple of weeks, but none of them had made the connection. Only Lore, the one member of the team who'd spent real time with the creature, could see that there was magicks at play, and that the depth-raider was responsible for them. He'd resisted the dreams, too, at first, discounting them as coming about because of stress or the like, but only once he'd embraced them did he see that there was more meaning to them.

His own depth-raider-induced dreams had so often been about the malae, and for that reason, he'd thought they were just nightmares. He'd never told the rest of his friends about his own previous encounter with those creatures—the only ones he didn't think deserved to live. He'd kept it all to himself. For a moment, he'd thought these dreams were punishing him for that.

But over time, when he'd stopped resisting the dreams, he'd realized that they weren't nightmares but warnings. He dreamt of malae, yes, but he also dreamt of old friends, and towering devices like those they'd seen in the witchfinder village. The images were erratic, and abstract, but that was just how the depth-raider spoke—it couldn't help that. All Lore could do was try to interpret these warnings, and tell his friends once he understood them. But until then . . . he kept his dreams to himself. Until then, they might just think he was mad.

With enough distance between himself and his friends, Lore placed the depth-raider's cage down on the ground. He moved his hand to its latch, and then . . . hesitated, the creature's deep black eyes staring up at him.

"I've got to," Lore said, and it was as much for his own benefit as the depth-raider's. He flicked open the latch, expecting the creature to jump out, seizing its newfound freedom. Instead, it just continued to stare up at him with those gigantic eyes, and squeaked a confused noise.

"I've got to let you go, little guy. I've got to. Where we're headed . . . There's a Player there. And there won't be Duchess Yua and her soldiers around to watch you while we meet her. You're a lovely little guy now, but . . . what happens when you're around that much power? We've heard the stories. You, your type, you're world-enders. I can't risk you hurting anyone. Whether you mean to or not."

The depth-raider hopped out of its cage, then turned and looked up at him once more.

More images flashed through Lore's mind. He saw Coldharbor. He saw the Player that betrayed them. He saw Plyas's face, turning to dust. He saw the tieflings he'd grown up among, mourning. He saw his journey across the Coldwater, in search of new horizons. He saw Corminar, and Arzak, and Tokas, and Val. He saw the first Player they'd killed, and he saw his friends smile. He saw Seld, and Styk, and, finally, he saw the sheep he cared so deeply for. It was these last—the animals—that the depth-raider asked about.

"I'll find another way," Lore said. "I'll get them back. But I can't risk anyone else getting hurt in the process. Elandor seemed like a decent guy, really. Maybe he'll listen to reason. Maybe we'll find some other way to repay him and get the sheep back from his pocket world. Styk says he's got a new ability that could help if Elandor doesn't cooperate—we can do some kind of portal dimension heist? I don't really understand it, but Val seemed very excited about the possibility."

Lore caught himself. He was rambling. This wasn't like him, but he was distressed. It was like saying goodbye to an old friend. He drew in a deep breath, then waved the depth-raider away. "Go," he said. "Go now. Not before I change my mind, because I won't. I've thought about this a lot. This is what I have to do."

The barbarian reached down to the creature's tiny neck, took the witchfinder's clasp in his big, clumsy fingers, and undid the latch. The clasp fell to the ground at the depth-raider's side, and it blinked down at it.

Only then did the creature seem to understand what Lore intended.

Mental images, more erratic and vibrant than any that the depth-raider had pushed Lore's way before, filled his head. They flashed before him, growing faster and faster and faster, causing his head to erupt in searing pain. He clutched at it, trying to process the images, trying to understand what the depth-raider was trying to communicate. He pushed himself to focus despite the pain, and—

It stopped.

The depth-raider stared up at Lore for one last moment, then turned away. It hopped across the undergrowth, stopping to twitch its mouselike nose up in the air, like it had caught a scent, and then it . . . popped out of existence.

"You can *teleport?*" Lore exclaimed. "Why didn't you just do that all along?"

He shook his head to himself, then regretted it, because the pain from the flashing images hadn't quite faded.

The images—beautiful, horrifying.

Try as he might, Lore could only interpret the depth-raider's final message in one way:

I will see you before the world is born.

CHAPTER FIFTY-TWO

The Trapper's Mark

"You did *what*?" Val asked.

Lore blinked back at her, his face pale, and he shrugged—though I could tell he didn't mean it. "I let it go."

We'd woken in camp the morning after our meeting with Niamh to find a notable absence—the creature we'd crossed continents to find, one that we'd spilled blood over. We'd put in weeks of work, all for Lore to let the depth-raider go.

"And what, in all that is holy in Alterra, encouraged you to do such a thing?" Corminar asked. "Is there something left unresolved between us? Do you wish my debt to go unpaid?"

Lore shrugged again. "It wouldn't have been right, giving the creature away like that."

"That was the *whole point* of doing all this!" Val exclaimed.

At my side, perched next to me on a fallen tree that for whatever reason hadn't been removed with the rest, Arzak raised her eyebrows. Like me, she was more resigned to Lore having done what he'd done than the other two.

"It was . . . what's the word? Sentient?"

"All animals are sentient!"

Lore raised his hands in protest. "Well, I dunno, the other word, then! He was smart. Smarter than humans!"

"Smarter than *you*, maybe," Val snapped, and then her tense shoulders softened; she'd realized she'd gone too far there. "Sorry. Look. We put a lot of work into this, so you can imagine we'd be a bit miffed, yeah? And now how are we going to pay off the Red Thorn? Unless you want to go back to us getting them a mala, which . . . no. What's the plan here?"

"Sentience aside," Lore started.

"Sapience," Arzak called out to correct him.

"Sapience aside, what was *your* plan? Take it to meet a Player? I think that would've set it off, wouldn't it? Niamh is strong enough that if we brought it anywhere nearby . . ."

"He has a point, Val," I called out. "Unless you were planning on checking it in to an inn for a few nights or something."

Val shot me a glare. "Not helping."

It was my turn to hold up my hands—in surrender.

"It said it'd come back . . ." Lore mumbled.

"What was that?"

"Nothing."

"It *said it would come back*?" Val repeated. "It doesn't speak!"

"It does, just not in words."

"That's what speaking is! Words!"

Lore, looking increasingly distressed, shrugged again. "Well, it still said things! With pictures! What, did you think all those weird dreams you've been having was just us not eating so well?"

There was a moment of pause.

". . . How do you know about the dreams?" Val asked.

"Styk told me."

I held up my hands again in preemptive surrender.

"Styk . . ." Val growled.

"I meant, he told me about *his* dreams," Lore corrected himself. "You just talk in your sleep, Val."

I nodded my agreement. "Loudly."

"Look," Lore said, "I don't regret what I've done. You can shout at me all you want, but it's done now. He popped away. Teleported. We'll just have to find some other way of paying the Thorn back."

"After we kill Niamh," Val added. "I'm not letting her roam free any longer. You've seen the damage she's done already."

"Sure, after we do that."

They both turned to Corminar. "You on board?" the witch asked.

"I don't suppose that I have any other choice, do I?"

"You do not."

"Then, yes, Val, I am on board."

Lore looked relieved.

"Good. I'll get us some scouts, then," Val said, and she knelt to place her fingertips on the mossy ground. Her hands and eyes began to glow with that familiar green tint of *Witchcraft* magicks.

It wasn't long until our scouts arrived.

*   *   *

"Witch!" the soldier roared, finger pointing at the glowing Val, her wolf scouts circling around her.

We'd done well to avoid notice, even in the barren, deforested landscape, yet we hadn't been expecting anyone to be inside this abandoned barn. But the two men in Goldmarch armor who exited the barn were a low level, and both Arzak and I were out of sight.

I nodded for Arzak to take one soldier while I took the other, and we both crept up on the two soldiers before they could charge into battle with Val. With my level 2 *Stealth Attack* passive and my *Execution* ability activated, I took down my enemy in just a little over one hit—the first attack having alerted him to my presence but doing enough damage to him that the fight was already over. Arzak, for her part, had no trouble, but that didn't stop Corminar backing her up with a well-placed arrow.

At long last, this one enemy was enough to tip my *Knifework* progression over the edge.

Goldmarch Scout defeated!

Knifework: +1,500XP
Knifework increased to Level 35!
Base Points Gained: +1 DEX, +1 STR, +2 Free Points (VIT/DEX/STR)
Ability Selection Unlocked
Select an ability from the list below:

Val must have caught me smiling, because she asked, "You OK?"
"People who hate witches are really starting to get on my nerves," I replied.
"Tell me about it. Got yourself a new ability?"
"Oh yes."

Option 1: Ricochet (Knifework)—Throw blades at a hard surface for half your Stamina power to ricochet. Thrown blades retain 70 percent of speed with each bounce. Damage dealt scales with [DEX].

It was an ability that I'd chosen in a previous life, and one that had come in handy on numerous occasions. Back then, I hadn't had any *Worldbending* abilities, and so I'd leaned on this and *Throw* as my only real ranged attacks. In fact, if my memory was correct, this ability had been my very last attack the first time I'd faced down Jacob, Lev, and Tokas—that spoke for itself in terms of how much I used it.

But then again, it was the very same change—having *Worldbending* magicks now—that made this less useful. Not only did I have other options for range, namely either portaling myself next to an enemy or dropping them through a portal, I also hadn't invested in Dexterity to anywhere near the same extent as I had previously. And why would I? *Worldbending* had naturally become my primary skill tree, and I had my *Mana-Fueled* ability that allowed me to use mana in place of stamina for my *Knifework* attacks. Because *Ricochet's* damage scaled with Dexterity, this wasn't such a good choice this time around.

There, see? I do *sometimes* learn.

Hidden condition met! Alternative ability choice unlocked.
Option 2: Needle Blade (Knifework) [Requires: *Needlework* level 10]—You may use needles as weapons in place of knives. Needles deal 90 percent damage, but when dipped in poison, that poison is 100 percent effective.

It was an interesting selection for sure, and would have been *more* interesting should I have had an *Alchemy* skill tree. I could "borrow" Corminar's poisons, obviously, but that wasn't quite the same. If I was going to rely on something else for an ability to be effective, I wanted that something else to be fully under my control. I kept this one in the back of my mind as a possibility as I looked at the third and final option.

Hidden condition met! Alternative ability choice unlocked.
Option 3: Knifestorm (Knifework) [Requires: Dexterity over 90]—*Replaces Slice*. Lash out at all surrounding enemies in a tornado of blades, using either one or two daggers. All enemies within arm's reach receive physical damage worth the weapon's base damage and additional damage scaling on [STR].

It was always nice to get two hidden ability choices on one level-up, but that did always make the decision harder. I'd been given the choice to select this ability early on in a previous life, and I hadn't picked it. I think I'd only ever been given the choice once more, and on that level there was another ability that was more vital. It might have even been *Ricochet*.

This time, though, it felt like the right decision to select this ability. I didn't have many other ways of dealing with enemies if I ever got surrounded. If these enemies were so close that they were in arm's reach, I couldn't even escape through a portal, as they would fall through with me.

After one last look over the other two options to check that I hadn't missed anything, I locked in my choice.

Ability Unlocked: Knifestorm
Knifestorm (Knifework): Lash out at all surrounding enemies in a tornado of

blades, using either one or two daggers. All enemies within arm's reach receive physical damage worth the weapon's base damage and additional damage scaling on [STR].

I felt immediately better for it, as though my range and versatility of abilities was growing with every week that passed. And I didn't worry all that much that I was only level 15; I'd been efficient with my ability growth, so maybe that wasn't *all* that big of a deal.

I concentrated once more on the road ahead, Val's eyes glowing green as she sensed our commandeered wolf scouts. Corminar and Lore were just behind her, playing a game where Corminar had to guess what object in sight Lore was thinking of—so far, the answers had been: *road*, *tree stump*, and *sky*. And Arzak was at the rear of the pack, in theory making sure that nobody snuck up on us, but in practice still gazing lovingly on the sword I'd given her.

Suddenly, Val stopped.

"What is it?" I asked, hurrying to her side.

"Over the next hill," she said. "Niamh's destination."

"Where?" Lore asked. "There's nothing here. Nothing on the map."

Val shook her head. "There is. But the wolves . . . they don't have a word for it. The closest they have is . . . *sea beasts.*

Anticipation—or was it dread?—was heavy in my stomach as we silently strode up to the crest of this next hill. When we got there, when we saw what lay before us, suddenly everything we'd seen over the past few months fell into place. It was like the last piece of the puzzle had been put down, only we'd not been able to see the full picture until it was among the rest of the pieces.

Below us, along the coast of the Iron Sea, was a camp of shipyards—recently built, and of a scale unlike anything I'd seen before. A makeshift fort in the middle looked down upon each of the yards. Some ships in these bays were only half built, some were in this very moment having glowing blue and orange enchantments placed upon them.

And most of the ships? They were already at sea.

The mass deforestation. The creatures forced from the Iron Sea. Both of them made sense now.

The timber was going here from all across the Gentle Tundras, building a fleet like nothing ever before seen in the Western Continents. And Niamh, with her Trapper class, had overseen powerful enchantments to be placed upon these ships to strengthen them still. It was this power that had disturbed the cephalopors, and the merfolk, and all the other creatures that rumor had it had emerged from the Iron Sea.

Here, before us, was Niamh's true plan.

We'd thought we'd been so clever, disrupting the food imports to weaken

Niamh's hold on Aptleed. But we'd disrupted by only those that had come via land, when so much more came via sea. There was an elegance to Niamh's plan: just what we'd been doing, except on a much, much grander scale.

We thought we'd won the battle for the Tundras, but the truth was that they'd only just begun.

CHAPTER FIFTY-THREE

To End It Once More

The five members of the Slayers lay across the crest of the hill, using the cover of one of the few bushes not deemed worth tearing down.

"This not good," Arzak said for maybe the fifth time.

"No," Val murmured back. "No, not good at all. It doesn't seem like . . . a *perfect* plan, though, does it? If Yua can create an alliance of all the Tundran factions, then surely they can hold off a sea force?"

"The food imports," I reminded her.

"Still, though. We can just increase the purchases coming in from elsewhere?"

"What, from the Goldmarch?" I retorted. "I'm sure Queen Amira will be happy to oblige."

Val stuck her tongue out at my sarcasm.

"You will have to eat orcish food. Nice produce grow in snow. Trust me. You will like," Arzak said. "Lots of weltroot."

I didn't much want to find out what something called *weltroot* tasted like, so I turned my attention back to the new shipyards and figuring out what to do about them. "I think this is it. We've got to go in and kill her before she really gets going."

"You think she's in there?" Lore asked.

"I think it's our best bet, sure. If she's launching a fresh attack on the Tundras, where better than from a new base that nobody knows exists?"

Val nodded. "And if she's smart—and she is, trust me—she won't want to be at the front line. So she won't be on one of those ships unless she absolutely has to be."

"I had hoped to have a sufficient bow before we faced her, however if this is what needs to happen," Corminar grumbled, "then happen it shall. We will need disguises." Before Val could pipe up, he clarified, "And not only Val; we all must be able to walk into Niamh's office without a soldier taking notice."

"We get uniforms," Arzak agreed.

"You thought about what happens once we start fighting?" Lore asked. "Cos all those soldiers down there are gonna come running."

"We—" Val started, but she didn't get to finish that sentence because suddenly war drums erupted from around the shipyards—a great thundering, echoing noise that I could feel in my bones.

We turned our attention back to the shipyards to see that this sound was announcing the departure of the fleet. They were already putting the next stage of the plan into motion. Those vessels in the shipyards that were already completed rolled one by one into the sea on long, round wooden rollers, crashing into the water with an almighty splash. And those in the fleet that were already at sea—the vast majority of them—turned in the distance, pointing east.

"We're too late?" Lore wondered aloud.

But Val shook her head. "It makes no odds. We move now, we kill Niamh, and they'll have nobody capable of strategy. At least, nobody capable of it on her level. It doesn't change the plan." There was a shakiness to her voice that was subtle enough that only I—and from the furrowed brow, Arzak—noticed, and I squeezed her hand.

"It's gonna be over soon," I said.

She looked back at me and smiled a sad smile, one that showed she wasn't quite convinced. And she was right, of course. If we killed Niamh, then the woman who'd ruined Val's life would be gone, but she still had to deal with the fallout. She still wouldn't have a family. People the world over would still see witches dead and think that justice had been served.

The five of us turned our attention back to the shipyards once more.

"Are you ready?" Val asked.

"Never am."

She nodded, but still we snuck down the hill to do battle with a Player once again.

At the perimeter of the encampment, we used all our collective *Stealth* experience to keep out of sight through the advanced and elaborate strategy of hiding behind a wall.

"How many?" Val asked Corminar, who had somehow ended up with the responsibility of subtly poking his head around the corner.

"Only a small guard presence," the elf replied. "I am forced to assume that the majority of the Goldmarch army is aboard the ships."

"Could we fight our way through, then?" Lore asked.

"There are still too many for that to be a valid strategy."

"Hmm," Arzak said, and everyone but Corminar turned to face her.

"What is it?" Val asked.

"You not feel we always doing this? Sneaking into places, taking disguises? Must be better way of doing these things."

"If you have a better idea, we're all ears."

Arzak held her hands up in protest. "No better idea, just thinking aloud."

"I have it," Corminar said.

"An idea?"

"No, the location of the barracks. It is across the courtyard to our left; I saw the same man enter without uniform and exit with. Styk, would you care to do the honors?"

I shuffled over to his side. "Just tell me when." I poked my head around the corner of the wall underneath where Corminar was peering around, very conscious that if anyone spotted us, it would look ridiculous.

"Prepare yourself," Corminar said, where anyone else would have instead opted for "Get ready."

I raised one hand toward the side of the barracks closest to us and lowered the other to point at the floor at my feet. Arzak, Val, and Lore shuffled closer.

"And . . ." the elf started, and then a soldier suddenly came around a corner, who would see us if we were to open the portal in that moment. "Hold!"

"You know I can see, right?" I asked.

Corminar ignored me. "And . . . now!"

At his prompting, I opened the pair of portals and the five of us tumbled through, landing on the hard dirt outside of the barracks. I immediately whipped my hands backward to the barracks' wall, and again portaled us inside—this time, flying blind.

Last time we'd portaled our way into a barracks, we'd avoided detection, at least initially. It was only Val's poor acting skills that had given the game away, forcing Arzak and I to jump out of the wardrobe we'd been hiding in to help.

This time, we again tumbled out of a portal into the right room, but unlike last time, we did so in front of eight Goldmarch soldiers.

Lore raised a hand in greeting. ". . . Hi?" he said, a toothy grin on his face. But it wasn't enough to disarm this particular bunch.

One soldier looked to the exit.

"Arzak!" I shouted. "Door!"

She nodded, and I opened a portal beneath her—one that dropped her in front of the only exit to the room, and she slammed the door closed behind her. If we were about to fight, then we didn't want any reinforcements heading this way. We could only hope that nobody would overhear us, and not for the first time I regretted never picking *Silence* as a *Worldbending* ability, when I'd been given the option. I made a mental note.

"Soldiers . . ." a woman in the middle of the room said, her "gold" armor tinted by light blue magicks emanating from her hands. "Attack!"

There were enough people in this room that I didn't quite follow what happened next. All I know is that the soldiers nearest Lore and Arzak fell quickly, their builds being perfect for this kind of close quarters combat. Corminar and Val, however, were more hemmed in, so I joined them at their side, figuring three people who didn't like close quarters fighting was better than two.

Val twisted to one side to avoid an arcing greatsword, then ducked under it to knock the sword's owner in the stomach. But she didn't rely on bare-handed attacks alone, and she used her recently acquired lightning powers to drop the soldier to the ground.

Corminar, meanwhile, released arrow after arrow into the approaching soldiers, though at this range it was only a matter of time before the injured enemies overwhelmed him.

I jumped to support, portaling myself around the room and using the broken line of sight to quickly activate my *Stealth Attack* and *Execution* abilities on various targets, ignoring the experience point notifications as I did so. I didn't always take an enemy down in one hit—in fact, more often than not, I didn't—but it was enough to slow the soldiers down and thin them out some. Between my *stabs*, Corminar's arrows, and Val dealing magick damage, we weren't a half-bad team, even in this environment.

I'd thought the tide was turning, when the woman in the center of the room—who so far hadn't attacked anyone—whipped her glowing arms out to her sides. Echoes of the weapons of the fallen soldiers, formed of ghostly, light blue magicks, floated into the air.

"And what in Alterra is . . ." I started, but my question was soon answered.

After only a second of hesitation, the conjured weapons began flying toward all members of the Slayers at once.

We hadn't turned the tide at all. In fact, the fight had only just begun.

CHAPTER FIFTY-FOUR

Swords, Swords, & More Swords

"Uh-oh."

A half dozen floating, conjured swords stopped spinning in midair to point squarely at me, then shot in my direction. I surprised myself by jumping to the floor while the swords flew overhead, opening my usual portals not between me and the swords, but between Val and the ones flying toward her. The weapons shot through the portal and out at a wall, in which they became buried—but seconds later, they began trying to yank themselves back out again.

Somewhere between six and ten conjured weapons shot toward each member of the Slayers. I'd avoided the first wave, and I'd saved Val from the same, but the other three were having more trouble. Lore desperately swung his wide blade to parry the attacks of the floating weapons, and Corminar cowered behind the quartermaster's desk, frantically kicking the swords away as they approached. Only Arzak, of all of us, seemed to have a more viable long-term strategy.

The orc parried some of the conjured weapons away with her old sword, but she also used the enchanted sword I'd given her to absorb the floating blades. From the looks of it, she could only capture the magicks of one weapon at a time, but with every conjured weapon that she sucked in, her new sword glowed brighter. Even though it was a slow process, she was whittling down the enemy's attack, and every little bit helped.

The swords that had flown over my head turned in midair and swerved back toward me, and this time I again dove to the floor, but also opened a pair of portals to "catch" the attacks. The portal caught the conjured weapons in midattack and sent them soaring toward the last three Goldmarch soldiers—the conjurer included. While the weapons pierced two of the soldiers, sending them stumbling backward into the wall and pinning them there, the swords passed straight through the woman who had conjured them.

"Perhaps an ounce of assistance could be provided?" Corminar called out, his voice shaking, his legs frantically kicking the swords away.

The swords I'd just portaled turned around again, half pointing to me, and half splintering off toward Val. There wasn't much time to help them both, so I opened a portal below Val's feet without asking first—if she had a problem with that, then she'd have to bring it up later—and threw her into the corner behind where Arzak and Lore were successfully parrying or absorbing any attacks.

Next, I fixed my attention back to Corminar, dropping myself through a portal of my own just in time to avoid the conjured swords flying toward me. I dropped at Corminar's side and immediately grabbed two of the conjured weapons from the air—by the hilt, naturally, not the blade, though I'd once made that mistake in the past. I brought them down as I crouched and buried them deep in the wooden floor.

Corminar, recognizing what I was doing, took advantage of me slowing the attack. Instead of kicking the next sword away, he rolled out of its way at the last minute, hopped nimbly to his feet, and buried it in the floorboards in much the same way as I had just done.

Before long, this area of the room was clear besides the last sword, which Corminar and I were wrestling toward the wall. Out of the corner of my eye, I could see the conjuror with her arm stretched toward us, willing the magick sword away from the wall.

Corminar released his grip on the floating sword to pull out his bow once more, and he shot an arrow toward the enemy. She whipped another sword away from Lore to block the arrow, but in doing so she broke her concentration, and I was able to bury the sword in the wall.

I thought, for a moment, that we were on our way to victory. What a fool I was.

The conjuror roared, frustrated, and with a flick of her wrist she dematerialized the weapons that were buried in the wall or floor, and created new ones at her side to replace them. That was interesting, then; she had a limit as to how many swords she could conjure. And from the look of Arzak's sword, glowing brighter than ever, the conjuror wasn't able to unsummon those that Arzak had captured. If we could keep Arzak protected, doing her thing, then it was only a matter of time until this fight was won.

Unfortunately, the conjuror had just had the same realization.

All the remaining conjured weapons—a good twenty-five or so, though I didn't exactly have the time for a thorough count—ceased their attacks on Lore, Val, Corminar, and I, and all repositioned to point at Arzak instead.

"Err . . ." the orc mumbled, eyes wide. "Need help!"

Lore, standing closest to Arzak, rushed in the way of the soaring blades, knocking as many from the air as he could. Arzak, for her part, did her best to parry and absorb the rest, but it was clear that they were getting slowly overcome.

"Styk!" Val shouted to me, but I was already on it.

I reached to open another portal to shield my friends from the conjured weapons, but an idea struck me midway through. Instead of opening one of my usual *Local Portals*, I tried something else. I tried a *Pocket World.*

The floating swords, with no real minds of their own, did little to avoid the portal, and they shot straight into my pocket dimension, removing them from play. I felt through the magical connection with my ability that I was already eating well into my storage capacity—conjured weapons used up a lot of space, it seemed.

The conjuror's eyes widened as she saw her magicks disappear into the portal, and she tried first to pull the weapons back out again. But I was quicker than her, and I snapped the portal shut once more before the first sword tip could come through and wedge it open.

With so few swords left—only six or so, compared to the original number, which had been four times that—it crossed my mind again that the fight might now be turning. For a second time in the past five minutes, I was wrong. I really had to stop assuming things like that.

The conjuror, sensing that she wasn't going to be able to pin down—or kill— all five of us with so few weapons, changed up her tactic. All but one of the remaining conjured swords shot back toward the woman who'd magicked them, twisting at the last moment before hitting her to instead begin spinning around her, like some strange magical tornado. The last conjured weapon hovered in front of her, pointing at Lore, who happened to be closest. The sword hovered there as though daring Lore to attack, to find out what would happen if he did.

Lore took the dare.

The barbarian charged forward, swinging his heavy blade to knock the single floating sword out of the way, and then he swung it again at the conjuror. His blade met the spinning weapons, moving fast enough that he and the Bane Sword bounced away again—but not before he took a good few deep scratches in the process.

"Styk!" Val shouted. "Get her out of there!"

I nodded, then pressed my right hand forward to open a portal beneath the conjuror's feet. But just like what had happened a few times before when facing down an adept magick user, the conjuror was ready for this. One of the swords in the tornado tore off from its path and shot down below the woman's feet, stopping her from falling through. So these swords could touch her when she wanted them to.

I gritted my teeth together as I closed this futile portal. "Gonna need to try something else!"

Arzak, with her imbued blade, charged forward next, swinging her weapon into the tornado. But again, the storm of blades was moving fast enough that she only bounced off, unable to touch metal to spell for long enough to absorb the remaining swords.

"Reinforcements required!" the conjuror shouted. "Reinforcements required!"

Val's gaze flicked to me; she knew as well as I did that we needed to end this fight before someone actually heard us.

Corminar released an arrow over my shoulder, but again it was unable to get past the spinning weapons. It was seemingly impenetrable.

But there was still *one* thing left that I could try.

I made a show of roaring—and attracting the enemy's attention—as I pressed my right hand forward once more, looking as though I meant to open another portal beneath the woman's feet.

The conjuror immediately pulled one sword from her tornado, whizzing it toward the spot under her feet where my portal was about to be.

Or *would have been*, if I'd actually intended to open one there.

Instead, I opened a portal between the ground and the shifting blade. And I created its partner in front of the conjuror's chest.

The blade shot through, and because the woman had wanted to be able to stand on it, it was solid to her. She yelped as it pierced her chest. Her eyes bulged, and she let her conjured weapons fade as she instead shifted to yellow-white *Healing* magicks.

But Lore, Arzak, and Corminar weren't going to let her get out of this so easily. They seized the advantage of the break in the enemy's defense, letting her have sword and arrow and in plentiful supply. This time, the fight really *did* turn in our favor.

As the woman dropped to the floor, I let the notifications that had piled up come through.

4 x Goldmarch Soldiers defeated!
Goldmarch Bladebinder defeated!

Worldbending: +4,320XP
Worldbending increased to Level 43!
Base Points Gained: +2 INT, +2 Free Points (INT/WIS/CHA)
Knifework: +4,250XP
Knifework increased to Level 36!
Base Points Gained: +1 DEX, +1 STR, +2 Free Points (VIT/DEX/STR)
Stealth: +3,900XP

> *Stealth increased to Level 18!*
> *Stealth increased to Level 19!*
> **Base Points Gained**: +2 DEX, +2 WIS, +4 Free Points (DEX/WIS)

Nice, I thought, *up I go some more*. And then I returned my attention to the task at hand: killing a Player.

CHAPTER FIFTY-FIVE

The Mix-Up

Our borrowed Goldmarch armor now on, we set about marching across the new shipyards, doing our best to look as though we were striding with purpose. We hadn't bothered to clear up our mess in the barracks; chances were that the alarm would get raised soon enough anyway, when we took on Niamh. Once that alarm *was* raised, we just had to hope we finished her off quickly enough that I could portal us out of harm's way before the remaining soldiers swarmed us.

Admittedly, there weren't all that many Goldmarch soldiers left here. Most of Niamh's army had become her navy, taking positions on the ships built from Tundran timber. That explained why our earlier fight hadn't attracted any further attention, then.

We strode along the shipyards, the few remaining Goldmarch soldiers we passed nodding in our direction, or saluting to me. We hadn't realized when we picked out uniforms that fit us that I'd picked up a major's uniform, and all the respect I now commanded was really getting on Val's nerves.

So it was then that when we reached the tallest building in the new shipyards—Niamh's apparent makeshift fort—I nodded to the soldiers standing guard to give us access. And they stood aside in a hurry; I could really get used to this "commanding respect" business.

We walked through the corridors of the building, still doing our best to look like we knew where we were going, and soon we found the stairs. Val's logic had been that Niamh would be using the highest point of this building as her command center. It gave her the best view of her fleet, and why else would she build a fort so high if not to be at the top of it?

We climbed the staircase to the top level and found that the top floor was all one room. In the center of the room was a wooden table, intricately carved with a map of the western continents—everywhere from the Beached Armada to the Dawnwood—and on this table were small models of ships, just off the coast near where we were. And standing just across the table, staring at us . . . was an orc.

"Where is she?" Val spat. "Where's Niamh?"

The orc—the one I only at this moment placed as Niamh's assistant—looked up with a smirk on her face. "Not here," she replied.

"Not here in this room?" Lore asked. "Or not here at these shipyards?"

"Make no odds to you."

Val took another step forward, but the orc—Sulla, if I remembered her name correctly—held up an index finger.

"No. No, not come closer."

"And why the hells not?" Val asked.

"Niamh is Trapper, yes? Physical traps, strategy traps, yes. But also magick traps. You step closer and I activate."

The room went silent. Five Slayers stared down one Player's assistant.

"So . . ." Lore finally said, breaking the silence. "What's this trap do, then?"

"You not want find out."

Again, the room went silent. At least, until Arzak stepped forward.

"Woah, what are you doing?" Lore asked.

The friendly orc shrugged. "Maybe she lie. Maybe not. But trap or not, we do same thing? We attack and interrogate?"

Val thought about this for a moment, and then nodded. "Yep, fair enough." She and Arzak turned and launched themselves across the table, and in the same moment, Sulla slapped a hand down atop the carved wooden table.

A sigil glowed to life.

Something—some magical force—grabbed at my heart. It choked me, just for a moment, and from the look of the rest of the team, it was doing the same to them, too. And then . . .

Active Effect: Class Swap
Minutes remaining: 4 / 5
Your class and progression is temporarily swapped with another of target [5] entities.

Arzak and Val, choked by the trap, fell to the floor hard at Sulla's feet, and she smiled down at them before giving Val a good kick.

Snarling, I instinctively reached forward, meaning to open a portal beneath the enemy's feet that would stop her kicking Val again. But . . . nothing came.

"Err . . ." I said.

Corminar shot an arrow from his bow and managed to launch it into his own foot.

"What's going—" Lore began, and then suddenly accidentally opened a portal beneath his feet. He fell through it, then tumbled out of its partner on the ceiling above him. Then he fell back into it, and . . . Well, you can see where this was going.

I ran over to the edge of the portal, reaching out to catch him, but already he was moving too fast for me to have any chance of stopping him alone.

I stopped him. Alone.

As Lore clung to my outstretched arms, I stared down at them. I was . . . lifting him? Lifting *Lore*? About the largest human I'd ever encountered?

Sulla kicked Val in the stomach once more, and she spat out blood. Val clutched at her chest, desperately trying to *heal* it, but nothing happened.

Alright. I'm starting to understand what's happened here.

"Who's the Witch?" I cried out as Sulla strolled slowly to the other side of the room to draw an axe from atop a nearby table. "Who's the damned *Witch*?"

I looked to Arzak, who scrambled over to Val's side, meaning to *heal* her, but she shook her head—nothing happened. I reached within myself, searching for one of Val's powers, and tried to summon a wolf. But if I was doing it right— and I had no idea if I was, admittedly—nothing happened. I looked instead to Corminar, whose eyes glowed green.

"Oh, I *do not* approve of this at all," he said. Still, he leaped into the air and charged to the injured Val's side to heal her.

Sulla, meanwhile, approached the fallen Arzak with her great axe in hand. Arzak raised her dual blades to block the inevitable swing of the axe, but I already knew how that would end. She wasn't a Warrior anymore. Someone else was.

"No!" I shouted to Arzak, reaching forward to open a portal that I knew wouldn't come.

But it did.

Arzak fell through the portal on the floor and came out of one above Lore's head, crushing him. From the once-barbarian's hand, glowing purple, I realized he'd been quick to act; he'd been paying attention all these months.

"Oopsie," he said as Arzak pulled herself off him.

Sulla grunted, then turned her attention back to the injured Val and the elf leaning over her, who was trying to work out how her *Healing* magicks worked. "I require assistance!" Corminar shouted, sensing Sulla's approach without looking up. "Who among you is the Ranger?"

Arzak and I looked to each other, then shrugged at the same time. "Could be Val," I said.

Val roared with pain as she wrenched Corminar's bow off him and tried to fire it. She fumbled the arrow as she tried to nock it, tearing a gash in her palm in the process.

"It is not Val!" Corminar confirmed, then took the bow back from her and chucked it and his quiver toward Arzak and me. Arzak, being substantially taller, snatched the items out of the air first, and in a flash she nocked the arrow and fired it at Sulla. It hit the enemy squarely in the shoulder.

"I think it might be Arzak," Lore pointed out.

I'd started to put it all together by this point. Arzak had temporarily become a Ranger, Corminar had become a Witch, and Lore had become a Worldbender. Which meant that Val and I were either a Warrior or a Barbarian. Having never experienced either of those skill trees, I didn't quite understand what the difference between those two classes was, but I knew the gist of it: get a big weapon and swing it.

Arzak tossed me her two swords, and I snatched them nimbly out of the air. They felt . . . they just felt *right* in my hands. It was her class that I'd adopted.

"I have it!" Corminar suddenly cried, yellow-white *Healing* magicks pouring into Val's stomach. For his troubles, Sulla swung her axe his way, and the elf had just enough time to throw himself across Val—but not without suffering a deep gash wound in his back.

I charged in toward Sulla to prevent her landing another attack, jumping across the wooden table with more strength and athletic ability than I'd ever experienced before. I brought my borrowed swords down toward the enemy, and Sulla swung her axe up to block me, its metal handle able to hold off even my strong attacks.

"*Dual Swipe!*" Arzak called from behind me as I pushed against Sulla's axe, gritting my teeth with the strain.

"I don't know what that is!" I cried back. Just like Corminar had found, the swapped abilities weren't coming naturally to me, and it was for this reason that Sulla stood a very good chance of winning this fight. It was a stroke of genius, really; most magick-based traps would do damage to everyone in the room, friendly or otherwise. But this? This was more targeted—or at least Sulla, and likely Niamh, were excluded from it—and it weakened the enemies through means of making sure they had absolutely no idea what they were doing.

As if to punctuate this thought, Lore yelped as he accidentally fell through a portal again, though this time at least he was able to close them again before it got out of control. Meanwhile, Arzak loosed another arrow, narrowly avoiding hitting me but successfully catching Sulla in the chest.

This damage weakened the orc's attack for a moment, and I was able to press forward, knocking her to the ground. "*Dual Swipe!*" I cried, trying my best to activate this ability.

"You only moving one sword," Arzak noted.

Sulla released one hand from her axe and, rising, caught me hard in the throat. I stumbled backward, choking, my attack called off. The enemy rose back from her knees to her to her feet and pressed her own attack, swiping at me again and again with an axe that I was only *just* about quick enough to block.

"A little help here?" I cried out.

"Unless you want me to bleed on her, or Corminar to summon some wolves, it's gonna have to be from the others," Val replied, her voice weak from the damage she'd suffered.

Lore stumbled forward, and out of the corner of my eye I could see his brow furrowing like it did when he was really concentrating. He pressed one hand forward toward me and Sulla, and with the flick of his wrist . . .

. . . opened up a portal behind us. Corminar fell through it and came out tumbling toward Sulla. The movement of her axe once again narrowly caught him, dealing some damage but not enough to put him out of action.

Lore winced. "Sorry!"

"Lore, you've got to—" I started, but doing so distracted me just enough for Sulla to find an advantage. She knocked the bottom of her axe into my stomach, sending me falling backward toward the floor, and she raised her weapon high in the air.

As she stared down at me, she growled, and even Arzak burying another arrow in the enemy's leather armor wasn't enough to stop her.

She brought the axe down.

CHAPTER FIFTY-SIX

Niamh's True Plan

I winced as Sulla's axe came tumbling down toward me. In that fraction of a second, there wasn't enough time to block. There wasn't enough time to do much of anything, except wait for the inevitable. I could only hope I'd inherited enough Vitality from Arzak that I was going to survive the hit—even without armor.

I closed my eyes, preparing myself for the pain, and—

I fell.

Opening my eyes, I saw Lore's outstretched arms rushing up to meet me as I tumbled toward the floor. He caught me, found me too heavy, and then dropped me to the floor after all. I didn't like what this said about the number of Strength points he'd inherited from me.

"That's more like it, buddy," I said, looking up at him from the floor, and he responded with a thumbs-up and a goofy grin.

"Watch out!" Val shouted, and I rolled to the right just in time to avoid Sulla's flailing axe.

I raised my hands and . . . realized I'd dropped the swords when I'd fallen through the portal. Sulla approached, crazed eyes fixed on me, arrow after arrow hitting her in the back, swinging her axe closer and closer with every second. I retreated backward, toward the wall, my every instinct being to activate a portal to get me out of this mess, but of course . . . that wasn't possible. I flashed Lore a meaningful, wide-eyed look, and he tried to activate a portal beneath me, but lightning didn't strike twice—unpracticed at magicks, he missed again.

He'd saved me once, but very quickly I found myself pinned down again, this time with my back against a wall. I needed to think quickly. I needed to find some ability that Arzak had that I could use to get out of this. I needed—

> **Active Effect: Class Swap**
> Minutes remaining: 0 / 0
> *Effect removed!*

—portals.

I smiled, and fear flashed through Sulla's eyes. She'd realized what had happened. She realized she'd messed up, wasting time, not pressing the attack quickly enough.

Her advantage was gone.

Just as her swinging axe was about to meet my face, I opened a portal beneath us, and we both fell through, landing at Lore's feet. Arzak, moving quickly, reached for the Bane Sword and tossed it to the barbarian, who swung it down, holding it still only a fraction of an inch from the enemy's neck.

> *Level 18 Council Advisor defeated!*

> **Worldbending**: +750XP
> *Worldbending increased to Level 44!*
> **Base Points Gained**: +2 INT, +2 Free Points (INT/WIS/CHA)

A shame; that was a pitiful amount of experience points. Though I realized I couldn't exactly get experience for my two-handed attacks if I didn't have that skill tree unlocked any more. At least it had been enough for a level-up.

I turned my attention to Sulla, who was now totally restrained by means of three swords pointing at her head. "Drop the axe."

She did so without needing to be asked twice.

I saw the yellow-white glow of *Healing* magicks out of the corner of my eye, followed by Val bringing herself to her feet. She hadn't suffered that much damage, just more than Corminar had figured out how to fix. Val turned her attention next to the big wound in the ranger's back.

"I'll ask you again: where is she?" I demanded of Sulla.

"I tell you: not here," Sulla spat back at me. She'd surrendered then, but she wasn't going to give up any information that easily.

I sighed. "You know, I don't think that trap was all that good. You had all these threats at first, and you were all intimidating and such, and now . . . well, I just don't think you followed through on those promises."

Sulla spat upward at me, but at my height it didn't reach me.

"Unless . . . you didn't know what it did?" I suggested. "You just knew that Niamh had set a trap there, but she'd never told you what it did? Does she often keep stuff from you?"

This time, the orc didn't react. Though she didn't show it on her face, I suspected she was considering my words carefully.

"Was it intentional, do you think? Did she mean to leave you in the dark? Or did she simply not bother to tell you?"

"Not sure which worse," Arzak added, nodding along. "Must be hard not be trusted." She understood what was going on here, then. I was playing the bad guard, while she—a fellow orc—would play the good. Someone that Sulla might open up to.

"Do you even *know* where she is, your boss?" I asked. "Or did she not bother to tell you that, either?"

"I know where she is!" Sulla insisted.

I shook my head. "She doesn't know," I said, directing this over my shoulder at Val. "See, I told you she—"

"I *know*!" the enemy orc said again.

"You not convince unless you say," Arzak offered. "She here, yes?"

"Pfft. Why this be?"

"Because she would need to control her operations in the Tundras from somewhere, wouldn't she?" I said. "And I don't exactly think a ship is the best place to do it."

At this, the orc on the floor tipped her head back and laughed. I could almost see tears forming in her eyes. "She did say you stupid. You Lore, yes?"

"Hey!" Lore exclaimed.

". . . Oh," Sulla said. "You are Styk, then?" Sulla didn't wait for me to confirm. "She say you stupid, but I not believe it. Nobody can be this stupid, I say. But she right! You think all this is about Tundras still? This *never* about Tundras. Tundras just have wood we need."

I narrowed my eyes. If I hadn't heard the way Sulla had said this, I'd have thought she was lying. But this woman spoke like she had nothing to lose, like we were so far from the mark that she risked nothing by speaking the truth. "What do you mean, this isn't about the Tundras? You just wanted the wood?"

"You not see our ships? Big Goldmarch fleet. No fleet of this size seen for ages."

"We saw the fleet. It was about control of the Tundras—interrupting food transport links, starving us into submission."

Sulla laughed again—a bold move for someone with so many sword points to her neck. "Nobody *care* about Tundras. Nobody invade Tundras for generations, and know why? Because no point. Nothing to gain."

"You gained something."

"True. We gain wood. For ships."

"And the ships are for . . . ?" I asked, but I could sense I was losing her. I'd lost my advantage; she thought all of us were fools now.

Sulla stared up at me and smiled. I found this infuriating.

"Tell me what the ships are for, or we'll turn your neck into a bloody hedgehog." When Sulla looked up at me, confused, I clarified, ". . . Cos it'll be spiky. Cos of the swords in it."

The orc nodded. "Right."

"Still not telling us?"

Sulla stared up at me again, and at this, Arzak smashed the woman in the head with the pommel of her sword.

I blinked at her. "What . . . did you just do?"

"Knock her out," the orc said. "I learn it from Lore."

Lore nodded knowingly.

"And so what is it that you suppose we do next?" Corminar asked, staring at the unconscious orc.

Arzak shrugged. "She not speaking."

"Well of course she's not *now!*" Val cried.

"Not before, not now. But now nobody annoying me." Arzak gestured around the room. "We in command center. We look around."

I sighed; the whole point of interrogating this woman had been to avoid having to actually look around. After all, someone could stumble inside at any moment and raise the alarm. But I supposed there was no other option now.

I shifted to the side of the carved wooden table, staring down at the little models of ships with markers for the sailors standing upon them. They were sailing east, just as we'd seen them do in real life. Between them, there was enough to disrupt trade all across the Iron Sea, to hold the Gentle Tundras in Niamh's grasp.

Of course, Sulla had claimed they had no interest in the Tundras anymore.

Behind me, the rest of the team ruffled through paperwork. Lore tossed a big pile onto the floor. When everyone looked at him, eyebrow raised, he explained, "Tax returns."

I stared back down at the ships, the vessels with such power that they were driving creatures like cephalopors out of the water. Surely Sulla was just lying to us, trying to throw us off the scent. Because what was the alternative? What else could this fleet do?

A chill ran down my spine when I noticed a model under my right hand, in the southeast.

The Great Golden Canal Project. The canal network that connected the Iron Sea to the Sea of Roots, enabling trade all the way from the Tundras to the Dawnwood—a project sponsored by Queen Amira herself, in a display of gratitude to her supposed future allies.

Only, there was another way of looking at it, wasn't there?

You could send trade ships through the Goldmarch-controlled canals, yes. But you could also send warships. And when your shipyards were so far north, how could anyone at or beyond the canals expect the oncoming sea force?

This was an invasion, yes, but it really wasn't the Tundras that Amira wanted.

It was the Dawnwood.

"Guys," I said. "I think we've messed up."

CHAPTER FIFTY-SEVEN

Setting Sail

Corminar stared down at the wooden model of the Dawnwood, paling, the truth of what I'd just told him setting in. "No . . ." he whispered. "No."

"It's the only explanation, Cor," Val said, hand on his shoulder. "Sulla wasn't lying. And what else could the Golden Canal Project have been for? A real act of charity?"

The elven ranger shook his head. "Fools," he muttered.

"What?"

"Fools," he said again. "All of us. All of my kind, too, to have trusted Amira in these supposed 'diplomatic efforts.' We should have looked to the larger picture, to how the pieces interconnected. We should have known this was coming."

"Cor, we couldn't have—" Val started, but Corminar turned away from the table, snarling with anger.

"We most certainly *could* have! Or is it not our proclaimed occupations to distrust Players?"

"We *did* distrust her," I said, backing Val up. "We fought in a war to remove her from our home. That was our distrust."

"Your home," Corminar corrected me. "The Tundras are *your* home."

"And yours. You know as well as I do that you've not been welcome in the Dawnwood for a long time now. That's not your home anymore."

"Styk . . ." Val said. She flashed me a look that said she didn't think I was helping.

"OK, fine, look," I continued. "That's not the point, anyway. The point is that we've been fighting. We're not fools, we were just . . . misdirected. What matters is what we do next. And I reckon we've got to do what heroes do."

"And what's that?" Val asked.

"We follow."

"Cooee!" I shouted, standing on the docks by the last seaworthy ship, jumping up and down. "Over here, you big idiots!"

A face popped over the side of the ship—a woman wearing Goldmarch armor. "Oi!"

"What, should I not be here?" I asked, playing oblivious.

"No, you *bloody well* should not be here," she replied. Then she turned to others on the ship. "Enemy on the pier!"

This was what I'd set out to achieve, so at that I turned and jogged slowly away from the ship. The guards took their sweet time in following, balancing clumsily on the plank that joined the vessel to the docks.

I turned, running backward. "Nice secret bunch of dockyards you have here! Would be a shame if someone, I dunno, reported them to Duchess Yua of Lenktra, wouldn't it?" The guards were following already, but I couldn't resist rubbing it in a bit further.

Once my pursuers were on land, I began to sprint properly, turning around the corner of a tall wooden palisade wall . . . and bumping straight into more guards.

"Oops."

"Yeah, bloody *oops*," the tall soldier I'd just collided with replied, then he swung his sword toward me.

I responded by opening a portal beneath my feet, and I smiled and waved as I dropped through it, coming to land on the platform of a watchtower up above.

"Missed me!" I shouted, to both the pursuers from the ship and to the man I'd bumped into. I glanced back at the vessel, and the four familiar figures creeping onto it, rushing for the capstan. They'd needed a few minutes of peace before they could raise the anchor and drop the sails. They'd needed someone to goad the guards into chasing them away from the last seaworthy vessel.

Fortunately, I could be very annoying when I wanted to be—and I had the portal magicks to evade capture. It really hadn't taken the Slayers very long at all to realize that this was the correct course of action.

"He's up there!" the woman who'd first spotted me shouted, pointing up to the watchtower.

"Hi!" I waved back at them, conscious of the soldier at her side raising his bow to point at me. Just as the ranger could fire, I opened another portal in the way of the attack, pointing the arrow back at the man who'd shot it.

He stumbled backward, looking at the arrow pointing out of his right upper arm. "Oh," he mumbled.

I risked another look at the ship, not wanting to look too much in case it tipped off the Goldmarch soldiers. Val, Lore, Arzak, and Corminar were all now at the capstan, beginning to turn it, though it looked like the warrior and the barbarian were doing most of the heavy lifting. There was a *clunk, clunk, clunk* noise as they lifted the anchor, and if I wasn't distracting enough, the soldiers were going to realize this wasn't being done by people from the Goldmarch.

"Well?" I asked. "What are you waiting for? Come up here! We can have a nice chat."

The woman in charge gestured for her soldiers to climb up the ladder, but it was a long way to go.

I made a show of tapping my foot impatiently—an act that *really* got on the woman's nerves—before calling out, "This is taking too long! Want me to help?" Before she could answer, I opened a portal underneath the first soldier's feet, bringing her up to the top of the watchtower with me, where I proceeded to push my knife forward in a *stab*.

But the soldier recovered quickly, and she brought her blade around to meet mine, smashing it out of the path of attack, but not quite out of my grasp. I attacked again, hoping my weapon being smaller meant that I'd be quicker on the attack, but that hope was unfounded. She turned on the spot to avoid the attack, and as she came back around to face me once more, she lunged with her sword.

I was rapidly running out of time to defeat her—four of her five colleagues would soon be up the ladder, and I'd be surrounded. In this enclosed environment, I wouldn't be able to guarantee portaling away without someone following. I had to act now.

But I'd planned for this. And it had been exciting to find a use for an ability that I didn't get to use all that often, what with most objects seeming to be magically reinforced these days.

With the flick of my wrist, I opened up a portal at the top of the ladder, but this wasn't one of my usual *Local Portals*. This was a *Portal Slice*. The metal ladder was sliced clean through and began to creak. The soldier up on the platform with me baulked, eyes wide, as she saw what had just happened. For a moment, when the ladder didn't immediately fall, I thought I was going to have to shift around the platform to get a look at the bottom of the ladder, too, and *Portal Slice* through there. But then the creaking got louder, and louder, and the base of the ladder began to warp and bend, sending the four soldiers tumbling toward the ground.

It wasn't enough to eliminate any of them, but it bought me some time.

The soldier on the platform lunged with her blade once more, and I had just enough time to lean to one side to avoid the attack. But I wouldn't keep being that lucky.

I risked a glance over to the deck of the seaworthy ship, and then I saw the signal: Val jumping up and down and waving both hands in the air. They were ready to go. As the soldier raised her blade to attack me once more, I opened a portal behind me and stepped through it, out onto the deck of the nowstolen ship.

But a hand poked through before I could close it.

The woman pushed herself through the closing portal, jaw gritted with determination, and stumbled out onto the deck. "Stop!" she cried. "In the name of Empress Amira, leader of the—"

She didn't finish that order because Lore collided with her chest, tackling her toward the wall of the captain's cabin. Before they could hit the wall, I opened another portal—conscious that I'd depleted a lot of my mana reserves already—and summoned its partner at the edge of the ship.

Lore and the Goldmarch soldier both fell through the portal and over the rail, tumbling toward the sea below. In a fraction of a second, I closed the last portals and opened one last pairing—one that caught Lore in midair and caused him to come out rolling across the deck.

From the water below, I heard a huge splash.

6 x Soldiers of the Golden Empire escaped!
Worldbending: +900XP

Between the soldier's barked order and the new notification, I realized that the Golden Kingdom was no more. It was the Golden Empire now, what with Amira having parts of the Gentle Tundras in her domain already, and the Dawnwood surely about to fall to a sea force they could not have seen coming.

Niamh's plan was coming together, and the only chance the elven homeland had was that she could be stopped by a witch, a gentle barbarian, a narcissistic ranger, an orc warrior who would really rather be knitting, and . . . me. Whatever I was these days—simply a bladespinner, a hero, or the spawn of a Player?

As the western banks of the Iron Sea faded into the distance behind us, I closed my eyes and breathed. At my side, Val squeezed my hand, though this time even she didn't say a word.

We were heading for war once more. The *real* war.

Except, this was one we had no hope of winning.

CHAPTER FIFTY-EIGHT

Payment

"Up," Arzak said, shaking me awake in my bunk. She and Corminar had been on sailing and watch duty, after we'd figured out that we could man the ship with just two people if need be. I hadn't voiced this thought, but I suspect the ships were designed that way so as many soldiers as possible could disembark and be part of the invading force.

Groggily, I looked to my side to find that Val had already risen for the day. "It's morning already?"

The orc shook her head. "No. We being followed."

At this, I sat bolt upright and narrowly avoided hitting my head on the bunk above this one. The designers had packed so many bunks onto these fairly compact ships—enough to carry an invading force as efficiently as possible for the two or three days it would take to reach the Dawnwood.

I followed Arzak up to the deck, where Lore was standing looking at the horizon. I narrowed my eyes, trying to adjust to the low light of the predawn morning. "How long has it been following?"

"Long enough that we know it *is* following," the barbarian replied.

"Goldmarch?" I asked. "Was there another seaworthy ship at the dockyards? One we missed?"

Lore shrugged. "Can't tell at this distance. Will know once it catches up, though."

"And how long until that happens?"

"At this rate? Maybe a couple of hours?"

I gulped. "You given any thought about what happens when they *do* catch up? Back on land, I could portal us away. Here, though . . . we'd be trapped."

"We know," Arzak said glumly.

I dwelled on this a moment. "Anything we can do to go faster? Something with the sails?"

"I look like sailor to you?" the orc replied, arms crossed.

"And I checked; there weren't any sailing guidebooks anywhere," Lore added helpfully. "You'd think there would be, on a ship, but . . ."

I looked about. "Where's Val? And Corminar? You asked them?"

"Val's up in the top bit," Lore said, pointing up the mainmast. "I asked her already."

"Crow nest," Arzak corrected him.

"And . . . Corminar? Dunno. Inside somewhere? Figure elves don't really sail much, though, do they? Like their feet on solid ground."

I nodded. "I'll go find him. See if he's got any thoughts. Otherwise . . . prepare to fight, I guess?" I couldn't help but sound defeated already. Resisting the urge to sigh, I turned and walked down into the hold of the ship, walking among the rows of bunks. There was an eerie quality to this ship being so empty, there being so many spots where people *should* have been, but weren't. In fact, the only figure I found was Corminar, holed up on a bunk at the very front of the ship.

"You doing OK?" I asked the elf with glazed-over eyes. "Lore says you don't like boats."

"My people do not, as a rule, enjoy being on water. Much preferable is it to feel the roots beneath our feet."

"Through shoes, you mean?" I asked.

Corminar didn't respond, not at all in the mood for jokes right at this moment.

"There's another—" I started, meaning to explain the situation, but at that second, the elf spoke.

"In the wildest of my dreams, I did not expect to return home in this manner. I *never* imagined it would be under these circumstances."

I nodded. "Can't blame you. Not sure I've ever read about an invasion of the Dawnwood. Not something that's happened in the past few generations, is it?"

"It has never been invaded, Styk. Never before has anyone had the gall, the malice, the . . . greed. And yet it is to happen in my lifetime. Chances are, I sail to watch my homeland fall."

"Others have underestimated us too, though, haven't they?" I retorted. "And look where they've ended up. We've got to stay confident, Corminar. We've got to remember that we are *heroes*. And heroes do not give up. Heroes always find a way to triumph. We will sail to the Dawnwood, we'll save them, and we'll make you a legend of the elves. Maybe we'll even get that birth seed of yours planted, make a proper bow for you. How does that sound?"

"Impossible," Corminar responded.

"So was killing the pyroknight. So was killing those other Players, before you met me, I imagine. We've faced the impossible before, and yeah, we face it again now. But I expect to live to see the other side."

The ranger remained quiet, then shook his head. "No."

"No?"

"No, not this time. This time, the odds are truly stacked against us. We no longer face one lone enemy, a situation wherein the enemy out-levels us, but we have a numerical advantage. In this scenario, the Goldmarch outnumbers us a hundred to one. These situations are not even comparable. You would be insane to treat them as such."

"I've been called insane before."

"Yes, I overhear you and Val flirting on occasion."

"That's not—" I shook my head; this wasn't a conversation there was any point having. "Look, Corminar. You're the Hero of Iranir. That means some-thing to your people. You can lead them to victory, if you'd do it."

"No," the elf said again. "That battle, in the Honey Wars . . . that was a onetime stroke of inspiration. Nothing more. I will never be that leader again."

"But Corminar, I've *seen* you be that—"

Before I could finish that sentence, I noticed Lore lurking down the cabin. He'd been peculiarly quiet, considering his large body type, as though he'd been approaching slowly, softly, delaying the moment until he'd have to deliver what-ever news he'd come with.

"Styk," he said. When I realized how pale his face was, my stomach churned.

"Yeah? What is it? What's wrong?"

"We were wrong," the barbarian explained. "About the ship."

"It's not following us? That's good news, isn't—"

"No. We were wrong; it's not *one* ship."

I began to feel sick, and it wasn't just from being at sea. At my side, Corminar didn't respond to this news, his eyes fixed on the floor, still glazed over. ". . . How many?"

"Six. At least."

"Then it is over," Corminar said, finally piping up. "It is over before it even begins. Our quest is futile. Hopeless. Who did we think we were, that we might sway the outcome of a war?" He paused for a moment, then looked pointedly at me. "Did we truly think we were heroes?"

"I did," I answered honestly. "I still do."

Lore nodded. "Me, too. But I think . . ." He paused, licking his lips. "I think it's just us two, though, Styk."

After a moment, the ranger rose from his bunk. "We should adjourn to the deck," he said. "Perhaps there is more that can be done to increase our speed."

Lore and I nodded our agreement, and followed him up to the deck, but I think we all knew in our heart of hearts that there was nothing we *could* do, that our capture was inevitable.

Our capture was inevitable.

By this point, it was clear. We'd done all we could—all we'd known to do—with the sails, but the truth was obvious: these ships were faster, and were always going to be faster.

This left us with only one question: if they were faster than the ship we were on, then they weren't other Goldmarch ships. So who in Alterra were they?

Corminar, the member of the Slayers with the best eyesight—this being a natural ability of the elven race—kept his gaze fixed on the nearest of the ships. I watched as he narrowed his eyes, trying to bring the ship into focus.

"You see it yet?" Lore asked.

"Please, Lore, will you stop asking?" Val answered on the elf's behalf. "He'll tell you when he sees it."

"OK, but it looks closer. I think. Surely he—"

"Enough, Lore."

"I just wanna know how quickly we're gonna die."

I moved to nudge Lore to follow me, to draw him away from the rest of the team. We already knew the plan for when the ships caught us. Or, at least, we knew enough of it; we'd fine-tune the details once we knew what we were up against. None of us had any faith in the plan—that much was clear—but we'd at least go down fighting.

I'd have felt a lot better about our odds if I could see land on the horizon. But instead, all I could see was a thin layer of fog over the gentle Iron Sea, the brightest of the Architects' stars shining up above.

"Come on, Lore. Let's talk a walk."

Lore nodded, and we moved away just as Corminar murmured something.

"What was that?" the barbarian asked, eyes wide, suddenly very interested once more.

"I know who it is," the ranger said.

"And just how screwed are we?" Val asked.

The elf kept his gaze on the nearest ship. "This remains to be seen."

"I don't . . ." Val said, shaking her head.

"You will see before long."

"Should we prepare to fight?"

"No," the elf said with a sigh. "I think our greatest chance of survival comes from not fighting, just this once. Drop the anchor."

"You sure?"

Corminar nodded.

After the ship had come to a halt, I and the other four members of the team stood in silence, watching out across the sea as the closest ship approached. One by one, we all realized who was chasing us, and once it was my turn, I wasn't sure how to feel. All I could do was trust that we could handle it.

Though, knowing them, the danger was very real—and very likely.

Finally, the ship approached, slowing down as it drew closer, before coming to a stop about as close to our vessel as any ship could come; it was sailed by some expert sailors. Almost to a person, these elven sailors had a bow in hand and a full quiver over one shoulder. And among these elves was a familiar face. A face from weeks long past, from a moment in time that had set us on an adventure once more.

The man to whom Corminar owed his debt.

"You think you can deceive the Red Thorn?" Elandor's voice boomed.

"We didn't deceive, we just—" Val started, but a raised index finger from the elf caused her to snap her mouth shut.

"I see no depth-raider aboard, sorcerer."

"Oh, that's my fault," Lore said. "I—"

"The time for explanations is over. No, now it is time that the Red Thorn collects its debt, one way or another. The world will not hear that the Thorn relinquishes their dues so easily." He signaled to the legion of elven rangers on the nearby ship, and in an instant, all four dozen raised their bows, aiming them at the members of the Slayers. "Your time is up. Payment is overdue."

CHAPTER FIFTY-NINE

Exile's End

"Payment is overdue."

I and the other four members of the Slayers stared him down, waiting for Corminar—the most familiar to the Red Thorn—to speak.

"There are more important matters to contend with," my ranger friend finally said.

Elandor's glare did not soften for a moment. "I assure you, nothing is more important to me—as the head of the Red Thorn in the Tundran region—than the respect that our organization commands. By failing to deliver on your debt, you call our various attributes into question."

Corminar considered the man before him, and all the rangers on the nearest ship. "Then you do not know."

"You would be a fool to assume so. I know who sails across this very sea, and I know of their destination. I know that Empress Amira seeks to add the Dawnwood to her empire."

It was so rare that I saw Corminar truly lost for words, but this was one of those moments. "And yet you consider a debt more important?"

"I consider our image more important. If the Hero of Iranir thinks he may default on our debt, then who else might follow suit? It is easier to dam the stream than protect against the flood."

"But surely you understand why payment may be delayed? Why our attention is drawn elsewhere?"

Elandor shook his head. "We cannot accept excuses. Even—"

"Even the fall of our shared homeland?" Corminar interrupted.

"It is our homeland no more," Elandor replied, then turned to look at the nearest squadron of his employees, bows still nocked and ready to fire. "Look upon your fellow elves. We have been without the trees for long enough now, that our fellow exiles have started families in these human realms. There are elves growing up today who will *never* think of the Dawnwood as home, only the Gentle Tundras. And, too, their parents begin to think of the Tundras as home. We speak of debt. What debt do we owe the Dawnwood, the land to which we can never return?"

Enough of this.

"You don't owe them anything," I shouted. "You do it because it is *right*. Because it's what you *should* do."

Elandor smirked. "You think we base such decisions on notions of right versus wrong? You know what we are, do you not?"

"Criminals," I replied. "But you don't have to be. You can be heroes instead."

The head of the Red Thorn in the Tundran region no longer made any attempt to stem his laughter. "As though it were so simple."

"Why isn't it? *I* did it! And if *I* can, surely the great Elandor can, too?"

The elf's smirk faded; I'd backed him into a corner here. Elandor glared back at me, eyes seeming to pierce into my very soul. "As I say . . . it is not so simple."

"Yes it bloody well—" I started, but Corminar gently grabbed my elbow, pulling me back.

The Hero of Iranir stepped forward once more. "I understand if you have no notions of heroism; that is a stance that I, too, share. Or, rather"—Corminar glanced to me—"shared. I do not quite know where I stand today. But perhaps I can provide a different motivation."

"A motivation to allow you leave to pay your debt?" Elandor asked.

"No," Corminar clarified, "a motivation to sail to war."

The two vessels went eerily quiet at this, and all I could hear was Val's breathing next to me, and the waves lapping against the hull of the ship.

"This would be quite the ask," Elandor finally replied.

"You sail seeking payment?" Corminar asked. "You wish for me to pay my debt? I can pay your debt a hundred times over, should you allow me to do so."

"Tell me."

"As payment, I will grant you all permission to return to the Dawnwood," Corminar shouted loud enough for all Thorn employees on the other ship to hear, loud and clear. "*All* of you. This is worth far more to you than any depth-raider, than any mala. I know this for certain."

Elandor paused, considering. He might not have necessarily found this offer appealing, but he had the other elves of the Red Thorn to think about. If his employees heard him turn down such an offer, then his leadership would be more in question than a single unpaid debt could ever cause. Corminar had played his hand well.

"How can you make such assurances?" the leader of the Tundran Thorn finally asked.

"You said it earlier: I was—*am*—the Hero of Iranir. If I save the Dawnwood again, the Red Thorn sailing at my side, the council will have no choice but to listen to me. You will regain your homeland. You will plant your birth seeds, and you will see them grown. A generation of exile will be over. *This* is my payment; do you accept these terms?"

Even considering the natural stoicism of the elves, I could see that Elandor was considering this from every side. What happened if he turned this down? With so many Thorn members having overheard this offer, there was no way he could avoid this information spreading. And if this news spread, then surely one member of his organization would take offence. At least one. And that surely wouldn't end well for him.

"You give me your word?" Elandor finally asked.

"You have your exile ended, or you have my life," Corminar replied.

Elandor nodded, and the rangers lowered their bows. "I will summon all those under my command. You will have your army; be sure to deliver to them all that you promise."

Seven ships sailed southeast. There were more on the way, sailing as fast as they could, summoned by means of magical signals—a *Worldbending* magick that I hadn't yet unlocked. Elandor's expectation was that the other Red Thorn vessels would catch up with us before we reached the Great Golden Canal Project, being that they were positioned further east and were faster than the slowest of our ships—the one that I and the rest of the Slayers had commandeered.

Tensions had settled, and in this temporary newfound state of "not feeling like we're about to die," I tracked down Val, to find her leaning against the railing at the bow of the ship.

I placed a hand on her back as she approached, and she flinched, having been so lost in thought. "How are you doing?" I asked.

"We ride for a war we're probably not gonna win, and I'm about to face down the woman who ruined my life." It was a pretty eloquent response.

"You've faced her once already," I pointed out.

"That was different; this time, we're going to kill her."

I raised my eyebrows. "Fair enough." I joined Val in leaning on the railing, staring into the misty distance. There was nothing to see, not really—just the gray sky and the sea disappearing into the horizon. Yet at the same time it was captivating. Something about it made me calm, allowing me to block out all thoughts of the terror we were about to encounter. I closed my eyes, focusing on the sea air washing over me and Val pressing herself into my side for feelings of comfort. Of safety.

"I want to kill her," Val said out of the blue.

"Niamh?"

"Who else? I want to kill her. I want to be the one to do it, to see the life fade from her eyes. I'm owed that."

"You've been spending too much time around the elves, I reckon. All that talk of who owes who what."

"I'm not joking, Styk. It needs to be me."

I fiddled with the Sisyphus Artifact, forever on a chain around my neck—the artifact that had saved my life twice, and was powered by the deaths of the Players. "What about . . ." I pulled the octahedron out of my shirt, gesturing to it.

"There are some things in life that are more important than progression. This is one of them. I know you want the experience buff, but . . ." She turned to look at me, those dark brown eyes staring into mine. "I need this. After what she did to me, after everything she took from me . . . I need to be the one to take something of equal value from her. Her life would do it, I think."

I shook my head. "What does it matter, as long as we win? As long as we eliminate her? A hero wouldn't—"

"We're not heroes, Styk," Val replied, her voice firm but her hands gently cradling my face. "We never will be. I think it's time you faced up to that." Before I could reply, she pressed her lips to mine, and we held each other for a time, the warmth of each other's bodies triumphing over the bitter sea air.

And then we released one another, not another word said, and looked back at the misty Iron Sea. Together with our newfound comrades, we sailed southeast, for the Great Golden Canal Project.

And war.

Relaar, Captain of the Rooted Guard

Distant footsteps echoed down the grand hallways of the Evergreen Palace. The sound reverberated around the palace's arching roofs and the large, open windows that allowed in not just the plentiful light of the sun, but the noises and aromas of all that the Dawnwood had to offer. As Captain Relaar of the Rooted Guard stood on the balcony of her great office in the western tower, she should, by all rights, have been at peace. For nothing was as peaceful as this, the view across the rooftops and trees of her home, the capital city of Sunalor, taken in with the accompaniment of elder tea, brewed from the finest of leaves.

There was just one problem: by custom, nobody ran in the Evergreen Palace. Yet these echoing footsteps grew closer with every moment that passed.

Captain Relaar retreated from the balcony to sit behind her desk, and she sipped the last of her cup of tea before the scout burst in the door. The young man had none of the grace and decorum that the world associated with the elves, and yet if he did not, there was surely good reason for it.

But what news could he possibly bring that would cause him to act in such a way? And what news could he bring that the Captain of the Rooted Guard was the first port of call? This was a near-honorary position, overseeing the capital's guard force, whose main responsibilities were to offer a form of ceremony to the opening of new libraries, public baths, and the like. This organization had not seen combat since the Honey Wars, and yet . . .

"What news, soldier?" Relaar forced herself to ask.

The scout opened his mouth, but at first, no sound emerged. And then he managed, only faintly, ". . . Attack."

Relaar rose to her feet. "The swarm?" she asked, memories of her battles with the *witchcraft*-imbued bees flooding her mind as it had so many nights over the past few years.

Yet the scout shook his head. "Goldmarch," he breathed.

"Goldmarch? Queen Amira thinks to march upon the Dawnwood? Where do your spies report such activity? I cannot imagine our neighbors in the Sundorn would allow such—"

"They do not march, captain, they sail. They sail through the Great Golden Canal as we speak."

Relaar felt her world flip on its head in that moment. She, of course, knew of the canal project—it had been labeled a beacon of cooperation between these two powerful nations. Her involvement in this project, however, had been minimal; no use was there for soldiers, even ceremonial, in matters of democracy. And yet even if she had been involved, could she have seen this coming? The Goldmarch, for decades, had no navy to speak of, their sea borders split in four, and therefore it being of much more significant military advantage to build a land army instead. Where could a Golden fleet have emerged from?

"How many?" she asked.

"Our scouts report thirty ships, somewhere between sixty and one hundred soldiers aboard each vessel. They should arrive by sunfall."

Relaar resisted the instinct to sink back into her chair; it would not do to show weakness, for that could ripple through the ranks like wildfire, and impact the result of this apparent inevitable war. Instead, she nodded and forced herself into action.

"Listen to me carefully," she said. "Find Lieutenant Seralin; tell him he is needed in my office at once, and tell him all that you have told me. Once you have done so, leave him and seek the Master of Alteration. Tell him nothing except to retrieve soldiers all across the Dawnwood as efficiently as possible. Once he has relayed these orders, he is to report to my office. The Master of Alteration is under Seralin's command, but he will have to excuse this singular misinterpretation of protocol. Understand?"

"Find Lieutenant Ser—" the scout began to repeat.

"Yes or no, private?" There was no time.

"Yes," the scout said with a nod, and Relaar gestured for him to carry out his duty.

Lieutenant Seralin appeared momentarily, his face paling for the first time that Relaar had seen in five years of working together. "Attack? From the sea?"

Relaar ignored the question. "I have asked the Master of Alteration to summon the national guard," she informed him, not apologizing for not looping Seralin in, considering the circumstances. "How many soldiers will he retrieve by sunfall?"

"I do not know, I . . ."

"How many?" Relaar repeated, more forcefully this time.

"Even *Worldbending* magicks only goes so far, captain. There are mana reserves to think of, and efficiencies of groupings to consider. I—"

"*How many?*"

"Perhaps one thousand."

"Then we are outnumbered three to one," Relaar said, this time sinking into her chair; she could trust Seralin to maintain morale. "And we must assume that the enemy has a plan. Seralin, command all alchemists in the city to create explosive potions, and every worldbender—soldier or otherwise—to relocate these potions to the sea."

"Mines, captain?"

Relaar nodded. "As best we can arrange. Though we should not count on this strategy; any good general will have anticipated this, and will have ensured the proper countermeasures. From our reports of disturbances in the Iron Sea, I am forced to assume that this means enchanted hulls—magicks that has the secondary impact of driving the natural away."

Lieutenant Seralin returned the nod and moved to leave the office.

"Those are not the extent of your orders, lieutenant."

Seralin paused at the threshold to the office, turning back to face Relaar.

"Provide all summoned troops with the best bows and lances in our arsenal. Position them atop the harbor walls; this is our more opportune defensive position. Should the harbor walls fall, there should be a standing order to retreat to the inner walls."

"What of those in the outer city? Should we evacuate?"

"No," Relaar replied. "Arm them."

"But captain, they are not soldiers. So few of them have combat skills at all."

"Only those who volunteer," Relaar said. "But we must arm as many as possible if we are to fend off the invaders." Before the lieutenant could protest further, she added, "And send word to the council. Matters of invasion are under our domain, but they must be informed. Perhaps there is work that can be done to maintain morale. Put this idea to them."

Seralin nodded. "I will." Once more, he turned toward the door to carry out the orders as Relaar had given them.

"There is . . . one more thing. I ask that you keep this as quiet as possible."

Seralin, hearing the tone of Relaar's voice, pressed the door closed. "Yes?"

"Pick out the tallest tree at each side of the harbor. Evacuate its residents. Arrange potions of rot at their base. As a last resort, we fell them, and we set them aflame."

"We . . ." Seralin started, his eyebrows raised. "The fire would . . ."

"The inner wall's enchantments will stop it."

"But those outside, their homes . . . They would be lost."

"If it comes to the felling of the trees, then those homes are *already* lost. Seralin, we must do as the Hero of Iranir once did. Should it come to this, we must commit treason to protect our home. Are you ready to pay the price of exile?"

The lieutenant nodded. "I . . . will arrange it as you say. Let us pray to the Architects that it is not needed."

CHAPTER SIXTY

The Great Golden Canal Project

Two Goldmarch ships were anchored at the canal.

For what it's worth, the Great Golden Canal Project was something to behold. I'd never been to this stretch of coastline on the southeast of the Iron Sea before, but I imagined it once looked like every other near-deserted bit of coastline in this part of the world, so close to the Badlands. But now there were two walls of shining white rock, imported from some faraway land, that seemed to part the land itself. Between these two massive walls was a giant metal gate, ornately designed. I supposed that this project was supposed to look like a diplomatic effort, and so no expense could be spared on such important things as aesthetics.

And there, before this great metal gate, were two imperial warships, like those we'd commandeered and were at this very moment sailing aboard.

"Wish my portals were bigger," I mumbled.

"What, you wanna stuff those ships in a pocket world?" Val asked, standing at my side at the prow of the ship.

"That or just portal our fleet past them. That'd be handy, wouldn't it?"

Val looked around at the six other ships, eyebrows raised. "Handy, sure. A little overpowered to be possible, though, don't you think?"

I shrugged. "With the artifact, who knows how strong I'll get?" I left out the part where I hadn't necessarily agreed to let Val kill Niamh—I did want that experience boost, after all.

"Besides, what about the rest of the Thorn ships that are coming? Best we fight and clear the path."

I sighed; I knew there was *a lot* of fighting in my near-future, and I hadn't anticipated it starting here and now. "Guess so."

Val turned to Elandor, still aboard our ship—and not letting Corminar out of his sight for a second—and nodded him over. He joined us at the front of the ship, along with the rest of the Slayers. "Any thoughts?"

"Two ships?" Elandor asked, eyebrow raised. "This is hardly enough to be concerning. We shall surely triumph."

"Well, yeah, but any thoughts on how we do it without losing anyone?" the witch asked.

Corminar opened his mouth to back Val up. "We will require every last soldier if we are to turn the tide of war."

Elandor remained quiet, his eyes fixed on the enemy ships that we were rapidly approaching. As I followed his gaze, a thought occurred to me.

"I do have . . . *one* idea," I said.

The Red Thorn ships furled their sails, slowing their pace, while our ship—once again hosting only the Slayers, Elandor this time allowing Corminar out of his sight—approached the enemy. With only five people aboard, there were reduced chances of significant losses. The flip side, however, was that there was a greater chance of losing the five people still aboard, which included *me*. So I had a pretty vested interest in my plan working out.

"You ready, bud?" Lore asked.

"Yeah, are they 'in sight' enough for you yet?" Val smirked, and from her expression I took that she was just teasing; she didn't *really* have any doubts.

I studied the ships we were rapidly approaching, and nodded. "Get ready to raise the sails." Val and Lore hurried off to join Arzak and Corminar at the ropes, and I raised my hands.

"Do it!" I shouted, and immediately the team slowed the ship while I set about executing my plan. I stretched a hand toward the hull of the nearest enemy vessel, and I activated *Portal Slice*.

. . . Nothing happened.

"Is it working?" Val cried out. "I don't see any holes in the hulls."

"Yes, I know." I tried again; maybe I'd missed.

"Still nothing!"

"Thanks for the update." I'd failed to consider something, clearly. My *Portal Slice* ability only worked on objects that weren't reinforced by magick. But if the hulls were enchanted to withstand damage . . . this ability wouldn't work. "Stop raising the sails!" I shouted.

"If we not raise sails now, we move in attack range," Arzak pointed out.

"That's the idea."

"That not *good* idea," the orc added.

"The hulls are reinforced. I can't *slice* them. But if we get within ten yards . . ." I let the rest of the team fill in the gap. Three of the Slayers nodded knowingly.

"If we get within ten yards, what?" Lore asked.

I blinked at him. ". . . Then I can open a portal beneath the deck. Pour the water in. Like we did with the pyroknight."

"Oh right. Yeah."

Once again, I regretted not upgrading *Local Portal II* when I had the chance. It would have been really nice not to need to be ten yards away right about now. The team raised the sails when we were much, much closer, waiting until the momentum threatened to cause us to crash.

"Ready? Again?"

"Yes, Val."

The other members of the Slayers raised their weapons to attack, and I stretched a hand toward the bottom deck of the enemy ship. "Got it!" I shouted as I opened one portal in the ship and one in the Iron Sea.

None of the Goldmarch soldiers aboard noticed, because they were distracted by the other four members of the Slayers hopping onto their ship. With a great leap—and really wishing that I could use my portals to get across—I joined them. All we needed to do was distract them long enough that their ship sank, and at the rate that I knew water came through my portals . . . that wasn't going to be very long.

"How *dare* you—" the captain started, eyes bulging, before Corminar released an arrow that landed squarely in the middle of his forehead.

And then twenty soldiers of the Goldmarch—fortunately a small contingent— were upon us. Lore and Arzak stood at the forefront of our group, defending us against the worst of the attacks, while Val sent powerful gusts of wind blasting the encroaching soldiers backward and Corminar loosed arrow after arrow, slowing or felling the enemies.

I stood at the back with my knife and concentrated on keeping the portal open; if I got hurt, I could lose my focus, and the portals would close.

At the far side of the ship, I saw a man, paling, stagger up onto the deck, into the midst of a fight.

"Err . . . boss?" said the soldier who'd just come up.

"Boss dead," an orcish soldier grunted back.

"OK, well . . . we're sinking. Pretty fast."

I glanced back to our ship, but found that it had drifted away; we weren't getting back aboard without my portals, and I couldn't close the current ones until the job was done. But the other enemy ship was approaching, and that one, we might just be able to reach.

"Lore, Arzak!" I shouted. "The mast!" I pointed to the approaching ship, and they nodded their understanding. The barbarian swung his Bane Sword hard into the side of the mast, chipping away at it with every strike until it cracked. Corminar and Val stepped up their attacks for just a moment to fend off the enemies while the largest two Slayers ran at the mast, hitting it with their shoulders. The remaining wood splintered, and the mast tumbled toward the enemy ship, sail ropes snapping from the weight and flying toward enemy soldiers, who ducked to avoid them. All the ropes snapped except for one—which held the mast tantalizingly close to falling on the other ship.

Corminar reacted first. He swung his bow upward, pointing it toward the rope. One arrow later, the mast fell, squarely onto the other enemy ship.

"Go!" I shouted, and we jumped onto the fallen mast, sprinting delicately across it to the other ship, where twenty more soldiers were waiting for us.

Arzak, first onto the mast, leaped off with a roar, bringing her two swords down into the deck, sending splinters of wood into the surrounding soldiers. This helped clear a spot for the rest of us aboard this ship—and not the sinking one—but this time around we didn't have the advantage of surprise.

The enemy were organized, and their captain barked strict orders to the sailors, which they followed without question. This put their strongest fighters at the front, with the archers delivering arrows in waves, making it harder for us to block.

"Any time now, Styk!" Val cried out, voice a bit shaky.

"I haven't got portals yet! They're not—"

15 x Goldmarch Sailors defeated!

Worldbending: +2,800XP

"—sunk."

It was a disappointingly small amount of experience, considering how many enemies I'd "defeated." But of course that was because I'd thrown them into the water—killing them would have been worth a lot more. I still got another *Worldbending* level out of it, and in this moment—with another ship to sink—I could be happy with that.

"OK, scratch that!" I shouted, and I shifted the portals from the first ship to the second. Based on how quickly the first ship had gone down—and this one being built to the same specifications—we just needed to last around three minutes. That, surely, we could do.

The encroaching enemies forced Arzak and Lore backward, my friend unable to fend all the enemies off at once. Between Corminar, Val, and myself, I was the next most able to manage being hit—what with my *Warped Shield* ability—and so I could see exactly what needed to happen next. I stepped forward, toward my two larger friends, and kept part of my focus on the portal filling up the hold with water.

"Styk, what are you . . ." It was almost touching to hear the note of concern in Val's voice.

"Buying some time!" I stepped between Arzak and Lore, weapon raised, and I activated a newly acquired skill that I hadn't had the opportunity to use yet—*Knifestorm*. Was this really why I was throwing myself into trouble? I didn't know, and there wasn't exactly time to give it much thought, all things considered.

I threw myself toward the nearest two enemies as I activated the ability, spinning on the spot and lashing out at the soldiers, landing hit after hit after hit after—

Another, third, soldier caught my arm and stopped me turning, the other two writhing on the floor from their many wounds.

"Uh-oh. Lore?"

The barbarian swung his blade into the soldier who had just grabbed me, leaving only an arm with its fingers wrapped around me. I shook it off and tried to ignore the rising nausea and the *Knifework* experience notification.

"How long?" Arzak asked, her voice strained with the energy of—just about—fending off the attacks of three Goldmarch sailors at once.

"Should be nearly there!" I replied, retreating back to behind the meat shield that was Lore. Not that he was *only* that, obviously.

"And yet not one of them seems to have noticed?" Corminar said.

"True," the orc replied, then turned back to the soldiers she was fighting off. "You should look down in ship."

Only one of the soldiers hesitated. ". . . Why?"

"New cargo. Very wet." She hesitated. "Is water wet?"

"Did you not notice how low we are in the water?" Val added.

More soldiers hesitated at this, enough that Lore and Arzak were able to stop retreating and still be able to fend off the attack. Which was pretty handy considering we were running out of space to retreat to.

"Ship's pretty far . . ." Lore said.

I could, of course, portal us back to it, but that would mean closing the current pair of portals, and the ship wasn't quite sunk. But we couldn't hold out much longer . . .

"Styk?" Lore asked. "You got anything?"

"Yeah," I replied. "Catch me." At that, I closed the current portals and opened a new one beneath Val and Corminar's feet, sending them tumbling back to the deck of our ship. Then I turned to do the same to Arzak and Lore and myself. "Bye!" I said, with a wave, to the Goldmarch soldiers, before leaving them on their mostly sunken ship.

They weren't going anywhere fast, of course, but there were enough rangers on board to potentially hurt anyone who came close—including us, right in that moment. It was far better to sink the ship entirely.

I opened a portal in the air above the top deck, that being the best I could do without being within ten yards of the lower decks, and I positioned the portals to blast down the open stairwell. Even as the many soldiers rushed to collect buckets and bail the water from their ship, it was too late.

---

23 x Goldmarch Sailors defeated!

Worldbending: +4,500XP
Worldbending increased to Level 45!
Base Points Gained: +2 INT, +2 Free Points (INT/WIS/CHA)
Ability Selection Unlocked
Select an ability from the list below:

. . .

Now, we were talking.

CHAPTER SIXTY-ONE

Last Orders

We put the Great Golden Canal Project behind us—after some fumbling with a new technology called locks, which split the sea level—and set sail across the wholly new horizons of The Sea of Roots. So far away from land, there was nothing to differentiate the old elven sea from the sea I'd stared out across for so many years of my youth, but still something had changed about the *feel* of the water.

Though, maybe that was simply because we were now so close to battle.

Other Red Thorn ships had joined us, as Elandor had promised, and we now numbered twelve—though some vessels carried more soldiers than the others. I could only hope that we were enough to make a difference to the outcome of this war, but when I'd asked Corminar for his thoughts on the matter, he hadn't committed either way. This didn't give me much hope.

But I couldn't control that. In fact, the only thing I could control as we sailed—the only thing that might have made the *slightest* difference to the battle ahead—was my ability selection. I brought up the notifications once more, but kept one eye on the horizon for signs of trouble.

Ability Selection Unlocked
Select an ability from the list below:
Hidden condition met! Alternative ability choice unlocked.
Option 1: Ripple Husk (Worldbending) [Requires: Any Husk *Worldbending* ability]—*Replaces Ash Husk.* Dynamically warp the fabric of your skin into materials best able to repel oncoming attacks for ten minutes. Gain 30 percent resistance to all attacks while active.

It was a strong start. A *very* strong start, in fact, though it being a hidden alternative choice usually had a lot to do with that. If I picked this, I would lose my *Ash Husk* ability, yes, but I barely used it anyway. And this? This was a lot more useful, being that it seemed to work against all types of attacks. The only downside was that it offered 30 percent resistance to these attacks, whereas my original *Ash Husk* offered 50 percent—if only against fire attacks, admittedly.

This basically worked as an extra 30 percent health, as far as I could see. I needed that. But did I need it more than the other options, considering I had *Warped Shield* doing a similar-ish thing already? Admittedly, that currently only worked against low-level melee weapons. I put a pin in this choice and turned to the other options.

> *Hidden condition met! Alternative ability choice unlocked.*
> **Option 2: Silence III (Worldbending)** [Requires: *Stealth* level 20]—Create a bubble of 20-yard radius in which sound is eradicated. Uses mana to cast, zero mana to maintain. You may only have one bubble active at any one time.

Here it was: an improved version to the ability I'd regretted passing over many times before. I'd told myself that next time this came up, I'd select it, because it was so useful when combined with my *Stealth* abilities. And yet, again, it was up against some very serious competition already.

I cast my eyes over the description again, to look for what had changed. It had been a 20-yard radius for the rank 2 version, if I remembered correctly. But what *had* changed was the mana cost. If I selected this, I wouldn't need to use mana to maintain the silent bubble, only to cast it, which was a very compelling new addition. Of course, there was still a restriction in that I could only have one bubble active at once—I couldn't just travel the world slowly eliminating any sound, as much as the idea amused me.

"What are you grinning about?" Val asked, raising an eyebrow at me.

"Nothing!" I said.

"Better be." She turned her attention back to the horizon.

With two very compelling options presented to me already—and whatever of those I didn't pick this time, I was definitely going to give real thought to when they came back around—I focused on the third and last ability.

> *Hidden condition met! Alternative ability choice unlocked.*
> **Option 3: Ultra Tamed Portals (Worldbending)** [Requires: *Tamed Portals*]—*Replaces Tamed Portals.* Focusing large volumes of mana allows you to reduce portal glow by 99 percent, for near-invisible portals at the cost of significant mana/second.

It was yet another hidden option—my build was apparently so effective that the stronger alternative ability choices had replaced every single standard option. I was clearly doing *something* right.

This one was an interesting one, as it replaced a passive ability with an active one. This wasn't *necessarily* an issue—it just meant I'd actually have to think about using it—and for what it afforded me in nearly invisible portals, that might just be worth it. I thought about the applications: sneaking into places more easily, maybe creating portals in front of someone and stabbing them through it.

But were these applications as good as those for the first two? The only problem with this great selection of abilities was that . . . I could only choose one.

I read through the three again, looking for which of the three I could eliminate first, before finally settling on removing *Ripple Husk* from the running. It was a good ability, don't get me wrong, it's just that it seemed to have fewer useful applications than the other two.

And as for the other two . . . There really was no obvious answer. I could reasonably pick either of these two and have that not be an incorrect choice. But considering I needed to make this selection now and not, you know, in the midst of a war, I stared at them both a while longer, before, finally, I picked . . .

Ability Unlocked: Silence III
Silence III (Worldbending): Create a bubble of 20-yard radius in which sound is eradicated. Uses mana to cast, zero mana to maintain. You may only have one bubble active at any one time.

I closed my eyes and sat with this decision for a moment, searching for a deep-rooted feeling that I'd chosen the wrong one. But none came. It really was a hard choice, and having this *Silence* ability meant that I could make more use out of my *Stealth Attack* and *Execution* abilities, both of which boosted damage as long as I was undetected.

It was, I decided, as good a choice as any.

Corminar spotted the distant, hazy shoreline first.

Of course it was him; he'd been the one who hadn't moved from the prow of the ship, his eyes fixed on the horizon ahead of us. And he had the elven eyesight to see what Val, Arzak, Lore, and I couldn't.

At least, not at first. But soon it came into view: not the city, but the fleet of Goldmarch ships beginning their attack. Each of them bore those familiar golden sails, making no attempt to hide where they'd come from. It didn't matter now, of course; the trap had snapped shut, and all the elves could do was defend their capital.

Next, the trees came into sight through the mist. Of course, trees *were* the buildings, in a way—every house, tavern, palace was built into or around one of the trees this part of the world was famous for. I was taken aback; I knew logically that the Dawnwood were tall, being so ancient, but I hadn't been prepared for quite how tall these trees were. Even the shortest of them would have towered over the Golden Palace in Auricia—the building which had given me vertigo just looking up at. I made a mental note not to look up when we got closer, as vertigo was the last thing I needed in the middle of a battle.

And then I started to make out the lights in the buildings, twinkling in the low evening sun. Corminar hadn't spoken about Sunalor much, but from what little he'd said, I'd known it was a beautiful city, full of—

A huge explosion erupted in the bay, powerful enough to blow one of the Goldmarch ships to one side. The sound made ripples across the surface of the sea as it traveled, and I had to put one foot back to stable myself from the blast. There were mines in the water, but—looking at the ship that had sailed into it—they weren't powerful enough to blow holes in the enchanted hulls of the Goldmarch ships. At least, *one* wasn't powerful enough. Multiple might yet do some damage, if the elves had planted that many of them.

Another explosion, then another, and another, immediately answered my question—the bay was filled with them. They might take down a Goldmarch ship or two yet.

"This poses a problem," Elandor said, still occupying our commandeered ship.

I turned to him. "Your hulls aren't magically reinforced."

"Indeed, they are not."

I turned back to the scene of the erupting battle, making out clouds of arrows raining down both upon Goldmarch ships and on the distant harbor walls. The war had well and truly started.

"Then I think—" I started, but Corminar, his brow intensely furrowed, stepped forward.

"We head east," he instructed. "Around the minefield. We disembark on the eastern coast, and from there, we march to Sunalor's aid."

Elandor nodded and turned to the nearest Red Thorn ship, bellowing the orders and demanding they be passed along.

Meanwhile, I saw Corminar grasp his bow so tightly that his fingers turned white. While the rest of the Slayers adjusted course, I stood by his side, my hand resting upon the pommel of my dagger. I watched as the land of the Dawnwood grew closer, the sound of explosions and shouting and screaming growing louder, the deep sounds of the war drums echoing through my heart. As we neared the coastline, I caught glimpses of elves running from the city they called home, dragging crying children and crates of precious belongings, some abandoning the latter as they realized they would need to move faster to outrun the grasping hand of the new Golden Empire.

I'd seen fighting before. The Architects knew I'd seen fighting. But I'd never seen a battle like this.

"So it is, then," the ranger said. "The battle for Sunalor has begun."

CHAPTER SIXTY-TWO

On Elven Soil

"Pull!" Val shouted, and the rest of the Slayers pulled an oar. "Pull! Pull!"

With every stroke of the oar, our rowboat grew further from our anchored ship and closer to the coastline. Around us, dozens—perhaps as many as a hundred—more rowboats, filled with members of the Red Thorn, did the same. Though I faced away from the shoreline, I could see the branches of the great elven trees towering overhead. If any of them fell, nobody underneath would survive—though Corminar had assured me that the trees of the Dawnwood never fell; the old magicks running through them was too strong.

I had wanted to crash our ships into the coast—partially because it would have been more immediate, and partially because I liked the drama of it—but that idea had been quickly overruled. Corminar had reminded me that we had no certainty of victory, and with that came a need for an escape route. So we left the ships safely moored off the coast, and not on the beach with their hulls in splinters.

"And . . ." Val said, making a change from the "Pull! Pull! Pull!" that had been echoing around my head for the past half hour. Before she could say any more, the rowboat knocked against the coast. We had landed.

All of us hopped out into the shallows, the water splashing beneath our feet, as the nearest of the Red Thorn did the same. We turned our attention toward the city. The suburbs sprawled as far out as where we'd landed, abandoned homes built out from the trees that towered high above us. There was no time to wait for our full contingent to land; we needed to start carving a path into the city. And between us and the outer city walls, soldiers in golden uniforms were waiting, terrorizing the citizens simply seeking to flee, robbing them of their valuables, slaughtering those who stood their ground.

Up until now, I'd thought that the new Empress Amira had been having her soldiers pose as bandits, but I'd gotten that wrong. In fact, it was the other way around: these were bandits posing as soldiers. With that realization, any semblance of merciful thoughts left me.

"On me," Corminar said, his voice booming with a confidence that was abnormal even for him, as though he was making an effort to project such a thing. We followed him without complaint, even Elandor taking no issue with his order, trudging up the sand onto sturdier ground. With hands on our weapons, we stepped onto the cobblestone road leading into Sunalor, weaving through the fleeing locals. My eyes remained upon the closest of the empire's soldiers, and so, too, did those of my allies.

"Drop it!" a Goldmarch soldier said, trying to tear an ornate chest from the hands of a young elven man, her allies sneering on, taking great joy in their pillaging. "I said—"

The enemy didn't get to finish that sentence, because in a flash, Corminar had drawn his bow and released an arrow which wedged itself firmly into the soldier's ear canal.

"And you say you want better bow?" Arzak asked, in the same moment that the lot of us charged into battle.

But this was just the first skirmish of many.

Heal him!" I roared to Val, only two dozen feet away but also separated by the clash of ten Red Thorn elves against twice that in golden uniforms. "*Heal* him!" I grunted as I heaved Lore with all my might, trying to get him out of trouble, unable to drop him through a portal in case he fell onto one of the two swords that were currently sticking out of his abdomen. At least he'd killed their owners already.

A bloodied Val pushed through the clashing soldiers, ducking to avoid a swinging blade before twisting to grab their arm and shock them with her lightning magicks.

"Like prickled pie," Lore mumbled hazily, and I only had the slightest clue what that meant because he'd once before mentioned this delicacy from his home—a pie baked with fruit skewers sticking through it.

"Stay with me, buddy . . ."

We'd been fighting for probably around two hours by this point, and even with Corminar's health, stamina, and mana potions, all our reserves had taken a hit. We had lost a good few Red Thorn elves by this point, though—if we thought about only our chances of success and not the loss in life—we at least had more joining us with every moment that passed. The path we'd attempted to carve hadn't remained clear, what with more Goldmarch soldiers spilling out from ships nearer the capital, so the Thorn elves behind us had still had to battle their way through.

Finally, Val arrived at our side, and immediately set about *healing* Lore. When she gave the nod, I pulled one of the swords from his stomach, and the witch tried to close the wounds fast enough that the loss in blood wasn't too great. But her eyes lingered on my arm, and the huge gash thereon.

"You're hurt," she said.

I shrugged it off; I really hadn't noticed the pain all that much in all the chaos. "It's not as bad as it looks."

"Still, though, I—"

"Focus on Lore," I replied, "he's the one looking like prickled pie."

Val raised an eyebrow. "Like what?"

I didn't have a chance to answer, because a Goldmarch soldier spotted that Val and Lore were vulnerable. I opened a portal beneath me and another over the charging soldier's head, coming down hard with my knife to wedge it in the top of their head. In the midst of the fight, my approach from the sky went unnoticed this time, and I was able to get the damage boost from my *Stealth Attack* and *Execution* abilities. Unlike the fights before this particular soldier, this enemy went down in one hit.

When I returned to Val and Lore's side, ready to defend them against any more attacks, the witch handed me a health potion.

"No," I said. "You need that, too. There aren't many."

"Just take it, will you?" Val snapped. "For me? So I don't have to worry?"

Who would have thought there would be acts of love at the center of a battle? I took the potion and drank it, and the familiar warm yellow-white light of *Healing* magicks wrapped around my wound.

Down on the ground, Lore was looking more with it. "Did someone mention pie?" he asked.

"You did," I reminded him.

"Oh. Damn," he replied, like if there was pie available in this moment then he would take a moment in the middle of his battle for a quick snack. This look faded from his face when I yanked the other sword from him, on Val's say-so. "That hurts!"

"Yes," Val agreed, and said nothing more.

Arzak shouldered the Goldmarch soldier through the portal, and they tumbled out of its other side—far in the sky above. They fell, spinning, until they clipped their arm on the top of the city wall, then impacted against the giant tree root protruding from the mud below. Again, I ignored the experience notification—there were going to be a few of these before we finally secured Sunalor, and there was no time to be reading them now.

"Open the damned gate, curse you!" Corminar bellowed to the elves in green and brown light armor at the top of the city wall.

"I am under strict instructions not to open this gate for—" the young elven soldier replied, her voice shaky. This was not someone who had seen battle before; even I could tell that.

"Do you not see what we are? Do you see that we do not wear the uniform of the Goldmarch? Do you not see the shapes of our ears?"

The soldier on the wall pointed to me. "Yet that one is human."

Corminar blinked and then gestured to the group of perhaps four dozen members of the Red Thorn who had already amassed at our side—with more coming every moment. "Perhaps focus on the majority rather than the—"

"How can I be sure he is not a saboteur? Or one of the other two? Or the orc?"

Elandor stepped forward from the crowd. "You are too young to remember the Honey Wars, are you not?"

The elf atop the gate hesitated before responding. "I was but a child."

"Do you have a superior near you? One who served during the Honey Wars? Retrieve them."

The elf blinked down at Elandor, weighing up the risk of doing as he said. But the bulk of the Goldmarch attack was on the coastal side of the city, and the walls were high and the gate strong. They could spare one other guard for this interaction, so she waved over an older-looking elf with a furrowed brow. He glanced down at the crowd outside the gate, did a double take when he spotted Corminar, and then his face paled.

"Open the gate," the older elf said, quietly at first, then shouting. "Open the gate!" She turned to the first guard. "See that they are escorted directly to Captain Relaar."

"But—"

"You will follow orders immediately, without question, or you will be stripped of your rank. Understand?"

The elf blinked, nodded, and then looked down at Corminar in awe, unable to comprehend who he was that he commanded such respect.

The city of Sunalor was both beautiful and desolate, and somehow also beautiful in its desolation. The buildings largely stood embedded into the trees, though not so much that the life of the plant was at risk—only cutting into the trees enough for support beams or the intricate artistic carvings that lined any bare bark. Not that I had much time to study it.

We'd been escorted through the empty city by the elf at the gate, Private

Ollaria, who I had since learned was a member of the so-called Rooted Guard, the almost ceremonial military service that watched over Sunalor. Though, I suspected, they'd been *entirely* ceremonial up until about twelve hours ago.

Ollaria kept us traveling away from the walls, and this was why it had been so quiet—the locals had either fled or were armed with bows on the city walls, giving their lives to protect their home. We cut toward the harbor walls down a wide road which might have once boasted a vibrant market, but now only had wooden frames of stores now abandoned. Our group approached the harbor wall, and the private pointed out where Relaar was.

"She is a glamorous woman, and should be wearing—"

Corminar raised a hand to cut her off. "We are old acquaintances; I will know her."

Ollaria nodded, then stepped aside for us to climb the steps to the top of the harbor wall. "Allies inbound!" she shouted up, to avoid the rangers on the wall immediately turning around and firing at us.

"You know Relaar?" Elandor asked Corminar quietly.

"She was promoted to captain at the same time that they delivered to me my notice of informal exile."

The head of the Red Thorn nodded. "Good, then she will know your intentions. I am afraid to say that she will know me as well."

"I understand." Corminar increased the speed of his climb, pushing to the front of the now hundred-plus-strong group of Thorn and Slayers, while Elandor dropped back.

When we reached the top of the wall, we found the apparent captain flanked by two other highly decorated elves, one of whom gripped a wooden staff that glowed gently with the familiar purple light of *Worldbending* magicks.

"The Hero of Iranir," Captain Relaar said with a nod, speaking clearly but quickly—elsewhere along the harbor wall, the enemy was beginning to raise ladders formed of Tundran wood, and she would need to deal with this sooner rather than later.

"We learned of the attack. I bring reinforcements."

"Yes, I see that," Relaar replied, her eyes skimming to Elandor. "Red Thorn, if I am not mistaken." She turned to one of the men at her side—the one in ornate armor, rather than the elf with the staff. "Lieutenant Seralin, just how many of these elves are exiled?"

"As the humans say, desperate times call for—" Corminar didn't finish that sentence, because a spray of red blood washed over him.

Captain Relaar blinked at Corminar, tilting her head to one side in confusion, unsure where the blood had come from. And then, slowly, she looked down, and she saw the giant bolt that had pierced her torso, protruding halfway out the other side.

"Oh," she said, and then dropped to the hard stone of the harbor wall.

The elf she'd called Lieutenant Seralin rushed to her side, cradling her, but my attention shifted to the man who had fired this bolt. A Knight of the Realm stood behind the dropped captain, holding a weapon that was mechanical in design, as though someone had taken a bow and rotated it on its side, using a gear mechanism to add more power to the fired bolt than any hand-drawn bow could achieve. And more soldiers in gold poured forth from the ladder resting against the wall next to him.

"Seralin!" the elf with the *Worldbending* staff shouted. "Seralin!"

But the man was cradling the now-dead captain, tears pouring down his face.

"Lieutenant!" Corminar shouted, and I rushed to the elf's side to shake him back to reality. But nothing changed; he just blinked up at me with glazed-over eyes.

"Corminar," Arzak said, and she met the ranger's gaze with such intensity that she communicated some prearranged elaborate message. It took me only a moment to realize what it was: the orc told him it was time to become the Hero of Iranir once more.

And then, Lieutenant Cladenor took command.

CHAPTER SIXTY-THREE

The Outer Wall

With every second that passed, dozens of Goldmarch soldiers spilled from the long wooden ladders over onto the top of the harbor walls. And that was to say nothing of the thousands more waiting to climb from down below. All that stood between this army and the elven capital of Sunalor falling to the Golden Empire was a few hundred elves, the Slayers, and Lieutenant Cladenor, Hero of Iranir.

"You two," Corminar said, pointing to Arzak and me. "Take down the ladders. Now."

"Err, there's like a few dozen soldiers in the—" I started to point out, but the ranger's glare stopped me.

"The remainder of our contingent will worry about the enemies."

It wasn't much of an answer, but I didn't exactly have any better ideas, and *someone* needed to take those ladders down before we were overwhelmed. I nodded to Arzak, and we charged across the wall for the nearest ladder.

I opened a portal ahead just as the soldiers were about to strike us, slipping our squad behind them and leaving them to follow through on their attacks—buying us approximately an extra second. I moved to *Portal Slice* through the ladder, but there was nothing doing; Niamh had thought to imbue this wood as well as the wood of the ships. She really had thought of everything.

Well, hopefully not everything, *or we were in real trouble.*

But pushing things was where Arzak excelled, and I figured that was probably why Corminar had paired up the two of us. The orc slammed her shoulders into the ladder, heaving it—and all the soldiers on it—away from the wall, pushing, pushing, straining as she—

"Help or just watch?" she asked.

"Right. Yep." I ran into the ladder in much the same way as Arzak, shoulder-first, and bashed it. It reverberated in the air for a second, balancing, and just as I thought it was about to fall back toward us again, the orc ripped a stone brick from the top of the wall and threw it at the ladder. This was the push it needed, and both the ladder and the dozen or so soldiers in gold uniform upon it plummeted toward the ground.

We spun back around just in time to see the soldiers swiping their swords at us once more, and the tip of one of these blades caught my stomach, ripping my clothes and slicing my stomach open. Hopefully it wasn't as bad a wound as it . . .

My legs gave way beneath me, and Arzak wasn't around to catch me because she had soldiers to ward off. Behind her, Corminar and the rest of the elves pressed the attack on this group and the other enemies spilling out from the other ladders. They were holding their ramp down from the wall effectively for now, but how long would that last?

I had a moment to breathe, fortunately, and I pulled the health potion from my pocket.

Thank the Architects that Val insisted on giving it to me.

I drank hungrily at the fluid, embracing the fizzing heat as it encompassed my stomach, closing the wound and reversing the darkening of my vision.

"Alive?" Arzak grunted. This question didn't seem to be short just due to her usual strange syntax; there wasn't the time to say much more.

"For now!"

"Then help."

I hopped back to my feet, dagger in hand, and charged into the midst of the enemy soldiers, activating *Knifestorm* before any of them could turn to attack. I didn't deal enough damage to fell any of them, but I distracted them enough that Arzak or an elven archer were able to see them off. I received more experience notifications as a result, but there wasn't time to read them. I may have helped take two or three soldiers down, but there were probably a thousand times still to go.

"Next ladder!" I shouted, and ripped Arzak from the middle of a skirmish by opening a portal beneath her feet. To her credit, though, she went with it.

We landed by the next ladder, this time amidst a small group of soldiers—those who had just reached the top of the wall and hadn't yet charged toward the elves defending the nearest ramp. I *knifestormed* again, slashing at them, pushing a group to the floor, and then Arzak roared—activating some Warrior-class skill, probably—and took on the lot of them with her dual swords.

She moved faster than I'd seen her move most times before, and I glimpsed the pupils in her eyes having expanded to cover nearly the whole eye. One of the Goldmarch soldiers, a mage, threw a fireball at her—why was it always a fireball?—and she blocked it with her sword, absorbing it. From there, her blade wasn't just dealing its usual damage, it was dealing fire damage, too.

As soon as we got a moment, we turned our attention to the ladder, just as a man in more elaborate golden armor and a glowing purple band of magicks around one ear reached the top. "Oh no you don't," the senior soldier said, grabbing onto the wall and using his feet to reinforce the ladder's position.

I began to push, but Arzak had other ideas, instead whipping her dual blades slashing inward, and . . . cleaving the soldier's hands clean off. "Yes we do," she said, and kicked the ladder. This time, there was no uncertainty about which way it would fall; it was another one down.

As I looked along the wall to the next ladder, I spotted something. Down below, two enemy mages let forth the blue glow of *Sorcery* magicks in a combined stream, blasting at the top of the nearest ladder. My eyes bulged when I saw what they were doing; they were morphing the stone bricks of the city walls as though it was dough, forming from it large stone clamps to hold the ladder in place. They'd changed up their strategy, and because they'd used magicks to do it, I couldn't use *Portal Slice* to remove the clamps once more.

"Problem," I said to Arzak, nodding toward the enemy's change in strategy.

"Mm."

"What now?"

"Back to Corminar. He in charge today."

I could have portaled us back, but Corminar had provided me with only so many mana potions, and we could well have been in this for the long haul. Instead, we ran, weaving through the remaining stragglers as the enemy side pushed up their siege ladders once more, rejoining our friends at the ramp. Arzak swiftly dealt with the last enemies of this wave, catching them unaware as we'd arrived at their rear.

"I cannot help but notice that ladders remain at the wall," Corminar said.

"Can't do anything about it," I replied. "They've learned. Got magicks holding them in place."

"Sir," one of the elven soldiers said. "Sir?"

"Yes?" Corminar replied. In his position, I would be snapping at someone trying to demand my attention, but the elf was keeping his cool.

The soldier nodded to the east, toward where another group of elves were struggling against a group of enemies only half their number.

Corminar turned back to me. "Styk. Traverse me to their side; I shall remind them to hold formation."

"If I may . . ." the elf with the staff—who had been standing at Relaar's side—offered. "Many of our soldiers, there, they have no combat background."

At this, Corminar's calm expression finally faded. "What in the name of Gaia do you mean?"

The other elf hesitated. "We have little standing army. In order to defend against such an unprecedented invasion, we were forced to ask for volunteers."

"Then what are they?" Val asked.

"Merchants. Farmers. Tradespeople. People who are willing to die for their home."

Corminar swallowed, glanced at the approaching swarm of soldiers—the siege ladders now back in place—and turned back to me and Val. He pointed to the elf with the staff. "This is Debayur, Sunalor's Master of Alteration. Work with him. See what you might yet do."

Corminar, Lore, Arzak, and the rest of this group of elven soldiers pushed forward to defend us, and I turned my attention to the Master of Alteration. "Alteration? *Worldbending?*"

"Correct," Debayur replied. "With two dozen more such specialists at my disposal. We were responsible for placing the explosives into the Sea of Roots, but alas that is where our usefulness has ended."

"Can we close up the ramps somehow?" Val asked.

"Open some portals, or . . . ?" I suggested.

Debayur shook his head. "I am afraid we have attempted this already. The enemy has *Worldbenders*; temporary portals are left alone, but any attempt to use them to stymie enemy progress attracts their attention. We would need . . ." He trailed off, but it was inspiration, not overwhelm, that burned in his eyes.

"What? Is there another way? What is it?" Val's eyes dashed over to the next ramp, where the enemy was about to break through.

"We might use voids, not portals," Debayur said, his face paling.

"Voids?" I asked. "What are—"

"Dark magicks. Portals that have no end, that spill out only into the void. They cannot be closed by another, only fading as time passes."

"Then what in the hells are we waiting for?" Val asked. "Do it."

"I have not the magicks. I—"

"Then I'll help," I cut in. "Can I feed you my power?"

Debayur shook his head. "No. But there is one way."

From the fact that his voice croaked when he said this, I imagined I wasn't much going to like what this "one way" was. But we were out of options, so I resisted the urge to ask.

"You must tell Corminar: order the retreat to the inner walls. If we time this correctly, then the voids might eat a few hundred soldiers before the enemy truly knows they are there."

I nodded; now wasn't the time to be questioning orders—the elven capital hung in the balance. Instead, I turned, and I portaled myself into the middle of the crowd of friendly soldiers, grateful that Corminar—being a ranger—wasn't at the front. "Order retreat."

"Styk, now is not the time for—"

"It comes from Debayur. Trust him. It's the only way to buy ourselves some time."

Corminar hesitated, lowering his bow to look at me, and then nodded. He turned to one of the elven soldiers. "Retreat," he said.

As the elf in question ran off to start ringing on a large metal bell—one that was soon echoed down the wall, and then further still—I ran back to Debayur's side. I nodded to the elf, and he nodded back in kind.

"Please," he said. "Win."

Before I could question why he was telling us this, Debayur whipped his hands out at his side and closed his eyes. When he opened them again, they were burning a vibrant purple.

"Oh," Val said. "*Oh.*"

"What? What's happening?"

Val staggered backward, away from Debayur, and nudged me back, too.

The Master of Alteration's glowing eyes grew brighter, as though burning with a purple fire. He rose into the air, slowly at first, but then higher and higher and higher, until he was towering over most of Sunalor, if not quite the Dawnwood itself.

And then, he exploded.

CHAPTER SIXTY-FOUR

Voidstorm

Debayur exploded with the light of a sun, raining down *Worldbending* magicks in arcs of fizzling purple fire. Each arc shot toward the top of the wall near the exit ramps, igniting into huge blazing portals. But though I was familiar with portals being purple, this one was filled with black. The sheer power of these voids being brought into existence made the ground shake, and the trees—sending giant seeds plummeting toward the city.

Goldmarch soldiers, charging after the retreating elves, were sucked into the voids—alongside a small handful of friendly soldiers, too. As far as I could see from here, at least a hundred soldiers of the empire fell into the darkness, and likely more still were eaten by the voids elsewhere along the wall. Debayur had been true to his word; we just needed to use the advantage he'd given us.

Lore grabbed Val and I by the arm as he ran past us. "Didn't you hear? We're retreating to the inner wall!"

"Yes, we heard, Lore," Val grumbled, running and shaking her arm free of the barbarian's grip. She whipped her arm free and accidentally slammed it into Elandor's side, who responded with a scowl but nothing else. I had no doubt that if we hadn't been in the middle of a battle, he would have berated her.

On we charged, the Slayers, the Red Thorn, and the Sunalorian elven contingent, running along cobbled streets on the ground level of this towering city. Platforms and houses and whole places of business loomed over us, wedged into the trees in the outskirts of the city. Dirt dripped from their foundations as the many voids created an extreme quake that was rippling through Sunalor.

"Watch out!" someone up ahead roared, and I looked up to see one of the tree-embedded struts sliding out of its position, the quakes having shaken it loose.

Nothing happened at first, and I carried on running, charging along the path through the trees and under where the foundation looked ready to fall. Just as I passed under it, an almighty creak announced not just the wooden strut beam falling, but the whole building it was supporting. Screams and shouts erupted from behind me, but I didn't look back, telling myself that I didn't have the time but really just not wanting to see. I glanced around quickly enough only to confirm that the Slayers were all still with me, and I kept going.

Up ahead, between the wide trees, I saw the inner wall, and the majority of the city towering up behind it. If the outskirts fell to the enemy, many would lose their homes and places of business, but it was nothing compared to if this inner city fell. At the center, low in this vertical city that stretched toward the treetops, between rope bridges that crossed between trees, I saw a beautiful and elaborate palace—one that looked like it had been conjured from the roots themselves, rather than built by elven hands. I almost missed my step, admiring it, before reminding myself that my being here wasn't exactly an act of tourism.

More buildings fell behind us as the quakes reached their highest intensity, the trees themselves creaking from the strain, before—all of a sudden—it . . . stopped. I could only imagine that the voids, too, had faded away behind us, which meant that the enemy would be charging us once more.

"Corminar," I shouted to the ranger running ahead.

"I know," he called back.

We piled into the city through one of three visible main gates in the inner city's wall, this bottleneck slowing our entry. Without speaking, the Slayers—as well as much of the Red Thorn, including Elandor—remained close to Corminar, who climbed atop the city wall to look down upon the field of battle.

"Corminar . . ." Val said.

"I am thinking," he said, his eyes intense, looking from the roads of the outer city to the elves, bunched up upon the wall. So few of them looked like real soldiers, so few of them seeming ready for the next wave of attack.

"Corminar!" the witch insisted. "What are we doing?"

The elf gulped, shaking his head, and then stopped. "Where is Debayur?" he asked me.

I shrugged. "Exploded."

"Of course he did." Corminar stared down the wall at the lines of soldiers so far from ready. "I suppose there is another way . . ." He rooted through his pack, pulling out an herb for his alchemy.

"What're you thinking?"

Corminar ignored Val, turning to the elves. "Do any of you still carry your birth seeds? I am looking for the seed of a babel tree."

Nobody responded, but Elandor was glaring at one of the members of the Thorn. "You will hand it over," he told them.

The elf in question approached. "Will I get it back?" they asked as they handed it over to Corminar.

The Hero of Iranir crushed the seed with a pestle. "You will not."

I cast my attention over the wall, back toward the harbor. There was no sign of the enemy wave yet, but it was coming. I could hear it.

"Any time now," Val muttered.

Corminar held up an index finger to demand her patience. He merged the two ingredients into a vial, shaking it and shaking it until it began to glow with the light of a completed potion—this one a dark yet vibrant blue. He drank the liquid without giving it a second thought, and didn't react to what was surely a disgusting flavor.

When he spoke next, everyone nearby grabbed their ears. His voice boomed across the city, louder than . . . well, pretty much anything I'd heard before. At least we now knew what sort of potion that was.

"Citizens of Sunalor," Corminar boomed, talking to all elves who still remained in the city. "My name is Corminar Cladenor, though I know that I am most often known as the Hero of Iranir. It is not a title I enjoy, but it is a title that has me standing before you, leading this defense.

"I know that many of you do not possess Warrior classes, or Mage classes, or Ranger classes. But that does not mean that you are not soldiers. That you stand here today, willing to give everything for the city you love—that is true heart, and *that* is what makes you a soldier."

Between Corminar's words, I heard the city was silent but for the sound of the charging invaders. He had a whole city's attention. They were listening.

"But there is more to be done, if we are to repel these Goldmarch invaders, and if we are to retain our home. Here, on this wall, we make our last stand. We hold this wall, or we die. Though I intend to do my best to ensure that the latter does not occur.

"I ask you now: form lines along the wall. Those with spears should stand at the front, and be ready to repel enemy siege ladders. Those with bows should stand behind, and should be prepared to fire upon my mark. We will rain a storm down upon the invaders."

The first of the enemy soldiers charged into view, followed by hundreds more. Thousands more, really. To look upon the remaining elven force, I couldn't imagine how we could hope to win. But all we could do was try.

"Arrows," Corminar ordered.

The enemies grew closer, charging the walls, war cries erupting around the city.

"Draw," the Hero of Iranir said.

I noticed that the soldiers began to sprint toward the gates, not the walls in general; they were targeting the weakest points. They carried no siege ladders with them—Corminar had gotten that wrong—but I supposed they were still clamped in place on the harbor wall.

"Corminar . . ." I began to point this out.

The ranger nodded; he knew.

"Fire!"

The elves released their first wave of arrows, and though so many fell short, dozens of enemy soldiers fell.

"Ready!" the Hero of Iranir demanded. "Fire!"

And again, more fell. But we were so severely outnumbered that even a dozen Goldmarch soldiers dying at a time would only get us so far. After three more waves, the enemy reached the gates, and Corminar gave the order to fire at will. While Goldmarch soldiers tore at the wooden gates, elves rained arrows down from above.

I poked my head over the wall for just a moment to see how many enemies had fallen, but realized that wasn't important. What was important was the number left—and how quickly they were disintegrating the wood with their axes and fire magicks.

"We need to reinforce it," I told Corminar. "It won't hold."

He responded by nodding, then giving his next order. "Those of you who do not have a clear shot: reinforce the gates. Use anything you can. The stones of the ground level buildings, wooden beams—anything that can add weight."

The elves followed his command, some continuing to kill while others stacked rocks and bricks against the gate. Before long, there was a pile there that the enemy couldn't hope to get through. At least, not quickly.

But then something exploded. This wasn't the explosion of advanced magick, like Debayur had given his last breath to summon; this was something far more basic. The wooden gate was torn apart by the blast, many of the stones and bricks behind it scattered with enough force to kill locals in one hit, and injuring others. I could only take *some* solace in the fact that we were atop the wall and out of the danger area.

"What in hells was—" Arzak started, and then another blast on the top of the nearby wall cut her off. This explosion threw off a dozen elves, and blasted debris over the lot of us.

My ears rang from the blast, and I blinked to keep my vision straight. "Wards!" I shouted. "We need wards!"

"Soldiers!" Corminar boomed. "Those of you with sufficient magicks should begin to summon—"

Another explosion hit the wall, closer this time, knocking Corminar, Val, and I from our feet. And at this point, Val realized what was going on.

"It's the mines!" she shouted. "It's the elven mines—they're launching them back at us!"

Arzak grunted as she helped Corminar and me to our feet. "Hm. Hate *Worldbenders.*" She looked at me. "Not you."

"Wards!" Corminar shouted, getting straight to the point this time. "Summon wards!"

Dotted along the wall, the few elven mages began to follow his command, balls of glowing blue light encompassing some of the soldiers. But there weren't enough of them. We couldn't keep everyone protected.

Another blast on the gate down below cleared the path for the enemy, a couple dozen spilling in instantly, some of them with those same glowing purple rings around one ear. I seized the moment to *Portal Slice* twice, grateful that the elves had never needed to magically reinforce these walls, and I dropped the top of the gate arch down onto the soldiers. But it would only slow them for a minute.

If these explosions kept coming, I couldn't comprehend how we could win this. It was a stroke of genius on the enemy's part, really, to use the elves' own tactics against them. I wasn't sure I would have thought of it, at least not in the midst of a battle. It took someone with—

I realized, then, what was going on.

Niamh was their commander. She was the strategic genius behind all of this. We'd assumed she would have been back on the ships, separated from the battle. And that was right, but we'd made one fatal assumption there. She was still giving orders. Those glowing purple rings around her field commanders' ears? That *Worldbending* magicks? She was using them to communicate. She was getting updates from the field of battle. She was updating her strategy in real time.

At that moment, I had to resist the urge to drop to my knees. All felt lost. How could we hope to compete with that? But I gulped, steadying my nerve, and focused on what needed to be done.

"I'm sorry," I told the Slayers. "I'm sorry, I need to go."

Val and Lore looked at me like I'd lost my mind. *Fair enough, really.*

"What?" the witch demanded. "What in the hells are you talking about?"

"There's only one way of winning this," I told her. "We need to go kill Niamh. We need to go now."

CHAPTER SIXTY-FIVE

Turning Tides

"I'm coming with you," Val shouted over the clashes and screams of battle. "If you're killing her, I'm coming with you."

"Me, too," Lore agreed. "You'll need someone who can take damage. And . . ." He looked to Corminar.

And then something surprising happened. Of all the people in the world, it was Elandor, head of the Red Thorn in the Gentle Tundras, who did something noble. He stepped forward. "You will require a fourth if you are to commandeer a ship, and you will need a ranger. And Sunalor needs the Hero of Iranir here. I will go with you."

Val and I made a meaningful sort of eye contact—*Do we have any other choice?*—and then nodded.

"Corminar Cladenor?" Elandor said, looking into the ranger's eyes. I expected him to reiterate the terms of the deal, to remind him—and the rest of the Slayers, by extension—what he owed. But instead, he said only, "Win."

Corminar responded with a nod, and then, as the four of us departed to take down the enemy general, he returned to giving orders. To saving his home city. Seralin, Relaar's lieutenant pushed past us to speak with him. "Cladenor," I just about heard him saying as we began to weave our way along the wall. "There is something else you should know . . ."

The four of us—including an honorary Slayer I'd never expected to have on our side, in Elandor—pushed through the elves desperately trying to defend their home, shifting away from the gate, where the enemy was concentrating their advance. The further along the inner wall we traveled, the sparser the enemy legions grew, until we were halfway between one gate and the next. There were still plenty of soldiers in our way, but now that this side of the inner city was practically surrounded, it was our only option to get to Niamh before she could deal any more damage.

Getting past this sparser coverage of soldiers was going to be down to me.

"Everyone ready?" I asked.

"I could never be prepared for this," Elandor said. "The defense of my city. The massacring of a people I could never truly leave behind. The—"

"He means 'are you ready to fall through a portal,'" Lore informed him.

Without waiting for the elf's response, I opened one between the four of us, and we fell onto the cobbled streets in the distance. The charging soldiers immediately closed upon us, and Lore bashed one away with the swing of his huge right arm before I could open another portal. We fell through it, the typically stoic Elandor stifling a yelp, and spilled out down the road, toward the rear of the invasion force. One of our attackers fell through with us, and Val leaped toward her to imbue lightning magicks into the soldier's uniform. If the Goldmarch invader had a hope of surviving the attack, it was put to bed by Elandor loosing an arrow into her head.

"You know," Elandor murmured to me. "I do sometimes regret my *Worldbending* ability selections, particularly having overlooked portals in favor of pocket worlds. If I were to do it all again . . ."

I suppressed the urge to agree that although I wished he *hadn't* picked *Pocket World* abilities and stolen Lore's sheep, we wouldn't be here to save Sunalor if he hadn't. Instead, I concentrated on opening the next portals—to the harbor walls—before the sparser nearby soldiers could deal us any damage. We spilled out atop the wall, all enemy soldiers having now long since passed this point, and turned our attentions to the distance.

"Where is she?" Lore asked, his eyes scanning the ships in the Sea of Roots. "Where's Niamh?"

"I'm gonna guess . . . *there*," I replied, pointing to the big one. For all of Niamh's strategic know-how, and her ability to anticipate or react quickly to changing enemy tactics, she'd failed on this account. She'd built herself a flagship, one that easily identified her location. If she'd ever expected a splinter force to tear off from the defense of Sunlar and bring the fight to her, then she had considered a smaller threat than ensuring she projected strength. I almost felt patronized.

"Worldbender," Elandor ordered, "summon one of your portals to allow us access to—"

"Styk," I corrected him.

"Clarify?"

"My name is Styk, not 'Worldbender.'"

The regional leader of the Red Thorn blinked at me. "Is now the correct time for such assertions?"

"Say *Styk*."

"Styk, summon one of your portals to allow us access to the nearest ship. Once aboard, we should—"

I opened a portal in front of me. "Yep," I said, "I know. I just wanted to hear you say it. Cos once all this is done, I'm thinking there's a whole continent who are gonna consider us heroes; I'd like for them to know our names."

Val cast a quick glare at me, but said nothing, and we stepped through the portal. We spilled out into the air above the ship, landing clumsily on the deck. I'd opened the portal a little *too* high in the air—that was the danger with creating portals at a distance; my accuracy at range wasn't great—and the shock of hitting the wood made pain flash through my ankles. As Lore and Elandor spilled through the portal, I considered asking Val for a quick *heal*, but then I spotted that the ship wasn't empty.

Two soldiers, still blinking with surprise, stumbled out of the main cabin into the low light of the evening sun. "Err . . ." one of them said, and then grabbed her sword while her colleague sent a fireball in Val's direction, knocking the witch from her feet.

As the soldier with a sword braced to meet the blade of the charging Lore, the mage turned to me, loosing a fireball. I opened a portal above her, and I activated *Ash Husk* as I fell through it. My skin rippled and changed into ash, limiting the damage any fire magicks could do to me—and had the added benefit of it being nice to get to use this fairly niche ability for once. I took a fireball to the arm, spinning me in the air, and I capitalized on this by shifting from using *Stab* to using *Knifestorm*. My dagger caught the woman a few times, but she was armored enough that it didn't kill her.

I landed on the wooden deck and shifted back to my feet, but in doing so I gave the enemy enough time to swing her sword. I moved to open a portal beneath me, to remove me from harm's way, but I knew I was going to be a split second too late—the enemy was about to deal decent damage.

But midswing, an arrow buried itself in the side of her head, and she fell to the floor, losing her grasp on the sword.

Looking behind her, I saw Elandor, bow in hand. He nodded.

"Thanks, Elandor."

"You are welcome, Worldbender." So he hadn't quite learned my name just yet.

A blast of air from Val made the other Goldmarch soldier stumble, and this was enough for Lore to break their block. Within seconds, we'd seized control of the ship. I supposed Niamh hadn't exactly been planning for anyone to attempt this; the two remaining soldiers were maybe there only to bring the ship into the harbor once the battle was over.

We set about turning the capstan to raise the anchor, fully conscious that time was of the essence. Only once the sails were down and we were moving steadily toward the flagship did I take a moment for myself, in the middle of all this madness.

Some notifications had piled up.

> *14 x Soldiers of the Golden Empire defeated!*

> **Worldbending**: +7,650XP
> *Worldbending increased to Level 46!*
> **Base Points Gained**: +2 INT, +2 Free Points (INT/WIS/CHA)

I marveled at how few experience points I'd received for fourteen soldiers defeated. Though, I supposed, in all cases I'd only contributed to their deaths, and not been the one to deal the most damage. There had been plenty of arrows flying around, not to mention the Master of Alteration's *Void* magicks, all of which had split the experience many ways. And of course, it was silly to be worrying about experience right now—both when there was a battle raging and when I was about to get a *ton* of it from taking down a Player. And I'd get more points to invest into the Sisyphus Artifact, too, boosting my experience gain from here on.

At least, if Val let me deal the final damage.

I turned to her, opening my mouth to remind her of the reasons I needed to be the one to kill Niamh, not her—but I hesitated when I saw her shaking. "Are you OK?"

"I'm fine."

"It's OK if you're a little scared. I mean, it's a Player, after all, and she is the one who—"

"I'm not afraid." Val turned to me then, and when I saw her eyes, I realized she wasn't lying. Those deep brown eyes weren't fearful, they were burning with a red-hot anger. "I want this done, Styk. I want this over. I've carried this with me for too long. But now, I'm going to get revenge on the woman who ruined my life."

I said nothing, leaving it at that. Val wasn't in the state of mind to be reminded of the power of the artifact, and saying anything now might only make her less likely to allow me the final blow. So instead we became silent, and we trained our eyes on the flagship that we were rapidly approaching.

The enemy was so close, and yet still out of reach, and all we could do was wait for the inevitable. Lore and Elandor joined us at our side, and together— a team even more ragtag than the last—we thought about ending the life of another Player.

Soon, we were close.

"So, any thoughts on what we do next?" I asked. "Anyone got a plan?"

Elandor blinked at me. "There is no *plan*?" he asked.

I shrugged. "I dunno, portal in, kill her . . . how hard can it be?"

"Incredibly difficult, Worldbender. It could be *incredibly* difficult."

"We've done it before," Lore said.

"You would not believe how little confidence that instils in me, Shepherd."

"Listen," Val said, cutting through the bickering, and not being a part of it, for once. "I know her. I know what she's about. We can do this, but we've got to be careful. She's got a broad range of abilities; that's part of why her level is so high. *Enchantment*, sure, but also *Stealth*, *Illusion*, even a bit of *Archery*. She's gonna hit us with all kinds of stuff, and we're not going to know what's coming next. Watch out for attacks, watch out for traps. Watch out for *anything*."

"The advice to 'watch out' does not a plan make."

"We'll use the element of surprise," I said. "We'll spring everything we have on her before she even knows we're there. Even someone as strong as her couldn't hope to survive that." I turned to Val. "What's her health situation like?"

The witch shrugged. "She's put most of her points into Intelligence and Dexterity rather than Vitality, as far as I could tell. Though, that might have changed. She's a fragile but powerful weapon—don't let her hit you, but if we can deal lots of damage fast, then . . . Yeah, we might have a shot."

"And as a backup plan?" Lore asked.

I nodded to him. "The usual. You at the fore, taking the damage. Val behind you, *healing*, keeping you strong. Elandor and I dealing damage at range."

"And if not," Val said, her eyes glazing over some as she thought of times long past. "I do have one other trick up my sleeve. Something that got me out of trouble last time."

I looked at her and shook my head. If she did *that*, then we'd never survive. Not on a ship. We'd have nowhere to run from it. "No. Not that. We'd die."

"But if we're dying anyway . . . You want to be a hero, Styk. What's more heroic than dying for a cause?"

"None of us are dying. Not today." I thought of the rest of the Council, and their mysterious scheme that could only spell trouble for the rest of the poor souls in this world. "We still have so much work to do."

Elandor raised his hand, index finger pointing upward. "If I may ask . . . Your initial plan hinges upon us retaining the element of surprise. Do you not think that a vessel sailing straight toward the Player's flagship might alert her to our presence?"

"Sure, but I have a plan for that. Something to distract."

"Yeah?" Lore asked, his eyes lighting up.

"I'm gonna portal us aboard," I said. "And then, this ship is going to ram them."

CHAPTER SIXTY-SIX

The Trapper

Lore wrenched on the wheel, shifting the ship a little to the left. "How's that?" he shouted out.

Val, at the front of the ship with me, narrowed her eyes, staring at the enemy flagship. "Yeah," she cried back, "yeah, that's it! Hold it there!"

Back at the helm, Elandor plunged a sword—stolen from the soldier we'd killed earlier—through the wheel and buried it into the wooden deck, holding the wheel in place. "It is done."

Lore tested the wheel anyway, trying to nudge it this way, then the other. He nodded to confirm, and then the pair of them joined me at the ship's bow. We were close now, the flagship well in sight, and I could just about make out one figure standing on the deck. Hopefully Niamh was too distracted by managing the invasion of Sunalor to notice there was a ship coming for her—one not sailed by Goldmarch soldiers—but I wasn't going to count on it.

"Shall we?" Elandor asked, adjusting the bow on his shoulder and flexing his hands.

"Not yet. Just a little closer," I told him. "Unless you want me accidentally dropping us in the water."

"With every second that passes—" Elandor started.

"I know, I know."

"Are *you* ready?" Val asked the elf. "This isn't some normal fight. This is a Player." When Elandor was about to protest, Val waved him back down. "I know you know that. But it's worth saying. You got any other tricks up your sleeve? Don't suppose you can throw her into a pocket world, never to be seen again? Or can you only do that with Lore's sheep?"

"The power of sheep is near enough the limit of those abilities, alas. I cannot use it on any creature with particular sapience."

"Sentience," Lore corrected him.

Elandor blinked at the barbarian. "No, *sapience*."

"Oh. Yeah."

"Worldbender, if you will—"

"Alright, now," I said, opening a portal beneath the four of us. We fell through it and out its partner's side, onto a balcony of the quarter galley protruding at the rear of the ship. We landed with heavy thumps, and I twisted to look for any sign that we'd been spotted, but when I peered inside, I saw no one.

"Distracted by the ship coming straight for them, I imagine," Val whispered.

"How long till it gets here?" Lore asked.

"Maybe thirty seconds. Let's go."

I led the group into the captain's cabin, finding it deserted. Wherever Niamh was managing the invasion from, it wasn't here. But what I did see were dozens of maps pinned to the walls, with all kinds of markings on them, looking to be plans for different scenarios: for if the elves mustered a sufficient fleet, for if the harbor walls did not fall, for if they needed to blank their enemy, and more. She'd really accounted for every permutation of events. Except, I could only hope, this one—four idiots ramming her ship and trying to take her down.

Wasting no time, I crept forward, Lore, Val, and Elandor following closely at my heels. At the exit to the room, I hesitated—the moment we stepped out into the light, there was much more chance of being spotted. I kept close to the doorframe as I peered out, looking for signs of trouble. But I saw only three: two Knights of the Realm, and the Player herself.

Niamh stood in the center of the deck, flanked by her borrowed knights, bow and quiver over her shoulder, and small glowing portals floating all around her. Through these portals, she might hear reports from and give instructions to her commanders in the field—but her attention wasn't on the portals. It was on the ship now only moments from crashing into her.

"Alright, ready?" I asked the team, and I edged onto the deck.

At that moment, an almighty noise erupted—a squeal like a siren's wail— and Niamh's head snapped to face me.

"Ah," I said, looking down at the sigil glowing on the floor beneath me. A trap.

At that moment, before Niamh could react, the ships collided.

Splinters of wood shot into the air, some of them burying themselves in the bodies both of the enemies and of myself. I could hear water begin to rush in below, the hull having splintered, having been enchanted against enemy attacks and not against other enchanted hulls. And the flagship itself jolted to one side, throwing six of the seven people aboard off their feet—only Niamh remaining effortlessly upright.

As the flagship jolted back the other way, the knights rushed us.

We retreated back into the cabin as planned, in the case of other soldiers being aboard, and Elandor loosed an arrow that hit one of the knights squarely between the brows. But these were Knights of the Realm; it would take more than a well-placed arrow to stop them.

I swung a hand forward to open a portal in front of the two giant, burly Knights of the Realm, and they and their great axes fell through, coming out the other side to collide with one of the cabin's walls.

Lore slammed the door to the captain's quarters shut, delaying Niamh's entry into the fight, and giving us a few extra seconds to eliminate the knights. We could only hope that out across the bay, Corminar was giving her trouble to contend with—because any further seconds might be the difference between life and death.

The Knights of the Realm regathered themselves, one of them turning to swing their axe at the nearest Slayer. Val dived out of the way of the axe, narrowly avoiding getting hurt, and blasted them with a wave of air that knocked them staggering backward.

For our plan to work, we needed at least one knight still aboard. And we had two.

"Oi!" I shouted to the knights, and then I charged them.

But this was a fake out; I hadn't suddenly grown suicidal. As I sprinted across the luxurious cabin, I opened a portal beneath one of them, and they were distracted enough by my feigned attack that they fell through it. I heard a splash in the near distance as they landed in the water.

"One down . . ." Lore said, and suddenly there was a bash on the door. His eyes widened, and he reinforced himself again it. "I thought you said this would buy us enough time!"

"I said it *might*!" I shouted back, but my attention was on the other knight.

"Styk?" Val prompted me.

"On it!" I flung a hand downward, opening a portal in the deep sea beneath the ship, and I opened its partner inside the cabin, only for the briefest of seconds. A heavy blast of water knocked the Knight of the Realm backward, against the wooden wall once more, and I breathed a sigh of relief that the wall held. When I closed the portal a second later, we were wading in a thin layer of water, but the enemy was absolutely drenched.

"Now!" Val shouted, and the four of us leaped up to grab onto the rafters above, separating ourselves from the layer of water. Except the witch also used her new lightning magicks.

The knight shook as the lightning shot through them and their wet covering, dropping to the floor as Val released the magicks. Elandor and I released ourselves from the rafters, and I portaled us over to the enemy, meaning to waste not a second. We released attack after attack after attack of arrow and blade, and it didn't take long for the elimination notification to pop up—one that I swiftly minimized.

A heavy thud announced another attack on the cabin door, and Lore grunted with the strain of resisting. "Hurry!" he cried.

The other three of us got to work.

"Ready?" Lore asked.

We nodded, and the barbarian took a deep breath before standing back from the door. The door blasted open immediately, and he, Elandor, and I stared at the silhouette standing before us. Niamh was a small, thin woman, and yet we already knew enough of her to know this was deceiving. Even Jacob, the pyroknight and the strongest person we'd ever fought, couldn't measure up to the trapper.

"Knock knock . . ." she muttered. "You know, I really did hope you would stay out of this. I had sympathy for you before, back when you were only defending your home. But now that you threaten my plans, I am forced to cast you down. For this, I do sincerely apologize."

"Yeah, I bet," Lore replied.

"Doubt me all you like, Barbarian, but I do mean it. Perhaps as an act of—" Niamh suddenly stopped talking, her attention diverted by someone talking through one of the portals. She held up an index finger to demand that we wait. It was infuriating, but if the next stage of the plan was going to work, then we had to bite our tongues.

"No matter," she told someone through one of the small portals. "Order a fifth of the remaining force to splinter away, to circle the city and approach from the rear. They are few; if we stretch them far enough, the city will fall."

It was good to know that Corminar was still holding the enemy off, at least.

Niamh turned back to us. "Now, where were we?"

"Something about an act?"

"Ah, yes. An act of small mercy," she said, then stepped aside, gesturing us past. "Would you like to bathe in the sunlight one last time before I cut you down?"

What an exciting opportunity.

I glanced to Lore and Elandor, who nodded, and then in silence we stepped outside onto the main deck. We'd not intended for this, but we could work with it—more space to fight in was always handy.

"I am sorry to see that your witch friend has fallen already," Niamh said. "I once thought she would someday die at my hand, when she finally tracked me down, and yet . . ." She shook her head and turned to face the three of us standing and staring her down—port versus starboard.

The flagship suddenly lurched to one side as water broke away at one of the lower decks.

"I suppose I will have to transit to another ship. A shame; a copy of my personal library is aboard, and printing does not come cheap. Especially when you are forced to eliminate those involved."

At that moment, I saw a flash of movement to my left. It was time.

"Now!" I shouted, and the three of us charged. Two of us began to glow with purple magicks, while one of us used the tried and tested strategy of swinging a big sword.

I hopped through a portal to attack Niamh from behind, but the moment I touched her, an invisible sigil glowed into life—one that blasted me across the deck and out over the water. It was only my portal magicks that stopped me falling into the depths, instead stumbling back out onto the deck.

Elandor, meanwhile, opened a portal world entrance above the Player's head, dumping a rain of arrows onto her head. But with the flick of her wrist, more sigils still glowed into life all around the ship, and the arrows diverted toward them, as though compelled.

Only Lore, using the simplest of all the attacking techniques, came close to hurting Niamh. But as he charged, a Knight of the Realm sprinted into action, crossing the deck in a flash and putting themselves between Niamh and Lore, knocking him to the floor with almost performative ease.

A Knight of the Realm with a dead woman's face, that is.

As Niamh grimaced down at the barbarian, the knight retreated to the Player's side. And when the knight got close, she grabbed Niamh by the throat and revealed her true face. Val's face. Val, who Elandor and I had hurriedly helped dress in Goldmarch armor, then portaled her across the ship.

Val imbued Niamh's throat with her lightning magicks. "Surprise, bi—"

But any cocky retort was cut short.

The body in her grasp didn't react to the magick attack at all. In fact, it only smiled at Val, and then . . . it faded from existence.

Val retreated, stumbling backward in her oversized armor, blinking at the spot where Niamh had been standing only seconds earlier. "An . . . an illusion," she said.

"But you touched her!"

"A *powerful* illusion," she said. "A decoy."

The implications sunk in. Niamh really had planned for everything; she'd planned for *this*, too.

And then another Niamh appeared, at the other end of the deck. "Surprise, Witch," she said. But there was no real malice in it, and even a smile on her face. The Player clapped. "Oh, very good, very good! I thought I had the constructs of this world all figured out, but you surprise me. You are capable of meaningful thought after all! Of course, this doesn't change what I have to do, you understand."

"Doesn't change much for *us*, either," Val spat back at her.

Niamh's smile didn't fade. "So, the witch lives after all. And she still has quite the sharp tongue on her. Is that what all this is, then? Not the defending of a region, but revenge?"

"No," Val replied. "Not revenge. Justice. Delivered by *Witchcraft*." She pulled a small, seemingly insignificant flower from her pocket, plucked from the ground with roots intact, and she threw it to the deck. "*Witchcraft* isn't all that powerful away from nature, you know? And out here . . . well, I don't have all my plant life to work with. So I thought I'd bring some with me."

Val thrust both hands forward, and they glowed a vibrant green as she worked her magicks. Roots sprang forth from the tiny, limp flower, shooting in every direction. A hundred. A thousand. Each of them buried themselves in the wood of the deck, piercing a hundred trap sigils that glowed as they were shattered.

Finally, the smile faded from the enemy's face.

CHAPTER SIXTY-SEVEN

The Mice & The Lion

Niamh pulled her bow from her shoulder, though she still snarled down at her broken traps. "A rare treat, I suppose, to be able to indulge in the more primitive skill trees."

Before she could draw her bow, the four of us charged across the deck, bringing the fight once more. I opened a portal beneath Lore, as the slowest of us, to close the gap between him and the enemy—which also meant that the person able to withstand the most damage was at the front. As Lore swung the Bane Sword at the enemy, Elandor loosed arrow after arrow at Niamh, while Val pre-emptively started her *Healing* magicks.

Niamh blocked the swipes of Lore's sword not just with ease, but using her bow, of all things—though the glowing wood was another giveaway that something magick was at play here. The limbs of her bow blocked the Bane Sword's strikes without suffering any chips to the wood, and not only that, but the bow seemed to push back against the sheer force of Lore's attacks, meaning that Niamh didn't need to put her body weight behind the blocks.

Sigils shattered in the air around her as Niamh's enchanted traps blocked shot after shot of Elandor's arrow, these being the only traps left that Val's roots couldn't destroy. But she surely had to have a limited supply, right? Either she had manually made them all, or they were powered by mana—either way, there had to be an end to them.

We just had to live that long.

I leaped into the air, knife raised above my head in two hands, and I moved to *stab* down with it—but Niamh batted me out of the way with the swipe of her hand. I landed on the hard wooden deck, tumbling head over heels.

"Don't you see?" Niamh said through clenched teeth, the fight apparently not quite as simple as she'd maybe imagined. "You are *mice* to me. Rodents. Vermin. Barely worth the effort it takes to kill you. I offered you mercy before out of the kindness of my own heart—but I treat such creatures with respect only while they do not stand in the way of progress."

"Oh yeah?" I said, stumbling back to my feet. "And just what is this 'progress,' then?"

"You think I would divulge the Council's plans so easily? Perhaps you are a fool after all."

"He is," Val said, "but I'm not." At that moment, she leaped over Lore's shoulder, putting a foot on his back to get purchase as she jumped into the air. She landed on the Player's back, grasping onto the woman's neck for dear life, and she screamed with fury as she sent lightning magicks into the *real* Niamh this time.

Another sigil activated, sending Val's magicks shooting back through the witch's body. She screamed her head off, but still she hung on for dear life, pushing the magicks back into the enemy. Niamh screamed, too, then, and this was just the opening that Lore needed to land a swipe of his blade.

Lore nicked Niamh, a spray of blood whipping across the deck. Niamh screeched further, ripping Val from her back with her bare hand and throwing her away. The damage didn't last long, because one of Niamh's sigils activated, and a glowing yellow-white light encompassed the wound in her side. But it was evidence that she could be hurt. And if she could be hurt, she could be killed.

It was the morale boost we needed.

As Val, Lore, and I charged once more, Niamh fired an arrow toward the barbarian. In midair, the arrow split into ten, and the arrows' trajectories changed to tear off toward each of the Slayers—honorary or otherwise. And if that wasn't enough, they suddenly erupted with magicks of all kinds, shapes, and colors.

Lore was hit first, taking the arrows to his chiseled torso, flame encompassing his left side while a dark corruption took his right. Val leaped to heal him, and in doing so avoided the two arrows sent her way, just about. Meanwhile, I opened a portal beneath me and allowed myself to drop through it and out of danger—but Elandor wasn't so lucky.

The leader of the Tundran Red Thorn took three hits—one arrow that dealt frost damage to his legs, another which made his eyes glow with the red of *Illusion* magicks, and one more: a plain old arrow crafted from the finest of metals. This one hit him in the neck.

Elandor staggered backward, eyes bulging, clasping his wound to stop the blood flowing as best he could.

"Val!" I shouted, but she was busy *healing* Lore's wounds, so instead I portaled myself to the elf's side. I yanked my one and only remaining health potion from my pocket, pulled the cork free, and forced it down Elandor's throat, closing the man's jaw with my hands. He coughed and gulped, but it did the work. At least, enough to ensure the damage from the arrows only knocked him out, rather than kill him outright.

We were down to three.

Val had Lore stood back up, the worst of the enchanted arrows' effect now faded, though he was still looking a little worse for wear.

"How do we beat this?" I shouted to her. "We don't know what's coming next!"

"Indeed, you don't," Niamh agreed, and fired another three arrows at once. Again, these arrows changed direction in midair—one of them shooting toward each of us. I opened another portal to avoid the shot, but too late I realized that the arrow wasn't aiming directly for me. As I was about to fall through the portal, the arrow exploded in a blaze of blue, forming a pillar of light from which . . .

I couldn't move out.

I glanced around at my two remaining friends, and saw that they, too, were caught by Niamh's latest trick up her sleeve. I tried to pull myself free, but the magick pulled back, meeting any force I used with an even greater force. I tried to cut through the pillar of light with my knife, but it made no difference. I tried to *Portal Slice* my way out of it, and then simply open a portal to get out . . . but neither worked. Looking across the deck, I saw Niamh, her eyes on Val, taking her time as she approached the witch, as though savoring the moment. I saw Val struggling against the trap, but having about as much luck as me.

And then I saw Lore. Big, lovely, strong Lore.

Lore was having *much* more luck. He strained against the pillar of light, pushing himself to one side, and then part way out of it. But as he strained, he was grunting, and any moment now he could grunt loud enough to attract the distracted Player's attention.

So it was at this moment that I got to use my most recently acquired ability. I pushed an arm forward as much as I could, but couldn't outstretch it within the confines of this trap. But when Val had taught me the basics of magicks, she'd told me to use my arms to control the aim of the magicks—she had said explicitly that they weren't required.

I twisted my hand to point roughly toward Lore, doing the best that I could, but then . . . I closed my eyes. I concentrated on where I wanted the magick to go in my mind's eye, not with my outstretched hands. I imagined it—a bubble around Lore, one that prevented any sound from escaping—and as soon as I thought I could see it, I activated *Silence III*.

When I opened my eyes, it was there. I couldn't see it—this particular ability not giving off a glow of any kind—but I knew it was there. Mostly because Lore was by this point shouting, his mouth wide open, as he forced his body through the portal.

With her eyes on Val, Niamh drew a bow from her quiver.

Lore looked from Val, to me, and then back to Val again, and I had to bite my tongue to stop myself from shouting at him—and drawing the Player's attention. Finally making a decision, Lore charged across the deck toward me, then threw himself into the pillar to tackle me from it. We came rolling out the other side just as Niamh drew her arrow. I immediately opened a portal below where Lore had fallen, catapulting him toward Val.

The great barbarian collided with the witch, knocking her from the pillar trap just in time for the arrow to breeze harmlessly past the both of them.

"The mice flee, but they cannot hope to defeat the lion," Niamh proclaimed.

I skirted around the fight to join Lore and Val at their side. "Alright," I told them. "One big push. Everything we've got."

"Everything?" Val repeated.

"No. Not that." If she did *that*, then chances were that one of them would be dead long before Niamh was.

"Ready?" Lore asked, eyes bearing into Niamh, and then without waiting for a response, he rushed her.

Val and I had no choice but to follow suit. The witch blasted Niamh with waves of air, while I reached for the water below. We'd sunk a good way by this point, the flagship now sitting a lot lower in the sea, so I didn't need to reach far to find water. As with the Knight of the Realm and the pyroknight before her, I opened a portal to empty the contents of the sea onto Niamh. From the force, she staggered backward, but a moment later she'd wrenched her bow forward to hover vertically before her, the limbs of the weapon splitting and parting the water attacks.

I closed the portal a half second before Lore reached Niamh, and he swung his Bane Sword once more, this time again managing to bury it deep in the enemy's side.

She screamed with a combination of pain and surprise, and this time—while *Healing* magicks engulfed the wound once more—she snarled at Lore. She pulled an arrow from her quiver and shot it immediately into Lore's chest.

Lightning engulfed him.

Niamh pulled another arrow, and once again she concentrated her fire on Lore. This time, his right arm twisted inhumanly . . . and then snapped.

I opened a portal beneath my feet, launching myself into an attack of Niamh, activating *Execution* alongside *Stab* even though she had to know I was there. I buried the knife in between her shoulders, and she howled, shaking me and the dagger loose, but didn't stop firing arrows at Lore.

The barbarian sank to his knees as the third hit him, and bright yellow ghost-like echoes of the depth-raider appeared before him. And then, giant ghostly pillars like those we'd seen in the witchfinders' village, but a hundred times their size, their spectral images bursting from the water. Only at this did Niamh suddenly stop, eyes wide, and hesitate.

"Then it's true . . ." she said. "It will work. Tana's plan will work. But . . ." she looked down at Lore. "You will need to be there to witness it?"

She hesitated, then pushed over to Lore while Val blasted her with magick attacks—whatever that was, whatever she'd seen . . . it was enough to distract her from the literal attempt on her life. Niamh crouched down at Lore's side and wrapped her hands around his head.

"No!" I shouted.

But Niamh didn't attack Lore. No, quite the opposite. Whatever she had seen . . . whatever she had conjured with her yellow *Divination* magicks . . . It had convinced her that Lore needed to survive. A white sigil appeared on her forehead, and then traversed down one of her arms to Lore's own head, where it activated. She wasn't *hurting* him; she was *healing* him. Lore closed his eyes, drifting not from life, but from consciousness.

We were down to two.

I turned to Val and I told her something with my eyes, and my eyes alone.

The woman I loved responded with a nod. She understood. She knew what needed to be done—the one thing we could count on, when all else failed.

It was time to summon the bogspawn.

CHAPTER SIXTY-EIGHT

Forbidden Magicks

Val would need time to summon the bogspawn; this I knew.

I also knew that Niamh wouldn't freely *give* us time, so it was going to be up to someone else to buy Val this time. I looked with regret at Lore and Elandor, both unconscious on the deck of the sinking ship—if they were still with us, this would have been so much easier.

So there was only one thing for it: it was time for an all-out attack. With one eye on my mana reserves—and grateful for one of Corminar's mana potions still in my pocket—I opened a portal next to me and dropped through it, coming out behind Niamh for just long enough to get a quick *stab* in. As she turned, enraged, I stepped back through another portal and came out behind her again, once again able to land a *stab* before she could meet me with her enchanted bow.

Niamh, scowling, quickly drew a bow and fired an arrow toward me. Or, at least, toward the spot where I would have been if I hadn't just disappeared through a portal. Out of the corner of my eye, I'd seen Val's hands and eyes begin to glow in that bright green that said she was working on a powerful ritual— she was already at work, I just needed to survive long enough for her to see it through.

I reappeared from a portal above Niamh, mixing it up a bit, and just like I had with the pyroknight, I used gravity to improve the damage dealt by a *stab* of my blade. But this woman was far stronger than that Player had ever been, and it was going to take a lot more than that to bring her down.

I landed on her shoulder, and it felt stronger than it looked, hitting me hard in the chest and sending me spinning to the deck. I wasted no time in looking back at Niamh, knowing that she would easily hit me if I stayed still too long, and I opened a portal in the root-bound wooden deck. I fell through back to behind Niamh, where I brought my knife arm around to—

Without looking back, the Player caught my wrist in midair. Her hand was tight around me. Strong. I couldn't break free, not easily. Not by myself.

"Enough, now," Niamh said. "It's time for this to be over."

"Agreed," Val replied, and streams of crackling green energy poured forth from her hands. Niamh turned and saw this, and moments later she recognized it for what it was—for something she'd seen already, all those years ago.

And now I was seeing it for the first time, too. The streams of green *Witchcraft* magicks didn't form the bogspawn itself, but seemed to grab a hold of the very edge of reality—in a way not unlike I'd seen in the witchfinder villages. Those glowing green arcs tore the borders of this world open, and through this tear, I saw . . . nothing. The void. Not darkness, but the absence of reality.

And, from out there, in the nothingness, a paw grabbed at the edge of reality. The paw looked like that of a large cat, but when the head appeared, it looked like anything but. It had the antlers of a stag atop a long, leathery face. The lion-like paws tore away at the entrance into reality that Val had created for it, revealing the rest of its form. It stood on four long legs, its large body seeming to be made of rotting flesh—any number of beasts stitched together like some lunatic's attempt at replicating the Architects' act of creation. When it stepped forth, into our world, I half expected flies to buzz around it, but of course there was nothing. I got the sense that even if flies had been interested in its rotting flesh, the creature would have struck such fear into them that they would have flown away.

That was precisely what I wanted to do right now, presented by this foul creature, but I forced myself to stand my ground.

Finally, Niamh released my wrist—she'd realized that there were greater dangers around now—and I staggered backward, putting as much space between myself and the enemy as possible.

The bogspawn surveyed those surrounding it. It looked first at Val, then at me, and then at Niamh. I knew that there was only a one in three chance that it would pounce on the Player first, that it would kill her before either of us, and I didn't much love those chances.

But it was all we had now.

All three of us, the Player included, remained still and quiet as the beast considered each of us—not wanting to do anything to make the bogspawn choose us over the others. Then, the bogspawn stopped surveying us, and it concentrated its attention on none other than the Player.

"I've escaped you once before . . ." Niamh growled to the creature.

We'd done it. We'd won. We'd lucked out. I resisted the urge to jump with joy, to cheer, to—

The bogspawn snapped its head to me. Then, it turned.

As soon as it pounced, I ran. I sprinted, without really knowing where my feet were taking me, down the stairs to the lower decks of Niamh's flagship. I could hear the heavy footsteps of the bogspawn chasing after me, making the wood shake with every step. When it grew too close to bear, I flicked a portal open ahead of me and slipped out of range of its long antlers and sharp teeth.

I collided with the wall of the ship as I tumbled out the other side, and put my hands against it to steady myself. While I had increased the distance between myself and the horrific monster, the bogspawn was fast, and it was only a matter of time before it found me once more. I sprinted onward, but found myself delayed by the rising water levels. This ship was well and truly sinking, and it was only a matter of time until we were all in the water. Would the bogspawn do so well in that scenario? And would I live long enough to find out?

I moved to open another portal as the bogspawn drew closer, hoping to buy myself some time to figure out how we might still use the creature's appearance to our advantage, but I caught sight of my mana reserves as I did so. After all this fighting, they were nearly empty. I pulled the glass vial filled with mana potion from my pocket, and I yanked the cork free in a hurry.

But the bogspawn was too near, and I had to suddenly open a portal beneath me to escape its swiping paw. As I fell through the portal, the bogspawn's claws caught my hand . . . and as they sliced through my flesh, I dropped the potion.

Falling out the other side of the portal, closing it behind me, I reached out to catch the potion in midair, but it was out of reach. It smashed upon the hard wooden deck.

"Val!" I shouted across the top deck. "I'm almost out! I'm almost out of mana!"

The witch nodded as she faced down Niamh—the latter still willing to fight despite the presence of an admittedly distracted bogspawn on the ship. Maybe that was precisely *why* she wanted to fight then; she could take Val down before focusing on the bogspawn and me. "Then we need to end this. Now."

"Well, *yeah*. Any ideas?" It really, *really* wasn't looking good.

"How many portals?" the witch cried back, blasting Niamh with air.

"Maybe two? Three? Depends how long I keep them open. Why, what are you thinking?"

"I don't know yet. I—" Val stopped midsentence, and both Niamh and I immediately knew why.

We followed Val's gaze to the stairs, where the bogspawn had appeared once more. I turned back to the witch. "Val! Any ideas? What are you thinking?" I repeated.

But Val looked pale. She shook her head. "I don't know! I . . . I . . ."

I looked back to the bogspawn, who looked around ready to pounce once more, but as I skimmed over the deck, I saw something.

Elandor.

Elandor was still alive, if unconscious, laying on the wooden deck. And maybe, just maybe, he held the key to evening out the odds. If what I suspected about my *Pocket Worlds* ability was true, then . . .

I shook my head. It didn't matter. We were out of other options; it was time to try something else.

As the bogspawn pounced toward me, I charged at it—an action that both the monster and I seemed genuinely surprised by. The monster bounded, and I slipped to the ground, opening a portal above me that the bogspawn had no choice but to slide through—landing it next to Niamh. But it had its eye on its prize already, and it turned back to me.

Meanwhile, I slid to Elandor's side, and I grabbed his head with both hands. "Let's hope this works . . ." I activated my *Pocket Worlds* ability, hoping against all hope that "Open and access pocket dimensions" really *did* mean those that I hadn't created. I put almost all my remaining mana into this attempt, saving only the tiniest amount, doing everything I could to make sure that this worked.

And . . . it did.

As the first of the sheep fell through the pocket world's exit portal, I thanked the Architects that Lore wasn't awake to see this. Two dozen sheep fell, bleating, from the portal to the pocket portal, landing in a huge pile . . . on top of Niamh.

Suddenly, the bogspawn needed to reassess its choice of prey.

It looked from me to the pile of sheep—with a Player buried, shouting, beneath them—and it reconsidered. And this time, it was an easy decision to make.

The bogspawn pounced into the pile of sheep, tearing their flesh apart with its wide, toothy mouth . . . but making no distinction between sheep flesh and human flesh. Blood splattered the deck, beginning to to pool beneath the dying sheep, trickling across the roots and the wooden planks.

With so little mana remaining, all I could do was stand and stare at the chaos before me, apologizing to Lore a hundred times over in my head for what I'd had to do. It really *had* been the only way.

And then, from the pile, a human shape staggered out.

When she emerged from the madness, Niamh was covered in blood—both hers and the sheep's—and was down one arm. Instead of concentrating her traps on her wound, she spat toward me, "I'll deal with you next," and then turned her attention back to the monster.

She approached it while it was busying itself with a sheep, and she reached her remaining arm forward. Niamh weaved a sigil into life in the air before her, this one glowing blue with *Sorcery* magicks, and when she was done, she pressed her hand into the bogspawn's rotten side, and the sigil attached itself to the creature's flesh.

From the look of it, this had taken most of Niamh's remaining mana to craft—it was no simple magick—and her legs shook beneath her as she stumbled backward, away from the monster. The sigil began to grow brighter and brighter, glowing to life.

But just before it could activate, the bogspawn whipped its head up to face the Player. It looked from Niamh to the symbol on its chest, and then it understood—on some primal level—what was about to happen. It pounced at Niamh at the same moment that the sigil activated.

"No, no, no!" Niamh shouted.

And then the bogspawn exploded.

Niamh was caught in the center of the blast, and was blown to the floor. Even Val and I, at some distance, suffered some major damage, and I had to put my weight on the witch as she gave me a quick *healing* boost to keep me conscious. A shrill noise rang through my ears from the explosion, and I chewed my jaw on the empty air to try to get my hearing back.

When the dust finally settled, the bogspawn was gone—but Niamh, still, was not. I checked my notifications—surely that had been enough to kill the Player, surely she was not still with us—but I only had those for the Knights of the Realm.

Niamh was still alive, for now. If deathly injured.

Val and I took a moment to regather control of our breathing, the battle now finally over, before we strolled over to Niamh's body.

The Player looked up at us as she tried to reach toward her wound, the yellow-white light of *Healing* magicks flickering in and out of existence—she was too weak.

"No," Val said, her voice gentle. "Don't bother. It's over now."

CHAPTER SIXTY-NINE

One of Many

"It's over now."

Val and I hurried over to Niamh's side, and only when I was satisfied that she really was dying, rather than faking it, I allowed myself to breathe. When the Player saw us standing over her, she didn't move to strike, or to spit at us. In fact, she smiled.

"Does she know what you are, Styk?" Niamh asked through a bloody mouth. "She might be a witch, but I think she would believe what you are to be so much worse."

I hesitated, then. Every instinct told me to end the Player's life, there and then, before she could reveal to Val what she knew of me. But I hesitated. I hesitated at possibly the most important moment of my life.

"Does she know you are the spawn of a Player?" Niamh finished.

Val stumbled backward, face paling, and I watched as she looked from the Player to me, unbelieving. "Is it true?"

Niamh answered for me. "Cleo, her name is. A member of my Council. A smart woman, though I see that never . . ." The Player had to stop to cough up blood. "I see that attribute did not get passed on." And then, to Val, she continued, "Did you never wonder why he could use that artifact? An artifact meant only for Players? He has our blood within him. He is one of us."

Val's eyes remained on Niamh, apparently unable to tear them away—or, perhaps, to look at me.

"Val, you know me," I said to her. "You know what I am. What I believe in. You know I'm nothing like one of *them*."

Only then did the witch look up at me.

"We're both ashamed of what we are," I said. "But we both know that we're more than what we were born as, right? Right?" *Was I convincing her, or convincing myself?*

Slowly, Val nodded.

"You understand?"

"I . . ." she started, her voice croaking. "I'll need some time to process. You . . . understand that, right?"

I thought about reminding her of my reaction to the news that she was a witch—it didn't bother me for a second. But that wasn't helpful right now. "I understand," I said, and turned back to Niamh. "Was that your final ploy? Turn us against each other by telling her what I am? That I'm the man who is part human, part god?"

"The man?" Niamh repeated, beginning to laugh. "*The* man? You thought it was just you? You thought you were special?" The Player stopped her laughing only when the coughing and spluttering became too great, and for a moment it looked like she might slip away from this world then.

"I thought . . ."

"Our kind have roamed these lands for generations. From the days that your so-called Architects created it. You must know that our lives are far longer than yours. Did you really think that only *one* of us would have birthed children with the locals, that only one of us might have accidentally blessed her spawn with the magicks of our homeworld? There are hundreds with Player blood in them, if not thousands. Any one of them could have used the artifact." She laughed again. "And you thought you were special?"

"I am special," I said, raising my dagger. "I *have* the artifact." I moved forward as if to kill her, and at that moment the fear came out.

Niamh's eyes widened at last. "Stop!" she croaked. "Stop. I've made arrangements. I created a standing order, after our encounter in the Tundras. If I should die, the Council are to be notified that you and your friends are coming for them. You will be hunted to your last breath."

"So what?" Val asked, and I saw that her eyes were on my dagger point; she hadn't forgotten our discussion about who should be the one to end the Player's life. About who *deserved* to.

"If I die here, in this world, more Creations remain to me. And once Tana is successful in this one, I will be practically immortal. If you die, however, it is over—whether you have Player blood in you or otherwise."

"I best not die, then." With that, I plunged my knife down, activating the simplest of all my abilities: *Stab.* As I twisted the knife in Niamh's stomach, watching the life fade from her eyes, Val didn't complain; that she was here to see it seemed to be enough. Either that, or she was still sidetracked by the news of my ancestry. The reason didn't matter, because there was something else far more important: that I leveled up the Sisyphus Artifact once more, whatever the cost.

As I twisted once more, Niamh drew her last breath, and a single tear dripped from Val's right eye.

---

2 x Knights of the Realm defeated!
Level 46 Expert Trapper defeated!

Worldbending: +21,050XP
Worldbending increased to Level 50!
Base Points Gained: +8 INT, +8 Free Points (INT/WIS/CHA)
Ability Selection Unlocked
Select an ability from the list below . . .
Knifework: +13,200XP
Knifework increased to Level 39!
Base Points Gained: +3 DEX, +3 STR, +6 Free Points (VIT/DEX/STR)
Level up!
You increased to level 17
Descendant of the Architects defeated!
Sisyphus Artifact: Charge replenished!
Sisyphus Artifact: Leveled up!
Artifact Upgrade Unlocked
Select [2] upgrades from the list below . . .
1. Increase Charges VI [8 > 9]
2. Extend Active Period II [1,000 > 1,500]
3. Increase Effect I [+900 percent > +1,400 percent]
4. Add Experience Preservation Charge IV [+1]

This time around, I knew exactly what to pick. If Niamh was telling the truth—and for all her faults, she didn't strike me as a liar—the Council would be coming for us now. If they came, there was a good chance I'd need to use the Sisyphus Artifact again. So I might as well keep the experience when I *did* die. But until then, I was going to want to grow stronger as quickly as possible.

Artifact upgraded confirmed!
Sisyphus Artifact
Charges Remaining: (1 / 8)
Active Effect: Legacy of Sisyphus
Days remaining: 902 / 1,000
XP gain increased by +1,400 percent

The rest of the notifications weren't time-sensitive; I could deal with those later. For now, Val and I had to turn our attention to the two unconscious men lying on the deck of the sinking ship.

Unsurprisingly, it was Lore that we ran to first, though we quickly established that he was . . . absolutely fine? Sleeping, but fine. Niamh really had spent so much of her mana healing his wounds—but why? I had the worrying feeling that we'd find out before long. We'd need to wake Lore up soon, before the ship sank entirely, but that was nothing a bucket of cold water over the head couldn't fix.

Elandor, however, was much worse for wear. He'd taken some very heavy wounds, wounds which Val poured all her *Healing* magicks into . . . but it wasn't enough to fix them. The witch did just enough to bring Elandor conscious, to face down his rapidly approaching end.

For what it was worth, the elf did so with honor.

"Worldbender," he croaked, and this time I let it slide. "My bow . . ."

"The battle's over, Elandor. We won. We killed her."

"And . . . Sunalor?"

I cast a glance over my shoulder at the coastline, but I simply couldn't tell; it was too far. "I'm sorry. I don't know."

Elandor forced a smile to his face. "You might have lied to me, but I respect that you did not. My bow . . . do you see it?"

In answer, I nodded.

"Please, take it. As a gift."

I slid the bow out from under his hand. "For . . . me?"

Elandor laughed. "I never will understand human humor. No, Worldbender. Not for you. For the Hero of Iranir. For Lieutenant Cladenor. I think . . . he has earned it."

These would turn out to be the last words of Elandor, leader of the Red Thorn.

As it happened, waking Lore up had ended up being much more difficult than I'd expected. Splashing cold water on him hadn't done it, and I'd been about out of ideas when it had occurred to Val to slap him in the face—several times.

When Lore awoke, sporting a bright red patch on his right cheek, he blinked at the situation around him. "Did I kill her?" he asked.

Val and I couldn't help but laugh, and the witch clapped the barbarian around the shoulder. "You did a good job, buddy."

From the bright smile that emerged on his face, Lore was happy enough with that result. I tried to smile at Val, too, but though she was otherwise acting normally to me, she didn't seem to quite be able to meet my eye.

What with me still having so little mana left in my reserves, we'd had to swim to the nearest ship—with the now-fresh Lore doing most of the work. After we tired ourselves beyond all belief, Val and I clinged onto the barbarian's loose-fitting top as he continued swimming, not slowing down even slightly. Lore even considered climbing the rope ladder at the side of the ship with us still hanging on, but ultimately asked us to get on by ourselves.

I grunted my teeth as I pushed my exhausted legs up one by one, and then staggered onto the deck of a ship without any holes in the hull. Only then could the three of us look back at the city of Sunalor, and hope that our friends had been successful in their quest to save it. We sailed back toward it as the invasion continued, Val and I admittedly unlikely to make any difference to the tide of war, so exhausted were we by our encounter with Niamh, but we went anyway—determined to see this journey through to its end.

And then an explosion—no, *two*—rang out across the harbor. I thought at first that this was another mine—perhaps we'd hit something, even—but then the noise was followed up by an almighty screech, and a crack. We watched on as two of the towering Dawnwood trees began to fall, one on each side of the city, plummeting toward the dirt. Even at this distance, we could hear the smashing of buildings beneath them, homes sacrificed in the name of the defense of Sunalor.

But we also knew that to fell a tree of the Dawnwood was heresy. It was the act of a desperate man, an act that Corminar had needed to resort to once before.

"It wasn't enough," I breathed, and though neither Val nor Lore replied, I knew that they agreed.

All we had done, by killing Niamh, was take their general away. But we'd been too late, and the new Golden Empire's army had been too great in number. In those latter stages of the invasion, they'd been powerful enough even without Niamh to ensure that the elves hadn't stood a chance.

Corminar had failed. Sunalor had fallen.

CHAPTER SEVENTY

Extraction

"Are you sure about this?" Val asked me, her eyes on the city and not on mine.

"We've got to give them something to aim for. And I can think of nothing better. Unless you want to go into the city yourself, and find them?"

Lore raised his hand. "If it's all the same to you, I quite like it here on this ship and not surrounded by thousands of enemies. I've had enough of enemies."

Val sighed; she knew the alternatives. Either we produced a signal for Corminar and Arzak to run toward—assuming they were still alive—or we go in and get them ourselves. And I think even Val was getting tired of jailbreaks by this point. Of course, there was a third option: we could have turned our ship around and sailed away—but it was so far from the heroic thing to do that I didn't even bother to voice it.

The witch closed her eyes, gathering her remaining mana and then beginning a ritual. It didn't matter what the ritual was—Val had chosen one that took a little while—because what we really were after was . . .

Val shot the green glowing *Witchcraft* magicks into the air—a pillar of light that lit up the harbor for all to see. Of those in the city, many would know it was *Witchcraft*, but only Corminar and Arzak would realize that Val was the one doing it. When the pillar of light had shone brilliantly for a good half a minute, I tapped Val gently on the shoulder, bringing her back down to Alterra.

Unless I was mistaken, she flinched at my touch.

Our signal released; all we could do now was wait—and see whether it was friend or foe that reached us first.

With nothing but time to kill now, I brought up some recent notifications once more—my *Worldbending* ability selection window. This time, I'd leveled up my skill to level 50, and I knew from past lives that this could only be a big one.

Ability Selection Unlocked
Select an ability from the list below:
Option 1: Portal Relay (Worldbending) [Requires: any *Portals* ability]—*Passive.* Up to ten smallscale portals can now be positioned relative to an entity, and used to communicate sound.

This ability had to be what Niamh had ordered casted on her, so that she could manage the invasion from afar. There were definitely use cases, particularly because I worked in a team—though whether the rest of the Slayers would like me being the hub that provided orders was another matter entirely. Having access to more portals at once definitely had its upside, too, but they were smallscale, so I imagined I wouldn't exactly be able to fit through them. Still, if it meant I could put my hand through and steal things . . .

I shook my head, reminding myself that I wasn't a thief anymore; I was a hero. A hero. After taking down not one but *two* Players, how could I be anything else?

This was already a high bar in terms of ability choice, but I could see that there were still three more options to come, so I put it aside mentally for now.

Hidden condition met! Alternative ability choice unlocked.
Option 2: Pocket World Transit (Worldbending) [Requires: *Pocket Worlds* ability]—Enter your pocket worlds. When you exit once more, any distance you cover within your pocket world will be reflected on the outside.

I had to resist the urge to smile at this one, but its applications were definitely appealing. It meant that I could cover huge distances undisturbed, appearing out of nowhere in, perhaps, the middle of an enemy camp, or a bank vault. There were just two issues with it. First, would I be able to properly measure distance from within a pocket world, with no landmarks to speak of. And secondly . . . was I really sure I *wanted* to go inside them?

I kept my mind open to it, and moved on to the next option.

Hidden condition met! Alternative ability choice unlocked.
Option 3: Needle Dart (Worldbending) [Requires: *Needlework* level 10]—Launch needles through minimized portals. Can be targeted to any location excluding living beings and magick-imbued objects. Uses mana per use.

This was quite a fun one, but perhaps not as game-changing as the previous two. I could already throw needles through portals if I really wanted to, though this ability would presumably have these "minimized" portals be much subtler. And the targeting exclusions were more limiting than they initially appeared. Without them, I could launch needles at vital organs. But with them . . . not so much.

But there was still one option left to me.

Hidden condition met! Alternative ability choice unlocked.
Option 4: Enhanced Portals (Worldbending) [Requires: *Local Portals* ability]— *Replaces Local Portals.* Create a portal to another location within current range of sight or within a 30-yard radius. Support up to two pairs of portals at once. Uses mana to open portals only.

"Wow," I mouthed to myself. At first glance, this was a decent improvement to an already vital ability of mine. But then I'd thought about it further, reading it through again and again so that I could see everything that it changed.

Having two pairs of portals instead of one essentially doubled the *Local Portals* ability's power alone—though I'd have to practice holding four portals in my mind's eye at the same time. But this wasn't all that this ability replacement achieved.

Instead of requiring mana per second to keep a portal open, the mana cost was only to *open* them. This meant that my mana went a lot further, and I could keep more back for my *Warped Shield* ability, or to power my dagger attacks through my *Mana-Fueled* passive.

Also, when combined with the whole "having two pairs of portals" thing, it meant that I could keep one half of a pair open at a safe location without doing myself in. We could always have an exit open to us at any time, simply by having me move or open its partner.

All these possibilities appeared to me immediately, and I could only imagine that there were more still to come. My selection was obvious to me.

Ability Unlocked: Enhanced Portals
Enhanced Portals (Worldbending): Create a portal to another location within current range of sight or within a 30-yard radius. Support up to two pairs of portals at once. Uses mana to open portals only.

I closed my eyes, allowing myself to feel the upgraded ability seeping in through my body. Was it my imagination, or could I really feel it?

At that moment, Val cried out, pointing into the water. I followed her line of sight. There, in the distance, was a figure, swimming through the Sea of Roots.

No, I realized. *Two* figures; one was carrying the other on their back.

We couldn't help but cheer when we saw who it was—Arzak, covered in injuries, straining herself to carry an unconscious Corminar on her back as she swam through the water.

Lore ran to roll down the ladder on the side of the ship, then leaped down it, offering an outstretched hand.

Arzak took it. "Nice see you," she said.

"Yeah, you too," replied the barbarian, and heaved Arzak onto the ladder before pulling Corminar from her exhausted frame.

"*Heal*," Arzak said, holding her wounds. "*Heal* him now."

Val ran to Corminar's side as Lore lowered him to the deck, rifling through his robe. I saw the injuries he'd suffered in the pursuit of defending his homeland—tears, bruises, broken bones. He'd given everything.

And still, we'd failed.

Val pulled a small blue vial from Corminar's pocket and downed it. The vial didn't even hit the deck before she began *healing* him, pulling him back from the verge of death.

"We lose," Arzak said.

"We know," Val replied. "I'm sorry; we weren't fast enough."

"You kill her?" the orc asked.

"Styk did." Arzak didn't celebrate this, only holding Val's gaze before casting a glance in my direction, presumably too exhausted to find joy in this.

Corminar stirred while Val *healed* him, mumbling about the invasion, and how he'd "had to do it." There was distress in the elf's voice—distress that wouldn't fade once he finally did wake up.

"Guys," Lore said.

I looked immediately to the horizon, not to him, thinking that he was saying an enemy was approaching. But there was no one. "What's up?"

"I . . . have an active effect."

Arzak and I blinked back at him. "What?"

"*Man of Prophesy*," Lore read from the System messages before him. "I think . . . I think Niamh did it to me, before she died. When you said she was *healing* me? Cos I saw what she saw—something huge, something I don't understand yet. Something that the depth-raider showed me, too. Something's coming, and I think . . . I have to be there."

Silence crossed the ship for a moment.

"What does it do, this effect?" Val asked.

"It gives me . . ." Lore swallowed. "It gives me visions of destiny. I only found the effect cos I saw one. Something flashed in front of my eyes—a woman. Cleo."

My mother. I felt Val's eyes bearing into me.

"I think we were fighting alongside her? We were fighting with . . . a Player? Or against Cleo, too? I can't tell, I think there's . . . I think there's two futures, one good, one bad. I think this effect, it tells us what we need to do to get to where Niamh saw me. She wanted me there so much, she gave me a glimpse into my future."

"You know what we need do next?" Arzak asked.

Lore shook his head. "No, I don't think it works like that. I think . . . I don't know, I think we just have to wait, see what the visions say when they come, and make the right decisions in the moment."

"Or the 'wrong' ones," Val said. "We should make sure Niamh doesn't get her way."

"But if we make the wrong ones, maybe we don't make it to the Council's grand plan. Maybe we don't get to stop it."

The ship fell quiet once more, before I spoke.

"The 'why' is important, sure. I want to know why Niamh wanted you there as much as the rest of you. But there's something else we're missing: this effect, it seems to be leading you to the Players. It's leading us to the fight. Niamh said that the Council would be hunting us, but we have a weapon of our own now.

"Now, we can hunt *them*, too."

Val

Val held Styk's *Blade of Samal* in her hand, balancing it on her fingers as she stared down at her sleeping lover.

They were sailing north at a rapid pace, the Great Golden Canal Project not far ahead of them. Corminar, who Val had just about saved from death—not that anyone had thanked her for it—thought the canal would be abandoned now, it having served its singular purpose. Arzak wasn't so sure, and had volunteered to keep watch on the upper deck just to ensure they didn't run into any trouble.

But none of this was of concern to Val in that moment; she had bigger things to worry about. Like what to do with the information that Niamh had handed her on the flagship—that Styk was the son of a Player.

He'd been so kind to her after learning what her real class had been, and she would have loved to return that favor, but . . . There was a difference between being naturally gifted at *Witchcraft* and being the spawn of the invaders from the Ascended World. That was something that ran in the blood. Something that, maybe, couldn't be overlooked.

Val adjusted her grip on the knife, holding it like Styk would, when he intended to use it.

None of the others knew. Not yet, at least. Val had considered telling them, warning them of what they were traveling with. They had the right to know. But Val . . . just couldn't bring herself to say the words.

Who really was he? What did she *really* know about Styk, truth be told? He'd always glossed over his past life, and the people he'd killed. Not to mention how he reacted to any talk of his parents, though at least Val understood why, now. Styk might have been content to not know where he'd come from, but Val wasn't.

Could she really trust a man like that?

Val toyed with the knife, knowing she wasn't going to do it. Knowing she *couldn't* do it. No matter Styk's sins, no matter who he was . . . she couldn't hurt the man she loved.

She placed the knife gently down next to Styk, where she'd found it, and turned away.

A large figure loomed in the doorway. Val's heart skipped a beat at first, expecting danger, but then she recognized the shape as Arzak.

"How much of that did you see?" she whispered, thankful that Styk was a heavy sleeper. Maybe not as heavy a sleeper as *Lore*, but heavy nonetheless.

In answer, Arzak, gestured for Val to follow her up onto deck. This . . . probably wasn't a good sign. If her orc friend had seen her with the knife, playing with the idea of . . . Well, best not to think about it, really.

Up on deck, Arzak turned to her. "You know?"

Val took a very literal step back. "*You* know?" she threw back at her friend.

"For some time. Do research of own back in Rose Home. About Sisyphus Artifact. About who can use. About . . . *him*. Thought better to keep close. To watch." The orc looked down at the newest of her pair of swords. "He not show sign of turning out like Players."

Val wished she could agree. "You sure? Have you not heard all this stuff he's been spouting about us being heroes? He's really beginning to see himself that way. As a hero."

"Is problem? Long as he do good . . ."

"He thinks we . . . he thinks *he* is better than everyone else. Don't you see it?"

Arzak stared back at her for a moment. "Mm-hmm." She nodded.

"Do we really think that's not how Players start out? We know they think they're being honorable. We know they do stuff for people, get people lauding them. But then, as time passes . . . suddenly they think themselves heroes without actually doing anything heroic."

Arzak remained quiet, allowing Val to sit with this thought for a time. The waves splashed against the hull. The lights of the canal glowed just ahead of them. It was this, the sight of the Great Golden Canal Project, that made Val realize what she had to do.

"I'm . . . going, Arzak."

The orc nodded, taking this in her stride. "No. You not go. *We* go."

About the Author

O. S. Marrow is a progression fantasy author with a particular interest in the philosophical and metaphysical. His passion for writing started at a very young age, as he scribbled down fan fiction inspired by his favorite books (none of which should ever see the light of day). Marrow currently lives in London, United Kingdom, and is often seen staring out of his study window, searching for the perfect next word.

RESPAWN YOUR CURIOSITY

follow us on our socials

podiumentertainment.com

@podiumentertainment

/podiumentertainment

@podium_ent

@podiumentertainment